The
Spiced
Cocoa Café

BOOKS BY HARPER GRAHAM

The
Spiced Cocoa Café

Harper Graham

Bookouture

Published by Bookouture in 2025

An imprint of Storyfire Ltd.
Carmelite House
50 Victoria Embankment
London EC4Y 0DZ

www.bookouture.com

The authorised representative in the EEA is Hachette Ireland
8 Castlecourt Centre
Dublin 15 D15 XTP3
Ireland
(email: info@hbgi.ie)

Written by Harper Graham

ISBN: 978-1-80550-288-3
eBook ISBN: 978-1-80550-287-6

For anyone who likes their romance—and their books—with a little spice.

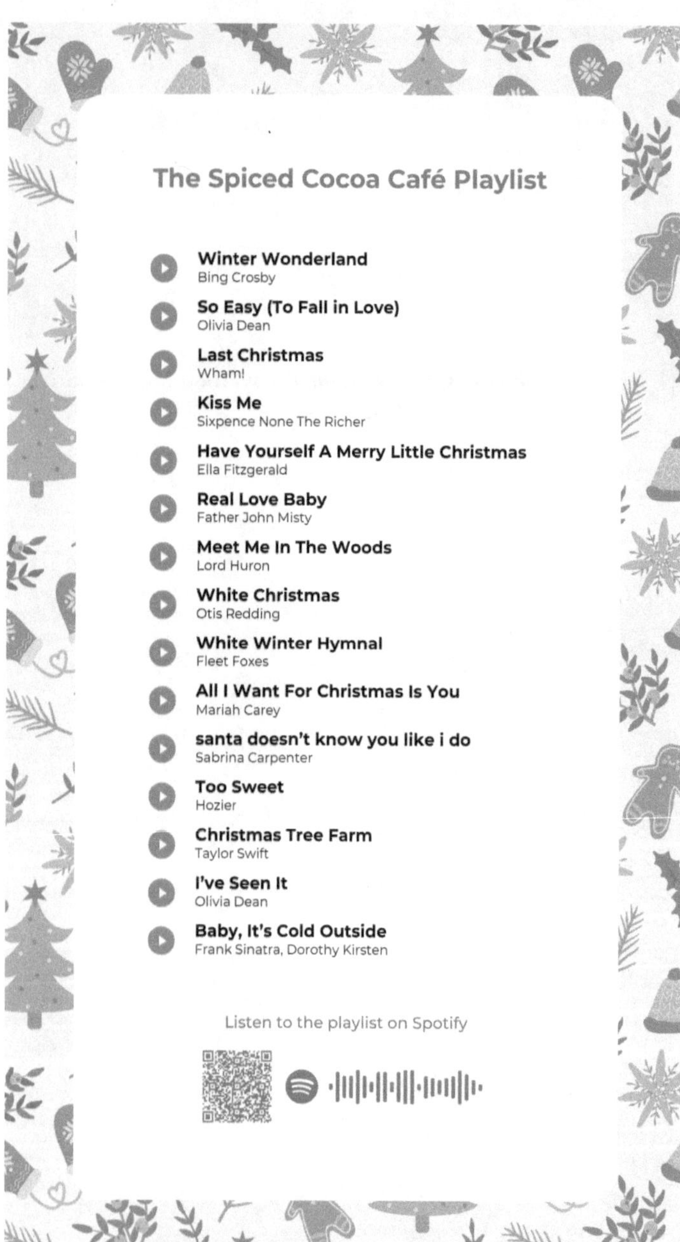
The Spiced Cocoa Café Playlist

Winter Wonderland
Bing Crosby

So Easy (To Fall in Love)
Olivia Dean

Last Christmas
Wham!

Kiss Me
Sixpence None The Richer

Have Yourself A Merry Little Christmas
Ella Fitzgerald

Real Love Baby
Father John Misty

Meet Me In The Woods
Lord Huron

White Christmas
Otis Redding

White Winter Hymnal
Fleet Foxes

All I Want For Christmas Is You
Mariah Carey

santa doesn't know you like i do
Sabrina Carpenter

Too Sweet
Hozier

Christmas Tree Farm
Taylor Swift

I've Seen It
Olivia Dean

Baby, It's Cold Outside
Frank Sinatra, Dorothy Kirsten

Listen to the playlist on Spotify

ONE

CASSIDY

"Chocolate. Spice. The magic of Christmas in the air," Cassidy whispered, her crystal-blue eyes sparkling. "I'm ready."

She stood in the middle of her new chocolate shop and turned in a slow circle in an oversized sweater, arms outstretched. It probably looked like she was starring in a one-woman holiday musical, but she didn't care. Everyone else in the small town of Maple Falls was fast asleep. When they woke up on the first day of December, her doors would be open, waiting for them.

Cassidy closed her eyes and inhaled deeply. She had been up for... was it twenty hours now? But it was all worth it. Her lifelong dream was finally coming true—if she didn't screw it all up.

Everything was set up as well as it could be. The Cocoa Corner was a chocolate lover's cozy paradise. It was decorated in warm browns and soft creams, with pops of color—vintage teal and peppermint pink. A thread of tiny copper twinkle lights lined the shelves, casting a soft glow against the glass jars of dipped caramels and handmade truffles made from dark chocolate, flaky sea salt and bourbon.

Her shop would offer all the chocolates she'd perfected during her years working as a chocolatier in Paris, plus a few old local favorites, thanks to the former owner, who'd generously passed on her recipes.

But the Cocoa Corner's pièce de résistance was her festive hot cocoa pop-up, the Spiced Cocoa Café. The signature dark spiced cocoa was the highlight. It was Cassidy's French grand-maman, Genevieve, who had gifted her the secret, handwritten recipe, passed down through generations and carried over to the US. The one she now kept folded in the locket that hung over her heart. The scent of melted chocolate mingled with cinnamon, cloves, and nutmeg would wrap around customers like a hug from her grand-maman.

A hand-painted sign above the bar read "Warm Up Here" with tiny snowflakes and stars dotting the corners. A few café tables nestled by the window, spruced up with pine and holly.

The Spiced Cocoa Café bar was stocked with fluffy homemade marshmallows, chocolate curls, crushed peppermint, and red and green sprinkles. For those who preferred a traditional approach, she would serve the cocoa with thick, buttery croissants from the Pumpkin Pie Bakery.

Cassidy's stomach fluttered as she looked around. She was practically dead on her feet but somehow still exhilarated. It was probably the caffeine. She'd drunk countless cups of cocoa while finalizing every last detail. Crossing her fingers, she silently pleaded for opening day to be a success. Her only wish was that her grand-maman and her parents were still around to see it.

She walked over to the calendar hidden safely behind the counter, a gift from her new friend, Madison, who recently moved back to town to help run her family's inn. Strategically placed ribbons and bows did little to hide a whole lot of holiday spirit from Mr. December. Cassidy could appreciate a man who knew how to celebrate Christmas.

In the corner of the calendar, Cassidy had pinned a golden piece of paper in the shape of a star. That star meant the Cocoa Corner was one of four local businesses selected to take part in the annual Light-Up Display Competition, which took place across four evenings in December. This competition was part of the town's wider Christmas Countdown of events— Cassidy had learned that this town cherished its seasonal festivities.

Each of the four businesses would decorate their storefront outside and in with a unique festive theme, and locals would gather to watch as they turned the lights on and had their chance to shine. Donations would happen throughout, with voting and the winner being announced on Christmas Eve.

Her slot was the third Friday before Christmas. So, as well as launching the Cocoa Corner and the pop-up café, over the next few weeks Cassidy had to organize the most spectacular light-up event the town had *ever* seen.

She walked toward the window and let herself dream for a moment. Soon, this front display would be transformed into something magical. Maybe she'd build a chocolate sleigh and fill it with handmade truffles. She imagined music playing softly through the speakers, laughter on the street, and a hush falling over the crowd as her display flickered to life.

It would be cozy. Enchanting. Unforgettable.

She had always loved a bit of competition, even if it was just a board game with her brother, Julian. But this was so much more than just for fun. If she won the contest, the Cocoa Corner would be named Maple Falls Business of the Year.

That would give her fledgling chocolate shop the visibility and community trust it needed to survive. She'd get to host the town's New Year's Eve party, drawing in customers and solidi-fying her place here so that she'd really, truly feel like she belonged here in Maple Falls. Best of all, she would get to choose which charity received all the donated money.

And Cassidy knew exactly where she would send it. There was a children's hospital just outside Maple Falls that had cared for her when she was a little girl recovering from the accident that took her parents' lives, long before she moved to Paris. It had been a safe haven in the hardest chapter of her life.

This event was everything. The culmination of her opening weeks. A chance to give back, and to prove she could really do this. She could build a life here, in her own way, without Jean-Paul, a.k.a. the French Bastard.

She refused to think about her cheating ex. Instead, she looked around the shop—at the gleaming wooden floors, the glass jars lining the counters filled with star-shaped marshmallows (she may have eaten dozens of them), toffee truffles, and chocolate-covered almonds.

"We did it, Grand-maman," she whispered to the room. If she could see her now, she'd be so proud.

This place was hers. Not Jean-Paul's. Not her brother's. Not some half-finished dream she'd left behind in Paris.

She just had to ignore the doubts. Her ex's voice, whispering, "You're not good enough. You don't belong here. Everyone will figure that out sooner or later." She had to *believe*. That was what the spirit of Christmas was all about, wasn't it?

Cassidy had worked so hard to make this place as magical as it was. Now her heart squeezed, knowing that her grand-maman would never see it. And that her fresh start meant that she was very much alone.

Her brother and his husband were hundreds of miles away. There was no one to step in and help her if she needed it. No one she could rely on.

Big, fat snowflakes were tumbling heavily from the sky now, drawing her attention back to the front window. Cassidy could only imagine how beautiful everything would look once the town was lit up for the holidays.

She inhaled deeply before blowing her thoughts away with a slow exhale.

It was pitch-dark outside, but the snow called to her. She turned, filled her mug up with the rich spiced cocoa, and stepped outside to look up at the beautiful starry sky.

Snow had been falling off and on since she'd moved to Maple Falls, but tonight felt different. It was the kind of snow she'd loved since she was a little girl, when she would press her face to the frosty window of her childhood home, waiting for the first flakes to fall.

She tipped her face up now, letting the big, fluffy flakes land on her lashes and cling to her hair. The chilly wind tickled her face. It was a cold that woke her up from the inside, reminding her she was here, alive, chasing a dream she'd carried in her heart since she was old enough to hold a cup of cocoa with both hands.

Sure, it snowed in Paris, but not like this. There was nothing like the hush of a small town wrapped in Christmas lights, where the world seemed to hold its breath and time slowed.

Moments like this were why she was here in Maple Falls, cocoa in hand, heart wide open. Christmas. Snow. Magic. It was everything she wanted her life to be.

Her heart had been broken last Christmas and she had sworn this year would be different. No more people-pleasing. No more rolling over for others. She had even made a vow: No men for an entire year. She needed to focus on herself, and so far, it had worked out perfectly.

Her dog, Muffin Marie, or Muff for short, had trotted outside with her and seemed to love the snow just as much as she did. The energetic goldendoodle bounded a few steps forward, then crouched low, ready to pounce on a fresh pile of snow.

"Whatcha see, girl?" she asked her pup.

Muff took that as her cue, spinning in wild circles along the sidewalk, nose buried in the snow one second then springing up the next with a playful bark, a full-blown case of the zoomies taking over as her curly white coat turned into a blur.

Cassidy couldn't help but look up at the stars and smile. In that moment, the snow felt like a sign. "Okay, universe. I see you. I feel you. You're giving soft Hallmark energy, and I am here for it."

Aside from Muff, the street was silent. Wisps of smoke curled from chimneys and soft lights flickered behind shop windows. Across the street, the darkened window of the Hot Honey Farm Shop reflected the glow of the streetlights, a wreath hanging on the door, and a few pine garlands draped over the entry. Next door, the Maple Leaf Café had a single string of lights, while the Pumpkin Pie Bakery boasted a swaying inflatable gingerbread man. Here and there, hints of Christmas had already arrived. But soon, the whole street would come alive with garlands and glowing lights, like the town itself was stepping into its own fairy tale.

Suddenly Cassidy realized she was barefoot in the snow. Her feet were turning into popsicles, and she was rather fond of her toes.

"C'mon, Muff. Let's head back in." She turned back to the door, when a quick twist of the knob had her frantically shaking her head.

She jiggled the handle. Nothing.

Tried again. Still locked.

"Oh no. No, no, no…"

She peered through the frosty glass out of habit. She lived alone now—there'd be no one to rescue her—and her keys were safely in her purse inside.

"How? Why?" she asked the stars. Muff replied with a playful woof.

Cassidy stepped back and placed both hands on her hips. "I am a grown woman. I have lived in another country and started my own business. I will not be defeated by a door."

Muff barked supportively from the snowbank.

She turned to her. "Thank you. That's one vote of confidence."

The cold seeped into her bare toes, and she shivered. "Great. First day, and I'm going to lose a toe."

She glanced up at the dark second-story apartment window. "Should I climb up?" she asked Muff.

Muff barked softly, wagging her tail in encouragement.

"You going to catch me if I fall?" she asked the pup.

"She won't. But I will," came a warm, deep voice.

Cassidy froze, as if she had forgotten how her legs worked. Which definitely wasn't a good thing, in case this man turned out to be a complete psycho. It was the middle of the night, after all.

Muff barked and pranced over to greet the probable psycho and she turned to call her pup back. Her voice caught in her throat.

Psycho or not, this guy was tall, broad-shouldered, and dusted in snowflakes as if Santa Claus himself had conjured him.

His flannel shirt peeked out beneath a heavy coat, his dark hair was tousled, and a pair of worn boots crunched the snow, packing it into the earth as he strode toward her confidently.

He had that rugged, just-rolled-out-of-bed-but-still-unreasonably-hot thing going on. He had a rough voice that warmed her faster than cocoa ever could.

Cassidy hadn't missed guys at all this past year. No dates, no kisses. In fact, she'd found her relationship with herself far more... satisfying... than it had been with Jean-Paul. But my God, this guy was something.

"Liam Hawthorne. I own the Hot Honey Farm Shop, across the street." He outstretched his hand.

Of course. She knew who he was, and he was competing in the light-up contest too. Somehow, in a town this small, she hadn't officially met him yet, but she'd heard he was absolutely determined to win.

So right now, he was Christmas Enemy Number One. Figured he was gorgeous.

"Oh." She forced a smile. "Cassidy St. Clair. The Cocoa Corner." She slipped her hand into his and desperately tried to ignore the warm buzzing sensation that traveled up her arm. But there was only room in her thoughts for the feel of his strong, warm hand cradled in hers. Cassidy forced herself to break the spell, pulling her hand back.

"I know who you are." Liam slid both hands into his coat pockets.

She squared her shoulders, reminding herself she had a new life and a cocoa empire to build, kicking off with winning the Light-Up Display Competition.

Then their eyes met. His were not full of festive cheer, not at all. Her sunshine hit his storm cloud, and for a breath, everything stilled.

And she knew right then, her vow was in trouble.

TWO

LIAM

Liam hadn't planned to end up standing in the snow, in front of a woman who looked like Christmas personified, but here he was.

She stared at him, wide-eyed, cheeks pink from the cold, messy blonde braid falling over her shoulder, barefoot, and holding a steaming mug like it was the answer to life's problems. There was chocolate on her cheek—actual chocolate.

It would've been funny if it weren't so ridiculous.

He swore under his breath. This was exactly what he didn't need. A woman who looked like a holiday movie heroine, blue eyes bright with Christmas cheer. Like her soul was made of snow and cocoa with a dash of magic.

She was a walking holiday card. And he would rather walk barefoot over hot coals than get caught in that.

Because Christmas didn't mean magic for him. Not anymore. It meant heartbreak and hollow traditions that made everyone else smile while he pretended to do the same.

Normally, Liam would drown out the holiday cheer with

long runs and work on the family farm. He was the king of the Jingle Bell 5k, after all. But his hamstring had other ideas, tearing during last week's training session. The injury had left him limping around with nothing but frustration and the town's Light-Up Display Competition to tackle. At least that was one area where he could put his competitive nature to good use, even if it did mean he had to fake some Christmas joy. His farm shop was guaranteed to take first place. He was doing it for his family, who ran the local farm, and nothing was going to get in the way of that.

Especially not a newcomer like her.

It was all the dog's fault. Five minutes ago, he'd been working late on woodwork in his farm shop, trying to pretend his hamstring wasn't throbbing like hell, when a deep, cheerful woof echoed down the sleepy street. Normally, he'd have ignored it. But something had nudged at him—a sense that something wasn't right.

He'd slightly limped to the window and peered out into the snow. And there she was.

Cassidy St. Clair. The new girl in town and the owner of the Cocoa Corner chocolate shop with that spiced cocoa everyone couldn't wait to try.

Their shops were across the street from each other and she'd moved last month, but he hadn't met her yet. He'd been busy helping his twin brother, Jackson, at the family farm, while his mom ran the shop. They'd only opened it at the beginning of November and everything they did really was a family affair. At the farm, the fall harvest rolled right into pumpkins and hayrides, then straight into selling Christmas trees. It had been nonstop, not much time for socializing.

But he'd heard all about her. Hell, she was now friends with all of his friends. His friend Zoe, who ran the local flower shop, had even added her to their group chat on WhatsApp. And Liam was sure he'd get on with her just fine, like he did with everyone. If only she weren't obsessed with his least favorite time of year. *Christmas.*

So, given everything he'd heard about her festive spirit, perhaps it was for the best he hadn't made it to any friend hangouts lately.

Christmas brought out the worst in him. The anniversary of the day his world fell apart was rolling around again. As much as he wanted to, he could never just smile and push through. He wished he could project the same carefree, life-of-the-party Liam everyone knew most of the year. Then there'd be no questions. No sympathy. But he simply couldn't, and he also didn't want to talk about why.

No one knew exactly how much pain this time of year caused him.

Well, no one except his best friend, Zach. It was freakish how well they read each other. Liam swore he knew him better than even his twin, Jackson.

Zach would have known exactly how annoyed Liam had felt when he'd looked out of his window and seen a beautiful woman pacing barefoot in heavily falling snow. Snow was not something to be trifled with. This time of year, people ought to be careful, and he knew that more than most.

She'd checked her door handle multiple times, then peered through the windows. And while he didn't know her personally, he could tell she was the type who'd try to break into her own shop just to avoid asking for help.

So, he'd sighed, tugged on his boots and flannel jacket, and made his way outside.

And now, introductions over, she was beaming back at him like he was the angel Gabriel.

This woman was gorgeous—too gorgeous, in fact, for a man trying very hard not to notice things like the fullness of her lips or the red polish on her toes.

But he was no angel, not this time of year. He did not smile back.

"You alright?" His voice came out low and rough, with a barely masked touch of frustration.

She nodded, her smile slipping, mug clutched to her chest in a defensive pose. "Totally fine. Just... bonding with my door."

"Is that so?" He huffed a laugh despite himself, which only annoyed him more.

She was flustered, trying so hard to pretend she had everything under control. But her lip quirked, and she looked to be one sarcastic comment away from either laughing or crying, and his frustration cracked just a bit.

"I'm guessing you're locked out?" he asked.

"Yes. But it's fine. I was just about to scale that drainpipe," she said, pointing at it confidently, then squinting up. "Okay, maybe not. But it did seem like a viable option five seconds ago." She lifted her mug. "Hot cocoa is a gateway beverage to all sorts of poor decisions."

"Going out barefoot in the snow being one of them?" He raised an eyebrow.

She glanced down at her feet and wiggled her toes with a wince. "It would appear so. Don't suppose you have a magical spare key?"

"Rita didn't mention one?"

"Not that I remember. And if she did, I have no idea where it'd be." She glanced toward the shop's front door. "Maybe there's a flowerpot or a fake rock or something?"

"Something like that," he said, already walking. He motioned for her to follow him around the side of the building, where the gutter met the curb. He bent down, peeled a small magnetic key box off the back of the downspout, and handed it over.

"Rita had a tendency to lock herself out too," he added as an explanation.

"Kindred spirit," she said with a smile.

They made their way back to the front door and Liam watched her turn the key, saw the tension drain from her shoulders when the lock clicked open. She turned to him, snowflakes in her hair, chocolate still on her cheek, and she looked so happy. Bright. Full of hope.

It was the kind of hope he hadn't let himself feel in years—four years, to be exact. He should have walked away then, should have left once he saw she was safely back inside. But he didn't. Because when her eyes met his, something sharp and hot cut through the layers he'd built around his heart, leaving him exposed in a way he hadn't expected.

It wasn't just attraction. It was gravity. The kind that pulled a man down and made him forget his better judgment.

And the worst part was, a reckless part of him—buried deep and aching—wanted her to keep going. To tear through every last wall until there was nothing left to hide behind.

THREE
CASSIDY

"It's showtime," Cassidy told herself while instinctively reaching for her grand-maman's gold locket around her neck. "Wish you could see this," she added before adjusting her braids and taking a calming breath.

It was Monday morning, and she was ready. In the last few weeks she'd posted about the grand opening on the Maple Falls community board, pinned a flyer outside the hardware store, and run a promotion on the shop's brand-new social media page, offering a free hot spiced cocoa to the first ten customers. She'd even practiced saying, "Welcome to the Cocoa Corner," in the mirror.

Before her nerves could get the best of her, she marched to the front door and flipped the sign to "Open." She refused to acknowledge her trembling hands.

Snowflakes sparkled like glitter in the sunlight outside the shop's giant floor-to-ceiling window. Outside, the early December morning was dusted in frost, and just across the street, she could see Liam's farm shop with its wood crates stacked neatly out front.

Within minutes, customers began to trickle in, eager to see what she had done to Rita's store.

"Well, this is just the coziest place I've ever seen. Don't you agree, Mrs. C.?" Mrs. Bishop asked as she walked in and did a full three-sixty turn.

"Is that hot cocoa I smell?" Mrs. C. asked, stepping closer to examine the bubbling cauldron of spiced cocoa.

"It is! It's my grand-maman's recipe," Cassidy explained. "Spiced and dark, but I also have a lighter white chocolate option if you prefer." The white chocolate one was her own creation, inspired by her love of the delicate petit fours she'd crafted in Paris.

"I'll take whatever one is your favorite," Mrs. C. said.

"Make that two cups," Mrs. Bishop called, already drifting toward the front display case. The long glass case was filled with handcrafted truffles, creamy pralines, caramel cashew clusters, peppermint bark, and chocolate-dipped pretzels. "Oh, I see you have pralines. Those look just like Rita's, and hers were heavenly."

"I hope they live up to the memory."

"I'm sure they will, dear, and I'll happily take the risk."

Cassidy laughed, going over to the pop-up café bar. "I'll give you the dark spiced cocoa. It's wonderful. A recipe passed down through generations. Would you like them for here or to go?"

Mrs. C. glanced at Mrs. Bishop, eyes twinkling. Cassidy gestured to the row of mismatched vintage mugs hanging from hooks behind the counter.

"Don't ask me. You know I can't make up my mind," Mrs. Bishop said honestly.

"Ain't that the truth," Mrs. C. said to her friend. "We do have a busy morning—lots of presents to buy—but those mugs are darling. Let's sit for a minute," she decided for them, motioning to the seating area off to the side.

Cassidy's heart gave a little swell of pride. She'd created that space with care: a round café table with two chairs positioned just so, the winter morning light pouring in at the perfect angle.

Behind it, on the second side window of her shop, was a little reading nook with two overstuffed velvet armchairs in cranberry and a quilt stitched in holly reds and snowy whites draped over the side. Between the chairs sat a low table stacked with some festive novels, a few classic romances, and a vase of greenery.

It was the warm and inviting space she had always dreamed of. And soon, she hoped, it would be filled with regulars who thought of the Cocoa Corner as their own cozy escape.

"Two mugs coming right up." She ladled two cups of steaming spiced dark cocoa out of an oversized copper saucepan.

"Here, it's even better with one of Emily's croissants. She baked them fresh this morning." She added the croissants to the saucers and brought them over.

On the outside, she looked normal, or at least she thought she did. Inside, she was screaming, *Please let them like it! Please let them like it!*

They were the first official customers to try her spiced cocoa. Madison had loved it, but would they?

She started rambling about the chocolates instead of studying the ladies' first sips like she wanted to. "The praline recipe was Rita's, as are the turtles and the espresso truffles." She nodded toward the framed photo of Rita, which was displayed behind the register. "I owe her everything for selling the shop to me."

Mrs. C. took a sip of the cocoa, and her eyebrows shot up.

"Now, isn't this something? Who would've thought cocoa could taste so rich and flavorful?"

"We might have to stop here every day on our way to the bakery," Mrs. Bishop added, dipping the corner of her croissant in the warm, velvety liquid.

"What is that? Ginger?" Mrs. C. asked, cocking her head. She shook her head.

"Well, there's definitely cinnamon in it." Mrs. Bishop looked up for confirmation, but Cassidy's lips were sealed.

"Cardamom?" Mrs. C. asked after taking a second sip.

"Sorry, secret family recipe. Even my brother doesn't know it," she confessed. "It's been passed down by the women in my family," she explained.

"If I had a recipe this good, I'd probably keep it a secret, too," Mrs. C. declared, lifting the mug and inhaling deeply.

"Is there anything else I can get you two?" Cassidy asked, wanting to leave the ladies to enjoy their cocoa in private.

"Well, a praline and a turtle, of course. Have to see if they're as good as Rita's," Mrs. C. said, not caring if it offended her.

Cassidy forced her smile not to slip. She knew everyone would be coming in to compare her chocolates to Rita's. It came with the territory. Theoretically, she knew she could make chocolate with the best of them. But the locals in Maple Falls might have a very specific idea of what fine chocolate should taste like.

"Do you like candied pecans?" Mrs. Bishop asked, pulling her from her thoughts.

"Hm?"

"Candied pecans, dear. Do you like them?" Mrs. Bishop repeated impatiently.

"I've never made them, but I enjoy eating them," she replied.

"Perfect. I'm making some for the holidays. I'll drop off a jar."

Cassidy started to protest. "Oh, you don't have to do that..."

"Nonsense. You're one of us now. Consider it your official welcome to Maple Falls," Mrs. Bishop insisted.

Cassidy beamed—she was off to a great start.

She thought she might have a minute to plan out her Christmas window display after the ladies left, but customers kept on pouring in. Within minutes, she had a line almost out the door of folks who wanted to sample her hot cocoa. Some came for the freebie but didn't mind when they'd missed the boat. They swooned over their cups and by the time the first batch of cocoa ran dry and the last croissant disappeared from the case, she was exhausted but buzzing.

Now, the shop had finally gone quiet. She took a breath and moved to the window display, restocking the rows of glossy truffles and peppermint bark, considering how to make the front look even more festive. Maybe garlands of cinnamon sticks and dried orange slices?

She glanced out the frosty front window—and froze. Across the street, Liam stood just outside his farm shop, sleeves rolled up, unloading crates of honey from his truck like they weighed nothing at all. His shirt clung to his shoulders, and his breath misted in the cold air as he adjusted the crates.

Cassidy tried—really tried—not to think about all the fun she could have with Liam and a jar of his famous hot honey, but her imagination wasn't cooperating.

The front door jingled, snapping her out of her thoughts as Mr. Alders walked in.

She recognized him instantly. She'd seen the older man a few times at the hardware store when she was picking up bits for the café over the last few weeks, and had first assumed he worked there. He was always hovering near the front counter like he owned the place. But it turned out he was recently retired from the store and had nothing else to do.

"Good morning, Mr. Alders," she called, brushing a strand of hair from her face. "Would you like some hot spiced cocoa? Freshly made with my secret family recipe."

"Hot cocoa?" he grumbled. "Rita never sold that."

Her smile wavered for half a second before she pasted it back on.

Mr. Alders wandered further into the shop, eyes narrowed. He wasn't admiring the displays so much as scrutinizing them—the shelves she'd added, all the glass jars, the shaped marshmallows, the splashes of color. The deeper he walked in, the deeper his scowl grew.

"Looking for a gift?" she asked brightly. "Something sweet for the season?"

"Got any maple fudge?" he asked. "Rita used to make the best maple fudge."

"I'm afraid not. I have pralines made with Rita's recipe, though. Would you like one of those?"

Before he could answer, Mr. Alders stumbled slightly, catching his foot on the box she had just brought down. It was overflowing with decorations—tinsel, twinkle lights, and the foam head of a half-assembled snowman peeking out the top.

He stared down at it like it had personally offended him.

"Don't tell me you're going all out with Christmas too."

She laughed softly. "Guilty as charged. I'm decorating for the Christmas Light-Up Display Competition. Will you be coming to see the displays?"

"Not unless I'm dragged," he muttered. "This whole town's lost its mind. Christmas on every corner. All a man wants is a piece of fudge and a little peace and quiet." He stood there, staring at her. Whatever he saw, he didn't like.

His glare only made her smile brighter, her chin lifting a fraction higher. *Not today, Mr. Alders. Not on my first day.*

She had to look like a complete and total fool to him, hands on her hips, Christmas sweater lights flashing. But she was absolutely determined not to care. If the man didn't like Christmas, he was in the wrong spot, talking to the wrong woman.

"Just let me know if you want to sample anything," she said, daring him to find fault with her or her shop.

Mr. Alders grunted, gave the shop one last look of disapproval, and turned on his heel.

Her new friend Zoe breezed in before the door had even clicked shut. She felt her shoulders drop, a breath she hadn't realized she was holding easing out as Zoe's energy filled the room.

"What in the world did you do to Mr. Alders?" she asked, rushing in, arms full with a bouquet from her flower shop. It was full of red carnations and white lilies, with sprigs of evergreen and holly arranged in a gold vase.

"I have no idea." Cassidy shrugged.

"Well, these are for you! Opening day flowers. Thought they might give you an extra pinch of good luck—not that you need it. This place looks amazing, and it smells like heaven."

"Aren't I a lucky girl." Cassidy reached over and accepted the flowers. "These are perfect, and so Christmassy."

"I try." Zoe beamed.

"Hot cocoa?" Cassidy offered, walking over to the makeshift cocoa station.

"I'd love some. It's freezing outside. I heard we're supposed to get six inches of snow tonight."

"That much? Really?" She'd forgotten how much snow fell in the Midwest. Would it distract customers or bring in more locals? Should she make an extra batch of white hot chocolate if school was called off?

"That much and probably more," Zoe said. "Looks like we'll have a couple of storms roll through in the next few days. Hopefully they'll hold off until after the Santa House opening tonight. You are coming, right?"

"Wouldn't miss it," Cassidy replied.

"Can I get one of those chocolate-covered graham crackers to go with this?" Zoe asked.

"I've got croissants, too," Cassidy said, pulling a fresh tray from the back.

"Then why didn't you say so? Give me one of those."

"It's even better if you dip it in the cocoa. Trust me—I had three of them before the shop even opened," Cassidy confessed with no shame whatsoever.

She waited until Zoe dipped the croissant and took a bite, making a sound that could only be called pornographic.

"It's good, isn't it?" Cassidy asked with a laugh.

"'Good' doesn't do it justice. You, my friend, have a gift."

"Just like you and these flowers. Thank you—it was really very sweet of you."

"You're welcome. I know you've been nervous about opening day. But by the taste of this cocoa, you have nothing to worry about." Zoe looked around. "Have you given any thought to how you're going to decorate for your light-up night?"

"I'm working on it. I just wanted to get the shop open first before diving into full-blown window display holiday mania."

She paused, then added, "I met Liam, by the way."

Zoe's eyebrows rose, a knowing look in her eyes. "Oh? And what did you think?"

Cassidy let out a half-laugh, half-groan. "Tall, grumpy, and somehow still manages to look like a lumberjack who could model for a flannel ad." She shrugged, trying to sound casual. "He's up against me in the light-up contest. Figures he'd be annoyingly attractive."

Zoe smirked. "Hey, I'm competing too, you know. And Emily."

"Yeah, neither of you is planning a full light show with

cocoa flights and a marshmallow bar," Cassidy teased. "Liam's got all that competitive energy going on. I can tell. You're both just in it for a bit of fun."

"And you're in it to win," Zoe said, amused.

"Someone has to," Cassidy shot back with a grin, then sighed, staring into her cocoa. "I just didn't expect my biggest rival to have that whole rugged, sexy thing going for him."

Zoe's eyes sparkled. "So, you think he's cute."

"I think he's going to be a pain in my ass," Cassidy corrected, ignoring the way her cheeks warmed. "Anyway, I'm here to launch my shop and win this competition, not get distracted by a guy with broody eyes."

"Whatever you say." Zoe lifted her mug in a toast.

Cassidy narrowed her eyes but couldn't stop the smile tugging at her lips. "Don't start."

But the truth was, even as she said it, she couldn't stop fantasizing about Liam. She'd thought about him all through the early hours of this morning, as she lay wide awake in bed after he'd helped her get back inside. He'd made for some very interesting thoughts indeed.

She supposed that's what you got when you took a year off of men.

No matter how many times she scolded herself, her mind kept drifting. Back to the way Liam had looked standing in the snow, boots planted wide, jaw set, looking every inch the grumpy lumberjack.

And now she couldn't stop picturing him hauling wood through the forest, flannel shirt rolled up to reveal forearms that could probably split logs without an axe. Sweat beading at his collarbone, those stormy eyes locking on her as he set down the bundle. Reaching for her, pressing her back against a pine, his rough hands on her hips. His mouth taking hers with the same quiet intensity he seemed to carry in everything he did.

In her mind, his fingers would find the button of her jeans, flicking it open with practiced ease, and she'd arch into him, the cold pine at her back contrasting with the heat of his body, giving him access.

Fantasy Liam wasn't slow or patient.

His rough, callused fingers would slip under the waistband of her panties, finding her with a sure touch, stroking exactly where she needed it most—where only she knew she liked it, until now.

She imagined gasping against his mouth, her hands tangling in his messy hair as he pressed her harder into the tree, taking control, giving her everything she hadn't even known she'd been craving during her year off men.

And in that secret, wicked daydream, Cassidy didn't care about the Christmas Light-Up Display Competition, or her vow to go a whole year with no men.

All she wanted for Christmas was Liam.

As if he could sense her desire, the man himself walked in.

She froze, the bell above the door chiming as if to mock her. Liam stood there in jeans and a long thermal shirt, snow dusting his boots, those storm-cloud eyes taking in everything. Including her.

Zoe, catching the shift in the air, made a quick excuse and ducked into the back kitchen.

Cassidy forced herself to move, her cheeks flaming, her pulse throbbing in places she'd rather not acknowledge. She propped a hand on the counter and it slipped a little, trying and failing to look casual. "Scoping out the competition, are we?"

Liam's gaze flicked over her, slow and infuriatingly unreadable. "Please. Like I'm worried."

Her eyes narrowed. "You should be."

He stepped closer, and the air snapped between them. "That so?"

"Mm-hmm." She swallowed, refusing to back down. "Your

grinch energy won't save you when the lights go up and the cocoa starts flowing."

A muscle ticked in his jaw, but his mouth curved, just barely. "You think you're tough, don't you, Sugarplum?"

She lifted her chin, ignoring the warmth curling low in her belly. "Tough enough to beat you."

Liam smirked, stepping even closer, close enough that she could smell the cold air and cedar clinging to him, close enough that her brain stuttered. "I'm not the one who should be worried about getting beaten."

"Oh, you'll see." She jabbed a finger at his chest, regretting it the second her finger met warm, hard muscle beneath the thermal. "I've been dreaming about this—Maple Falls, my shop, having the best Christmas window display ever—since I was a kid. You don't stand a chance. You're going down."

His eyes darkened, his gaze dropping to her lips before sliding back up. "Dreaming about me going down, huh?"

"Don't flatter yourself."

"Too late." His smirk was pure trouble.

She glared at him. "Can I get you anything?" She turned, flipping a braid over her shoulder as she moved behind the cocoa bar. "I've got a spiced French hot cocoa that's *heavenly*, but maybe that's too much holiday spirit for you."

His eyes flicked to the simmering pot, then back to her. "I'll pass. Just wanted to come and congratulate you on your big opening day, neighborly soul that I am."

She narrowed her eyes. "Not man enough to handle it dark and spicy, I guess?"

That earned her a sharp laugh. "You'd be surprised. Just not a fan of fancy chocolate."

"Oh really? I bet I can change that. Let me guess your favorite. I'm freakishly good at it."

"Oh yeah? What do you peg me as?"

Cassidy bit her bottom lip thoughtfully and eyed Liam up

and down. *Focus on your chocolate spidey senses*, she reminded herself. *Do not picture this gorgeous man naked and standing between your—*

"You good there?" He cocked an eyebrow.

She snapped her head up. "Perfect. Never better. Sometimes it just takes a minute. The chocolate goddess and all..." Cassidy marched confidently over to the display case and plucked out a single square of milk chocolate sprinkled with sea salt. She was pretty sure this would do the trick. "Here, try this."

Liam stepped forward. His eyes didn't leave hers as he took the chocolate, brushing her fingers in the process, sending a zing of heat up her arm.

He bit into it, chewed, and *shrugged*. "It's fine."

Cassidy's mouth fell open. "*Fine?* That chocolate won me a Parisian chocolatier award!"

She wasn't just offended—she was personally attacked. That chocolate was blood, sweat, and hours of tempering perfection, and this flannel-wrapped farm boy had reduced it to "fine"?

Liam wiped his thumb across his lower lip, where a fleck of chocolate had caught, completely unbothered. "Huh. Maybe it's a French thing."

Indignation sparked in her chest. *Who is this man?* Her first instinct had been right: He was definitely a psycho.

Then he added, "I told you, I'm not a fancy kind of guy. You'd probably be better off handing me a Snickers," and Cassidy's patience snapped.

"A Snickers? A *Snickers?*" she repeated, her voice rising. She planted her hand on her hip, glaring at him. "Are you kidding me right now?"

His mouth twitched, but he didn't smile, dark eyes steady and infuriating. "Just not into luxury chocolate. Never saw the point. Not in chocolate, and not in Christmas either."

She was actually scowling at this point. She couldn't help it. "I bet you think *Die Hard* is a Christmas movie!"

"Only one I like. Anyway, what's that got to do with anything? Does it matter?"

"Of course it matters! How else are you supposed to plan your Christmas movie checklist?" She looked at him like this was the most obvious thing in the world.

"Christmas movie checklist." He repeated it flatly, as if tasting words he wasn't sure he liked.

"You don't have one?" she asked, horrified.

"You do?" He raised a brow, unimpressed.

"Obviously. Tonight is *The Santa Clause*—parts one and two. Tomorrow is *Home Alone*."

"Yeah..." He shook his head. "Like I said, I'm not really into Christmas. Hate it, actually." His jaw tightened, daring her to comment.

"Hate it?" She threw her hands up. "What is wrong with you?"

"Nothing." His voice was low, edged. "Last time I checked."

To Cassidy, Christmas had always been special, but even more so after the accident that took her parents' lives. It was the one thing that still held magic after everything she'd lost. Lights twinkling through tears. The smell of Grand-maman's cocoa when she brought it to her in a flask, in a quiet hospital room. A nurse who made her a handmade stocking.

Christmas had been her lifeline. Her anchor.

Cassidy swallowed that emotion down and gave him a mock glare instead. "That's basically blasphemy in Maple Falls, you know."

His eyes softened just slightly, one corner of his mouth lifting. "Whatever you say, Sugarplum."

Zoe reappeared, her gaze flickering between her two friends.

"Guess that's my cue," Liam said. "Gotta get back to the

store and serve people their Christmas presents. 'Tis the season and all. Five dollars cover the chocolate?" He didn't wait, placing the five-dollar bill on the counter. "See you later," he said, turning and waving on his way out.

Cassidy quickly stepped behind the counter, ignoring the cash. Her eyes were too busy following Liam across the street.

Zoe didn't say anything for a beat. She just sipped her cocoa and smiled.

"What?" Cassidy said, trying to sound nonchalant.

Zoe leaned on the counter and whispered conspiratorially, "If you stare any harder, you're going to fog up the glass."

Cassidy shook her head and pocketed the five. "I wasn't staring. I was glaring."

"Staring, glaring, what's the difference?" Zoe laughed. "Both require passion, don't they?"

"Passion, ha! I'll show him passion, Mr. I-Don't-Have-a-Christmas-Movie-Checklist." Cassidy grabbed a cloth and started wiping down the already spotless counter.

"You realize that's not really a thing, right? And here I thought you said you were off men for the year?"

"I am," Cassidy said firmly. "Anyway, Liam is definitely not my type. And he's clearly not into me."

"Ha, whatever you say, *Sugarplum.*"

"Whatever. It doesn't matter. I *am* off men."

She'd thrown everything away, including her identity, on a man before. She couldn't afford to lose focus now. That's what her year of abstinence was all about. "No men. No distractions. No charming, rugged, stupidly good-looking farm boys who show up when you're barefoot and brain-dead."

"Don't forget that tousled hair and those long, long lashes."

Cassidy peeked toward the window again, even though Liam was long gone. "I promise you I am *not* getting involved with that grumpy grinch of a man."

Zoe patted her hand. "Famous last words, honey."

FOUR

LIAM

Liam's hamstring was killing him. And it wasn't the only part of his body that was throbbing. Ever since he'd left Cassidy's shop two hours ago, he hadn't been able to get her out of his head. She'd been angry—no, furious—when he'd dismissed her chocolate. If only she knew the truth...

Outside, snowflakes brushed softly against the wide front windows of the Hot Honey Farm Shop. The scent of pine from the crates of fresh wreaths near the door mixed with the faint sweetness of apples and cinnamon courtesy of the wax melter his mother had plugged in as a new business gift.

"You want the shop to smell comforting, like home," she'd said, dropping off the wax melts and the porcelain heater.

Liam knew she was right. If there was anything Beth Hawthorne knew, it was how to make a place feel like home with her weekly family meals, the way she slipped fresh flowers into Mason jars for the table, or how she could turn a plain room into something warm just by being there.

Liam leaned on the counter, shifting his weight off his bad

leg, the reclaimed wood cool and solid beneath his palms. He scrolled through Christmas display ideas on his laptop, a well-worn sketch pad open beside it, filled with scribbled measurements and rough pencil drawings of window displays and light arrangements he wasn't sure he'd actually build.

Three weeks. That was all he had until it was his light-up night. Three weeks of pretending his new farm shop was the holly-jolliest place this side of the North Pole.

Three weeks of faking the Christmas spirit he couldn't quite bring himself to feel anymore.

Some people have way too much time on their hands, he thought, grumbling over every over-the-top Pinterest suggestion. There were houses with displays set to music, thousands of lights timed to flashing snowflake beats, all color-coordinated to perfection.

Some even went full monochrome. All white.

Sterile, Liam thought, *like a hospital.* Cassidy would never go for anything so plain. No, he had a feeling she loved color bursts of red and gold lights, and loads of greenery. And there'd be glitter, no doubt about it.

He needed something with a more down-to-earth feel. Still eye-catching, still beautiful, but true to who he was, like this shop. Liam's family's farm business had been booming these past few years, but now, with his brother finally home, he could focus on bringing the farm's goods closer to town. When he'd bought the space, he'd renovated it to look like a rustic barn with wooden beams overhead, lantern-style lights, and shelves made from reclaimed barn wood. The shelves showcased jars of honey, homemade jams, and locally crafted alpaca scarves and mittens, which hung from black wrought-iron hooks below. Out front, he had a red tin roof overhang that he planned to string up lights around.

The space already told a story. He just had to add a bit of holiday charm to it.

He could do that, couldn't he?

His competitive spirit said, *Hell yeah, I can.*

He had to win. It was the perfect way to raise funds for the llama sanctuary that he, Jackson, and Madison's dad, George, were developing on the family farm.

Liam wasn't the type to stress under pressure. Usually, he was a go-with-the-flow kind of guy. But since Jackson had returned, everything had shifted. He'd seen what war had done to his brother. The way he flinched at loud sounds. The way he didn't meet anyone's eye for long.

So, now, more than ever, Liam wanted this to work—not just for the shop, not just to win the competition for the sake of it, but for the llama sanctuary. A place where Jackson could heal, a place where the animals Jackson loved could do what no one else could.

He didn't want Jackson feeling like a burden, like the way Liam had after the accident four years ago. His family would never see it that way, but he had. Liam had been useless for months. Everyone had dropped everything to check on him, make sure he was okay. They'd upended their lives like he needed a caregiver and all he'd felt was hollow inside.

He knew Jackson needed a purpose, something to occupy him, and the llama sanctuary was the perfect project. So Liam shook thoughts of those dark days away and forced himself to focus on the present. The llama sanctuary, the farm shop, the Light-Up Display Competition.

He tried to picture his window display: festive garlands with red and gold accents, velvet ribbons, oversized bulbs suspended from the ceiling in the front window. Could there be llamas? Liam was wondering if the llamas would eat a Christmas tree when the bell over the door jingled.

Zach strolled in, bringing a swirl of cold air and snowflakes that clung to the shoulders of his flannel jacket. His sandy-blonde hair was wind-tousled, and his hazel eyes scanned the shop with easy curiosity before landing on Liam with a crooked grin.

And wouldn't you know it, the man was carrying a gift bag from the Cocoa Corner.

The chocolate shop's logo stared back at him, smug as hell.

Liam tried not to scowl. He couldn't stop replaying the look on Cassidy's face when she had tried to guess his favorite chocolate, standing there with that fresh confidence, all bright eyes and sass. So sure she had him figured out. Holding out that tiny square of chocolate like it was the holy grail, waiting for his approval. Thinking she could bribe him into loving Christmas with one little chocolatey treat.

And then the way her mouth had fallen open, eyes flashing with outrage when he'd told her it was "fine." The way she'd planted her hands on her hips, fire in her eyes, telling him that piece had won her an award in Paris and how dare he compare it to a Snickers.

She was infuriating. But he'd nearly kissed her then, just to get a taste of that fire.

And right now? She was across the street, a temptation wrapped in chocolate and peppermint, laughing with customers while she fixed a wreath that kept falling down inside on her window. He'd watched her try to pin it back up three times already, golden hair falling across her cheek.

It was a problem. She was a problem.

Because even though her Christmas spirit drove him up the wall, he wanted more. Cassidy St. Clair wasn't the kind of woman he could flirt with for fun and forget about by New Year's Day. And Liam wasn't the kind of man who could give her what she deserved.

Even as he greeted Zach, Liam couldn't help it—his eyes drifted back to Cassidy, who was now waving goodbye to customers, her laughter drifting across the street when the door opened.

"Duuude," Zach said, dragging out the word. "You've got it bad."

"I don't have *anything*," Liam shot back, grabbing the broom and sweeping up pine needles near the entrance. "She's not my type. And she's downright annoying."

Zach snorted. "Sure. That's why you've been staring at her shop all morning."

"I'm not staring. I'm keeping an eye on the competition," Liam growled.

"Uh-huh," Zach said. "You know, Madison thinks the two of you are perfect for each other. She's hoping you'll get together at the Santa House opening tonight."

"Great. Tell Madison to focus on her own love life," Liam muttered.

Zach grinned. "Oh, she is. Our love life is going just fine, breaking in every room in the new house..."

Liam didn't want to think about his best friend having sex all over his house. Madison ran the Cinnamon Spice Inn, but she'd recently moved into Zach's place. A handyman by trade, Zach had built them the home of their dreams.

Liam glanced toward Cassidy's shop again. She was still at the window, adjusting the wreath that had fallen—again. She stood on her tiptoes, cheeks flushed, lips parted, eyes flashing with frustration and determination.

Liam swallowed hard.

Nope. He couldn't go to the Santa House opening. Because Madison was right, he might end up inviting Cassidy back here afterwards, to his farm shop. It didn't take much for his mind to wander—to picture her exactly where he'd want her: perched on the edge of his shop counter. She'd tilt her head in that mischievous way. He'd step between her legs, hands sliding under her hips, tugging her to the edge.

And then—

She'd wrap her legs around him. Tight. Hungry.

Her breath would catch when he kissed her, the way it had earlier, like she hadn't expected to be caught off guard. His mouth would trail down her throat. Her hands in his hair.

He could see it so clearly, it made him groan under his breath.

Liam shifted, adjusting himself, heat crawling up his neck.

"Yeah, you're real subtle," Zach said, laughing.

"Shut up," Liam commanded unconvincingly, his eyes drifting once again across the street.

Just as Cassidy managed to get the wreath back up, it fell again, pulling down a strand of lights with it. She stomped her foot, then glanced up—catching him watching her.

For a moment, their eyes locked through the glass.

Cassidy's lips parted. She cocked her head, challenging him.

Liam lifted his chin, smirked, and pointed to the wreath, silently offering her a hand.

She rolled her eyes, flipped her braid over her shoulder, and turned her back to him.

Zach let out a bark of laughter. "Right. Nothing going on there at all."

"Go home," Liam said, unable to hide his grin as he turned back to the honey display.

But inside, he was buzzing.

He'd only met the woman twice, and already Cassidy annoyed the hell out of him. She distracted him, frustrated him.

And I want her so damn badly.

Zach motioned to Liam's sketch pad and the computer. "You sure you've got this under control, man?"

Liam glanced over, drumming a pencil lightly against the edge of the counter.

Zach turned serious. "Look, I know how you feel about Christmas. You want some help with all this?"

"Thanks. I'm probably going to need it."

"Alright, then. You got it."

"Thanks, man."

"When do you want to start?"

"Sooner the better," Liam said, crossing his arms, eyes flicking toward the window across the street. "I really want to win."

Zach wandered over to the honey tasting table, ignoring the spoons and dipping toast bites straight into the samples, because of course he did.

"How's Jackson doing now that he's back home?" Zach asked, brushing crumbs from his hands.

"Better," Liam said. "Keeps to himself mostly, but he's good with the animals. The llama sanctuary's helping." Liam glanced up. "Thanks for getting George involved."

"There wasn't much convincing needed. Madison's dad has a soft spot for animals. And having your family farm as another rescue site will help a lot. The inn's already got more than enough animals."

"Things are going well over there, though?" Liam asked.

"Better than ever since the Halloween reopening."

Zach wandered to a display of handmade goods, his eye catching on a pair of green fleece-lined mittens. A matching scarf hung above. It took him all of ten seconds to decide they were perfect for Madison.

"Look at you, picking out more Christmas presents," Liam ribbed his buddy back.

"When you love a woman, buying for her is easy. You'll see."

Cassidy flashed through Liam's mind again. He brushed it off quickly.

He'd just met her. And as had been the case with every woman in the last four years, there was no love in their future. At most there'd be a bit of flirting, a kiss that burned hot and fast, a few nights tangled in sheets.

That was the kind of thing he knew how to handle. Something easy and uncomplicated, just enough to take the edge off the holidays.

But that was as far as it could go. He wasn't going to allow himself to care for someone, go deeper, be vulnerable. He'd built up walls to protect himself from that, for very good reason.

The thing was, something about Cassidy didn't feel like fun for now.

Which was exactly why his brain knew he needed to keep his distance.

If only his body didn't crave the taste of chocolate and spice on his tongue.

FIVE

CASSIDY

Later that afternoon, Cassidy had just ordered a neon sign for the Spiced Cocoa Café featuring a steaming mug and marshmallows when Emily from the bakery, a few shops down, rushed through the door. She did a full three-sixty, cataloging the shop.

"Please tell me everything down here is okay," Emily said without preamble, brushing snowflakes off her coat sleeves. Her cheeks were flushed, either from the wind or fury—or both.

"Yeah, I'm all good. First day's going well. What's going on?"

"Nothing's broken? Missing?"

"Not unless you count my sanity."

Emily didn't laugh. "I'm serious, Cassidy. Someone destroyed my decorations."

"Your Christmas decorations? Why?"

"God knows. And I only have until Friday to redo it all." Emily groaned.

Cassidy thought back to Emily's display, which was all ready for her slot on Friday, the first one of the year. She'd created the most adorable tree outside her shop, made of stacked upside-down pie tins and twinkle lights. Cassidy had loved it instantly.

"What about your tree? Tell me it survived!"

"Afraid not. I found parts of it behind the bakery dumpster!"

Cassidy gasped.

"I know. It was so cute! What am I going to do? It took me a week to make that thing."

"I'm so sorry, Emily."

"And my inflatable gingerbread man? Slashed. Just lying there in the snow, deflated, like a sad crime scene."

Cassidy covered her mouth. "No!"

"Yes. Do you know what this means?"

"No, what?"

"We have a grinch among us! A real-life Gingerbread Jerk!" Emily declared.

"A Gingerbread Jerk? Here?" Cassidy had just started settling into the idea that Maple Falls was made of snowflakes and sugar cookies. The idea that someone was sabotaging Christmas displays felt like something out of a big-city headline. It just didn't fit in this winter village come to life.

"Mark my words! Something fishy is underfoot."

If it was true… her mind started racing through possibilities. The only two Scrooges she'd come across in this town were Liam and Mr. Alders. Liam would never destroy personal property, would he? He might have a weird personal vendetta against Christmas, and he was determined to win the contest. But he'd grown up in this town. He was close to his friends; he wouldn't do something to hurt one of them. The older man, on the other hand, well, he had quite an opinion on Christmas décor.

"Do you have any suspects?" she asked, not quite ready to throw Mr. Alders under the bus.

"Not yet, but you can guarantee I'll be keeping an eye out."

"Yeah, absolutely. I don't blame you," Cassidy said slowly. "I'll do the same."

"Thanks," Emily said. "And if you hear anything—kids messing around, suspicious snowmen, whatever—say something. People are starting to talk."

Cassidy leaned in. "What are they saying?"

Emily shrugged. "It's mostly just speculation. We all love a little Christmas competition around here, but this is something else. I smell sabotage."

"You think it's personal?"

"I think it's petty and horrible. Probably someone who's mad they weren't asked to participate." She glanced pointedly at Cassidy's front window, which, aside from a small display, was still pretty empty. Soon it would be filled with lights, garlands, and a chocolate display fit for first place. But right now, it was a blank canvas, not exactly a vandal's playground. "Although I doubt it's aimed at you. Yet."

Cassidy twisted her lips. "Yeah, I know. I need to get with the program..." It had just been such a busy few weeks since she'd moved here from New York, what with redecorating the shop and making all the chocolates. Her to-do list was never-ending. She'd been focused on getting her business up and running, and not on the light-up contest. But that had to change. She needed to design something that would draw customers to her shop, and their votes.

"Promise you'll let me know if you hear anything," Emily said, walking toward the door.

"I will, promise."

Cassidy's heart broke for Emily. She knew how stressful it was to start from scratch with the clock ticking. Speaking of which...

She ladled a fresh mug of cocoa, put on her coat and stepped outside to survey the front of her shop. The Cocoa Corner looked cozy enough with its striped awning, the soft glow of pendant lights inside, and the rich scent of chocolate wafting out every time the door opened. The tables she'd set up were charming, with mismatched chairs and soft, plaid cushions she'd found at the flea market. It was warm. Welcoming.

But it wasn't Christmas.

Not yet.

Emily was right, she was behind. Everyone else had decked their storefronts with garlands, window scenes, and themed displays, even if they weren't taking part in the contest. In less than two hours, the sun would be setting and Oak Way would light up.

Meanwhile, the Cocoa Corner looked like it hadn't even heard of Christmas, except that annoying wreath that kept falling down.

She took a sip of cocoa, the warmth not quite reaching the knot in her stomach.

A vandal in Maple Falls just didn't fit. This town was all twinkly lights, kind neighbors, and friendly gossip. But the word "sabotage" kept echoing in her ears.

Cassidy glanced at the café tables, the ones she'd dragged out on a whim, thinking they might attract cocoa drinkers with strong constitutions. They looked so plain now. Exposed.

She lowered her mug. "Okay. Time to sparkle."

She only had a few crates of holiday odds and ends out of storage, but nobody should underestimate what can be achieved by some twinkle lights, garlands, and the slightly chaotic energy of a woman who's just been warned of small-town sabotage.

If someone was trying to mess with the competition, she wasn't going to make it easy.

Because Cassidy St. Clair didn't back down from a challenge, especially a festive one. Oh no. She was going to make her shop sparkle so bright that no grinch would even dream of touching it.

She was halfway through wrapping a candy-cane-striped garland around one of the front café tables when Muff gave a dramatic huff and flopped in front of the door, as if all this decorating was all work and no play.

"You're not exactly helping," she muttered, nudging the loose end of the garland around the table leg while Muff let out a groan that sounded suspiciously like a yawn.

That's when she saw Liam stepping out from his shop across the street, coffee in hand.

His beard looked freshly trimmed, dark eyes shaded under thick brows as he crossed the street with easy confidence, like he had nowhere to be and knew everyone would wait for him anyway. The cold didn't seem to touch him.

"Ah, I see you've finally stepped up your game," he said, coming to a stop beside her. He took a sip from a black ceramic mug that read "Bee Cool," with a tiny cartoon honeybee on the front.

She caught herself biting her lip and narrowed her eyes at him. "Is that supposed to be a threat or a flex?" Cassidy refused to look at his shop and catalog the amount of decorating he'd already done today. She liked it better when he just had a wreath and a bit of garland. Now he was showing her up.

"Bit of both," he said, flashing a slow, infuriating grin.

"For your information, these are more than decorations. I'm making a statement."

He quirked a brow, but before he could respond, Muff trotted over, tail wagging furiously. His entire posture softened as he crouched down, ruffling the pup's ears.

"Well, hey there, sweetheart," he murmured, the corners of his mouth lifting into a relaxed, genuine smile Cassidy hadn't seen before.

Muff licked his chin, and Liam chuckled, the sound low and warm.

"You're a traitor, you know that?" Cassidy muttered to her dog, but she couldn't help noticing the way Liam's dimples showed when his face lit up.

She was smiling in return before she could even help herself.

Liam glanced up from Muff. "So what's this big statement, then? The dollar store's named you their holiday princess?"

Her smile turned to a scowl. "Hey! I'll have you know these decorations were expensive!" She stopped and looked around at the cheap tinsel and lights she'd rounded up. "Okay, that's a lie. But that's not the point."

Liam scratched under Muff's chin, the pup leaning into him with blissful abandon. "Then what's the statement about?" he asked, still smiling at the dog.

She crossed her arms. "No Gingerbread Jerk is going to dim my holiday sparkle."

"What's a gingerbread jerk?"

"Not *a* gingerbread jerk. *The* Gingerbread Jerk." She sighed. "Emily stopped by in full crisis mode. Said someone trashed her pie tin tree and told me to keep an eye on my things."

He let out a short laugh. "She made a tree out of pie tins?"

"It was *charming*," she defended, eyes flashing. "And now it's a pile of twisted metal behind her bakery." She may have taken poetic liberties with that last line.

He took a sip of coffee, the corner of his mouth twitching. "Maybe the saboteur's just doing the town a favor. Christmas around here can be a little... much."

She paused mid-wrap. "Wow. Okay. Now you sound like Mr. Alders."

"Mr. Alders? The sweet old guy at the hardware store?"

"Sweet?" She huffed. "He came into my shop and said I was

ruining everything. That it was all 'too much like the rest of Maple Falls.' You should've seen the way he looked at my sweater." She flung her coat open to reveal her bright green sweater with flashing lights and a cartoon gingerbread man giving a thumbs-up.

Liam burst out laughing, Muff barking happily as if in agreement.

"What?" she demanded, hands on hips.

"You didn't flash him like that, did you?" he asked, eyes dancing with mischief.

"Shut up." She couldn't hide the flush in her cheeks.

He stood, brushing snow from his jeans. "I'm just saying, that sweater is a lot."

"At least I'm not hiding behind 'bah humbug' to avoid Christmas."

That wiped the smile from his face, his jaw tightening as he looked away, the warmth he'd shown Muff retreating as quickly as it had come.

"Sorry," Cassidy said, seeming to realize she'd hit a nerve. "It's just... this place... this competition, it matters to me. I'm just getting started, and if someone's out there destroying things—"

Muff barked once, as if to break the tension, and he ruffled her ears one last time before stepping back.

"I really don't think it's that deep. The wind could've taken Emily's tree. Or it's a bunch of bored teens messing around. As for Mr. Alders..." He paused, then smiled. "He probably just misses Rita. He had a soft spot for her."

"Sure, take his side. I can see how you two would get along," she grumbled.

"Trust me. He's one of the kindest people in town. A little cranky, sure, but harmless."

Cassidy wasn't convinced.

Liam took another sip of coffee, watching her. "But... if it turns out that the man's on a holiday rampage, I'll be the first to help you take him down."

That earned him a reluctant grin.

"Promise?"

He sighed. "Promise."

She hesitated, then nudged his boot with the toe of hers. "Thanks, I appreciate it. Even if you are a traitor to holiday fun."

"Oh, I've got plenty of time for fun," he said, his voice dropping half an octave, eyes locked on hers. "Just depends on the kind of games we're playing."

The air between them pulsed with heat, visible even in the cold.

Cassidy rolled her eyes. "You're ridiculous."

"You like it," he said, letting the corner of his mouth curl just slightly.

She reached down to scratch Muff's ears, looking away before she gave in to the urge to move closer to those lips.

SIX

LIAM

"Oh, since I've got you here, do you have a second to pop in real quick?" Cassidy asked, looking up from her dog.

Liam looked a little surprised. "I suppose so. Zach's over at the farm shop untangling some lights for me."

"This will just take a second, promise."

Warm air, rich with the scent of melted chocolate and warming spices, wrapped around them as she held the door open. He followed in behind Muff, realizing just then how much he missed having a dog around.

His yellow Lab, Chance, had passed away last year. Liam had debated getting a puppy, but with all the work at the farm and opening a new shop, it wouldn't be fair to the pup. In the end he'd decided to wait. But seeing Muff had him rethinking that decision.

A soft instrumental version of "Silver Bells" played in the background while the pup dashed through the kitchen and directly upstairs to the apartment.

"Over here, if you please." She waved him to the front counter.

"Well, now you've really got me intrigued," he said.

He followed her to the counter, watching as she opened the glass case and pulled out a dome-shaped dark chocolate with a glossy, polished shell.

"I know the sea salt milk chocolate wasn't your favorite," Cassidy said, cupping the treat in her palms. "Try this one."

"You must be a glutton for punishment," Liam said with a smirk.

"You don't understand. This is personal now. I've never not been able to pick the perfect chocolate for someone. You will not be my Achilles' heel. Now go on—try it."

He started to take a bite when she stopped him.

"Whole thing," she advised. "Trust me. That way you get all the layers."

He raised an eyebrow but obliged. "Alright. You're the expert."

He popped the chocolate in his mouth and bit down. The flavors burst across his tongue—it was *good*. Too good.

Cassidy was watching him like a hawk, eyes bright with anticipation.

"Chocolate... coffee... is that brandy?"

She beamed. "Exactly! It's my mocha brandy truffle. So? What do you think?"

He hesitated. "It's great. But... not quite my favorite."

Cassidy slumped in mock defeat.

"Sorry," Liam said with a sheepish shrug.

The truth was, Cassidy had nailed it the first time. That sea salt milk chocolate had nearly blown his mind.

Rich. Smooth. Unexpectedly complex.

But he couldn't tell her that. Because the second he admitted she'd gotten it right, this little game would be over. And he wasn't ready for that.

There was something very sexy about watching her work him out. The way her brow furrowed in concentration, the sparkle in her eyes. He'd never had anyone study him like that—not with curiosity and determination and a kind of joy that made his chest ache.

Her chocolates weren't just good—they were something else. A whole different level. And yeah, maybe he hadn't grown up with things like that. Maybe a part of him still believed he didn't deserve them, or her.

But he wanted her. Badly.

"I will get it right," she vowed, pointing at him like a challenge.

He gave her a slow smile. "I'm looking forward to it."

And God help him, he really was.

Before she could respond, the bell above the door jingled and the mayor's great-niece and personal assistant, Elsie, breezed in.

Elsie had heels that were too high for the ice outside and a coat that looked more New York than Maple Falls. She was all business, all the time, striding in like she had an agenda and everyone else better get out of her way. "Perfect!" she exclaimed, seeing them together. "I'm so glad I caught you both!"

Liam clocked the plastic bin tucked under her arm and braced himself. Whatever she had planned, he already suspected it wasn't going to be good.

"I was just talking to Mayor Bloomfield," she said, "and while he might not fully appreciate what I'm doing, you will."

Her words were aimed at both of them, but only Cassidy was smiling.

"What are you working on?" Cassidy asked.

"An online, town-wide spotlight series," Elsie explained, taking off the bin lid. "I want to feature every participating business in the Christmas Light-Up Display Competition. We'll post cute write-ups and festive photos—social media gold. I even brought props!"

She pulled out Santa hats, felt reindeer antlers, and glitter-covered glasses shaped like Christmas trees.

Cassidy leaned over with interest. "Ooh, I love this one," she said, pulling out a green felt elf hat and placing it on her head. "What do you think?" she asked Liam, posing with her hands on her hips.

On anyone else, it would've looked silly. On Cassidy, it was... charming.

He tried not to show it. "You make it work." Understatement of the year. She looked like a flirty, mischievous Christmas elf, and now his brain was full of thoughts it absolutely shouldn't be having in a public space.

Thoughts that included the hat staying on... and not much else.

Elsie held up the glitter glasses. "And what about these for you?"

"No. Absolutely not."

Cassidy rolled her eyes. "Don't mind him. He's just a grinch."

Elsie looked momentarily deflated but quickly rallied. "No problem, not everyone needs a prop."

"Do you mind if I keep this?" Cassidy adjusted her hat. "I want to wear it to the Santa House opening tonight."

"Of course! It looks adorable on you," Elsie said.

Cassidy looked back at Liam. "You coming?"

"The Santa House? No." He would rather run the Jingle Bell 5k with his torn hamstring.

The Santa House, a small cottage next to the courthouse grounds, looked like a real-life gingerbread house. It was decorated in Bavarian style with whites and browns and plenty of oversized lollipops and gumdrops lining the walkway. The house opened tonight and would be available for kids, and kids at heart, to stop by and visit the head elf himself. There was even a paddock off to the side that housed his reindeer. Well, two of them anyway.

Cassidy shrugged and turned back to Elsie. "So, what are you thinking?"

"Just a quick chat here. I've got some great hashtags lined up —#MapleFallsMagic, #CocoaCorner, and I was thinking maybe #SpicedCocoa?"

Cassidy nodded. "I love that idea."

Elsie beamed. "Perfect. I'll talk to Cassidy first, and then I'll pop across the street to your shop, Liam, for a few quick quotes."

"Sure. Whatever you need," he said, far less enthusiastically.

Elsie turned away, her attention already locked on Cassidy, leaving him standing off to the side.

He should've felt relieved, escaping from Christmas hell, but he didn't.

He glanced at Cassidy, watching as she laughed and adjusted her elf hat while Elsie fired off questions. She looked radiant. Confident. Like she belonged in the center of this holiday scene.

Liam was out of his depth here. Christmas wasn't his thing and it hadn't been for a long time. The lights, the fanfare, the endless holiday cheer... it all reminded him of what he'd once had and knew he'd never find again.

But somehow, standing in the Cocoa Corner watching Cassidy shine, he found himself wondering if maybe this season wouldn't always have to hurt quite so much.

SEVEN

CASSIDY

Cassidy was happily wearing the green elf hat around the shop when Madison and her grandmother Edith popped in. She'd met Edith a few times, and she'd loved her instantly.

"Happy opening day!" Madison said, walking in and giving Cassidy a side hug.

"My granddaughter tells me I have to try your hot spiced cocoa," Edith said, her eyes twinkling. Her hair was pinned up into a classic twist with loose wisps framing her face. Her eyes were the same rich green as Madison's with the same spark of fearlessness. "If it's good enough to convince her to give up coffee, then it must be something special."

"Hold up," Madison said, lifting a hand. "Let's not get ahead of ourselves. I never said I was giving up coffee."

Cassidy laughed. "She didn't. But she did go through plenty of mugs while she was helping me repaint the shelves."

Madison rolled her eyes. "You kept the cocoa coming, and I wasn't about to say no to free taste-testing."

"And now I'm here," Edith replied, waving her off. "Where is this famous cocoa of yours?"

Cassidy ladled up two steaming mugs of cocoa from the festive pop-up café counter and let them top them however they pleased. Madison went for whipped cream, red sprinkles, and a caramel drizzle. Edith added whipped cream, chocolate sauce, a shot of peppermint, and crushed hazelnuts.

Edith glanced around the shop, taking it all in. "I just love what you've done with the place. It's got such a cozy, old-fashioned chocolate shop feel—and the Spiced Cocoa Café pop-up is just delightful. What a wonderful idea. It makes you feel like you've stepped right into one of those festive storybook towns."

"Thank you," Cassidy replied, smiling. "That's exactly the look I was going for."

"Well, you nailed it. You fit right in here in Maple Falls."

Cassidy's heart warmed at the compliment. Mr. Alders might not be a fan, but at least not everyone resented her for renovating after Rita's retirement.

She thought briefly about bringing up the mysterious festive sabotage and her worry about Mr. Alders but decided against it. She wasn't going to be a town busybody. She was still getting to know everyone and didn't want to start spreading gossip.

"Oh! Before I forget," Edith said, peering into the display case, "do you have any pralines? Or maybe caramel clusters?"

"I do." Cassidy smiled. "What would you like?"

"I'll take both. Poor Hank's stressed up to his eyeballs." Edith chuckled.

Cassidy glanced at Madison for clarification.

"Mayor Bloomfield," Madison supplied. "Gram's dating him."

"And he's a fine lover, too," Edith added with a wicked grin and a twinkle in her eye.

"Gram!" Madison covered her ears.

Cassidy snorted.

"I do not want to hear about your love life," Madison groaned.

"Well, maybe I do," Cassidy teased, grinning.

"I knew I liked you," Edith said, reaching over to pat Cassidy's hand. "You *are* coming to the crafting club this month, aren't you? It's on the sixteenth. We're making sock snowmen in the inn's dining room."

She leaned in, eyes twinkling. "Madison found the cutest tiny scarves and button noses for them, and we've got enough glitter to cover half of Maple Falls if we're not careful."

Cassidy remembered the first crafting club she'd attended —back when she had only been visiting Maple Falls. It was right then, making wreaths in Mrs. Humphrey's kitchen, that she'd realized she could imagine a life here. A small town with an artistic soul... and a chocolate shop for sale? It had felt like fate.

"I'm really going to try. I've got so much going on with the light-up contest coming up too, but I want to be there."

"Good. And I can tell you all about my latest rendezvous with Hank. He can do this thing with his tongue..." Edith shivered, just to make Madison groan and cover her ears again.

"I just love messing with her," Edith added, laughing. "Like I haven't had to hear her and Zach going at it every five minutes."

Madison turned beet red. "We don't even live at the inn anymore, Gram!"

"No," Edith agreed, "but you still have an old bedroom... the pantry... the laundry room. Don't forget the firepit. I've debated wearing a bell around my neck so you can hear me coming!"

Cassidy couldn't stop laughing. Edith was hilarious. Watching Madison and her grandmother filled her with warmth and longing. It reminded her of her own dear grand-maman. Would they have teased each other like that, too, if she were still alive?

"Anyway!" Madison declared, trying to change the subject. "You're coming to the Santa House opening tonight, right?"

"Wouldn't miss it," Cassidy said, still smiling from Edith's comments.

"Excellent. We're meeting at Zoe's at five," Madison said.

"Do you know who all's coming?" Cassidy couldn't stop herself from looking across the street, wondering if Liam might have changed his mind.

Nothing got by Madison. "Why? Is there a certain someone you hope to run into?" she asked, all too innocently.

"What? No!" Cassidy's voice cracked halfway through the denial.

Madison arched a brow. "Are you sure? Liam might've mentioned something to Zach about meeting you last night..."

Cassidy groaned. "Oh my God. I hate everyone."

"You get used to it," Edith said with a chuckle.

"I just got here," Cassidy mumbled. "The last thing I need is a distraction wrapped up in strong forearms and a growly voice and a beard that probably feels amazing—"

Madison's eyes widened in delight. "Ohhh. You've thought about the beard."

"You're leaving!" Cassidy laughed, waving them toward the door. "This conversation is over. Anyway, Liam already said he isn't coming."

"Alright, alright. We'll see you just before five," Madison said.

Cassidy waved as the ladies disappeared down the sidewalk. She needed to get back to work while there weren't any customers, prepping chocolates for tomorrow. Instead she lingered, her gaze drifting back to Liam's shop.

Absolutely not, she told herself.

She didn't have time for a slow-smiling, sharp-witted farm boy with broad shoulders and secrets in his eyes. Especially one who made her brain feel like it was full of cocoa.

Her mind flicked, uninvited, to the way he'd tasted that truffle earlier, lips parting around the chocolate like it was something sacred. How he'd gone quiet afterward, tongue sweeping across the corner of his mouth as if savoring every last bit.

Cassidy swallowed hard.

She was definitely not thinking about what else that tongue might be good at.

Nope. Not even a little.

EIGHT

LIAM

Later that day, after closing the Hot Honey Farm Shop, Liam stood behind the front register. He was keeping weight off his bad leg while he sketched the storefront in his notebook, wondering what else he could add to the display. Maybe a few pine trees, more garlands draped along the façade, some hand-made ornaments—rustic and festive. He would need to do a lot more than that to win the light-up competition, but it was a start.

He envisioned turning the front of his shop into a small-town Christmas market, something cozy and nostalgic that brought the farm right into downtown Maple Falls. Multicolored lights would frame his shop, small twinkly ones around the windows and the icicle type too. They'd drip down from the roof line in a warm cascade. Strings of soft white bulbs would wind around wooden crates stacked with jars of honey and bundles of wool, and he'd place glowing lanterns on the sidewalk out front, welcoming people home.

The idea was still rough, but the more he drew, the more it took shape in his mind.

The Santa House opening sure was popular. He could see more and more locals were flooding into the area, lining up along Oak Way. Families were bundled up, kids in puffy coats and knit hats chasing each other while parents sipped steaming cups of mulled wine from the local tavern—the Kettle—across the road.

He wondered if he should open up shop again when Cassidy, Zach, Madison, and Kit, the new chef at the Cinnamon Spice Inn, walked by the front of his store. Madison leaned in, cupping her eye to look through, while Zach knocked on the window.

"It's open," Liam called.

Zach pushed down the gold handle and opened the door, and Cassidy followed after him.

She was bundled in a deep red coat that hugged her curves, cheeks flushed from the cold, blonde hair braided, a few snowflakes still clinging to the ends. And, somehow, that felt elf hat she wore still looked perfect. The way her eyes sparkled under the shop lights made something tighten low in Liam's gut.

She was chocolate and sunshine, warm and alive, lighting up the dim shop just by standing there, and it threw him completely off balance.

"We're headed to Zoe's and then the Santa House," Madison said. "Thought we'd stop by and see if we could change your mind."

"I told them you already passed," Cassidy said, tugging off one glove. "But hope springs eternal."

"I still don't know what the Santa House is exactly," Kit admitted. "But Zach promised there'd be cocktails at the end of it, so I'm down."

"Zoe said Jackson might meet her there, too," Zach added.

That surprised Liam. Jackson hated crowds—especially since he'd come home. Even the farmers' market made him twitchy sometimes. If his brother was going, maybe he *should* go too.

But the idea of standing side by side with laughing strangers, families with toddlers on their shoulders, couples holding hands under strings of lights... it made Liam's chest go tight. He didn't belong in that kind of festive joy. Not anymore.

"Emily bowed out, seeing as she's still fixing her display," Madison continued.

"And she won't let us help," Zach added.

"I heard the bookstore got hit, too," Kit added, nonchalantly.

"What!?" Cassidy exclaimed with wide eyes and an indignant expression.

"Someone stole all the lights from the front of the shop," Kit explained.

"That's, what, the second attack now?" Cassidy asked. "And still no sign of the Gingerbread Jerk."

Liam leaned back against the counter, folding his arms. "If there even is one."

Cassidy raised a brow. "Seriously?"

"I'm just saying," he said with a shrug. "It's windy. It's December. People forget to anchor things. Doesn't mean there's a saboteur lurking in the shadows with a Christmas vendetta."

Zach snorted. "You sound just like the mayor. Anyway, come with us, and afterward I'll buy you a drink at the Kettle."

Liam smiled but shook his head. "Nah. Thanks, but y'all go ahead. I've got work to catch up on. Maybe next time."

Liam followed them to the door and locked it. But he didn't feel any better once they were gone. Watching people walk past the window, laughing and cheerful, only made the ache worse. The world felt too bright, too loud. He needed space. Quiet.

He grabbed his sketchbook, a pouch of pencils, and his coat and headed for his truck. He didn't know where he was going, only that it wouldn't be downtown.

The road up the mountain was winding, dusted in fresh snow, and the forest around him glowed faintly in the fading light. The sun had already dipped behind the ridge, leaving the sky streaked in lavender and pale gold, and below, the town twinkled faintly. It looked like a snow globe brought to life. Smoke curled from chimneys, drifting lazily into the twilight, and for a moment, the world felt hushed, like it was holding its breath, waiting.

Some people drank to escape. Liam drew.

He parked near one of the scenic overlooks and killed the engine. For a while, he just sat there, soaking in the silence. A few deer picked their way through the snowy underbrush nearby, and a cardinal darted past the windshield, a flash of red against the gray.

He'd planned to sketch the pines, or the way the snow clung to the branches... but instead, his pencil moved on its own.

Cassidy.

She had the brightest eyes he'd ever seen. But he'd seen something else there, too—a flicker of sadness just beneath all that glittering warmth, like she was trying to outrun something she didn't talk about.

Line by line, he tried to capture it. The tilt of her head when she listened. The flush in her cheeks from the cold. The way her lips curved into a smile.

It wasn't perfect. The lighting was all wrong.

But he kept drawing.

Because, somehow, she made the cold less sharp.

Finally, with a quiet breath, he started the engine again, the truck rumbling to life beneath him. As he eased back onto the mountain road, Liam looked back at the glow of the town, a faint, shimmering promise beneath the winter sky.

And for the first time in a long while, he felt a flicker of something like hope—warm, fragile, and just within reach.

NINE

CASSIDY

"We have a lovely new town, don't we?" Cassidy said to Muff as she bent down and scratched behind her fluffy white ears. Last night had felt like a Christmas movie come to life with the Christmas carolers, reindeer paddock, and Santa's house. The only thing that had been missing was Liam. And Cassidy *had* missed him. Trying to figure him out was quickly becoming the best part of her day. But even without him there, she'd had a marvelous time. If she wasn't so run off her feet, she'd volunteer at the house to be an elf. *I do have the hat already*, she thought as she tugged her stocking cap lower.

She and Muff had just taken a much-needed break in a loop around the lake near the inn, the frozen water shimmering under the pale winter sun, before heading into town to let the pup sniff every garland-wrapped lamppost and snowbank in sight.

Cassidy had flipped the shop sign to "Closed," along with a handwritten note that said, "Back in 30 minutes." If her shop continued to stay this busy, she'd have to come up with a plan for Muff. Cassidy was hesitant to hire someone, not when her shop was still a baby. Rita had had a couple of longtime employees, but they'd decided to retire when she did.

Maple Falls was starting to come alive with holiday magic, even on an ordinary weekday afternoon. Zoe's flower shop, Cherry Crush, had a stand of mini holiday bouquets and mistletoe bundles tied with red-and-white twine, the scent of pine and eucalyptus drifting onto the sidewalk. The Little Lantern Bookshop had a book tree in its window, stacked high and wrapped in twinkle lights, topped with a shimmering silver star that reflected the snow outside.

She paused to admire the oversized silver snowflake clings decorating the Maple Leaf Café windows, where the owner, Zach and Emily's mom, Anita, had tucked faux poinsettias, evergreen branches, and birch twigs into her sidewalk planters, creating a splash of color against the winter white.

Muff pranced beside her on their walk back. The entire time, Cassidy took in the heartwarming decorations and reflected on how welcoming Maple Falls had been. Anita had dropped off a grilled cheese and tomato bisque just before noon. "Just wanted to make sure you took time to eat," she'd said, buying twenty dollars' worth of handmade peanut butter cups on her way out.

Even Mayor Bloomfield had stopped in to see how Maple Falls' newest business owner was doing and to see if there was anything he could do to help. Cassidy had assured him she was all set.

She honestly couldn't believe how kind everyone was being.

But a part of her—and if she was being honest, it was a rather large part—wondered how long it would last.

Cassidy had been told many times that she was a bit much, especially this time of year, with her oversized holiday sweaters, random Christmas trivia, and her tendency to talk to marshmallows. The Midwest didn't always do quirky. And she hadn't lived here since she was a little girl. A lot had changed since then, including her.

But she'd also learned that she had to be true to herself. Anything less would end in heartbreak. The French Bastard had taught her that lesson.

They'd met at culinary school. At first, he'd found her adorable, endearing even. He'd swept her off her feet with his charm. Told her she was beautiful. He'd opened her eyes to the world—fine dining in Paris, lavish gifts, last-minute getaways. They'd been to so many places—Monaco, the Swiss Alps, Iceland, Tuscany, Bora Bora.

But little by little, he'd chipped away at her confidence.

"Are you sure you're going to wear that?"

"Have you ever thought about contacts?"

"Braids again? What are you, five?"

It hadn't just been about her appearance. He'd second-guessed her every creative instinct. Her ideas. Her spark.

"Citrus and white chocolate? No. Never."

"Do you even pay attention in school?"

"That will never work."

Soon, she'd stopped defending herself. Stopped offering ideas. In the end, she wasn't even a partner in the shop they ran together. She was just an employee. Worse than that, her opinions didn't matter. She didn't matter.

She'd lost herself. And it still hadn't been enough.

He'd tossed her aside, cheating on her with an intern in their apartment. She'd walked in last year to see Santa's little helper riding her boyfriend in their bed wearing nothing but a big red bow.

Cassidy couldn't believe that it had taken losing everything to make her realize she didn't want any of it.

Now, she wouldn't dim her light again. Not for anyone. She'd fought hard to get here—to Maple Falls, to this shop, to this moment. She was rebuilding something real, something hers. And anyone who couldn't see her magic didn't deserve a seat at her table.

She just needed a reminder every now and then.

Back at the shop, she climbed the narrow staircase to the small apartment above the Cocoa Corner to drop Muff off before heading back to work. Muff's paws tapped the wooden stairs beside her. She opened the door to her new home—a snug one-bedroom apartment that smelled faintly of cocoa from the shop below.

The space was simple but hers, and that meant everything. A tiny galley kitchen with pale blue cabinets she planned to repaint, a well-worn loveseat, and a small pine table tucked under the window where Muff's bed lay.

The pup padded over to the window, circling on her blanket before settling in for a nap.

Cassidy glanced around, taking in the plain white walls and bare windows. *It could use a little Christmas*, she thought, promising to tackle her apartment next. She imagined twinkle lights draped around the windows, a wreath on the door with red velvet ribbon, a full-size Christmas tree in the corner, twinkling with multicolored lights.

Outside, flurries of snow danced past the window, catching the glow from the streetlights, while inside, the warmth of the radiator hummed softly beneath the windowsill.

She had plenty more boxes in storage. Christmas décor handed down from her parents and her grand-maman that had sat untouched for almost four years. She'd packed them away when she'd moved to Paris, telling herself she'd get them out again when the time was right. But Jean-Paul's sleek, modern style didn't fit with twinkly lights or mismatched ornaments. And when it came down to it, he didn't care about the little things that mattered to her.

But this was her space now. Her fresh start. Her chance to create a home that felt like her—cozy, warm, unapologetically festive.

She pressed a hand to her chest, feeling the weight of her locket with its spiced cocoa recipe beneath her sweater, and smiled softly. This year, she promised herself, she would celebrate Christmas the way she wanted.

On the landing, she practiced again: "Welcome to the Cocoa Corner!" Her voice was light, but hesitation still crept in.

"Did I take on too much?" she questioned her reflection.

She wanted to believe the answer was no. But then she thought about that morning—how she'd been rushing, distracted, trying to serve people and prep a fresh batch of marshmallows when she'd caught sight of Liam through the front window, laughing with someone outside his shop. One second of watching him—one second too long—and she'd accidentally knocked a full mug of hot cocoa onto a customer's lap.

She'd apologized profusely, offered a full refund and a free box of truffles, but it had rattled her more than she wanted to admit.

She told herself it was just exhaustion. That she hadn't had a full night's sleep in days. But deep down, it felt like a crack in her façade, and everything she'd built threatened to slip through her fingers.

Her mirrored self had no response.

"You're no help," she said to her reflection as her phone rang. She shook off the uncertainties and put on a happy face.

She answered the video call and was immediately greeted by the two familiar faces she missed most—her brother, Julian, and his husband, Miles. Julian, with his crisp white shirt and black V-neck sweater, while Miles wore a hot-pink button-up and matching glasses. The men were a case study in opposites attract.

"Hey! We just wanted to see how our favorite sister was doing," Julian said.

"I'm good! How are you guys?" she asked, trying to sound chipper as she walked the rest of the way downstairs and into her shop.

"Uh-oh," Julian said, narrowing his eyes. "What's with the fake voice?"

"What fake voice? I don't have a fake voice. It's been a great first couple days."

Julian didn't look convinced. Cassidy couldn't have that. Her brother, in all his loving, protective ways, hadn't wanted her to go. He and Miles had wanted her to stay in New York and keep working at their patisserie, even running her own store when they expanded.

But she wanted something different, something that was just her own. She was eternally grateful to them. They'd been there when her Parisian world had fallen apart, but now she was ready to branch out on her own. And she was doing just fine. They'd just caught her in a moment of weakness, thinking about Jean-Paul and how much he'd royally screwed with her life.

"Here, wanna see?" Cassidy offered before they could ask any more questions. She turned the video around; the less time her brother had to study her expression, the better.

She walked around her shop, showing off the cute pop-up café with its spiced cocoa sign, its glass jar of Christmas tree-shaped marshmallows and candy cane twists, before turning the camera on her handwritten chalkboard and display case.

"I've sold a little bit of everything, and look, it's snowing out!" Cassidy didn't have to feign excitement in that as she panned the phone to the front window. She was counting on a white Christmas this year; it had been years since she'd had one. Paris wasn't exactly known for its holiday snowfall.

"What about you guys? How's it going?" she asked quickly.

"Cass," Miles said gently, "you know you don't have to pretend with us."

She sighed and flipped the camera back around.

"I'm okay. Just tired. That's all. And, you know... apparently there's a Gingerbread Jerk on the loose."

Julian's sculpted brows rose. "A what now?"

"Someone's been messing with people's holiday displays," she explained. "Knocking things over, breaking stuff. The bakery and bookshop were both hit."

Miles leaned closer to the camera. "Cass, that doesn't sound like harmless Christmas mischief. Do you have security? Locks? Maybe a festive taser?"

"I'm fine," she said quickly. "It's probably just bored teenagers or the wind or... whatever. I've got Muff, I've got marshmallows, and I've got backup cocoa. I'm good."

Julian didn't look convinced. "Just promise us you'll be careful, okay?"

She nodded, even as her stomach fluttered. She didn't want them to worry—not when she'd fought so hard to come here and prove she could do this on her own.

"I promise," she said. "Besides, if the Gingerbread Jerk wants to come for me, they better bring it. I'm scrappy when provoked."

The shop's bell jingled. Cassidy looked up, relieved to see Madison step through the door. Her fiery red hair spilled out of the beanie she had tucked on her head. "Sorry, I have to let you go. I have a customer." She panned the camera to her friend to prove she wasn't lying.

Madison played along, waving back.

"Fine, fine. We'll call you later," Miles insisted.

"Looking forward to it," she said with a wave before hanging up.

She turned her attention to Madison. "Thank you for coming in when you did."

"Happy to help. What's that all about?"

Unlike with her family, Cassidy didn't feel like she had to hide her feelings around Madison. Perhaps because they had something in common, coming back to the Midwest after being away for so long.

"My brother. He and his husband, Miles, are worried about me."

Madison nodded. "It's a big leap. Starting over."

Cassidy leaned against the counter. "Yeah. And honestly? I was a mess when I came home from Paris, so I get it."

Her friend stepped closer as if imparting a secret. "Well, for what it's worth... your chocolate is magic. Trust me, I know these things."

Cassidy brightened. Madison was a food critic for one of the country's top culinary magazines, and she didn't sugarcoat things. If she said it was good, it had to be.

"Thanks. I needed to hear that." Cassidy stood up taller. "So, what can I get for you?"

"An extra-large cup of your spiced hot cocoa to go. Kit's assembling a massive gingerbread house in the lobby, and her visions of grandeur are giving me anxiety."

"That's saying something."

"You haven't seen this house." Madison lowered her voice. "She's got gumdrop turrets, Cassidy. Turrets."

"Is that even structurally possible?"

"Not according to physics. But Kit doesn't believe in physics. Or rules. Or the limitations of icing."

Cassidy grinned, ladling the cocoa. She liked Kit and could appreciate her enthusiasm for the season, unlike some people she knew.

As though she'd summoned him with her thoughts, she caught sight of Liam as he stepped outside his shop. All rugged with his red checkered flannel, worn jeans, and leather work boots. He stood, hands on his hips, surveying his space.

Then he pulled out a measuring tape and Cassidy's throat went dry.

She decided right then that there was something very sexy about a man with a plan—especially when that man looked like a living lumberjack and smelled faintly of cedar and honey.

She almost smiled—until he scowled at the string of Christmas lights hanging off his awning, shook his head like the lights had personally offended him, and muttered something she couldn't hear but was *definitely* not in the Christmas spirit.

She forced herself to tear her gaze away, rolling her eyes as she did.

Mr. Grumpy Lumberjack was clearly working on his display for the Christmas Countdown, and the irony was infuriating. He didn't even like Christmas. What right did he have to win a competition that was all about community, joy, and actual festive cheer?

That first-place prize should be hers based on her energy alone.

And it *would* be hers if she could just keep her focus in this year of no men.

Because that man was clearly a big distraction wrapped in flannel.

And she couldn't afford to lose herself for a man, especially not a grinch. No matter how good he looked holding a measuring tape.

TEN

LIAM

So far, so good. He'd stayed away all day. So, Liam tried—and failed—not to give himself too much shit for stopping by the chocolate shop yesterday.

"You couldn't even hold out one day," he muttered, shaking his head as he tightened his grip on the steering wheel.

He'd told himself maybe it had been a fluke. That what Cassidy did to him—the way she'd looked in the snow on Sunday night, barefoot, braided hair, smiling like magic had dropped straight from the sky—was some kind of sleep-deprived moment of madness. A temporary spell conjured from the scent of cocoa and cold air.

Yeah. No.

He'd been dead wrong.

The image of her yesterday, flushed and flustered, trying to impress him with chocolates, had been playing on loop in his head ever since. The way she'd lit up when he'd bitten into that truffle and deflated when he hadn't given her the reaction she'd wanted.

How she'd insisted they had a crazed vandal running among them.

God, she was so damn fierce about it. Like everything she did had to mean something. Like she couldn't not care. He hadn't seen that kind of fire in a long time. He wanted to feed it. Push her buttons. Watch her unravel.

He couldn't stop wondering how her passion would translate when she wasn't pouring it into cocoa or trying to win a light-up contest. What would she sound like when she wasn't trying to impress anyone? When she let go completely?

He imagined her mouth on his, hot and demanding. But this time, it wasn't on the counter in his shop. No, this time, it was his truck.

The image hit him like a snowstorm. Cassidy, waiting for him on the backseat of his truck after closing, wrapped in one of his old flannel blankets. The kind that smelled faintly like pine and woodsmoke. She'd be sipping cocoa, cheeks flushed, her breath fogging up in the cold night air. Her braid would be undone, golden waves spilling over her shoulders, and when he climbed in beside her, she'd look at him with that fire in her eyes —the one that made him forget how to think.

"You took your time," she'd whisper, voice low and full of intent.

She'd pull him down by the collar, lips crashing into his. Her hands would slide beneath his coat, finding the edge of his thermal shirt, slipping underneath to touch bare skin.

And then she'd straddle him.

Right there, in the backseat of the truck, hips rolling in slow circles against his lap, grinding down just enough to drive him insane but not enough to give him what he needed. Her hands tangled in his hair, her mouth tracing the shell of his ear.

"You want me?" she'd breathe. "Prove it."

And he would. God, he would.

His hands would slide up her thighs beneath that extra

Christmas skirt she wore. He'd tug it higher, revealing lace-trimmed stockings—or maybe nothing at all. Her body would be hot against the cold night, her moans fogging up the truck windows as he made her come apart beneath the winter sky.

It would be all breath and steam and the creak of the suspension as they moved, as he pushed into her, slow and deep, her back arching beneath him. The town silent. Just the two of them and the heat they couldn't outrun anymore.

A muscle ticked in his jaw as he shifted in his seat, the steering wheel gripped too tight in his hands.

He was not going to think about Cassidy St. Clair riding him in the back of his truck.

He tried to reroute his thoughts. He didn't know Cassidy well. He'd heard things around town, snippets from Madison and Zach, even his mom. She'd lived in Paris. Owned a shop there. Something about a breakup. She was a happy, bright, and smiling kind of person, and to his great annoyance, she was the town's biggest fan of Christmas, which was saying a lot.

But there was more to her, he could sense it. She had a darker kind of depth. He wanted to know her story. Not just the one wrapped in silky sheets and cocoa-smudged kisses, but the kind of story that shaped a person.

Liam's truck rumbled as it turned onto the gravel drive leading to the family farm. The wrought-iron archway above the entrance was strung with evergreen garlands, white twinkle lights, and a red bow nearly as wide as his wingspan.

His mom's handiwork, of course. She still believed in the magic of the season. Beth handled all the farm's decorating, right down to the gift barn, where they sold the same goods he now offered in town: honey, jams, alpaca knits, hand-poured candles. They sold the type of gifts that made you feel appreciated, remembered.

Coming out to the farm today hadn't exactly been on Liam's list. He'd just been here on Sunday for lunch. A tradition his mom insisted on keeping alive. One o'clock sharp, every Sunday. Open-door policy. Anyone from town could drop in and usually did.

It had started back when Jackson was deployed, and their sister, Lily, was always somewhere across the globe chasing sunshine and Wi-Fi. Liam never missed a Sunday, not even now, when he'd rather skip right over the holidays.

On Sunday, Beth had served up country-fried steak, mashed potatoes, gravy, and apple pie for dessert. Mayor Bloomfield had dropped by, along with his lady friend, Edith, and Mrs. Bishop. Her kitchen renovation still wasn't done, despite Zach's best efforts. Mrs. Bishop had decided to rearrange everything, including the kitchen sink, and Liam had since learned not to ask his best friend how things were going.

His mom had a habit of filling the table with guests. "The more, the merrier," she always said. And no one loved a full house more than she did.

But today, Liam was here for a different reason.

The town Christmas tree.

His family had supplied the massive spruce that stood in Maple Falls' center square for generations. He should've delivered it yesterday, but he'd avoided the crowds—the Christmas cheer, the Santa House, Cassidy. Now, with just a few hours until the tree lighting ceremony, he had to get it loaded and into town.

He pulled into the gravel lot, parked, and stepped out. A cold gust hit his face, and he inhaled the sharp scent of pine and woodsmoke. Over by the barn, Jackson was already tying down the last of the netting around the spruce.

"Hey, man," Liam called, walking over. "Thanks for getting that started."

"Figured I'd make your life easier for once," Jackson replied, tugging the twine taut. Typical Jackson—stoic, efficient. His way of saying he cared without actually saying it.

"You sure you don't want to come into town with me?"

Jackson paused. "Nah, once last night was enough."

Liam nodded, not pushing. He understood that heaviness that no amount of holiday cheer could lift.

They were twins but completely different. Always had been. Liam had been the joker, the flirt, the fun one. And he still was, except for this time of year. Jackson was quiet, serious, and methodical year-round. The war had only deepened that divide.

Their mom came out just then, sweater wrapped tightly around her, ladle in hand. The smell of onion, garlic, and thyme drifted toward him.

"I was hoping to catch you before you left," she said. "I made beef stew. There's plenty extra. Come in and eat before you go."

Liam leaned down so she could kiss his cheek. It was automatic, like muscle memory.

"I'd love to," he said, "but I'm already behind. If I don't get that tree into town before four, Mayor Bloomfield will come knocking on my door."

She gave him a look. "Then you'll take it to go."

Before he could argue, she was already heading back inside.

Liam turned back to Jackson, who was stacking firewood beside the oversized pit they kept burning from fall through winter. It gave customers a place to warm up after tree shopping, but mostly, it made outdoor work a little more bearable.

"Where's Dad?"

"Fixing one of the sleigh tracks. They've been working overtime since Friday," Jackson said, tossing another log onto the flames.

Liam nodded. Sleigh rides were one of the farm's biggest draws. Pair that with cocoa, fresh-cut trees, and photo ops by the barn, and they had a holiday destination.

As Liam turned back toward his truck and loaded the tree,

Cassidy's laugh from yesterday echoed in his memory. Bright and unapologetic, like her smile. Like snowflakes falling in sunshine.

Why was he so drawn to her?

How could he even bring himself to feel like this, especially at this time of year?

They'd met two days ago. That was it. And yet...

His phone buzzed in his coat pocket.

He ignored it, hoisted the tree into the truck bed.

Buzz.

Then again.

With a grunt, he tugged his gloves off and pulled out his phone. The screen lit up with notifications from his friends' group chat.

Madison: Guys. Emily's shop was targeted again. This time they messed up her lights and her wreath.

Zoe: I don't like this. It's starting to feel personal.

Kit: I saw that! Emily posted it on Insta. It got 200 likes in the first hour and dozens of comments. #GingerbreadJerk

Cassidy: Unless the wind has a grudge and impeccable aim, it's definitely sabotage. This has to end!

Liam's thumb hovered over the reply bubble, then didn't type anything. Instead, he stared at Cassidy's message: *Unless the wind has a grudge...*

She'd added a wink emoji. Light, teasing. But Liam could imagine her face when she wrote it—spark in her eyes, hair falling into her face, biting her lip.

He scrolled back up and stared at the hashtag: *#GingerbreadJerk*

Was it funny? Yeah. A little. But the truth was, if there was someone out there trying to mess with businesses—wreck displays, ruin people's shot at the competition—it wouldn't take much to cause real harm.

He hated to think of Cassidy's shop being targeted next. He could picture her up bright and early, working on her chocolates alone in her kitchen while someone watched outside, waiting for the opportunity to strike.

Not that there was any real danger. Probably.

Still, something tightened in his chest at the thought of it. A sharp, defensive pull.

"You good?" Jackson asked from behind him. He was holding a container of beef stew for Liam to take.

Liam shoved his phone back in his pocket. "Yeah," he muttered, accepting the leftovers. "Thanks for the help. I better get going."

He climbed into the truck, but his thoughts stayed with Cassidy. He told himself it was just concern for a fellow competitor. But the need to make sure she was safe had already burrowed under his skin.

ELEVEN

CASSIDY

"Cassidy! Business going well?" Mayor Bloomfield called out as she arrived in the town square, just a stone's throw from her shop.

The mayor wore a red velvet sport coat over a white satin vest embroidered with tiny candy canes. She could appreciate the man's dedication to the season. Honestly, she should really find out where he shopped.

"First two days have been great," she said brightly. "I'm excited to see what the rest of the week brings."

"Good, good." He gave a jolly nod.

Late afternoon would soon turn to evening in Maple Falls, and the Christmas tree lighting ceremony was supposed to take place at the center of the town square, yet there was no tree in sight.

Cassidy looked around. The culinary shop had gone all out with a massive, eight-foot-tall nutcracker next to its door. She could have sworn it had given her a little salute when she'd passed earlier.

The Cinnamon Spice Inn looked even more impressive. Lanterns with flickering lights lined the walkway. The stately columns were wrapped in evergreen and lights with two full-size Christmas trees between them. An oversized wreath dominated the front door. Cassidy had had a chance to admire it earlier with its gold-painted pinecones, sugared cranberries, and burgundy velvet ribbon. Madison had truly made the inn feel like a home.

It was the same all down Oak Way. From nearly every awning and doorway hung garlands of evergreen and white twinkle lights. Even the lampposts were wrapped in gold-lined red ribbon and oversized bows.

But no Christmas tree in the town square.

"Can I help you with something?" Mayor Bloomfield raised his eyebrows.

"I was just looking for the Christmas tree. Isn't the lighting tonight?" According to the Maple Falls website, there were all sorts of activities planned to celebrate the tree lighting tonight: a Christmas wish fire, an ornament raffle, sleigh rides through town.

She stood up on her tiptoes, peering over his shoulder. Maybe it wasn't in the town square. Had she misread the location? That wouldn't be a shock. She was running on six hours of sleep. Tonight, she was definitely soaking in a bubble bath, crawling into fleece pajamas, and watching *Home Alone*. And no more cocoa. Her cocoa consumption was way too high. Almost as high as her lack of patience in uncovering and apprehending the Gingerbread Jerk before they succeeded in harming this beautiful town's Christmas spirit.

"Afraid you're a bit early," Mayor Bloomfield said with a chuckle. He brought a hand to his brow and scanned the street. "But it should be here any second now. He sent me a text about fifteen minutes ago."

"He?" Cassidy asked.

The mayor ignored her question. "Ah, there he is."

Cassidy followed his gaze just as a dark gray pickup truck rumbled into view at the end of the blocked-off road. She didn't need to look twice to recognize the man.

Do not think about his candy cane. Or his snowballs. Or tying him up with tinsel, she reminded herself.

But then Liam stepped out of the truck and all bets were off.

He ate up the pavement in three long strides, boots crunching through packed snow. Without a word, without looking at her, he dropped the tailgate and got to work loosening the tie-downs, unhooking the rope. His entire routine was smooth, practiced. He could probably do a lot with those straps.

He might be a grinch, and he might be way sexier than should ever be allowed, but Cassidy was determined to get on with everyone in this town. Liam was friends with all her new friends, and she was going to make him like her.

"Hey, neighbor," Cassidy said, walking over and trying to sound casual, but her voice came out all breathless instead.

Good Lord. It was happening again. Cocoa brain was back.

She cleared her throat. "Do you want help?" she asked in a perkier voice, and, before he could answer, she climbed right up into the truck bed to help him wrangle the tree.

He moved over to the side. "Um, sure."

"Alright, let me just hoist this sucker up and we'll be golden," she said, getting into position.

"You sure? You want some gloves?" Liam reached for a pair in the back pocket of his jeans.

"It's all good. I've got—wait! Hang on. It's caught on my sweater! Let me just..." Cassidy yelped, half laughing, half panicking as a spruce branch snagged the sleeve of her favorite Christmas sweater. It was green with a felt elf on the front, wearing a hat just like the one the mayor's assistant had given her. The jumper elf had actual fur around his hat and jingle bells on his toes.

"Let me go, Mr. Evergreen. I did not agree to restraints," she said to the tree, trying to break free. But the spruce needles only dug deeper.

"Enjoying a bit of role-play up there, are we?" Liam called over.

But she couldn't reply. She sneezed not once but twice.

"Bless you," he said, wincing sympathetically.

"Thanks." Cassidy turned her head and sneezed some more. She lost count after five.

Oh no. Of course. Stupid freaking tree. It had to be a Norway spruce. There was no other explanation. And if that man didn't make her brain-dead, she would've thought to check before now.

"What is your safe word?" she grumbled to the tree.

"You know," he said casually, "if you're gonna invoke safe words this early in the relationship, I feel like I should at least get a say in what they are."

ACHOO! Cassidy sneezed again. "This is not how this ends!" she declared.

"You good there, Sugarplum?" Liam sounded a bit more concerned now as he called from the back of the truck, where he was still holding up his end of the tree.

"No," Cassidy confessed as her eyes started watering. "I'm allergic to Norway spruces, and this—*ACHOO!*—tree is holding me hostage."

Through her stinging eyes Cassidy saw Zach and Madison arriving from the inn across the street.

"You okay?" Zach called up to Cassidy.

"No, she's allergic to Christmas," Liam answered for her.

"Not Christmas, just some Christmas trees—*ACHOO!*—just Norway—*ACHOO!*—spruces."

"Here, take this," Liam said to Zach.

Zach stepped in and lifted up the back of the tree while Liam climbed into the truck bed beside Cassidy.

He quickly assessed the situation. "You're tangled up pretty good, but don't worry. I got you."

Liam reached for something under his flannel. Cassidy's eyes might have been itchy and watery, but she still appreciated the waistband of his jeans and the sliver of skin above. Liam unclipped the utility knife from his jeans and flipped it open with the flick of his wrist.

Cassidy never knew she had a thing for a man with a knife, but now she knew.

"Hold still," he commanded, using the knife to cut the offending branches to free her.

The needles were still woven into her sweater, but at least she was now free from the tree.

"Let's get you out of here," he added, jumping out of the back of his truck and lifting his arms up to help her down.

Cassidy was going to protest, say she didn't need the help, but a larger part of her wanted to feel his hands on her waist.

She sat on the edge of the truck bed, swung her legs over, and allowed Liam to lift her down.

It was better than she'd imagined. His hands felt warm and strong. She leaned into him, feeling the heat of his body. It would be all too easy to wrap herself around him like tinsel, but she restrained herself.

Because she was off men. Yep, completely, one hundred percent off them until January 1st. And anyway, Liam clearly wasn't into her. How could he be? She radiated Christmas joy and he hated the holiday.

"You okay?" Liam asked, picking the needles off her sweater.

"I will be now that I'm away from the tree." Cassidy rolled up her sleeve to reveal a trail of hives already forming up her forearm. "Or maybe not."

"You guys go," Zach offered. "Madison and I have got the tree. You should take care of that arm."

"I'm fine," Cassidy said quickly. "I just need to rinse it."

Still, Liam frowned. "I'd feel better if I went with you. Allergic reactions are no joke. My dad's allergic to nuts," he added.

Cassidy sighed. "Fine. But only because you have that protective, bossy eyebrow thing going on."

He raised a brow in response. "This one?"

"Exactly," she replied. "That one is especially persuasive."

She hurried toward her shop with Liam trailing right behind her, his hand lightly hovering at her back, not touching, but definitely close enough to feel.

"You sure you're okay?" he asked again as she fumbled with her keys, trying to unlock the door.

"Just dandy," she replied, still unable to open the lock.

"Let me," Liam said behind her, his voice low and firm as he reached around her to take the keys.

His hand brushed hers. Warm. Solid.

She froze. Not because of her arm but because he didn't move away. He was still close. Too close. Deliciously close.

The door swung open, and she practically stumbled inside, half from nerves, half from the fact that Liam's presence was now fully short-circuiting her brain. She headed straight for the kitchen in the back.

At the center of the room stood a long, marble-topped work-table, cool and smooth to the touch, its surface usually dusted lightly with cocoa powder and powdered sugar. Copper mixing bowls hung from a rack overhead, swaying slightly as she brushed past them, and beneath the table were rows of drawers filled with candy molds, piping bags, and carefully labeled ingredients.

Cassidy made a beeline for the farmhouse-style sink

beneath the window, flipping the tap on and running cold water over her arm.

Liam followed with that swagger of his, his gaze never leaving her. "Let me see."

She held her arm under the water, trying to pretend this was normal. Trying not to look up and notice how good he looked in the soft glow of the twinkle lights she'd left on. Trying not to care that his voice had gone husky.

"I'm fine," she said, but it came out as a whisper.

"You keep saying that. But you're shaking."

She swallowed. It was true, she was practically vibrating inside. But not from the hives.

"It's nothing," she added with a soft smile.

He stepped closer, his hand coming to rest gently on her waist as he leaned in to look at her arm. "You broke out in hives. That's not nothing. Maybe you should have a doctor check it out."

"No, trust me, I'm fine. Just a little allergic reaction, no big deal. I once had an asthma attack from a holiday spruce-scented candle, so really, this is nothing," she rambled. "It's totally fine. I mean, it's not fine, but it's like... normal not-fine. You know?"

He huffed a quiet laugh, but his hand didn't move. Neither did hers, which had somehow settled on the front of his coat. She didn't even remember putting it there.

He was so close. She could smell him—woodsmoke and pine and something undeniably him. Her gaze dropped to his mouth.

"This isn't just in my head, is it?" she asked before she could stop herself. Her other hand was now on his waist. The water still running in the background.

He went very still. Then his voice came, low and rough. "No. It's not."

Her heart skipped.

In one whisper of a second, everything shifted.

The heat in his gaze made her dizzy. Her arm might've been on fire, but the rest of her was burning for entirely different reasons.

His fingers slid up her arm, careful to avoid her hives, but tender all the same. She tipped her face up just as he leaned in. His hand cupped her cheek.

And then—

"Cassidy, honey? Are you back here? I brought that jar of candied pecans," Mrs. Bishop's voice called out.

Cassidy jumped back from Liam like she'd been hit with a snowball. He stepped back just as quickly, one hand scratching awkwardly at the back of his neck.

"Oh hey, Mrs. Bishop," Cassidy called out, voice an octave too high. "I was just trying not to be killed by a Christmas tree!"

Mrs. Bishop's head popped into the kitchen, holding a festive Mason jar with a bow tied on top. She took one look at Cassidy's flushed face and Liam standing there looking very much like he'd been about to do something worth blushing over.

"Well," Mrs. Bishop said, taking in the scene. "Didn't mean to interrupt whatever... medicinal treatment was happening back here."

Liam cleared his throat. "Cassidy was having an allergic reaction."

"Uh-huh," Mrs. Bishop said, setting the jar on the counter with a wink. "I'll just... let myself out."

Cassidy groaned, covering her face with both hands.

Liam leaned in again, but this time, his mouth brushed her ear.

"Next time," he said, "you should probably avoid spruce trees. Dim lighting. And me."

Cassidy was pretty sure her knees melted into marshmallow fluff.

She didn't say a word. But as she turned back to the sink and the cool water and her steadily flushing cheeks, she knew one thing for certain: This man was a walking temptation. He was endangering her promised year of no men. He was doing things to her that Jean-Paul never did. Not even close. Jean-Paul had been a cold, calculated performance. Liam was heat and passion. There was promise in his eyes of the wicked things he could do. And heaven help her, she wanted to experience them all.

TWELVE

LIAM

Liam knew it was best to put as much distance between him and Cassidy as possible.

What in the hell were you doing? he chastised himself as he stepped outside the Cocoa Corner.

The cold wind whipped across his face and Liam prayed it would cool the hot, raw energy that had been building in his veins. He had been mere seconds away from crushing his lips to Cassidy's, pulling her close, and taking everything she would've given him. He would've tried to be gentle, but he couldn't make any promises. She smelled like chocolate and caramel—and a whisper of spice.

It was madness. There was no other explanation. There was no reason a woman he'd just met should have this much pull on him. But he couldn't deny it.

She was so full of life. So vibrant. So damn joyful. Liam had forgotten what it was like to see that spark in someone's eyes. He used to have that, genuinely, deep down inside him. But since meeting Cassidy, he felt more and more like he had been faking it, playing a role in Maple Falls. Until Christmas and the anniversary came around, he fulfilled that role dutifully. The charm. The flirting. The parties. But the happiness? That was surface level. A performance. To him and everyone else. It had been like that for the last four years.

All show. No substance.

And he'd built that persona himself. Hyped it up, even.

He didn't date, not long-term. Bachelor parties. Girls' weekend trips. If a woman came to Maple Falls looking for a Midwestern romantic fantasy, Liam was her guy. They'd both get what they wanted, and she'd leave by Monday morning.

No strings. No complications.

Liam preferred it that way. It was safer. And he hadn't been ready for anything deeper, not after what had happened that Christmas, years ago.

Deep down, he didn't believe he deserved love again.

And yet... there was Cassidy.

The way she moved through town with that bright-eyed determination, cocoa in hand, cheeks pink from the cold, calling out greetings to everyone she passed. The way she wore that elf hat with zero self-consciousness, like she couldn't help but dive headfirst into joy, even when she had every reason not to.

It should have annoyed him. Should have had him running a mile in the opposite direction.

But it didn't.

And Liam didn't understand why.

The downtown area was steadily filling up with locals and tourists for the tree lighting festival. The town's gas fireplaces were blazing, and people stood around them with knit hats pulled low and scarves wrapped tight, socializing with steaming cups of boozy hot toddies or mugs of hot buttered rum from the Kettle.

Cassidy might've cornered the market on hot cocoa, but the Kettle still had the best hot cocktails in town.

The square also had miniature trees set up in stands, and bins of plastic ornaments for kids to decorate them with while their parents mingled. A saxophone player stood on the corner wearing a Santa hat, playing "Here Comes Santa Claus," while the holiday trolley pulled up to the end of the street. The trolley, bright green and decorated with multicolored lights, brought locals from the residential district to the downtown area so they wouldn't have to drive over and find a place to park.

Laughter echoed through the streets, the scent of cinnamon was thick in the air, and it was only the beginning of the holiday season.

Liam smiled at Mr. Alders from the hardware store, waved at Zach's mom, Anita, and purposely avoided meeting Mrs. Bishop's eye, despite her best attempts.

He wondered how quickly word would get around that he was into Cassidy.

Knowing the locals, it would be common knowledge by nightfall.

He'd have to be careful. Keep his distance. Play it safe.

He had, though... hadn't he? He hadn't sought her out. Not this time.

He'd just been trying to deliver the damn Christmas tree, and the next thing he knew, she'd jumped up into his truck, offered to lend a hand, and look where that had landed him.

He shook his head.

This time wasn't his fault.

He'd just have to make sure there wasn't a next time.

Liam picked up his pace, weaving through the growing crowd, and joined Zach, who was just finishing securing the tree in the stand.

"Cassidy okay?" Zach asked, standing up from underneath the tree.

"Yeah, she's great," Liam said a bit too quickly.

He put his gloves on and tried to casually survey the scene, which meant he *was* casually surveying the scene. There were kids bundled up in puffy coats, throwing snowballs while parents stood off to the side, keeping an eye on things. One tyke in particular tried to break free and scale the tree Liam had just delivered. The kid shrieked as his parents ran after him.

Liam smiled. *That's better*, he thought, because if Zach had seen his earlier expression, he'd know Cassidy had him all torn up inside.

Liam couldn't give him the satisfaction.

After all the shit Liam had given Zach over Madison, he knew he deserved it. He just couldn't listen to it. Not right now.

And Zach wouldn't hold back. That was just how they were.

"Hey, guys, did you get the lights?" Madison asked, joining them. "The crafting club said they left them in the gazebo yesterday," Madison said. "They were all labeled and ready to go."

Liam strode around to the back of the gazebo, his boots crunching over fresh snow. A second later, his angry voice cut through the chatter.

"Found them," he called. "Or what's left of them."

Madison rushed over, Zach following behind. The large plastic bin was cracked open down the middle like someone had forced it apart. Shattered pieces of the lid were buried in the snow, and inside, the contents had been ransacked—some lights were still tangled around broken bits of garland, but half were missing entirely. A handful of crushed ornaments were scattered on the ground nearby, as if someone had stomped on them.

"Looks like the Gingerbread Jerk has struck again," Zach said.

"Everything okay?" Cassidy asked, walking over to join the group.

Liam hadn't even seen her approach. But the second he saw

her, every nerve in his body, nerves he'd fought hard to control, jolted back to life.

She'd switched her coat out for a deep green one that shouldn't have been sexy, but something about the way the wool hugged her curves made him fight not to stare.

He caught her eyes. They were bright, excited for the evening's festivities. She looked like Christmas come to life.

"Are you okay?" Madison asked, instinctively reaching for Cassidy's arm.

"Yep. Totally fine. I put some cream on it and changed my sweater. The rash is probably gone by now." She smiled. "What's going on?"

"The Gingerbread Jerk struck again," Madison explained. "We have forty-five minutes to get the tree strung, and no lights."

"What? No!" Cassidy looked over at the broken-bulbed mess and Liam could swear he saw steam coming out of her ears.

"I have a bin of Christmas decorations upstairs in my bedroom," she offered. "I don't know if I have enough lights, but it's something."

Madison turned to Liam. "Why don't you run back and help her grab it?"

The question was innocent enough, but God help him, he couldn't do it. The thought of being upstairs, in Cassidy's bedroom—where she slept, where the scent of her would linger in the air, on the sheets, in every corner of that small space...

Liam had been going crazy with need, and that was when they were fully clothed in public.

The idea of being alone with her in that bedroom, tension crackling like a live wire between them, the door closing behind him, her standing there with her soft sweater and flushed cheeks, looking at him like she wanted him as badly as he wanted her—

It was too much.

He thought back to earlier, when he'd almost kissed her. She had whispered, "This isn't just in my head, is it?"

And Liam had known right then that she felt every ounce of desire he did.

But he couldn't act on it. Wouldn't.

Cassidy was full of hope, love, and Christmas magic.

And he was full of emptiness and grief.

He wouldn't bring his heaviness into her light and bright holiday cheer.

She deserved better than that.

"I'll go to the hardware store," Liam blurted. Hell, he'd walk one town over before setting foot in Cassidy's bedroom. There was only so much temptation one man could handle.

Her face fell. "If you'd rather?" She looked away.

Liam cursed under his breath.

She'd offered to help, and now she looked shut out, as if he'd rejected her.

"It's just... they probably have more lights, and we can pick out exactly what we need. If we hurry, we can be back before the ceremony even starts," he amended. "You want to come?"

Cassidy's face lit up, and, by God, he felt something break loose in his chest.

All he could think was, *God help me, the next time we're alone, I'm not going to be able to walk away.*

THIRTEEN

CASSIDY

Cassidy tried to keep up with Liam as they quickly made their way down the icy sidewalk. Snowflakes were falling freely now. They were the big, thick, white ones that floated down in oversized crystals.

Maple Falls looked like a Christmas card that evening. Twinkle lights stretched across the street in zigzagging strands. Shop windows glowed warmly against the cold with paper snowflakes and wreaths with plaid ribbons. The scent of woodsmoke drifted through the air from the Kettle, where people cradled steaming cups as they waited for the tree lighting ceremony to begin.

Her breath puffed out in little clouds as she matched Liam's pace, which—because of his long legs—was practically a light jog for her.

"Who do you think did it? You already shot down Mr. Alders—"

"He's a nice guy," Liam interrupted.

"Yes, I know, you said that. But who else could it be? You've lived here your whole life. Surely you've got to have some idea?"

Liam shook his head. "Not a clue."

"Well..." She tilted her head and gave him a mock-serious look. "You do hate Christmas. You're grumpy. You always look like you're about two seconds from throwing an inflatable reindeer into oncoming traffic. Honestly, if I were writing a cozy mystery, you'd be suspect number one."

Liam scoffed. "That's rich coming from the mysterious new girl with a chocolate empire and zero background info. No one even knows where you came from."

"Excuse me," she said, hands on hips. "I came from two towns over. Before I went to Paris, I was a Midwestern girl through and through. And I'm a delight."

"Exactly what a criminal mastermind would say."

Cassidy gasped, mock offended. "Wow. I shared my chocolates with you and everything."

"I'm just saying..." Liam gave her a sideways glance, the corners of his mouth twitching. "If another string of lights goes missing, people are going to start asking questions about the new girl in town."

Then he looked at her—really looked at her. His gaze flicked from her flushed cheeks to the curve of her smile, then lingered just a second too long on her mouth.

"And don't think those sugar-coated lips of yours would get you out of trouble." He winked.

Cassidy's breath caught at the same time her foot hit a patch of ice.

"WHOOPS!" It came out like a shriek.

She slipped and pitched forward. Her back foot didn't have enough purchase to stop her.

Liam caught her before she could faceplant on the pavement —but the momentum and the sheer amount of ice were too much.

The air whooshed out of her lungs. Christmas lights blurred in front of her eyes.

One second, she was upright. The next, she was flat on top of him, sprawled chest to chest. Her cheek pressed into the soft flannel of his shirt. Warm. Familiar.

The rest of him was solid muscle.

Liam groaned. "You okay?"

"Oh my God. I'm so sorry."

Cassidy tried to scramble off him, but as she pushed herself up, her feet slipped again. And somehow—really, it was rather unfair at this point—she ended up straddling him, right in the middle of Oak Way.

And that's when she felt him, the undeniable hardness of him pressing up between her thighs.

"Well, that's one way to do it," Mrs. C. said, looking down at them with a mug of mulled wine in her hand.

"But you might want to go somewhere private. Lots of families around," Mrs. Bishop added with a whisper.

Cassidy's cheeks flamed.

Liam, on the other hand, just tipped an imaginary hat. "Evening, ladies."

"I cannot believe my luck," she said, moving more slowly this time to stand. "I swear this wasn't the plan," she mumbled.

Liam's lips twitched. "If it were, I'd say it was rather impressive."

"I'm not usually this clumsy... Actually, that's a lie. I'm always clumsy. But you were walking so fast, and I was thinking about the Gingerbread Jerk..." Or not exactly, but that was close enough to the truth. "Wait, are you hurt? Of course you're hurt." Cassidy reached out her hand to help Liam the rest of the way up.

"I'm fine," he answered through his teeth, pushing off the frozen ground back to standing.

Cassidy decided it was best that he hadn't accepted her help. There was no guarantee she wouldn't slip on the ice again.

"I didn't break your leg, did I?" Cassidy thought back to how hard she'd landed on him and winced.

"No. I hurt it last week on a run. Hamstring injury," he added, taking a tentative step, which resulted in a pronounced limp. He definitely didn't have that before.

Cassidy felt awful. So far her opening week had been a rollercoaster. From the high of launching her dream shop to the low of sneezing herself silly in front of the town, slipping on ice, and—let's not forget—literally crushing on a Christmas hater.

Because that's what this was, wasn't it? A crush. A full-blown crush on Liam freaking Hawthorne—a man who scowled at Christmas lights and said things that made her knees feel like melted chocolate.

And now, as if her pride wasn't bruised enough, someone out there was sabotaging holiday displays. The Gingerbread Jerk mystery had everyone buzzing, and she couldn't shake the creeping feeling that her cozy new world might be more fragile than she thought.

Cassidy knew she was putting a lot of pressure on herself, but she couldn't help it. Last year had been such a dumpster fire, and she wanted this Christmas to be perfect. It was more than the opening of her chocolate shop; it was the official launch of her new life.

"You good there?" Liam asked, slowing to a stop as they reached the hardware store.

"Hmm? Oh, just plotting a crime," she said lightly. "You know. Standard newcomer stuff. Sabotage. Maybe a little theft."

"Ah, so the usual."

"Exactly."

Liam didn't press, just like how she didn't press him. She knew he had to have one heck of a reason for not liking Christmas, but if he didn't want to tell her his story, that was fine with her.

They stopped in front of the light display.

"Alright," she said, hands on her hips. "Warm white or multicolored?"

"You?" He looked her up and down. "Multicolored. Obviously."

She raised her brows. "What's that supposed to mean?"

"All those plain lights wouldn't know what to do with you."

Her heart skipped. Their arms brushed as they both reached for a box. Fingers collided. Heat sparked.

"Sorry," she murmured.

"Go ahead," he said gruffly. "Take it."

Their eyes met.

"We'll need a few," he added, grabbing another box like it would anchor him.

Cassidy tilted her head, lips twitching. "Yeah, the tree's pretty big, huh?"

He couldn't help himself. "Oh, you have no idea..." He grinned, noticing how her cheeks flushed pink.

FOURTEEN

LIAM

Cassidy isn't all cocoa and candy canes, Liam thought as he fed her Christmas lights. He could see that now: She carried her own darkness, a pain she hid from the world.

One moment, she looked like she had unquenchable confidence, like when she was welcoming him into her shop. She beamed like the whole world was made for her. And the next, she seemed so small and unsure, like when he'd rejected her offer to grab the lights from her apartment. He hadn't meant to hurt her. He just... couldn't go into her bedroom.

Then there were the quieter moments. The way she watched people, as if memorizing how to belong. There wasn't much he missed when it came to Cassidy.

Sure, there had been an instant attraction between them. And the truth was, he wanted to know her. Really know her.

But that's exactly why he had to be careful.

She couldn't be a weekend fling. She was in Maple Falls to stay. He couldn't hook up with her and then pretend things were casual, not when every moment with her felt anything but.

He wasn't ready for something real, something long-lasting, and he might never be. Liam had loved someone once, and it had shattered him beyond repair. He wouldn't make that mistake again. Cassidy deserved someone whole.

Maybe he could just be her friend?

He just had to keep his damn boundaries intact.

No matter how good it felt to be near her, how tempted he was to kiss her.

Friendship was the best he could offer. But he wasn't going to suddenly pretend that he loved Christmas. Just like he wasn't going to ask her to dim her holiday sparkle to suit him.

They worked together in silence, stringing the lights around the tree. Cassidy was on the ladder; Liam was on the ground. He fed her the strands as they moved from branch to branch. Somehow, among the gathering crowd and falling snow, they got it done right on time.

"Perfection. I had all the faith in the world in you two," Mayor Bloomfield said, strolling over. He tugged down on the red velvet lapels of his sport coat and rocked back on his heels, admiring the tree. "That's a gorgeous spruce, son. Your family should be proud."

"Always an honor," Liam replied.

"And those lights?" Mayor Bloomfield clapped. "You do have an eye for Christmas décor." He nodded to Cassidy.

Liam watched her beam under the mayor's praise.

"Thanks. I wanted it to be perfect," she confessed.

"Well, you two certainly saved the day," the mayor said, voice booming just enough to carry to the nearby onlookers. "And after the recent... disruptions, I know the whole town appreciates it. Whoever's behind these incidents—we'll get to the bottom of it. Mark my words. The so-called Gingerbread Jerk won't ruin another Maple Falls tradition on my watch."

He gave a meaningful pause and then added, "Let's just

hope there aren't any more surprises hiding in the shadows, hmm?"

Cassidy's eyes flicked toward Liam. "Fingers crossed," she murmured.

Liam took a step back and watched as Cassidy surveyed the tree. She was still arranging lights here and there, making sure it was just so. She was such a perfectionist, and the mayor was right—she really had a talent for this. Something shifted in his chest as he felt equal parts admiration and dread. If he hadn't realized it before, he realized it now. Friend or not, Cassidy was going to be hard to beat for the Christmas Light-Up Display Competition.

As much as he liked her and could not get enough of her contagious smile, he couldn't let her win. His family needed that prize money. The llama rescue project was too important to him, to Jackson. His brother deserved it after the hell he'd been through. Not to mention the promotion that winning the competition would bring to the family farm shop. He knew how important the first year of business was to a new store, and just like Cassidy, he had a lot to prove.

He had to win, and that meant Cassidy had to lose. But tonight, he didn't want to think about any of that.

All he wanted was to have fun at the tree lighting ceremony —for Cassidy's sake. For their new friendship that felt so natural despite their differences, and seemed to be building very fast.

For the first time in four years, Liam felt like he could put aside the dark memories that surfaced this time of year, the bitterness and guilt it dragged up. He knew he couldn't let it go completely. But he could go back to being a grinch tomorrow.

"What are your plans for after they light this beauty up?" Liam motioned to the tree.

Before Cassidy could answer, Madison, Zach, and Kit appeared from the Kettle, bottles of spiked cider in hand.

"There you are," Madison said. "Kit's trying to wrangle us all for sleigh photos before the crowd gets worse."

"Like you don't want to get in Santa's sleigh. Look at that thing." Kit used her cider to motion down the street at the candy-apple-red sleigh in front of the Santa House. The volunteers had gone all out with the sleigh, a wall of wrapped presents, and a glittery backdrop.

"You want one?" Zach asked, offering Cassidy a bottle of cider.

She reached over and accepted it.

"Hey, where's mine?" Liam asked.

"Probably back at the Kettle." But even as Zach said those words, he was opening his coat pocket and taking the third and final bottle out of his inside pocket. "I figured we'd all want one."

They twisted off their caps and clinked their drinks.

"To Christmas," Kit said.

"To Christmas," everyone echoed—except Liam, who simply couldn't go that far. He took a sip and glanced away, pretending not to notice the way Cassidy was watching him.

The group stayed huddled together, chatting, sipping their ciders, and then, with the crowd gathered, the countdown began.

"Three... two... one..."

Mayor Bloomfield flipped the switch.

For a heartbeat, everything was still.

Then—*whoosh*—the tree came to life in a dazzling cascade of color. Multicolored lights rippled from the topmost star down through the thick evergreen branches. The hush that followed was unexpected. Like the whole town had stopped breathing for a moment. A kind of reverence hanging in the air. All that warmth. All that hope. It hit him harder than he'd expected. He'd skipped this moment for the last four years.

Out of the corner of his eye, he saw Cassidy. Her hands

were clasped together, chin resting on her fingers, eyes wide and glowing in the soft light.

"It's beautiful," she said reverently.

Beautiful, Liam thought, looking at her.

"Oh no," Madison said suddenly, turning to Zach with faux alarm. "I completely forgot to turn on the, um... Christmas tree in the great room."

"Tragic," Kit deadpanned, sipping her cider.

Madison ignored her. "Zach, do you think you might be able to help me with that?"

Zach didn't hesitate. "I'd be crazy not to."

Cassidy watched as Madison laced her fingers through his, tugging him toward the inn with a look that made it very clear the tree wasn't the only thing she needed help with.

"You sure it needs two people?" Liam called after them.

"You haven't seen how many lights she strung on that thing," Zach tossed over his shoulder with an unapologetic grin.

Madison laughed, bumping into him as they disappeared down the street, hands locked, the rest of the festival forgotten.

"They're so cute," Kit said, watching them walk away.

Cassidy smiled then glanced around the square. Liam followed her gaze.

The crowd had really grown. The jazz soloist had been replaced by a brass quartet and a group of carolers. The festive singers were dressed in 1800s Dickens-style apparel, complete with bonnets, plaid throws, and full wool skirts.

Kit tilted her head. "Hold up. Is that Rachel from Zoe's wreath class? The one with the red beret?"

"I think so..." Cassidy said, finding the woman in question.

"Wait, is she eying me up?" Kit stood a bit taller, tucked her hands in her wide-legged jeans pockets, trying to look cool and casual. "I thought I picked up a vibe from her."

"She was one hundred percent flirting with you last week," Cassidy confirmed.

Kit grinned. "Ha, I knew it. I haven't had a woman look at me like that in a *long time*." Kit drew out the last two words.

Cassidy laughed. "Go. Maybe you'll find some mistletoe over there."

"Mama can hope." Kit winked at Cassidy. "You two have fun. Don't do anything I wouldn't do—which, to be fair, is a short list."

And just like that, she slipped into the crowd, leaving Cassidy and Liam alone in the middle of the square.

Cassidy looked over at Liam. "Go on. You can leave. I'm fine hanging out by myself. I know you're not into all this."

"Listen, I don't even know what all this entails."

"Why am I not surprised?"

"How about you just be nice and tell me what's on the agenda?" He nudged her elbow with his. "That way I can brace myself."

"I might have memorized the Chamber of Commerce brochure..." Cassidy confessed.

"Why am I not surprised?" he replied, copying her.

She rolled her eyes. "Do you want to know what's going on or not?"

"Sorry. Continue."

"Let's see, for starters, there's the tree ornament raffle."

"Ah, yes, a classic. Did you donate one?" Local businesses each donated a special ornament for the raffle. Liam had included a handcrafted snow-covered tree from the Hot Honey Farm Shop.

"No, I found out about it too late," Cassidy said, a little deflated.

"Well then, you're allowed to enter. What else?"

She perked up. "There's the Christmas wish tags. You write something down, toss it in the bonfire, and your wish is magically granted."

Liam exhaled, casting a skeptical glance toward the community park where the fire crackled at the center of the square.

Cassidy sighed. "You don't have to do it. It's just... kind of fun. Or you can just go home, and I'll walk around by myself. I told you—I don't mind. I know you hate Christmas."

Her voice was casual, but Liam caught the flicker of disappointment beneath it. And that, more than anything, was what made him stay.

Liam wanted to make Cassidy happy, he really did. He just wished it involved something less Christmassy, like a pitcher of beer and a round of darts at the Kettle. He shouldn't be here—shouldn't let her get too close. But he was here. And what if tonight gave him a good memory in a season that hadn't been kind to him?

"'Hate' is a pretty strong word. Besides, it's been a hell of a day. Let's end it on a high note."

"Are you sure?"

"Positive. You pick. I'll do anything."

"Even the sleigh photo op?" Cassidy teased.

"No. Anything but that."

"Oh, come on. It's got a red velvet seat and everything."

"I'm not climbing into a giant fake sleigh, Cassidy."

"Okay, fine. But will you do the Christmas wish?"

Liam bobbed his head from side to side, weighing his options. "Fine. One wish."

"Deal." She beamed and linked her arm through his. "Baby steps."

Liam could see the bonfire and feel the warmth of it before they even got in line.

Cassidy picked up a tag, tapping her pen against her chin. "What should I write?" She looked over at Liam's tag. "Wait, you already have something? Let me see!"

"Nope, that's not how this works." Liam scrawled something quickly and folded it in half.

"Oh, no fair! You have to show me."

"Nope. It's a wish. If I tell you, it won't come true."

Cassidy rolled her eyes but smiled.

Liam caught sight of her tag—"Don't screw this up"—and his teasing faded. His gaze met hers. He wanted to tell her that she wouldn't. That she belonged here, in Maple Falls. That her shop would thrive. That her life would be filled with love and joy, because that's what she was filled with. She was brave in ways that had nothing to do with chocolate or Christmas lights. She was opening herself up to a whole new life.

But he didn't say any of that. Because if he did, she might think he meant more than friendship. And right now, that was all he could give her.

"Ready?" he asked, folding his wish a second time.

Together, they walked toward the fire.

"On the count of three?" Cassidy asked.

Liam nodded. "One, two, three," they counted together, and then tossed their tags into the fire.

The blue and orange flames licked at the edges of the paper, scattering their wishes into the night. He wondered—just for a moment—if it was possible to ever truly forgive himself. To stop living in the past. To stop measuring every happy moment against what he'd lost.

To let go of the guilt. The what-ifs. The endless replays.

Probably not, he thought.

But maybe... maybe his past didn't have to haunt him every time the snow started to fall.

He glanced at Cassidy. The way she smiled at the firelight. The way she made space for joy, for life. Trained her gaze to focus on that.

Maybe he wasn't ready to let go of his past yet.

But for one night, he could show up for someone who was living in the present.

And that was something.

FIFTEEN

CASSIDY

Tuesday, December 2nd

Cassidy still couldn't believe Liam was being such a good sport about everything.

Sure, he'd agreed to the tree lighting ceremony, the Christmas wish tags. But was it because he actually wanted to hang out with her? Or because he felt sorry for her because she was new?

That part she wasn't sure about, and it was driving her just a little bit crazy.

There were moments, though, quick, quiet ones, when she caught his eye and it felt like something shifted. Like a flicker of understanding passed between them. Not just attraction—though there was still plenty of that—but something else. It felt like he understood her. There was just this sense of a growing attraction between them that she could neither explain nor deny. She had never felt so intensely, so quickly, for someone else before.

But then he'd step back. Or keep his voice even. Or walk a little farther away than he had to.

And Cassidy hated to say it, but it kind of felt like Liam had quietly friend-zoned her.

If he'd been into her, wouldn't he be flirting more? Walking closer? Maybe brushing her hand by accident, or not by accident? But no. He wasn't doing any of that.

Cassidy told herself that was a good thing. She was off men until the start of next year. She was focusing on her fledgling business and the upcoming Christmas Light-Up Display Competition. That's where her attention should be. She didn't want to screw things up.

These were the thoughts swirling in her head as they walked side by side from the Christmas wish station back toward the sleigh while kids beelined in front of them to visit the Santa House.

As they crossed the square, Cassidy noticed how everyone seemed to know Liam. People waved from all directions. There were older couples, teens, parents juggling toddlers. He high-fived kids, exchanged cheerful hellos with parents, and even got a greeting from a minister.

"Liam, good to see you. Heard you made a Christmas wish this year," Pastor Rodgers said, giving him a pat on the back.

Liam seemed to tense under the touch.

The clergy member didn't seem to notice. But Cassidy did. Just like the way she noticed his forced smile and fake laugh when Mrs. Humphrey said she was surprised to see him out and about this time of year, and Mrs. Bishop asked Cassidy how much she'd had to pay him to take a stroll with her down Christmas Lane.

Yeah, this was not going to work.

"We don't have to do the sleigh thing," Cassidy said quietly. "Actually... would you rather skip all this and go for a walk? There's that path behind the shops that loops around the lake?"

"You'd give up your Christmas cheer for me?"

"Just pressing pause. It'll all still be here later."

His shoulders lowered a fraction, just enough for her to know how much he appreciated the out.

"Then yeah," he said, nodding once. "A walk sounds good."

They detoured toward the side street, weaving past glowing shop windows and vendors handing out gingerbread and cider. Cassidy snagged two steaming cups of hot cider from a stand, offering one to Liam with a smile.

"It's not as good as my cocoa, obviously," she said, "but it'll do in a pinch."

Liam grinned and took the cup, their fingers brushing just briefly. Cassidy felt the spark move up her arm and straight to her heart, warming her quicker than any cider or cocoa ever could.

They fell into step, the noise and color of the square slowly fading behind them as they turned onto the winding path that curved around Bear Lake. Solar lanterns lit the way, casting a halo of light that reflected the icy snowflakes that drifted gently down.

"I meant what I said back there," she said after a quiet minute. "You don't have to force a smile for me. I can tell this time of year's hard for you, even if I don't know why."

Liam was quiet for a beat, watching his boots leave tracks in the snow. "Thanks. I'm trying. It's just... some years are easier than others."

"You don't have to tell me anything. I just didn't want to drag you into a sleigh photo shoot with fake reindeer and a glitter-sprinkled Santa if your heart wasn't in it."

He smiled. "Honestly, the glitter might've been my breaking point."

She burst out laughing and they walked a few more steps in companionable silence, the snow crunching under their boots, steam curling from their cider.

"How's the shop going?" he asked. "It looks busy from my side of the street."

She tilted her head side to side. "It's good—I love it. But yeah, it's been a lot. I'm pretty much running on empty at this point."

"Sounds familiar," he said. "The shop. The farm. The llama sanctuary we're setting up. The paperwork. There's just not enough hours in the day."

They shared a look—exhausted but proud.

"Is it weird that I love it?" she asked. "Even when I'm so tired I accidentally put chili powder in the cocoa?"

Liam raised a brow. "Was it at least good?"

"I liked it, but it was definitely spicy," she said, eyes twinkling. "Not recommended for kids."

He laughed again, and Cassidy noticed he looked more like himself out here, away from the lights and music and well-meaning but intrusive questions.

"What made you want to open the farm shop?" she asked. "I mean, you've got the whole farm already. What made you want to add to it?"

Liam took a sip of cider, thinking. "I knew Jackson would come back to the farm and both of us wouldn't be needed, and I guess I wanted to create something of my own that felt... lasting. Not just selling our produce, and my own crafts, at market but building something that belonged to the town."

She nodded, not pushing.

"What about you?" he asked. "Paris to Maple Falls is kind of a leap."

Cassidy smiled, looking out over the lake, where the light reflected off the ice. "It is. But I needed a change. And I missed my grand-maman. She raised me in a town just like this, and it felt like she was calling me home. She passed away two years ago, and she made the most incredible spiced cocoa—it's her recipe I'm using now."

"She sounds like she was special."

"She was. She wore red lipstick every day and told

everyone chocolate was the cure for most of life's problems. She believed in magic. Not in the wand-waving way, but in small things. The kind of magic you find in shared traditions. Like cocoa. Or decorating sugar cookies. Or standing out in the snow with someone who makes your heart feel weird and fluttery."

Liam's eyes darkened just slightly, and she quickly added, "Not that I mean you do that—I mean, I'm just saying in general—"

He stopped walking.

She nearly bumped into him, her cheeks flushing.

"I know what you meant," he said, voice low.

The words sank into the silence between them, warm and weighty. Her heart thudded so loudly it was a wonder the whole town couldn't hear it.

She looked down at her now-empty cup and forced herself to breathe.

"I should probably get back," she said softly. "I need to make another batch of cocoa for tomorrow. And prep some chocolates. I've been selling out."

"Want some help?" he asked, not missing a beat. "I mean... if you don't mind."

"You want to help me make cocoa?"

"I want to see this magical recipe in action."

She grinned. "In that case... let's go."

Cassidy unlocked the side door to the shop and gestured him inside. The warmth hit them immediately—soft and rich, laced with cocoa, vanilla, and the faintest trace of cinnamon and orange zest.

"I still can't believe this is yours," he said, pausing in the middle of the kitchen space. "It looks like something out of a Christmas story."

Cassidy smirked as she pulled her coat off and tossed it over a stool. "I'll take that as a compliment."

He followed, shrugging out of his puffer jacket. "It is one. It's... cozy. Thoughtful. Smells like actual heaven."

Cassidy grinned, then got to work. "Alright. First, spiced cocoa prep. If I'm going to keep up with demand, I need at least three batches ready by morning."

She handed him a small apron—pink, with candy canes on it.

He eyed it. "You're serious?"

"You want in on the magic-making or not?"

He slid it on. "I feel ridiculous."

"You look festive."

He shot her a look, but there was a smile tugging at his lips.

Cassidy pulled out a bowl of pre-chopped dark chocolate and set it on the counter. "Start chopping the next batch while I prep the spice mix. Don't rush it—smaller chunks melt more smoothly."

"Yes, chef."

She glanced over her shoulder at him, surprised. "You watch cooking shows?"

He shrugged as he carefully began chopping. "My brother and I used to watch *The Great British Bake Off* to annoy our dad. Then we got weirdly into it."

Cassidy laughed. "That's so wholesome."

"Don't let it get around."

She turned back to her spice rack and began mixing cinnamon, nutmeg, cloves, and just the tiniest pinch of cayenne into a bowl. The scent rose instantly—warm, nostalgic, with just enough bite to make it irresistible.

"So," he said, still focused on chopping, "what exactly makes this cocoa recipe so special? Besides being slightly dangerous if you add too much chili?"

She measured the blend into a pot of warming milk. "It's

about layering. The right kind of chocolate. The balance of spice. And the energy you put into it in the moment. Grand-maman always said cocoa tastes better when someone made it with love."

Liam looked up, and their eyes met over the rim of the pot. Cassidy felt the air shift again. She turned away to stir, her cheeks heating.

"What would your grand-maman think if she saw all this?" he asked after a moment.

Cassidy smiled softly. "She'd be proud. And also slightly horrified that I've started using orange zest in her sacred recipe."

"She'd forgive you."

"She'd scold me in French first."

They worked in comfortable silence for a while on the cocoa prep and adding to her supply of chocolates. He moved beside her, steady and present, helping where he could—chopping chocolate, filling molds, watching her temper the mixture with reverence.

"You're really good at this," he said quietly.

She glanced up. "It's the one thing I've never questioned about myself. Even when everything else fell apart... this always made sense."

Liam didn't ask what had fallen apart. Cassidy appreciated that.

Instead, he set down his spatula and gently brushed a smear of chocolate from her cheek with his thumb.

She stilled, her breath catching.

His hand lingered for just a second too long. Long enough to turn something simple into something else entirely.

I could fall in love with this man. The thought rushed in unbidden and had her taking a step back.

Liam did the same. "Well... I should probably leave you to it, then," he started to say just as Cassidy heard her name.

It was Mrs. Bishop and Mrs. C., standing in front of her chocolate shop, talking loudly to a young family.

She tensed, not sure what to expect.

"I'm telling you, best hot cocoa I've ever had. Hands down!" Mrs. C.'s voice rang out, full of praise.

Mrs. Bishop nodded in agreement, pointing at her front door. "You must try it. I'm sure she'll be back open in the morning."

"I will be," Cassidy said, opening the door with a smile.

"Perfect! We've decided your cocoa could bring about world peace, or at the very least get my son-in-law to do the dishes," Mrs. C. added.

"Thank you so much. I'll be sure to have plenty of cocoa tomorrow. Stop in anytime before five."

"We'll be sure to do that," the dad said.

She glanced back at Liam, who had just joined them.

Mrs. Bishop and Mrs. C. gave one another a knowing look.

"Liam, didn't expect to see you here tonight," a woman with a bright red wool coat said behind the older ladies.

"Mom, Dad," Liam said, caught off guard.

Cassidy stepped forward to meet Liam's parents, a twist of nerves in her stomach.

"Hi, I'm Cassidy," she said with an awkward wave.

"I'm Beth," the woman said, giving Cassidy a warm hug before she had time to process it. "And this grump beside me is my husband, Tom."

"I'm not a grump, just cold," Tom replied with a smile.

"Do you want me to open back up? I can make you some cocoa."

"Nonsense, dear. Tom should've listened to me when I told him to wear his heavy coat," Beth replied with a head nod.

"Now, I'm happy I ran into you," Beth started saying to Liam. "I assume you told Cassidy here about our family baking night on the thirteenth?"

"I... uh..." Liam stammered. "You know I don't usually go to that."

"We just met," Cassidy explained, shooting him a sympathetic look.

"Even better. We welcome new friends and old," Beth continued. "Isn't that right, dear?" She turned to her husband, who was already talking to another local. Beth waved a dismissive hand. "Trust me, the more the merrier."

Cassidy knew Liam must hate being put on the spot, and she didn't want to impose. She was about to come up with some excuse, any excuse, why she couldn't make it when Liam spoke up. "It would be great if you could come," he said casually.

"Really?" Cassidy didn't hide her surprise.

Beth ran with it. "Oh, sure. The whole gang will be there. I don't think you've met our Jackson yet, but he's home, and there's Zach and Madison, I think Emily and Kit are coming, maybe some of the crafting club too."

"That sounds fun." Cassidy smiled.

Beth beamed back. "Perfect! I'll text Madison so she can loop you in. Six o'clock sharp!" She gave Cassidy another hug before pulling Tom off toward the hot buttered rum stand.

"Sorry, if you don't want me there that's totally okay..." Cassidy let her words trail off.

"No, you'll love it, and better yet, so will my mom. Truly. She loves this sort of thing."

Cassidy smiled softly. "It's a date then. Well, not a *date* date. You know what I mean."

He didn't say anything, just held her gaze for a beat, the air between them charged, the glow of the Christmas lights catching in his eyes.

She cleared her throat and stepped back, tucking a piece of hair behind her ear. She needed to end the night before she did something she'd regret.

Like close the small space between them and kiss him.

Because the only thing that would top tonight would be Liam in her bed, his hands on her, his mouth on her neck, and that thought alone was tempting enough.

If she let that happen, she might never want him to leave. Her heart would be exposed to being broken all over again.

And that was the last thing her carefully rebuilt life could handle.

SIXTEEN

LIAM

Today was Emily's light-up night, the first in the competition. Liam told himself he was only there to scope out the competition, not because he was hoping to run into Cassidy. The fact that she was there too was just a bonus.

All week they'd been rushed off their feet running their shops. He'd caught glimpses of her, outside, shoveling her sidewalk, or opening her door to greet customers with a smile. It was a good thing, this forced distance, given how strong Liam's feelings were becoming. He needed to cool his mind and the heat that pumped through his veins every time he hung out with her.

Now he spotted her across the square, bundled in a red puffer coat, a to-go cup cradled between her gloved hands. Black leggings, gray hiking boots with fur at the top. A green knit beanie pulled low over her ears, a braid slipping out the back.

He shouldn't have been thinking about how amazing she looked. But he was.

If she were just a tourist, a woman passing through, he'd approach her casually. Bump into her. Say something about the weather and how cold it had turned. Maybe mention the lake, frozen solid this time of year. If she was the outdoorsy type, she might want to try ice fishing.

He imagined the conversation. Her curious smile. Her laughter.

In the winter, small ice shanties—like miniature cabins on the ice—popped up across the frozen surface, giving people a place to fish or warm up while the snow fell around them. They'd head out to his shanty on the lake, his little wood-paneled escape, insulated and warm, tucked away from the world.

His had a space heater, soft fleece blankets, and a small cot. He'd start the heater. Offer her a drink. Maybe bourbon. Maybe cocoa. Watch her lips curl around the rim of the mug.

They'd fish, or pretend to, sitting on the cot, shoulder to shoulder.

Maybe she'd tease him.

He'd flirt back, playful, fun, like she was.

First, it would just be their legs brushing, then his hand on her knee, then she'd lean into him, laugh.

Then, when the sexual tension crackled and popped, he'd cradle her face in his hands and kiss her. Softly and slowly. Not rushed. No, he'd let it build. Let her feel how much he wanted her. How long he'd been holding back.

Outside, the snow would blow across the lake, ice crystals building on the windows, reminding them of how cold it was.

But inside it would be blazing.

She'd pull back and give him the look, the one that said *more*—and he'd oblige, laying her back on the cot, peeling her coat off, and her sweater.

Her nipples would be hard and stiff with nothing but the

ice surrounding them. But his mouth? It would be hot as he kissed and sucked, making love to her breasts.

Her breath would hitch as he ran his hands along her thighs, fingers brushing the edge of those soft black leggings. His finger would trace the center, and she'd arch into him, still wanting more.

He'd slide the fabric down, inch by inch, revealing the body he'd been fantasizing about since the moment he saw her.

He'd explore her like he had all the time in the world—touching, teasing, learning every gasp and whimper. His lips would replace his fingers, licking, tasting, driving her to the edge. And then, when she was needy and breathless, begging for more, he'd kneel between her legs, pull her to the edge of the cot, lift her up just a bit, and slide into her in one deep stroke. He'd fill her over and over again until she moaned his name from her lips and her body quaked around him.

It would be everything he wanted. Everything he thought he needed.

But then the fantasy shifted.

She'd shiver after, and he'd wrap her in a blanket, carry her to his truck. Drive her back to his place. He'd make her lasagna, the kind that took hours to bake. Pour a glass of red wine. Ask her about her favorite books, music, the place in Paris she missed most. He'd play her a record, maybe old jazz, and she'd spin slowly around his kitchen, teasing him, laughing.

Maybe they'd take a shower.

God, he really wanted to see her in his shower.

The image alone had his pulse pounding and blood rushing south. He shifted where he stood, fighting to come back to reality. This was not the place for his imagination to get the best of him.

Liam looked around him at all the good, small-town charm that he always tried to avoid this time of year. But not tonight, not when he was trying anything and everything to keep his mind off of Cassidy and all the things he wanted to do with her, because honestly, fantasy Liam was just getting started. Right now, the Christmas carolers, the sea of Santa hats, the smell of cinnamon-roasted almonds—they were all a welcome distraction.

"Hey, you," Cassidy said, bumping her hip into him.

Liam startled and then felt like an idiot, wondering if she could tell how hard he still was from thinking about her.

She raised an eyebrow. "You okay there?"

"Yeah, just—uh—thinking about strategy." Liam motioned to the bakery before him. "I take competition seriously."

She grinned. "Well, if you're referring to me, you should know that it's nothing personal, just business."

He gave a tight smile. "That's what they all say, right before someone ends up naked on a cot in the middle of a frozen lake."

"Wait, what?"

"Nothing," he said quickly. "Forget it."

But he couldn't forget. And judging by the tightness still in his jeans, he was pretty sure he'd never look at his ice shanty the same way again.

"Anyway, you ready for this?" he asked, willing himself to focus on anything else.

"I was born ready," she replied confidently, swinging her arm in front of her like a strongman.

"Really?"

"No, I just always wanted to say that. But how hard can this be? We throw up some lights, do a cute window display, and raise a bunch of money for charity..."

Liam huffed a quiet laugh. Cassidy had no idea what she was in for or how seriously people took competitions in this town.

Just then, lights began to swirl in front of the Pumpkin Pie Bakery. Large snowflake projections shimmered on the windows, which were draped in orange fabric to match the bakery's pumpkin theme.

The front door swung open, and Emily stepped outside, giving a little wave to the gathering crowd. Zach, Madison, and Anita were right up front to cheer Emily on. She wore a chunky cream sweater and a pair of dark jeans under a pumpkin-colored apron. Her blonde hair was piled into a messy bun with wisps and bangs framing her heart-shaped face. She tucked a strand of hair behind her ear as she smiled, the glow from the swirling lights catching in her blue eyes, making her look every bit the friendly, small-town baker she was.

Mayor Bloomfield stood beside her, microphone in hand, looking festive as ever. Tonight, he wore a green velvet sport coat topped off with a Santa hat, and a grin that showed how much he lived for moments like this.

His great-niece and assistant, Elsie, stood by, phone at the ready to livestream the entire event.

"Uncle Hank, can you angle slightly left? We need the logo in the shot for the thumbnail." Elsie tugged him a half-step sideways, earning a chuckle from the mayor.

Emily glanced over, her smile tightening as she noticed Elsie filming. "Do we really need this live?" she whispered.

"It's for brand reach," Elsie shot back, not taking her eyes off her screen. "We have to modernize these events if Maple Falls wants to stay relevant."

From her spot in the crowd, Cassidy heard Elsie's commentary and rolled her eyes, muttering to Liam, "Relevant? It's Christmas in Maple Falls, not an influencer launch."

Liam's mouth twitched. "Just smile for the camera, Sugarplum."

Cassidy shot him a look but couldn't suppress the small, reluctant grin as the lights dimmed and the snowflake projections grew brighter, casting gentle reflections across the street and over the gathered neighbors, all bundled in scarves and mittens.

"Thank you all so much for coming out to our first Christmas light-up night of the season!" the mayor boomed. "Emily would like to remind you that her charity of choice is the City Rescue Mission, a local organization that helps families in need. You can place your donations in..." Mayor Bloomfield looked around for Emily's donation box.

"Over here," Emily said, showcasing her oversized, hand-made gingerbread house. It was beautifully decorated with icing trim, gumdrop windows, and candy-cane railings. But instead of being purely decorative, the front door was actually a mail-slot-style opening for donations.

"Perfect! Yes, drop your donations off in the gingerbread house. The winning business and charity will be announced following our annual Christmas Eve walk."

Elsie took the mic from the mayor. "And don't forget, this year you can donate and vote online! On Christmas Eve, just go onto the competition website to cast your vote!"

Mayor Bloomfield took the mic back. "Er, right, or you can vote at City Hall anytime on Christmas Eve before five o'clock. That's what I plan to do!" He raised his hand with theatrical flair. "Now, if you'll all count down with me from five, we'll see the dazzling display Emily and her crew have created for you!"

The crowd joined in enthusiastically. "Five... four... three... two... one!"

Inside, Emily tugged a gold-tasseled rope, and the orange curtain dropped.

Right as the curtain fell, a brass quartet launched into "Joy to the World," their bright sound cutting through the nighttime air. At the same moment, gold glitter shot out of hidden cannons, raining sparkles all around them.

Everyone oohed and ahhed as the window display lit up.

The bakery had gone with an elegant silver and gold theme.

Faux snow and shimmering silver glitter dusted the front steps. Oversized gold and silver ornaments dangled from the awning. The front window featured a towering five-layer white cake, adorned with gold and silver marzipan snowflakes, sugared cranberries, and tiny candied oranges flanked by two silver Christmas trees that were decorated with miniature clay ornaments—tiny pumpkin pies, cupcakes, and coffees. The other window showcased a dazzling display of holiday desserts that appeared to be floating on top of fluffy artificial snow. The dessert plates rotated, bringing each one under the spotlight.

Even Liam had to admit—Emily had pulled out all the stops.

He glanced at Cassidy.

Judging by the stunned expression on her face, she'd just realized the competition was very, very real.

"Woah," she whispered, taking it all in.

Liam grinned. "Might as well quit now, no?"

She crossed her arms and tilted her chin. Her expression switched from awe to defiance in a heartbeat. "Please. I haven't even started yet."

"Uh-huh." He took a step closer, dropping his voice just enough to make her shiver. "Still time to back out. Save yourself the heartbreak."

She smirked. "You think I'm scared of that?" She motioned to the bakery. "It's lovely, sure. But it's missing one key ingredient."

"Oh yeah? What's that?"

"Me." She flashed him a grin that was pure challenge.

Liam laughed, low and warm. "Okay, Sugarplum. You talk a big game, but can you actually deliver?"

Cassidy leaned in, close enough that he could smell the peppermint on her breath, her eyes glittering with mischief. "Oh, I can deliver, alright. Because you want to know what else I've got?" She didn't give him a chance to answer. "A sprinkle of holiday magic. A secret recipe passed down through genera-tions. And cocoa bombs that explode with glittery marshmal-lows when you pour milk over them."

She stepped back, flipping her braid over her shoulder as she looked him dead in the eye. "So don't get too comfortable over there with your twinkle lights, Lumberjack. Because when I'm through, you'll be begging for mercy."

Saturday, December 6th

Cassidy was sketching ideas for her own Christmas light-up display between customers. She couldn't believe how gorgeous Emily's display had been, and that was *after* she'd been sabotaged *twice*.

She'd just had the idea of doing Twelve Days of Cocoa for her pop-up café, with a different themed cocoa every day leading up to her switch-on, alongside her signature dark spiced classic. She was making a list of all the different flavors: cinnamon swirl, peppermint bark, French lavender, white chocolate, gingerbread spice, and raspberry truffle.

Hopefully, locals would stop by each day to see and try the new flavor.

Then for her light-up event, she was thinking of running a Cocoa & Kisses-themed photo booth. She'd have tons of props, like oversized mugs, sparkly berets, mustaches, candy canes, Santa hats, and mistletoe. In the window, she could make a four-foot-tall snowman out of white chocolate, and in the other, an edible Christmas village. It would take a ton of work, but she could do it. She knew she could.

Just as she was beginning to feel the churn of anxiety, Zoe pushed open the door and walked over to the counter. "Wow, this is ambitious," Zoe said, peeking over at her designs. "Way more than I'm doing..."

"Do you think so? Will people in Maple Falls love it?" Cassidy chewed on her pencil. "We're up against Liam too, and he seems to be the poster child for the town. Is there anyone around here who doesn't love him? I mean, do I even have a shot?"

Zoe laughed. "I'll admit, it's going to be tough to beat him. But if anyone can do it, it's you. Who doesn't love chocolate and Christmas? The two are practically made for each other."

"Speaking of the competition..." Cassidy's fingers traced the rim of her cocoa mug, her brows knitting. "I really hope the Gingerbread Jerk doesn't strike again. I can't believe we haven't caught whoever it is yet."

Zoe nodded. "I know, right? Mayor Bloomfield thinks it's a bunch of teenagers being dumb."

"Maybe." Cassidy glanced out the window, watching snow swirl around the lampposts on Oak Way. "I hope you're right. It's just... this competition means so much to me. If someone trashed my display, I'd be livid, and not just because I want to win Business of the Year." She paused. "I really want to help the children's hospital this Christmas. It means so much to me."

Zoe reached over and squeezed her hand. "I know." She lowered her voice, a teasing smile playing at her lips. "I'll keep my eyes peeled for any gingerbread jerks lurking around."

Cassidy cracked a small smile, but the worry in her eyes didn't fully fade as she turned back to the window, watching the lights across the street flicker, wondering if someone out there wanted to see her fail.

"I wanted to ask you about the hospital you want to donate

the prize money to. How long were you there for, when you were a kid?"

"It was a lifetime ago... Honestly, I don't really remember," Cassidy said with a soft shrug. "I was just a little girl. But it was when I was in the hospital after the accident, after my parents died, that I fell in love with chocolate."

Zoe's expression softened as she waited for her to continue.

"My grand-maman used to sneak me these little flasks of thick, velvety, spiced hot cocoa using her special family recipe. She'd pass them to me like they were medicine." Cassidy smiled faintly at the memory. "And in a way, they were. That cocoa... it warmed me up from the inside out. Made me feel like maybe the world wasn't completely broken."

She looked down at her hands, then back at Zoe. "That's when I realized chocolate could be truly magical. I was so lucky to have Grand-maman, but I remember what it's like to spend Christmas in the hospital. If I can do anything to make those kiddos' Christmas a little bit merrier? Then you betcha I'm gonna do it."

Zoe remained silent, and Cassidy wondered what she was thinking.

"Sorry, probably a total bummer topic." Cassidy had learned that people don't necessarily like it when you talk about becoming an orphan at Christmastime. She picked up her pen and looked back at her sketch.

"It's not that," Zoe said gently. "I was just thinking about how grief transforms people differently. And how... well, it might not be my place to say anything, but I saw you and Liam together last night at Emily's light-up."

Cassidy stopped mid-doodling. "What does that have to do with anything? We're just friends," she said a little too quickly.

Honestly, she didn't know what they were. There were feelings, and some serious chemistry, but where was it all going?

"First of all," Zoe said, holding up a finger, "I'm pretty sure you two are going to be more than friends. I can see it. Everyone can see it. And it's not just because you were straddling him in the middle of Oak Way."

"That was an accident!" Cassidy held up her hands in mock surrender.

"Uh-huh. Suuure," Zoe said, drawing the word out. "You just slipped and fell on his dick."

"That's not what happened! We were... I was... The ice—"

She went to protest more, but Zoe stopped her.

"This is all beside the point. There's something I think you should know. I'm just debating if I'm the one who should tell you..."

Cassidy slapped her palms on the counter. "What the heck? You can't say something like that. Now you have to tell me. I need to know what I'm getting into here."

"I know. I know." Zoe's tone softened. "The thing is... you're not the only one who's had heartbreak at Christmas. Liam has, too, and it's torn him up. He hasn't been the same since the accident."

Cassidy's expression turned from intrigue to somber in a second. "Accident?"

"I think it was four years ago now," Zoe said, doing some mental math. "His girlfriend, Avery, was coming to spend Christmas with him. They were in college together, and Liam had finished exams early and come back to town. She stayed behind a few more days. Anyway, she was on her way to Maple Falls when her car hit black ice. She didn't make it."

Cassidy closed her eyes. So that was it, that was Liam's story. She'd known there was something, but this... this was just so heart-wrenching. She knew the ache of grief all too well. It got better, but it never really went away. Some days, it hit you out of nowhere and knocked you flat. Those were the bad days. But with time—and love—it grew quieter, easier to carry. She was thankful for that.

"Now I feel awful for calling him a grinch." Heat rose to her cheeks.

"Yeah," Zoe said, "the rest of the year, Liam's as bright and sunny as anyone. Life of the party. Always up for a good time. But come December?" She shook her head. "It just guts him."

"Trauma can do that." Cassidy frowned. It made sense now, didn't it? "God, he probably finds me completely annoying."

She motioned to her outfit: red corduroy overalls and a white-and-red striped tee. She looked like a human candy cane. And honestly, this was one of her tamer looks.

"Girl, no. Please. You are adorable. Not your fault he has Christmas PTSD."

"I know. I know." Still, she wondered if maybe—just around Liam—she should tone it down a little. She sighed. "I did think there was something deeper going on. I knew it couldn't just be that he was cranky about his hamstring."

"Oh, I'm sure he hates that too. We both ran cross-country in high school. He lives for running. He's the king of the Jingle Bell 5k. Not being able to do it this year is killing him. Trust me."

Cassidy nodded. "For the record, this is not where I thought this conversation was going," she said. "I figured you were about to tell me he had three baby mamas in the tri-city area."

"What?" Zoe snorted. "No!"

"I'm just saying. He's got that player energy. Tall, dark, and broody with a tortured soul, chiseled jaw, and dimples even the devil would be jealous of. Who knows how many Little Liams are out there?"

"Oh my God. You have to say that to his face. And I have to be there to watch."

Cassidy grinned. "Noted."

She drummed her fingers on the counter, her mind spinning, thinking of Liam and how she could help. "I wish there was something I could do. I know he can't do the 5k, and he'd probably hate anything too Christmassy, but... what if we did something outdoors?"

Zoe perked up. "I like where this is going."

"I don't know, what if we did a snow hike tomorrow? Nothing too crazy, just get a group together for a winter nature walk in the morning. You know the area. You were just out foraging. Maybe you could help plan the route? Then afterwards, snacks and cocoa, maybe a board game or two at my place? No holiday stuff. Just good company."

Zoe beamed. "I think that's a brilliant idea. He'd totally go for it."

"You really think so?"

"Positive."

"Alright then. I'll run across the street in a little bit and float it by him, see what he thinks."

"Great. I'll call around and see who else wants to join. What time tomorrow? Ten o'clock?"

"Ten o'clock is perfect," Cassidy agreed.

"I'll plan out the route and let you know."

"Perfect." Cassidy knew Zoe regularly hiked the area. If anyone could plan the best route, it would be her.

Truthfully, Cassidy was more of an indoor girl—puzzles, baking, watching holiday movies on repeat—but she wanted to give something back to Liam. Yes, she was wildly attracted to him. And sure, he'd been kind to her at the tree lighting festival. But it was more than that. She wanted to show him he didn't have to be alone in the shadows.

And maybe, just maybe... see if she could help him let the light in.

EIGHTEEN

LIAM

Liam was busy working on the front of his shop in between customers. He'd planned an all-natural, farm-inspired theme with everything real and rustic, including a large sweep of evergreen he was draping over the front façade.

He was up on the ladder, finalizing a corner of the garland, when Cassidy's voice called up to him.

"Does that mean your leg's feeling better?"

Liam had been so focused on the decorating that her voice startled him. His foot slipped down one rung, and he barely caught himself before falling the rest of the way.

"I'm so sorry! I didn't mean to scare you!" she said quickly.

"It doesn't count as a win if you kill me off," said Liam. He eased himself slowly off the ladder. It wasn't entirely her fault; the metal rungs were slick with snow, and his hands were half-numb from the cold. He hadn't planned on staying outside so long, but once he started decorating, it was hard to stop.

"Maybe I should start wearing bells on my shoes?" she offered, her cheeks flushed with embarrassment.

He glanced at her outfit, half expecting to see another one of her famous Christmas sweaters, or at least a bright red coat, but instead, she wore faded denim overalls and a cream-colored wool coat. No cute hat. No glitter. She looked... subdued.

"You feeling alright?" he asked, folding up the ladder and propping it against the building.

"Yeah? Why?"

"No reason," he said. He'd gotten used to seeing her Christmas sparkle, and prayed his gloom wasn't already rubbing off on her. Who knows, maybe he was reading into it too much. Cassidy didn't strike him as the kind of woman who cared what other people thought. No, she was the kind of woman who probably wore Christmas sweaters in August. He liked that about her, which was shocking. If it were anyone else, it would annoy the hell out of him.

He noticed she had a small square box in her hand.

"I just wanted to bring you a little thank-you gift for helping me with the chocolate earlier this week," Cassidy said. "I know hot cocoa isn't really your thing, and you were probably just feeling sorry for me, but still... it was nice."

Liam felt like an ass. Cassidy thought the only reason he'd spent time with her was pity? Maybe that's what had got him to hang out with her in the first place, but that wasn't the reason he'd stuck around. Maybe her wide, nervous eyes and that dumb sweater and the way she'd looked so hopeful in the middle of the town square had tugged at something deep in his chest.

No, it wasn't pity.

He'd stayed because of her.

Because she saw things he didn't—little things, like how the lights reflected in the snow, or the way the carolers' eyes shone as they sang. She didn't just go through the motions; she truly found the wonder in them, and, somehow, standing next to her, he'd felt it too, for the first time in years.

He'd lived in Maple Falls his whole life, but with Cassidy beside him, he'd experienced more of the town's magic than he ever had. Period.

And sure, yeah, he was going insane from wanting to kiss her, but it was more than that, too. So much more.

"Feeling sorry for you?" Liam repeated. "Not even close. Now, if you had suggested caroling, it would've been a different story."

"What? No caroling?"

"Dear God, no."

"Well, you're no fun."

"I wore that apron of yours, didn't I?"

He might've had a dream about her chocolate shop later that night. Only this time, she was the one in the apron—and nothing else. Not after he'd slid her leggings down, inch by inch, kissing his way along the soft skin of her thighs while she whispered his name like a prayer, a carol playing in the background.

He'd lifted her onto the counter, hands spreading her legs as he sank to his knees, mouth trailing closer, closer.

Her breath hitched when he finally tasted her, his tongue slow and certain, fingers gripping her hips. She moaned, one hand tangled in his hair.

And by the time he was done with her, there was nothing innocent left about hot cocoa—or "Silent Night."

He cleared his throat. "I had a good time, truly. Seeing Maple Falls through your eyes was... nice."

Cassidy smiled softly and held out the box. "Still. Here are a couple of chocolates. Just a small thank you."

He opened the box and laughed.

Inside were four individually wrapped bite-sized Snickers bars.

"Seeing as I haven't figured out your favorite yet..." Cassidy said with a smile.

"Can't go wrong with a Snickers." He unwrapped one and popped it in his mouth. "Hits the spot," he said after chewing.

"Anyway," she continued, "I know you're probably busy with your decorations, and I should be too, but I was talking to Zoe, and we were thinking about starting a Sunday hiking club. Nothing crazy. I don't know how your leg's feeling, but if you want to get outside and hit the trail, Zoe's plotting it out. We're thinking around ten o'clock tomorrow morning."

A hiking club. With Cassidy. Snow-covered trails. Her bright laughter echoing off the pines. Her flushed cheeks and blonde hair escaping her hat, falling in loose waves down her back.

Was it a bad idea? The more time he spent with her, the more he would want her, and he was already so far gone as it was. The pre-Cassidy Liam knew he should be putting distance between them, reminding himself why the boundaries he'd carefully constructed mattered, even if her presence made the weight of the holidays easier to bear.

He opened his mouth to say no. To walk away before it got harder.

But the thought of fresh air and crisp snow, of being outside with friends, of being outside with her, was too much to resist.

Hell.

"Yeah," he heard himself say, the word out before he could take it back. "Count me in."

"Really?"

"I'll come. If only to keep you from slipping on more ice." He quirked a smile.

Cassidy smacked him playfully on the shoulder and he laughed, watching the way her eyes sparkled with challenge.

He took a small step back, stuffing his hands in his coat pockets. "Ten o'clock tomorrow, then."

"Great! I invited everyone back to my place afterward.

There'll be snacks, board games, all that good stuff. No pressure; you can just come for the hike."

She was already backpedaling, probably assuming he'd come up with an excuse, that he'd bail. And yeah, he probably would have, if she hadn't looked up at him like that. Like she didn't expect anything from him but still hoped anyway.

"Actually, tomorrow's Sunday lunch at my parents'. We could head over there after the hike. My mom would be thrilled to have everyone," Liam said, surprising them both.

"Really?" Cassidy beamed.

And damn it, making her smile like that felt better than anything had in a long time.

NINETEEN

CASSIDY

Later that night, Cassidy's brother, Julian, wouldn't stop calling her. She was curled up in her flannel pajamas on her couch with a bowl of creamy chicken and dumplings when she finally answered on the third ring.

"Is everything okay?" she asked, tucking a fleece blanket around her while Muff jumped up and made herself cozy behind her knees.

"Everything's fine here. It's you we're worried about." In the background, she heard Miles call out a cheerful, "Hi!"

"Why? I told you everything is fine," Cassidy said—and this time, she meant it.

"Sure, that's what you said, but I wasn't convinced."

"I was just nervous. But my week took a turn for the better. I've spent time with some friends, met dozens of new customers... I've really started to feel like part of the community."

"Well, that's a relief. It's nothing like New York or Paris, is it?"

"It's not. But that's a good thing. The people are so kind, the shop and cocoa café pop-up are thriving... and there's a guy..."

She closed her eyes and sighed, wondering why she felt the need to tell her brother about Liam. But she did. Growing up, they'd only had each other and Grand-maman. They'd looked out for each other. Things had shifted a bit after Julian started dating Miles and then got married. But he was still her best friend.

"A guy, huh? Is he cute?"

"Hey now!" Miles called in the background.

"He's basically a sexy lumberjack... well, a farmer really. Broad shoulders, beard, rough hands," Cassidy said, just to give her brother a hard time.

"Shut the frick up. Maybe we will come to Maple Falls," Julian said with a laugh.

"Sorry to say, but I'm pretty sure he's just into girls, but you never know..." she teased. "Anyway, we're just friends. I'm trying to focus on the shop, and you know I made that 'no men until the new year' vow. But Liam did help me on Tuesday when I had an allergic reaction."

The men both sucked in a breath.

"I was trying to help set up the town Christmas tree, and I totally forgot how much Norway spruces make me itch." She downplayed the reaction, not wanting to worry them any further.

"How do you forget that?" Miles asked.

"Because this man makes me scatterbrained! I don't know how to describe it. But here's the thing, he kinda hates Christmas."

Another gasp. "Hates Christmas?" Julian said. "Oh honey, you can't date a grinch."

"I guess he's not a full-on grinch. Not year-round, anyway. It's just... his girlfriend died at Christmas a few years ago. And it's really messed him up."

The line went quiet for a moment.

"Well, that's just horrible," Julian said gently.

"Poor guy," Miles added.

Cassidy thought back to how she'd toned down her holiday outfit earlier. She just hadn't wanted to push Christmas on someone who clearly struggled with the season.

"I don't know... maybe I am a bit over-the-top with all the Christmas stuff."

"You shut your mouth," Julian said. "You better not change who you are just because this man has unresolved issues."

Julian sounded an awful lot like Zoe.

"Listen to your brother," Miles chimed in. "Don't let his walls make you think you have to shrink yourself. You've already played that game."

Cassidy sighed, tugging at the corner of her blanket. "I know I shouldn't. I know who I am, and I like that person. Or now I do, anyway. But... I guess part of me just wanted to help him. Make it easier. Even though I know I can't."

"That's your problem, Cassidy," Miles said gently. "You always try to fix people."

"Fatal character flaw," she muttered.

"No," Julian said. "It's not a flaw. It's one of your best traits. But there's a difference between helping others and hurting yourself."

She swallowed hard, eyes prickling. "Yeah. I know."

"Good," Julian said. "Because the Cassidy I know wears snowflake earrings in July and bakes Christmas cookies for the Easter Bunny."

"And don't you dare let some brooding lumberjack make you forget it," Miles added.

Cassidy laughed, the sound soft but real. "Thanks, you two. I needed that."

"Anytime," Julian said. "Now go hang up and put on something obnoxiously festive."

"I already am," she said with a smile. "And Muff's in a reindeer sweater, just for the record."

After they'd caught up a bit more, she hung up, her phone slipping from her hand as she leaned back against the couch, warmth still buzzing in her chest from the call. But the second her mind quieted, it shifted straight to Liam.

She wondered what he was wearing. Maybe that fitted thermal shirt that stretched across his broad shoulders, the sleeves pushed up over strong forearms dusted with a hint of dark hair. Maybe those worn jeans that hugged his hips in a way that made her mouth go dry.

Or maybe nothing at all.

Heat bloomed low in her belly, the thought of him fresh out of the shower, droplets of water sliding down the lines of muscle across his chest, disappearing beneath a towel slung low on his hips. She imagined the way his hair would be damp, curling at the ends, the scruff on his jaw darkening as he ran a hand over it, those deep eyes meeting hers, dark and hungry.

Cassidy squeezed her eyes shut, pressing a palm to her flushed cheek.

Get it together.

This was Maple Falls, not one of those steamy romance novels she kept hidden on her Kindle. But God, it was getting harder and harder to remember that when it came to Liam Hawthorne.

Was the no-men vow really that important to her anymore? The year was nearly up anyway.

Yes, she told herself. It had to be. She'd gone almost the whole year—she couldn't just give up now. And she couldn't afford to be swept away with romance. Her shop had only been open for a week. She had a major Christmas competition to get ready for: Her light-up slot was in just under two weeks.

And she couldn't lose herself again. She'd already toned down her Christmas outfit once for him. It didn't matter if she'd done it to be kind. She couldn't change herself, reduce herself, risk heartbreak all over again, for a man.

No, she needed to stick to her vow, stay true to herself, and focus on launching her cocoa empire.

She'd see him tomorrow on the hike, and she'd be ready—head held high, holiday earrings firmly in place.

TWENTY

LIAM

Liam had to admit, it felt good to be packing up his hiking gear that morning. Sure, they weren't going backpacking in the mountains. It was just a hike around the beautiful glacier lake in Maple Falls. Maybe a little bit of elevation, nothing too hard for his hamstring, but it felt good to get out of the downtown area and into the fresh, open air.

Everyone had agreed to meet at the trailhead and were already there when Liam pulled in with his truck. The parking lot was covered in snow, at least a few inches deep. The only treads in the lot were from their cars. The trees were bare, except for the evergreens, their branches weighed down by thick blankets of snow, and the air was silent, except for the call of a blue jay in the distance.

Liam was glad to see Cassidy back to her full Christmas self, wearing a bright green wool coat and a red knit stocking cap. Her blonde hair was braided into two neat plaits, and she'd even woven woolen tinsel into them.

Muff was there too, wearing a bright green bow on her collar and waiting patiently for the hike to begin.

"Hot cocoa?" Cassidy offered, holding out a flask.

Liam grinned. "Of course," he said, accepting it gratefully. He unscrewed the metal cap and took a swig. The warm, velvety liquid filled his mouth, and he shook his head. "You definitely have a winner here."

"Coming from a chocolate snob, that is a compliment." Cassidy pulled her stocking cap down further to cover her ears.

"I've got the granola bites!" Kit called, snapping her feet into a pair of snowshoes.

"You're being pretty serious with this hike," Liam said to Kit.

"Nah, I got them two years ago for Christmas and have never worn them. Figured if not today, when?" Kit laughed.

Kit had invited the new guy in town, Tyler, and his daughter, Emma. They arrived, hugs were exchanged, cocoa was passed round, and their group was complete.

Tyler was tall and broad-shouldered, his shaggy brown hair tucked beneath a knit beanie, a flannel jacket layered over a well-worn thermal. His easygoing grin made him instantly likable, the kind of man who felt like the solid center of any group.

Beside him, Emma practically bounced with each step, her pink snow boots leaving prints in the fresh powder, a rainbow pom-pom hat slightly askew on her head. She was around seven, with a sprinkle of freckles across her nose, her brown hair peeking out in messy braids.

As the group began the hike, they naturally paired off. Zoe and Kit were up front, along with Tyler and his daughter, who insisted on walking Muff, while Madison and Zach brought up the rear. Cassidy and Liam naturally fell in step together. Jackson had been invited but Zoe told Liam he'd decided to pass. That sounded more like his twin, keeping to himself, sticking close to the llamas, the work on the farm.

Zoe crouched beside a snow-covered shrub, brushing the frost off a cluster of red berries. "These are wintergreen. Totally edible—and they make a great tea, if you don't mind a little minty tang," she said, holding one up for the group to see.

Emma leaned in closer, her breath puffing clouds in the cold air. "Do they taste like gum?"

"Better," Zoe said with a wink. "Nature's version of it, anyway."

As they continued along the path, Zoe pointed out more hidden treasures beneath the snow—dried pine needles perfect for fire starters, bark that could be peeled for tinder, and mosses that held onto water in a pinch.

Snowflakes began to fall as they continued their hike. While Zoe talked about foraging for winter eats, Liam and Cassidy gradually fell further behind the group.

"Is your leg okay?" Cassidy asked, hoping the hike wasn't pushing him too hard.

"Yeah, this is helping actually. I probably should've started stretching more last week. I'm glad you suggested it."

"I figured it would do us both some good."

The snow started to fall faster, the flakes growing fat and heavy, drifting down in slow spirals. It clung to the tops of their hats and settled in the folds of their scarves, the world around them going quiet under the hush of fresh snowfall.

He watched as a dusting of snow caught in Cassidy's long blonde hair, the strands curling around her flushed cheeks. She looked like something out of a winter postcard, her cheeks pink and her eyes bright.

"Last Christmas was pretty rough for me," she said after a while, interrupting Liam's thoughts. "I'd been in Paris for years, but I decided I needed a fresh start." Her voice was soft as the group ahead drifted out of earshot. "I don't know if you know, but I grew up in Hope Valley, not far away."

"You said something about being nearby. I didn't realize it was that close."

Cassidy nodded. "I'd always planned on coming back to the Midwest one day, but I wasn't exactly sure where. My brother and I were raised by my grand-maman—she was French," she explained. "After my parents died."

"I didn't realize... about your parents."

"I was young. Almost nine." Her voice softened. "It was a car accident. Christmastime. We were all in the car. My brother was the only one who walked away unscathed." She looked down. "I spent quite a bit of time in the hospital."

His chest tightened. He pictured her, small and fragile, hair in messy braids, curled up in a too-big hospital bed while she stared out the window, waiting for parents who would never walk back through that door.

And God, hadn't he been there too?

Different year, but same season. Same unbearable silence on the other end of a phone call. He knew the way grief carved its name into your bones, how it changed the shape of a holiday forever.

It wasn't just a coincidence between them—that they'd both lost loved ones in a car accident—it was a thread, however painful, that connected something deep and unspoken.

"You don't have to..." he said gently, his voice lower, rougher, not wanting her to feel she had to share it all, even though part of him wanted to know everything.

"I know," she said, meeting his eyes. "I guess... I just wanted you to know more about me."

He swallowed, realizing that she was being vulnerable with him and not knowing if he could ever return the favor.

He wondered if she knew about Avery.

Was that why she was telling him this?

He wanted to ask, but something held him back.

Fear, probably. Fear of reliving his pain, of having to face it.

He looked at her, really looked.

She'd lost everything that mattered during the holidays. And yet, somehow... she'd found a way to love this time of year anyway.

He just wasn't sure he could do the same.

"Anyway," Cassidy said, forcing a lightness back into her voice, "that's my sad backstory. But it was when I was in the hospital that my grand-maman introduced me to our family's spiced cocoa. And the rest, like they say, is history."

Liam didn't say anything. He was too busy thinking how alike they were, both using lightness to soften the pain. He did it all the time.

They both knew what it was to lose someone suddenly and too soon, and to have Christmas forever marked by their absence. For every December 25th to feel bittersweet.

She was watching him, waiting for him to say something.

"Did your grand-maman teach you French? Or did you learn it in Paris? You're fluent, right?" he asked finally, remembering what he'd heard from the locals.

Cassidy nodded. "*J'ai adoré vivre à Paris... jusqu'au jour où je suis rentrée chez moi et j'ai trouvé mon petit ami au lit avec une autre femme.*"

"Should I be concerned that sounded both beautiful and terrifying?"

"Paris was great... until I came home one afternoon and found my boyfriend in bed with another woman." She gave a tight smile, then muttered under her breath, "*Le salaud.*"

"Loo saloo?"

She looked up at him, eyes glittering. "The bastard."

Liam's hands balled into fists, his knuckles cracking in his gloves. "Sounds fitting."

Cassidy nodded. "Don't worry, I got back at him."

"How?"

"I took the espresso machine."

"I highly doubt—"

"Oh no, he loved that thing more than me."

He let out a short laugh, but it faded quickly. She was joking, but he could see it in her eyes—the asshole had hurt her. Deeply.

Cassidy looked down, toying with the zipper of her coat, her breath catching before she forced herself to continue. "It shouldn't still bother me, but it does. It wasn't just that he cheated. He made me feel small, you know? Like every dream I had was silly. Like I was lucky just to be with him, and I should be grateful for the scraps of attention he threw my way. Every time I got excited about something—about a recipe or trying out a new flavor combination —he'd laugh, call it childish, tell me I didn't have what it took."

Her fingers tightened on the zipper, knuckles whitening. "And the worst part is, I believed him. For a long time."

Liam's jaw tightened. He hated knowing some smug, pretentious prick had made her doubt her worth.

She'd had her heart shattered by a man who didn't deserve her, but she still believed in love and the goodness in people anyway. She loved fiercely, lived boldly, and didn't let grief or betrayal make her bitter.

She was the kind of woman who would open her shop early if she saw someone waiting in the cold, who would deliver cocoa to the local snowplow crew before sunrise, who would remember your favorite chocolate even if you'd only mentioned it once. She faced the world with hope, even when it had let her down.

She deserved someone who saw that, who *cherished* that, who would protect her bright, unbreakable spirit instead of dimming it.

Liam didn't know if he could be that man.

But in that moment, watching her stand there in the falling snow, her eyes meeting his with that quiet strength...

God, he wanted to try.

They were silent for a moment. The wind picked up, blowing the loose snow around like frozen glitter, only it didn't stop. "Oh, wow, it's really coming down. Where is everybody?" Cassidy asked.

Liam hadn't realized that they had fallen so far behind the group. He'd been too caught up in listening to Cassidy's story. The trail was disappearing beneath the heavy snow, and if they weren't careful, they'd get turned around.

"I know right where we are," Liam said. "Or... I'm pretty sure I do. There's a shelter nearby—the llama barn."

Cassidy knew Liam's family was opening up a llama sanctuary, and truth be told, she'd been desperate to see it.

"On my family farm. Follow me."

They pushed on through the deepening snow. It was easily almost up to their knees by now, falling in thick flakes, making the trail harder and harder to see. The only sounds were the crunch of their boots and the whisper of the wind through snow-laden pines.

They moved in silence until the shape of the barn appeared ahead, its dark silhouette a welcome sight against the pale winter sky.

Liam pushed open the heavy wooden door. "We can keep going if you want," he said, brushing snow from his coat as they entered the barn, "but it's probably another fifteen minutes to the main house."

The air was warm, still, and quiet, carrying the faint, comforting scent of hay and wood shavings. "No, this is great. Let's stay here for a minute."

The barn was rustic, with exposed beams crisscrossing the ceiling and a row of four stalls lining one side. In the open area at the back, fresh hay had been spread in golden piles, and thick wool blankets were folded neatly on a bench.

The llamas barely acknowledged them at first. One looked up briefly then went right back to munching alfalfa from a trough, its ears flicking lazily.

Cassidy tiptoed closer, careful not to startle them.

One of the llamas—an especially fluffy one with lopsided bangs—wandered toward her, blinking slowly. Cassidy grinned then hesitated.

"Is she friendly?" she whispered.

"Mostly," Liam said, trying not to smile. "That's Daisy. She likes attention, but she's been known to nibble if she's feeling ignored."

"Good to know," Cassidy said, carefully extending her hand. Daisy sniffed it then pressed her velvety nose into her palm, as if granting her approval.

"Well, hello to you too," she murmured.

Just then, another llama—this one shorter and rounder— shuffled up behind her and started nosing at her coat pocket.

"Oh! Hey! That's not a snack!" she said with a laugh, gently nudging it away.

"That's Tinsel," Liam said. "He's obsessed with granola bars. If you have one on you, he's not above pickpocketing."

Liam pulled out his phone and texted Zoe. She replied within minutes—everyone had made it back safely, Tyler and his daughter were already in their truck, and the rest of the group had settled in at the farmhouse.

She looked around, her eyes catching on the string lights, the tidy stalls, the quiet glow of the space, and Liam swore the tension in his chest pulled tighter.

Because she was smiling, and the barn felt different with her standing in it.

It was just a shelter from the snowstorm, just a stop on the way home.

But with her there, it felt like more.

Liam knew she must be freezing. He was, and he had on far better gear than she'd brought.

He walked over to where the tools were stored and grabbed one of the thick blankets. He shook it out and brought it over, wrapping it around her shoulders.

"It's not Christmassy, but it looks good on you," he said, referring to the hot-pink, lime-green, and yellow-striped blanket they regularly used to keep the llamas warm.

"Thank you. And don't worry, I still have plenty of hot cocoa." She pulled a second flask from her back pocket.

"How many of those did you carry with you?"

"Wouldn't you like to know?" She winked and uncapped the flask, taking a long sip before handing it to Liam.

"It does hit the spot," he said, taking a drink and wiping his mouth with the back of his hand.

"It does, doesn't it?" Cassidy said, accepting the flask back.

As she did, the blanket slipped off her shoulders. He stepped forward and caught it, helping to secure it in place, but this time, he didn't let go.

The two of them stood face to face, alone in the barn, with nothing but straw surrounding them and the wind howling outside.

Liam should've stepped back. Should've made some awkward joke about the weather. Changed the subject. Distracted himself with anything but the look in her eyes. It was wide and searching, as if she was asking him a question. *Can you feel it too?*

And God help him, he could.

Being with her like this—alone, close, warm—was the closest thing to true happiness he'd felt in years.

What would happen if they kissed, if they gave in to the sizzling temptation that crackled and snapped between them?

He stepped closer, just enough to test the air between them.

She reacted by placing her hand gently at his waist and tilting her face up to him.

That one touch burned through every boundary he'd tried to build. Every reason not to... disappeared.

Liam bent his head slowly, giving her every second to pull away.

She didn't.

His lips brushed the corner of her mouth—gentle, tentative, testing.

She made a soft sound, full of longing.

He deepened the kiss.

Cassidy melted into him like she'd been waiting for this—like they both had. Her arms slipped around his neck, pulling him closer, and Liam was gone. His hands gripped her waist, anchoring himself to the one thing in the world that suddenly made sense.

She tasted like warmth and chocolate, like the promise of something real. Of something worth believing in again.

This wasn't just lust. He knew that. And that was what undid him. Because Cassidy wasn't someone you kissed to pass the time or to forget the ache in your chest. She was the kind of woman who could burn herself into your life, who made you want things you'd sworn you'd stopped wanting.

Liam still carried the ghost of a Christmas past that had ended in heartbreak. But with Cassidy in his arms, soft and alive and kissing him back like she wanted every part of him, the past felt quieter, the edges dulling beneath the heat rushing through him. She opened to him, and he didn't hold back.

He lifted her easily, her legs wrapping around his hips, her breath catching as he pressed her back against the post in the darkened corner of the barn. His body fit against hers, solid and hot, every nerve lit up as she rocked against him, kissing him deeper.

She let out a soft sound, half sigh, half plea, and it nearly undid him.

His hands roamed down her thighs, gripping, sliding back up to her hips, pulling her tighter, closer, until there was nothing between them but heat and need.

God, she felt good.

Her scent surrounded him—sweet cocoa and cold winter air, mixed with the warm, wild fragrance of her skin—and it made him dizzy, made him forget every reason he'd given himself to stay away.

Cassidy kissed him like she wanted this as much as he did, like she trusted him with this moment, her breath, her body.

And he wanted it all.

Her kisses. Her laughter. Her warmth pressed up against him in the quiet of the snow-dusted barn.

She'd tossed her gloves on the ground long ago, her fingers digging into his shirt.

His thumb brushed the waistband of her jeans, and he longed to continue to explore. He wanted to know every curve of her body, the softness of her skin, taste the sweetness between her legs. He wanted everything.

"Knock, knock! Rescue crew is here!" Zach's voice shouted from somewhere in the barn.

They froze, breaths coming in hard, unsteady bursts, hearts pounding so loud it was a wonder Zach couldn't hear them.

Cassidy's hands tightened in his shirt, her lips still parted, her eyes wide and glassy with want. His hands were still on her hips, her legs still wrapped around him, and for a moment neither of them moved, neither willing to break the spell that had been so abruptly shattered.

Liam let out a shaky breath, jaw clenching. *Of all the damn timing...*

He pressed his forehead to hers, closing his eyes, trying to catch a breath that wouldn't come.

He didn't move. Didn't want to. "Five more minutes."

"Liam..."

"Just five," he rasped, brushing his mouth against her jaw. "They can freeze. I'll warm you up."

Cassidy let out a breathless laugh—half flustered, half wrecked—but started to wriggle down anyway. Her cheeks were scarlet, her hair mussed, her lips kiss-swollen and tempting as sin. "I can't. I need..." She shook her head. "If I don't go greet them, they'll know exactly what we were doing."

"They'll know no matter what." Liam's hand slid over her hip again, holding her in place for one more second. "Next time, I'm tying you down."

"That a promise?" she shot back, voice low as she slipped past him.

She grabbed the fallen blanket, quickly smoothing her hair and trying to pull herself together.

Liam stayed frozen for a beat longer, pulse pounding, jaw tight.

His hands itched to reach for her again, but instead, he forced himself to call out, "Back here!"

Cassidy shot him a look over her shoulder—half *you're trouble*, half *I want more*—and damn it, he knew there was no going back now.

TWENTY-ONE

CASSIDY

"Do you want the good news or the bad news?" Liam's mom, Beth, asked once everyone was safely gathered in the kitchen.

Cassidy took in the entire space, her breath catching. Liam might no longer love Christmas, but his mom didn't hold back. A simmering pot filled with cinnamon, orange slices, and cranberries bubbled on the stove. Miniature evergreen wreaths, hanging on red ribbons, decorated the front of each of the kitchen's white cabinets. A porcelain Christmas tree with tiny multicolored bulbs was displayed at the center of a circular white cake stand, serving as the island's focal point.

Even the dish towels were green-and-white checkered to match the dining room table's runner, and the lights above them were intertwined with cranberry garlands and white twinkling lights.

Beth had passed out blankets to the group and tossed everyone's wet socks, sweatshirts, and mittens into the dryer. Everything else—coats, boots, scarves—was hanging by the door, dripping as they tried to get everything dry.

"There's bad news?" Cassidy asked.

"Well… I guess that depends on how you define 'bad,'" Beth said as she filled the coffee pot.

The group waited expectantly while she gathered her thoughts.

"Alright, I'll start with the bad news. The storm was a doozy. More than anyone expected, as you all well know. It dropped about six inches of snow, if you can believe that. Thankfully it's passed us now. We should be in the clear for the rest of the night."

Everyone exhaled.

"The bad news," she continued, "is that it knocked down several power lines across the main road. So, you're all kind of stuck here for the foreseeable future. There are downed wires everywhere; they all just blew down about twenty minutes ago."

"What about Tyler and Emma?" Zoe asked.

"Back home safe and sound. He texted me about ten minutes ago," Zach confirmed.

Liam's dad chimed in from the doorway. "The power company says they should have everything cleared soon, but you've got to give them a few hours. The wind's not expected to die down until after eight, so they won't even begin working on it until then."

"The good news," Beth said cheerfully, wiping her hands on her festive snowflake-print apron, "is that lunch is already underway. Kit, would you mind giving me a hand finishing things up?"

"On it, boss!" Kit hopped up and saluted Beth.

"Perfect. Liam and Cassidy, I'm sending you two to fetch the board games. I think they're in your old bedroom."

"Alright then…" Liam's voice was quiet.

Cassidy couldn't read the look behind his eyes, but she was dying to know what he was thinking.

"Madison and Zach? You get to pick out the movies."

"Perfect," Madison said, clapping her hands. "Let's go." She stood up and pulled Zach by the hand, disappearing into the living room.

Liam nodded for Cassidy to follow him.

Beth's love for Christmas décor continued in the living room. Cassidy was liking her more and more by the second. The room was adorned with evergreen, there was red ribbon along the mantel, and checkered flannel throw pillows sat on the brown leather sofas with Christmas quilts draped over the backs. A large spruce dominated the corner of the room, drawing her eye.

"Careful there, don't get too close," Liam warned.

"Ha, don't worry, I won't touch the tree. It's just... look at these ornaments, they're so beautiful." She reached out to touch one of the glass-blown bulbs. It was a dark metallic blue. Liam's name was scripted on the front of it, hand-painted white along with a snowflake.

"Those are a family tradition. My parents started it when they got married." He pointed to the top of the tree, where she could see a green bulb with the name "Tom" painted on it. Next to it was a red bulb with "Beth" scrawled across it.

"Then came Jackson and me." Liam pointed to his blue bulb and Jackson's gold one. "And then Lily." He pointed to a purple bulb at the bottom.

"You didn't tell me you had a sister."

Liam smirked. "Well, I just met you, so there's a lot of stuff I haven't told you."

Cassidy supposed that was true. Still, she loved looking at the bulbs and learning the tradition behind them. She missed this, this sense of family, of having traditions that you passed down from year to year.

Grand-maman had always tried to make Christmas special. Even after everything changed, after the hospital, the quieter holidays over the next few years, the casseroles brought over by neighbors with sad eyes, who knew what this time of year meant for them. She still lit the Advent candles and played old French carols, made hot cocoa from scratch and insisted on reading *'Twas the Night Before Christmas.*

But it hadn't been the same.

Cassidy had missed her parents every single day for the past eighteen years, but especially at Christmas. The memories were so distant, but she remembered her mother's laughter as she burned the sugar cookies *again*, the way her dad would lift her up to put the star on the tree. She remembered the way they'd all pile into the car to look at Christmas lights, her dad humming along to the radio while she and her brother voted for which house they loved best. These were her fondest family memories. The ones she missed the most.

She missed how safe it had felt, how warm, how *whole*.

And once Grand-maman had passed, Cassidy had been left with a strange silence where tradition used to be. Many of the old ones had gone with her, and there hadn't been anyone left to carry them on.

So, Cassidy made new ones. Small ones. Like her Christmas movie checklist, and her rotating lineup of hot cocoa flavors.

"Don't ask what happened to Hunter..." Liam added.

Cassidy's eyes got wide. "What? What happened to Hunter?"

"Lily called off the wedding. Smashed his bulb into a million pieces. The look on my mother's face." Liam shook his head. "It was priceless."

"Yikes!"

"My sister's what we call a free spirit. I think the last time she was home for the holidays was... six years ago? She's a bit of a traveler. If she's home, she's either sick or broke." He said it all with a fond smile as Cassidy followed him up the narrow staircase.

The house was laid out with the kitchen, dining room,

family room, and living room on the main floor, with the master suite off to the side, and three bedrooms and a bathroom upstairs.

Liam walked to the last room on the right and pushed open the door.

Cassidy smiled as she stepped inside. The twin-sized bed had a blue plaid comforter, and the shelves were lined with movie posters and action figures.

"I didn't peg you for an action figure kind of guy, but now that I see them here in your room..." She trailed off. "Nope. Still can't see it."

The broody lumberjack man she'd met definitely didn't fit that mold.

"I'll have you know a lot of these are worth a pretty penny," he replied, walking to the closet and sliding the wooden door along the track.

It was clear Beth had used the space for storage since her boys had moved out. There were duvets stored in plastic zipper bags, her sewing machine, bolts of fabric, and dozens of board games.

Liam focused on the shelf. "Which one do you like— Sequence?"

"Uh... I don't know if I've ever played that one," she said, scanning the titles.

"What about Monopoly?"

"I hate Monopoly. You win by bankrupting your friends. It never ends well."

"That's fair. Clue?"

"I love Clue. Yes. Grab Yahtzee because that's always fun, too." She kept scanning the titles in the closet. "What about Life?" she asked.

"Life is good," he said over his shoulder.

Their eyes met, and something shifted in the air. The look Cassidy gave him was soft, searching. She was acutely aware that they were standing in his childhood bedroom, alone, surrounded by memories—and possibility.

She bit her lip. "Listen, I'm not sure what's going on between the two of us, but I'm fighting really hard not to rip your clothes off if I'm being completely honest. You've got this whole sexy lumberjack thing going on."

Liam choked on a laugh. "Sexy lumberjack?"

"Okay, sexy farmer lumberjack. And I'm supposed to be in my 'year of no men,' but uh... there are things I really want to do to you."

He let out a low, nervous chuckle. "And I thought I was forward. So, this is a vow of yours? A whole year?"

"Self-imposed vow," Cassidy amended. "And there are only a few weeks left, but who's counting?"

Me, I'm counting, she thought.

She took a breath, her heart pounding. "Anyway, I just... wanted you to know that I'm into you."

His eyebrows lifted, his eyes sharpening, locking on her.

"Like... *really* into you," she continued, her voice softer now, her fingers fidgeting with the edge of her sleeve. "And sometimes it's really hard to remember why I made that vow in the first place when you look at me the way you do... But," she added, forcing herself to keep her voice steady, "I also want to take things slow. I want to focus on my business, on the Christmas Light-Up Display Competition. I need to prove to myself that I can do this. By the way, sorry to say, you are going to lose."

"Excuse me? You think you can beat me?"

"Oh, I know I can, Mr. I-Don't-Have-a-Christmas-Movie-Checklist."

"Again with the checklist," Liam said, shaking his head. "You don't need a checklist if the only Christmas movie you watch is *Die Hard*..."

"*Die Hard* is not a Christmas movie!" Cassidy stood tall,

hands on her hips. "There's no way a grinch is beating me in this competition."

"Grinch? I thought I was a sexy lumberjack." Liam cracked a smile, those dimples doing dangerous things to her resolve.

"Fine, you're a sexy grinch-lumberjack who drives me crazy, but I'm trying to ignore you so I can focus on everything else."

As much as she wanted to throw her vow and caution—and her clothes—to the wind, she couldn't. Not after what had happened with Jean-Paul. Not after letting her guard down and being shattered by someone who'd made promises with his lips and broken them with his actions. She wouldn't let that happen again. She was smarter now. Safer.

Even if her body was screaming otherwise.

Cassidy bent to grab a game off the bottom shelf, fully aware of Liam watching her. When she stood, she caught the way his throat visibly swallowed, drinking her in.

They weren't touching, but the air between them practically sparked.

Slow, she reminded herself. *Take things slow.*

God help her. Because if he looked at her like that again, she wasn't sure she'd make it out of this room without breaking the vow she'd sworn she'd keep until New Year's Day.

TWENTY-TWO

LIAM

Liam was still replaying the conversation with Cassidy after lunch as she sat beside him, curled up on the couch watching a Christmas movie, Muff at their feet. They'd decided to hold off on the board games for now and just relax before lunch. Liam watched as a log popped and cracked in the fireplace. In the corner, the tree glowed softly. The miniature multicolored lights reflected off the glass bulbs, creating a kaleidoscope of colors on the walls. The scent of cinnamon and citrus from the simmering pot on the stove drifted into the living room, mixing with the woodsmoke from the fire, making the farmhouse feel even cozier.

Liam felt like he was in high school again on winter break, all his friends piled into the living room, everyone finding a spot on the floor or the couch while a giant bowl of buttery popcorn made its way around.

Even Jackson had joined them. He'd come down from the loft for lunch; his usual guarded expression was loosening as Zoe handed him a mug of cider and teased him about his favorite band. When they moved to the living room, for a few minutes Jackson stayed, leaning against the wall near the fireplace as Zoe chatted about her plans for her flower shop's light-up event and how she'd love his help moving a delivery. Liam caught the way Jackson's shoulders eased, the lines around his eyes softening in the warm glow of the fire, as if Zoe's gentle energy made it easier for him to be there.

Cassidy looked perfectly at home, too. She was wearing a pair of his sister's sweatpants and his old high school sweatshirt—the faded blue one with the hawk mascot and stretched-out collar. The sweatshirt swallowed her whole, the hem coming down to her knees and the sleeves past her knuckles, but she seemed to love it, wrapping her arms around herself like it was her favorite blanket.

She shifted slightly, the edge of her knee brushing his thigh. It wasn't intentional—she was just reaching for the blanket—but Liam felt it. It was like a slow, steady pull in his core. He wanted to lean in, rest his arm around her shoulders, pull her just a little closer, but he didn't. The scene from the barn flashed before his eyes. Yeah, he wanted to pull her closer and then some.

Cassidy kept glancing over at him. Liam thought she was checking to see how he was handling all the holiday cheer, if he was doing okay. But truth be told, he wasn't really thinking about the movie.

No, he was thinking about how she'd told him—pretty bluntly and boldly, with some serious holiday innuendo—just how attracted she was to him. And yet, instead of acting on that attraction, she wanted to take it slow.

That should've been a relief. It should've made things easier. Safer.

But it didn't.

Because now Liam knew two things for sure: One, Cassidy wanted him. And two, she wasn't in it for a fling.

And the problem? Neither was he.

That realization scared the hell out of him.

He tried to walk it back. Tried to convince himself he wasn't looking for anything serious. That she was just a distraction. That she was new. That there was just something about her soft blonde hair and maybe that magical hot cocoa of hers that had thrown him off.

But that was a lie.

He'd been running from anything serious for four years, and now he was caught in an aching space between desire and fear. He wanted to know her, all of her secrets and her quirks and her stories from Paris, her memories of the small town nearby where she'd grown up. And he wanted to kiss her again. Not just a taste. Not fast and manic, pressed in the corner of the barn. No, he wanted to go slow. Find what made her shiver with desire. What made her sigh and moan and melt into him. He wanted to feel her body quake around him, to hear the way she said his name when she shattered.

To lose himself in the rhythm of her body, find something real and vulnerable, both of them cracked wide open. Something he thought he'd lost for good.

After, he'd want to hold her. He'd pull her against his chest, wrap the blanket around them both, and press a kiss to her temple. He'd feel her breath slow, her body soften, and he'd tuck her even closer like he could shield her from the world.

That wasn't a fling, it was real, and it was big. And that scared him.

If he had any sense, he'd say something tonight. Draw a line. Tell her that they shouldn't just take things slow; they should stop altogether. He could even picture himself doing it. They'd walk out into the snow, and he'd tell her how great he thought she was, but that he didn't want to wreck their friendship. He knew that's what he should do. Park her in the friend zone and never look back.

It was safer that way.

He had loved a girl before, deeply and completely. He'd brought that girl home for Christmas once. Or, he almost had.

Avery had been going to spend a week of their break at his house. He'd planned out all the things they'd do around Maple Falls—the hot cocoa crawl, making gingerbread houses at the bakery, throwing an epic snowball fight at the city park, sledding down the big hill outside of the library. Liam had always been a kid at heart, and once upon a time, Christmas had brought it out of him one hundred percent.

He'd wanted to give Avery a Christmas to remember.

Then, black ice, a highway pileup, a split second of fate that destroyed everything Liam had imagined for their future. The grief had swallowed him whole. He didn't go to the cocoa crawl that year. Didn't step foot in town or open a single present.

And ever since, the holidays had felt dimmer, shadowed. He'd faked his way through them, praying December would fly by as quickly as November had.

So yeah, romance at Christmas was never going to be his thing, and part of him knew what he should do. Protect himself, protect Cassidy.

Not just in the holidays, but always. Because getting close to someone, letting them in, meant risking everything again. Nothing was promised in this life. And Liam wasn't sure he had it in him to survive another loss like that.

But then Cassidy looked over at him, questioningly, and nuzzled a little closer. "This okay?" she asked.

His heart stopped. He should've said no.

But he couldn't. Not when every cell in his body was screaming *yes*.

So instead of pushing her away, he responded with a casual, "Yeah," and wrapped his arm around her shoulder, pulling her closer.

At that moment, there was nothing, not the ghosts of his

past, not the fear of what might come, not even the voice in his head that was warning him to be careful.

There was only Cassidy.

Warm, steady, real.

Liam closed his eyes. For the first time in a long while, he allowed himself to believe that maybe he hadn't lost every part of himself on that cold December night four years ago. That perhaps, beneath the layers he'd built to keep the world at bay, something had survived. Something waiting to be found.

And somehow, Cassidy had found it.

With her clear blue eyes that saw more than he wanted to admit, the easy confidence in the way she carried herself, the quiet strength behind her warmth. She was light and laughter and a fierce determination he couldn't look away from.

And whether he was ready or not, Liam was already falling —deep, hard, and headfirst—for the girl who he hadn't seen coming.

TWENTY-THREE

CASSIDY

Cassidy stood outside the community center late the next afternoon after closing up the Cocoa Corner, bundled tight against the cold. Snow drifted across the small front lawn in light, glittery flakes, swirling around the candy-cane-striped posts that framed the double doors.

The community center was just north of Oak Way, a short walk from the town square, tucked between the post office and the library. It was the kind of place that smelled like old wood floors and cinnamon coffee cake, where handmade flyers covered the bulletin board inside the entryway, announcing everything from bake sales and quilting circles to the Friday night bingo game.

It was where the town hosted chili cook-offs, game nights, and the annual mitten drive, where families gathered after the tree lighting to warm up with hot cocoa, and where neighbors dropped off casseroles when someone needed a helping hand.

Today, it was the site of the town's snowman-building competition, and Cassidy had zero regrets about skipping an evening of light-up display prep to be here. Because seriously, how was she supposed to miss this? Every event in the Maple Falls Christmas Countdown was truly a Christmas addict's dream come true, and she was *all in*.

She'd show discipline later that week and skip the lantern-lit garden walk at the community park, or the gingerbread baking class at the bakery, or next week's crafting club meeting at the inn.

Probably.

Maybe.

Okay, she didn't want to miss those either.

But *something* had to give.

Because the truth was, she was running out of time. She hadn't planned on spending all afternoon and evening yesterday at the Hawthornes'. Her light-up night was ticking closer by the day, and she still had half-finished decorations in the back of the shop and lists upon lists of tasks she hadn't checked off. The shop and her Spiced Cocoa Café pop-up were busier than she could have dreamed—customers piling in for thick, steaming mugs of cocoa and handcrafted truffles, leaving her completely run off her feet most days.

And she loved it, truly. Every sugar-dusted, cocoa-splattered minute of it. Even if it was a lot.

But it didn't matter how tired or busy she was. Cassidy wasn't going to miss an actual snowman-building competition. It was the type of community event she couldn't believe was even real. It was so wholesome that she had to pinch herself for how lucky she was to live here.

She had come prepared. Cassidy wore her red puffer coat, festive green leggings with tiny white Christmas trees printed on them, her faux fur-lined Santa hat, and heavy-duty ski gloves. She wasn't going to freeze today. And who knew? Her accessories just might help her team win the competition because everyone knew that when it came to making a winning snowman, it all came down to the accessories.

"I knew I'd see you here, Sugarplum," Liam said, appearing beside her and making her jump.

"You scared me!" she said, reaching for her hat to make sure it didn't slip off her head. "What are you doing here, Grinch?"

Liam chuckled, and those dimples were doing very unfair things to her.

"Nice to see you too." He pulled something out from inside his jacket. "You left your scarf at my parents' house. I wanted to run it over to you before, but you looked swamped this morning."

Before she could respond, Liam stepped closer and wrapped it snugly around her neck. His fingers lingered, just for a second, and she swore the world fell away. They were suddenly face to face, breath visible in the cold air.

Snowflakes caught in his dark hair, melting as they touched his skin, a droplet sliding down the curve of his jaw.

His eyes held hers, a deep forest brown, and Cassidy's pulse stuttered.

She wondered if "taking it slow" meant no public displays of affection, because right now, all she wanted was to fist her hands in the front of his jacket, pull him down, and taste the warmth of his mouth against hers. She wanted to know how it would feel to melt into him completely, to let the heat she saw flickering in his eyes match the heat building low in her belly.

But she'd made her vow for a reason. She needed to give herself space. To figure out who she was without anyone else clouding it.

Swearing off men had been easy for the past 341 days of the year, until Liam.

Until the way he looked at her like she was the only thing worth seeing. Until the way his touch felt like a promise of everything she'd almost convinced herself she didn't need.

Somehow, she resisted.

But only for now.

Because there were only a few weeks left until the New Year, and when the clock struck midnight, she wanted to see exactly where all this chemistry between them would take them.

"Hey, strangers!" Kit called, walking up with Madison and Zoe, each bundled in colorful scarves and knit hats already dusted with snow.

Kit dropped her voice dramatically. "You guys hear the latest? I heard Mayor Bloomfield had to replace *all* the lights on the town tree."

"What?" gasped Madison. "Don't tell me, the Gingerbread Jerk?"

"Yep," Kit said, eyes wide. "Snipped the wires at the bottom, left them dangling like tinsel."

"I'm not taking any chances," Madison said firmly, adjusting her knit hat. "I'm ordering security cameras for the inn."

Cassidy's eyes went wide. Cameras? She thought of her own cozy shop, the twinkle lights in the windows, the paper snowflakes taped to the glass. She hated the thought of not being able to trust her neighbors, of having to watch people who should feel like friends.

But what if it happened to her next?

Seeing the worry on her face, Liam gently bumped her shoulder with his. "Hey. Don't go spiraling. I'll talk to Mayor Bloomfield tomorrow, get the full story. For all we know, it's just gossip."

Cassidy let out a breath, nodding, though her mind was already ticking through possibilities. Because if someone really was out there, cutting Christmas lights and smashing displays, they were about to mess with the wrong chocolate shop.

The group changed the subject when Tyler and his daughter, Emma, approached. They were walking hand in hand through the snowdrifts.

"Dad, do you think we can build a whole snowman family or just one really big one?" Emma was saying, clutching a small reusable tote decorated with snowflakes and packed to bursting with supplies. "I brought enough crowns to make the entire royal family, but I only brought one cape if we do a superhero theme."

"Looks like we're going to have our work cut out for us," Cassidy replied, eying Emma.

"I just hope she's on my team." Liam grinned.

Before they could talk more, Mrs. C. clapped her hands, calling everyone's attention. The older woman wore a black wool coat, a matching stocking cap, and the largest rhinestone Santa pin Cassidy had ever seen. She was dying to know where the woman had got it from. It would go great with her ever-expanding collection. Her favorite was her Christmas tree pin, which was currently on her coat. After that, it was a three-way tie between Rudolph, a rhinestone snowflake, and her pearl snowman.

"Listen up, folks! Welcome to the twenty-third annual Maple Falls snowman-building competition!"

The crowd cheered.

Mrs. C. counted the participants and nodded approvingly, counting out popsicle sticks and dropping them in a tin can.

"We're doing teams again this year. Go ahead and pass the tin around. Pull a stick, and the color will tell you which team you're on. All accessories are fair game. There are hats, scarves, buttons, mittens—you name it."

Cassidy reached in and pulled out a green stick. She looked over to Liam as he pulled out red.

"Oh, you're going down," she said with a laugh.

Emma pulled out a red stick next and let out a squeal of delight. "Yes! I'm on Liam's team!"

Liam's lips curved, ruffling Emma's hat as she bounced beside him. "Looks like we've got the winning team, kiddo."

Around them, kids and parents pulled out sticks—blue, silver, gold, red, and green. Emily pulled out blue. Meg from the bookstore was on the gold team. Tyler joined them on red, while Zoe, Kit, and Madison joined Cassidy on green.

"You have thirty minutes to build the best snowman you've ever seen," Mrs. C. announced. "On my mark!" She blew her whistle.

Cassidy and Liam both sprinted toward the table of accessories.

"Wait, wait! We don't even have a plan yet!" Zoe called, but Cassidy wasn't listening. Her eyes were locked on a silver glitter scarf that was calling her name.

Liam reached it first.

"No way. That one's ours. I saw it first," Cassidy said, curling her fingers around the edge.

"You can't call dibs on a scarf," Liam shot back, but there was a spark in his eyes.

"Look at it. It's silver glitter! It's meant for me! Plus, it matches our theme!"

"Theme?"

"Mmm-hmm. It's, uh... Jingle Bells Jazz." Cassidy made it up on the spot.

Liam laughed. "That's not a theme."

"It is now," Cassidy said. "Jazz hands, glitter, little snowmen with saxophones—"

"That can't be real," he muttered. "You're making this up."

"Maybe," she said, batting her lashes. "But it's working, isn't it?"

Emma peeked up from where she was gathering buttons for the snowman's face. "Come on, Liam, let her have it. She's got that look."

"Oh, betrayal," he said dramatically, placing a hand on his chest.

Emma giggled, and Cassidy's heart squeezed watching them. Liam's expression softened as he glanced down at Emma, then back to Cassidy, and with a resigned sigh, he handed over the scarf. "You're lucky you're cute."

Cassidy smiled. She had been called a lot of adjectives—goofy, weird, funny, sweet. Never cute. Jean-Paul certainly never said that. Even when he was trying to woo her with his Shakespearean sonnets and pricey champagne.

Before she could overthink it, she leaned in and pressed a quick kiss to his cheek. "Thanks for the scarf."

Emma, still watching Liam, whispered, "Did she just kiss you?"

He cleared his throat, ears turning red. "Focus on the snowman, squirt."

She hurried back to their team, scarf raised high. "Victory!"

"I think you won more than a scarf," Kit replied with a laugh.

Maybe I did, Cassidy thought to herself.

"Don't we have a snowman to build?" Cassidy quickly replied.

They got to work immediately. Madison and Zoe began rolling the base while Cassidy and Kit gathered extra snow, determined to keep up with Liam's team, who were already building a snowman so big Emma was trying to climb on it to adjust the crown.

"You think we can beat them?" Kit asked, eyeing Liam's towering snowman.

"We have to," Cassidy said, breathless, snow in her hair. "We can't let him win."

Across the yard, Liam lifted Emma onto his shoulders so she could carefully place a button eye, and Emma squealed with delight, her boots swinging in the air.

Cassidy found herself watching them, unable to look away.

Liam's easy smile tugged at something deep inside her, the way he steadied Emma with careful hands, gently reminding her not to drop the button, letting her take her time.

He laughed at something Emma whispered, the sound soft and genuine.

And for a moment—a single, raw moment—Cassidy let herself imagine what it would be like to have that with him. To have *this*. A snowy afternoon, a yard full of laughter, a warm, steady man who would teach a child how to build the perfect snowman while she made cocoa in the kitchen, peeking out the window to watch them.

The thought squeezed her chest tightly with the realization of how badly she wanted that family life. The life that had been stolen from her.

"We've got to go bigger!" Kit shouted, snapping her out of her thoughts.

"You're right. More snow!" Madison agreed.

Thankfully, the storm yesterday had left them with plenty to work with.

Cassidy joined Madison and Zoe in rolling the middle ball, packing it tight and rolling it until it grew nearly too heavy to push.

"Wait—we're never getting this thing up there." Kit groaned, eyeing the massive snowball they had created.

"Yes, we are," Cassidy said, brushing snow from her gloves. "If we all work together! Ready?"

"I don't know if that's such a good idea..." Zoe said, the lone voice of reason.

"What? We've got this. On three. One, two, three—"

OOF!

They barely lifted it before dropping it back into the snow with a dull thud.

"My back," Madison wheezed, hunched over.

"My pants!" Kit yelped, reaching behind her to make sure she hadn't split them.

"Told you it was too much," Zoe muttered.

Cassidy shook her head, determined. "That was just a trial run. We can do this. One more time!"

Before she could rally them again, a familiar voice cut in.

"Need a hand?" he asked, already reaching for the oversized snowball.

"Hey! You can't help them!" Emma called from across the yard. "They're the enemy!"

Liam smirked but didn't stop. "Let's call it community service."

"Careful, watch your pants!" Kit called out.

Cassidy stepped back to give him room. Their eyes met for a beat longer than it needed to be. Her heart thudded. There was mischief in his eyes, and a steady confidence that made her stomach tighten and her breath catch.

Liam bent to lift the snowball, the muscles in his arms and shoulders flexing beneath his coat as he hoisted it up with a low grunt that sent a shiver racing through her.

"Here, this way." Cassidy stepped in to steady it and guide it onto the base.

It landed with a satisfying *thud*.

Madison whooped, Zoe let out a cheer, and Kit threw her hands in the air with a "Praise Jesus!"

Cassidy's pulse was still pounding as Liam leaned in, close enough for her to feel the heat radiating off him, his voice dropping to a teasing rumble meant for her alone. "Think I can get that scarf back now?"

Her breath hitched, her gaze dropping briefly to his lips before darting back up to meet his eyes. "Not a chance."

His mouth curved into a wicked smile, the kind that made her thighs clench. "That's too bad. I had plans for it."

The way he said it left no doubt in her mind that those

plans had nothing to do with building snowmen. Heat pulsed low in her belly, and for a split second, she nearly offered it to him just to find out what those plans were.

Twenty-three days until the New Year, she reminded herself, clutching the scarf tighter, even as her mind raced with images she absolutely shouldn't be having in the middle of a snowman competition.

Cassidy watched him walk away, broad shoulders moving under that flannel-lined coat, snowflakes clinging to his dark hair. She bit her bottom lip, forcing herself to look away.

But it was useless.

Because all she could think about was what it would feel like if he pressed her against the snow-covered fence, those strong hands on her waist, that wicked smile against her mouth.

Twenty-three days.

"Okay, let's finish this snowman before I do something stupid," she muttered under her breath.

"Like what?" Kit asked, raising a brow.

"Like tackle him in the snow and make out behind the pine trees," Cassidy replied honestly.

Kit smirked. "That could be pretty amusing..."

"And probably not fit for a child's eyes," Zoe added, motioning to Emma, who was working on the next snowball just out of earshot.

Cassidy sighed. "You're right."

She glanced over and caught Liam's eyes—eyes that said he wanted to kiss her as badly as she wanted to kiss him.

The heat from the barn, from yesterday's kiss, came flooding back to her. She didn't have much experience when it came to men. There was really only Jean-Paul. But she knew, knew it one thousand percent, that Liam would be a good lover. The way his hands had moved across her body. The way he'd pressed her up against that wooden beam in the barn.

The man knew exactly what he was doing.

And heaven help her, because she wanted to let him do *everything*.

The snowman competition wrapped up as the evening sun cast a soft pink glow over Maple Falls. Children were still darting around the yard, tugging at parents' hands to show off carrot noses and crooked stick arms, while Mrs. C. snapped photos for the town Facebook page.

In the end, Liam and Emma's towering snowman, complete with a superhero cape and a lopsided crown, took first place—though Cassidy's glittery, jazz-hands snowman won "Most Festive" and earned a stack of candy canes.

Liam crossed the yard in just a few long strides, his gloved hands shoved deep in his coat pockets, his expression unreadable but focused on her.

"Who knew," he said, low and casual, stopping just close enough that the crisp winter air between them practically crackled, "that you are just as competitive with snowmen as you are Christmas lights."

She raised a brow. "I take my snowmen seriously."

"I can tell." He hesitated then looked over her shoulder at the slowly dispersing crowd. "Hey, before everything kicks off again—want to go ice skating on Wednesday morning? Before the shops open. No crowds. Just us."

She could picture it already—the frozen lake, the morning frost still clinging to the branches, the two of them gliding across the ice as the town slowly woke up. Just them, the snow, and the hush of a new day.

"I'd like that," she said, her voice soft.

His gaze lingered, warm and unreadable. "Good. I'll pick you up at six thirty."

Cassidy nodded, but inside she was already lacing up her skates, breath fogging in the early-morning air, cheeks flushed from the cold—or maybe from him. And as she watched him walk away, hands in his pockets, that easy, quiet strength in every step, she knew Wednesday morning couldn't come fast enough.

TWENTY-FOUR

LIAM

Cassidy's door creaked open just as he reached it. She stepped outside, bundled in a white puffer coat, striped mittens, hair tucked into a knit hat, and that scarf Liam had returned to her yesterday. Her eyes lit up when she saw him. That look right there? It made the cold worth it.

"You're punctual," she said, voice bright as if she always woke up to go ice skating at dawn.

"I'm a man of my word," Liam replied, handing over a cup. "I figured we could both use some coffee."

Cassidy took it with a pleased smile. "You trying to bribe me into letting you win the competition?"

"Would it work?"

"Absolutely not."

They walked side by side down the snowy street, boots crunching in sync. The world around them was a still, blue hush. Even the lake, when it came into view, looked asleep beneath its smooth sheet of ice.

As they approached, the first hints of sunrise kissed the horizon. Pale gold bled into lavender and peach, casting soft light over the frozen water. It shimmered like glass, rimmed with frost-laced branches and a few early birds darting overhead. The rink was empty. Just them, the ice, and the slow, steady waking of the world.

Liam watched Cassidy take it all in, her breath fogging in the air. She turned to him with that look again—the one that made something in his chest pull tight.

"Come on," he said, nodding toward the rental shed, already unlocking it with the spare key. "Time to show off my moves."

"I should've stretched," she muttered, lacing up her skates.

"You think you'll be sore?" he asked, standing and offering a hand to help her up.

"I think I'll be sore, humiliated, and possibly concussed."

"I'll try not to laugh. Much."

Liam took off first, skating backward with practiced ease.

"Show-off," Cassidy called, trying not to topple forward. She took one tentative step at a time, like a toddler learning to walk.

"More like years of hockey." Liam skated toward her. "Here," he said, taking both of her hands so that they were face to face. "I've got you."

She gripped his hands tightly, cheeks flushed from the cold, or maybe, Liam thought, from something else.

He moved slowly, guiding her gently across the frozen lake, glancing over his shoulder now and then to make sure their path stayed clear.

"So, you played hockey?" Cassidy asked.

Liam found it impressive that she could carry on a conversation while trying not to lose her balance.

"I did," Liam confirmed, navigating a backwards turn, pulling Cassidy along with him.

"Jackson, too?" Cassidy wobbled forward, nearly losing her footing.

"Zach and Jackson," Liam replied, steadying her.

Cassidy tilted her head thoughtfully. "Jackson looks like a hockey player," she decided.

Liam laughed at her unexpected comment. "Oh yeah? How so?"

"He's the quiet type. You just know he'd rather solve things with his fists than talk it out."

Liam chuckled. It seemed Cassidy understood her brother pretty well.

"What about you? Did you play any sports?" Liam turned, letting go of her hands for a moment so they skated side by side instead of face to face. "Is this okay?" he asked, noting Cassidy's struggle to keep her balance.

She didn't answer; she was too busy concentrating now, and Liam knew she'd fall any second.

Liam fell in step behind her. His hands slid gently to her waist, fingers curling around her coat. "Or how about this? Is this better?"

She let out a breathy laugh, her body relaxing ever so slightly against his. "Yeah," she said. "This is better."

They skated like that for a few moments. Their movements in sync. The world narrowed to just the two of them. Liam heard the ice scraping under their blades, felt the wind blow across his face and the heat of Cassidy's skin under his fingertips.

He tried to focus on his breathing, the rhythm of their skates, and not on how much he never wanted to let go.

"As to your other question…" Her voice brought him back. "No, I didn't play sports. I took dance—mostly jazz and hip-hop. A little ballet to make my grand-maman happy." Her voice went soft at the mention. "But most of my time I spent with her doing puzzles, reading books… quieter stuff like that. Which suited my brother, Julian, and me just fine."

Liam smiled, picturing it. Cassidy in a tutu, probably talking a mile a minute. "Let me guess," he said. "You choreographed your own routines."

She nudged him with her elbow. "Maybe. And maybe they involved a lot of dramatic jazz hands."

He chuckled, but the image stuck with him, warm and a little bittersweet.

Because it was so different from his own childhood, where laughter came easily, sure, but so did noise and chaos. Siblings fighting over the last cookie, his mom hollering for them to get their boots off the table, his dad wrestling them into snow gear for skating on the lake. A house that had always felt full and loud.

Cassidy's stories felt softer, quieter, edged with a loneliness she didn't quite say out loud. A girl who had learned to make her own joy, who had clung to the light even after the world had tried to dim it.

And maybe that was what pulled him in the most.

"Tell me more about your brother," he said gently, because he wanted to know everything about her—about the people who made her who she was, about the family she missed, about the soft, hidden parts of her she didn't always let the world see.

Cassidy smiled. Liam could hear it in her voice. "Julian's great. He's really my best friend. After our parents died, we leaned on each other. I mean, we've always been close, but that changed things. Then after everything fell apart in Paris with Jean-Paul, Julian really wanted me to stay in New York. He and his husband own a patisserie there—they're brilliant at what they do. And I loved working with them, but the fast-paced city lifestyle? I was kind of over it. I wanted something different. Something for myself. The Midwest always felt like home, even though I hadn't lived here in years."

"Well, for what it's worth… I'm glad you came back."

"Me too. But I have to say… ice skating looks way more fun on TV. My ankles are killing me, and I'm pretty sure I'm going to take you down yet."

Liam laughed. "You want to head back?"

"I do. I really do."

Liam guided her off the rink, his hand steady on her back as they stepped carefully across the frosty edge, the blades of their skates clicking softly on the ice before they reached the snow-dusted path.

He didn't want the morning to end. Honestly, he could get used to starting every day with Cassidy—making her laugh, hearing her stories, drinking in those quiet moments when her eyes softened just for him.

The sun had fully risen now, painting the sky in shades of blush and gold. Liam knew that back in town, people were waking up, getting ready for work and school. But out here, it felt like a private world for just the two of them.

"Are you in a hurry to get back?" he asked, surprising even himself.

"I should be opening shop in a couple of hours," she replied. "But if you've got something else in mind, I'd love to hear it."

"It's just… talking about old times reminded me of a place nearby. Thought maybe you'd like to see?"

"Keeping it mysterious, are you?" Cassidy teased, bumping her shoulder into his side.

"Something like that."

She raised an eyebrow. "You know I'm dying to know what you're up to."

"Honestly? I'm just sort of winging it," he admitted with a grin.

Cassidy laughed, her eyes sparkling beneath the glow of the lampposts that lined the lakeside trail.

"You're not allergic to pine trees, are you?" he asked, remembering her earlier allergic reaction with sudden concern.

"Not at all," Cassidy assured him with a warm smile.

They set off, hand in hand, along the paved trail that wrapped around the lake. The city council had kept the main path clear, but where they were headed wasn't paved. Pines stood tall and dark against the brightening sky, their branches heavy with fresh snow, creating a tunnel of white and green that shimmered faintly.

Liam glanced down at Cassidy's boots.

"You checking out my footwear?" she asked with a smirk.

"Just making sure we're prepared." He grinned then turned off the trail, leading her through the snow toward a dense cluster of pines. They were still hand in hand, Liam in front, making a path through the snow for her to follow.

"You'd never see it from the paved trail—it's too buried—but I know right where it is," he continued, guiding her with sure steps.

Back here, the snowdrifts were dramatic. On one side, the snow was only inches deep, the other, several feet. Liam led her right down the middle, carving a path just for them.

Some people loved Maple Falls in the fall, with its fiery maples and woodsmoke from the campground. Others thought you couldn't beat it in the spring, when the town came alive with flowers and the promise of new beginnings. And it was beautiful in the summer, with the boats bobbing on the lake, the sun warming everyone through, the smell of honeysuckle in the air.

But if you asked Liam, he'd say there was nothing more beautiful than that moment, right there.

For years, he hadn't let himself see it. December had become a month he endured, a season that pressed on old wounds, turning all the twinkling lights and carols into reminders of what he'd lost. The snow-laden pine trees, the crystal ice rink, all the colorful lights—they'd been pushed into the background.

But now, with Cassidy's hand in his, it was like seeing Maple Falls in winter for the first time.

The bright morning light filtered through the trees, making the snow glitter in gold and silver. The entire scene looked enchanted.

"It's beautiful back here," she said, her voice soft, reverent.

He felt it too. The way the woods held the quiet, the stillness that settled deep in his bones, the kind that made you feel like the world had paused just for you.

They ducked through the trees, pine needles brushing their coats and caps, the scent of resin sharp and clean in the cold air. Branches hung low, heavy with snow, and Liam reached out to steady Cassidy as she stepped over a half-buried log, her gloved hand warm in his.

"Back in sixth grade, I was really into camping, survival training, all of it. I was convinced I'd find myself lost in the woods far more than I ever have," he explained.

"Lumberjack Liam." She grinned.

He let out a gentle laugh, the sound echoing softly between the trees. "Anyway, I don't even remember how I found it, but through middle school and high school... this was my spot." His voice went quiet, his gaze tracking the path ahead. "Whenever I needed space... I came here."

He held back a pine bough, revealing the hidden entrance.

She stepped inside and looked around in awe. They were underneath a massive white pine, its trunk at least a hundred feet tall. The first branch was above both of their heads, but its weight caused the tips of the branch to touch the ground, closing them off like a curtain.

The ground beneath their boots was soft, layered with thousands of dried pine needles. The air was thick with the scent of sap and damp earth.

Cassidy spun in a circle, eyes sparkling. "It's like a magical pine tree fort," she said, laughing softly.

Liam had known she'd love it, but seeing her here, cheeks pink from the cold, eyes wide with wonder... it undid him.

"It's beautiful," she said again, her voice low, like she didn't want to disturb the quiet. Then she looked up at him. "Really beautiful."

He looked at her, his throat tightening. He should say something meaningful, something about how much he liked being here with her, how special she made him feel. But even though romantic words weren't his thing, his hands knew what to do.

He reached for her scarf, gently adjusting it around her neck. His knuckles brushed her jaw.

Their eyes met. Neither of them looked away.

"You bring all the girls here?" she asked, teasing. Her voice was light, but he could hear the nerves beneath it.

He shook his head. "Only you."

Her smile faded into something softer, more real. She stepped closer until the front of her coat brushed his chest.

The space between them vanished.

Her gaze dropped to his lips. "So... are you gonna kiss me, or just keep holding onto my scarf?"

Her words broke something loose in him.

He cupped her jaw, brushing his thumb over her cheekbone, and kissed her.

Slow. Deep.

No barn walls, no frantic moments. Just this. The snow beneath their boots, pine above their heads, and the thrum of something real humming in his veins.

Liam pulled back, just a breath, resting his forehead against hers.

His voice was deep, ragged. "Cass."

She opened her eyes, dazed and bright, like someone waking from the best kind of dream.

"You okay?" he asked, gently brushing a loose curl from her cheek.

She nodded, slow. But the tension in her shoulders didn't ease.

He waited. Quiet. Steady. The way he always was with her.

"I know what I said," she said finally, her voice barely above a whisper. "About swearing off men until New Year's Day. About taking things slow even after that. I meant it."

He didn't move. He let the silence stretch, waiting.

She took a steadying breath. "I still want that," she said. "I mean—I did. But..."

"But?" he prompted, voice measured.

She exhaled sharply, her breath fogging in the air. "But you're ruining everything."

"Um... thanks?"

She laughed. It was a combination of frustration and fondness. "You're patient. And good. And effortlessly attractive. Do you know how annoying that is?"

"I'm sensing a compliment buried somewhere in there."

Cassidy groaned. "You are the worst. And also the best. And I'm trying to keep my head on straight, and you keep doing that thing with your thumb, and it's all very unfair."

His smile curved. "I could stop."

She looked at him flatly. "You could. But will you?"

His hand stilled. "Cass, I meant it. I don't know how that French guy was with you in the past, but whatever you want, I'll do. You want to stop, we stop. No guilt. No pressure. You say the word."

"But you want to," she said.

"I do. But not for the reason you think."

She raised a brow.

"I want to take care of you," Liam said softly. "This is about you finally getting what *you* want."

Cassidy froze, her lips parting slightly. For a long beat she didn't move, just watching him like she wasn't sure what to do with the words. "No one's ever said that to me before."

"Then it's about damn time."

She stared back at him, eyes wide and uncertain.

"This is a bad idea," she whispered.

"I'm a walking bad idea," Liam said, tilting his head. "But I'm also house-trained, good with dogs, and I make excellent lasagna."

She bit her lip, eyes sparkling. "And you think you can handle me?"

He leaned in, mouth brushing her ear. "Is that a challenge?"

Cassidy's breath caught, but she didn't look away. "Maybe."

Liam chuckled, low and dangerous. "You know how I feel about them."

"Then yeah," Cassidy said, standing taller, her voice steady. "Consider it a challenge."

TWENTY-FIVE
CASSIDY

Liam kissed her again, softer this time. Slower. His hands framed her face, thumbs brushing her cheeks like she was something precious. When she leaned into him, he deepened the kiss, one hand slipping down to the back of her neck, the other to the curve of her waist.

He pressed her gently against the pine's thick trunk, snow crunching softly beneath their boots. Her hands tangled in his jacket, fingers curling.

The kiss turned hungrier, but still controlled like he was holding himself back, making this about her.

His mouth trailed from her lips to her jaw, to the soft skin beneath her ear. Cassidy shivered, not from the cold.

He dropped to his knees in the pine needles. It wasn't rushed. Didn't feel desperate. He moved like this was worship.

With careful hands, he undid the button of her jeans.

Her vow whispered in the back of her mind, quiet but insistent. *No men. No sex. One year to focus on yourself.* It had been her anchor, her promise to herself that she would learn who she was without someone else defining her.

But as she stood there, with the cold air brushing her skin and Liam's warm hands on her hips, she realized she knew exactly who she was.

And what she wanted.

Liam looked up, his eyes dark, a question in them.

She let her hands slide into his hair, tugging him closer. "I want this," she said, her voice clear and certain, every word ringing like a promise in the hush of the pines.

Cassidy had never done anything like this before. Jean-Paul hadn't exactly been the outdoorsy type, and he certainly never cared about her needs. She'd spent half a year sleeping with him before realizing he didn't even try to give her pleasure.

She tried not to think about that now while Liam tugged down her jeans. She didn't want Jean-Paul in this moment, didn't want to drag his selfish shadow into something that felt so different. So new.

"Is this okay?" he asked.

"This is great," she blurted, the words tumbling out before she could think. It was all she could manage, because *God*, the way his touch felt—she couldn't think straight if she tried. It was more than great. It was amazing. Her toes curled in her boots, and if it felt this good with him teasing her, she could only imagine what else was in store.

Her flippant response made him grin against her skin, and the feel of that grin, warm and teasing, sent a rush of heat straight through her.

God, that grin should be illegal. So should this with how good it feels.

"You know..." he murmured, "I've been thinking about that scarf." He looked up at the material casually draped around her neck.

His hand slipped beneath the waistband of her panties.

"We could use it," he went on, his voice a delicious growl. "Could come in handy."

"Oh yeah?" she managed, her pulse thrumming.

"Mm-hm." He pulled back just enough to look up and meet her eyes, one brow lifting in mock innocence. "For wrapping. Tying. Holding you still."

A shiver ran through her, sharp and electric.

"Would you like that?"

Her eyes fluttered shut, and a soft, helpless sound escaped her lips—more confession than answer, the kind of sound that said yes without saying a word.

"What about this?" He tugged her panties to the side and stroked a finger over her.

She widened her stance without thinking, bracing herself against the tree, opening herself up to him.

He worked her slowly, carefully, like he was learning her reactions as he went. His thumb moved in gentle circles, his fingers slipping inside, patient and steady.

Cassidy gasped, but it wasn't just from the pleasure. It was from how it felt to be touched like this, like she mattered. Like she was worth this kind of attention. She held onto the bark, heart racing, breathing ragged.

He didn't rush. He just watched her, felt her. Responded to every sound and shift and breath.

She was close, closer than she'd ever been. Her body wound tight with tension, but something in her mind held back. That tiny wall she hadn't realized was still there.

She didn't want to compare it to Jean-Paul, not now, but the contrast was impossible to ignore. Of course, he'd touched her there, almost every time before sex, but it had always felt like a checklist: see if she was ready, maybe add lube, then get on with it.

Nothing like this.

A moan escaped her lips before she could stop it. Liam was

using both hands now, his thumb circling firm pressure over her clit while his fingers slid in and out. One finger was replaced by two, and heaven help her, she still wanted more.

Liam must've known. He could feel it just like she could. She was so turned on that she needed only a little more, the edge of release already tightening in her belly.

"Here," he said, gently helping her slip one leg out of her jeans. He lay back on the pine-needled ground and pulled her down until she straddled him.

She looked at him, confused, until he shifted beneath her, guiding her knees to either side of his face.

"Is this alright?" he asked, voice low. "If not, we can do it another way."

Yeah, she was definitely breaking the vow now. But she had never felt more alive, more herself. And wasn't that the point? Wasn't that what the vow was really about, finding who she was again?

"This is perfect," she breathed out.

His hands gripped her hips and drew her down to meet his mouth. The first stroke of his tongue made her gasp. It was slow and deep, like he had all the time in the world. His beard tickled against her sensitive skin, sending delicious shivers through her.

She let her head fall back, fingers gripping his at her waist as her hips moved in a slow, tentative rhythm. Liam responded with a low groan, tightening his grip, matching her movement with a hunger that made her dizzy.

She wanted to let go. God, she wanted to. But the closer she got, the tighter that wall pulled around her. Over and over again, she couldn't break through.

She whimpered, frustrated, but Liam just murmured a quiet, "That's okay."

Like he knew.

Like he felt what was happening inside her and didn't take it personally. Didn't blame her.

Cassidy leaned forward, pressing her palms to the tree behind him, breathing hard.

"I'm sorry," she whispered.

Liam slid his hands gently over her thighs, soothing and slow. "Hey," he said softly. "Don't be."

She looked down at him, eyes blinking against the sting of tears. She felt like an idiot. This man was doing everything right, and she still couldn't climax. And yet his expression held nothing but tenderness; there was no pressure, no demands.

She carefully stepped back, her movements a little unsteady as she stood and pulled up her jeans. He rose with her, brushing pine needles from his flannel.

"I didn't... it just..." She hesitated, glancing away. "It's not you. It's never happened. Not with anyone."

He reached out, cupping her cheek with one warm hand. "Cass." He waited until she looked at him. "That was incredible. Hearing you. Feeling you. I wouldn't trade it for anything."

Cassidy's chest tightened.

"I had an amazing time. Because it was you. Because you let me in."

She didn't say anything for a second. Just stood there, blinking at him.

Then finally, she nodded. A small, tentative smile pulled at the corner of her lips.

Liam leaned in, voice low and warm against her skin. "And don't worry," he murmured. "We'll get you there next time. That's another promise."

TWENTY-SIX

LIAM

One taste of her would never be enough.

That thought had hit Liam the moment his mouth touched her. She had gasped and squirmed, hesitant and unsure. He'd wanted to go slowly and gently, show her she could let go, that she was safe with him.

Cassidy was shy and more reserved than he'd expected, which only made him want her more. She looked at him like she wanted to trust him, like she wanted to believe this could be different.

When she'd confessed that she'd never climaxed with anyone, it had sucked the air from his lungs. He suddenly wanted that for her more than anything. He wanted to be the one to show her how it could be. Not just good, but transcendent.

Three years. She was with Jean-Paul for three years, and he never made her orgasm? Did the man even try?

She deserved to know what that kind of release with a partner felt like.

She deserved someone who cared whether she got there.

He didn't care how long it took. He had time. He had patience. And he was more than willing to earn every soft sound, every trembling sigh, every ounce of trust she offered him.

When they stepped out of the pine tree forest, fresh snow was falling, blowing effortlessly through the cloudless blue sky. She was bundled back into her coat, fingers laced in his, and he still wasn't ready for the morning to end.

"You hungry?" he asked, brushing his thumb gently over her gloved knuckles.

"I'm starving," she said, smiling up at him.

Real-life Liam was a lot like fantasy Liam, and he wanted to take her home. Liam could do a lot of things—he could woodwork like a master, grow the biggest pumpkin you've ever seen, and make a baby stop crying in five seconds flat—but cooking wasn't one of them. His go-to was eggs, toast, and a black coffee. If he wanted to get fancy, he could swing pancakes.

He offered her both options.

"Ooh, pancakes," she said with a grin as they climbed into his truck. "But only if there's maple syrup. And bacon. Or sausage. Or both."

Back in town, they stopped by the grocery store. They grabbed a carton of eggs, a box of pancake mix, bacon, and a bottle of the good syrup from the local maple farm. She added blueberries and whipped cream, saying they needed something sweet "to balance all that farm-boy protein." He tossed in fresh orange juice and a bag of coffee beans. She added holiday blend tea. It was easy. Domestic. It felt like they'd done it a dozen times before.

"What?" Cassidy asked, catching him looking at her. She glanced down at her outfit, puzzled. "Do I have pine sap on me still?"

He smiled. "No. Just... I was thinking about how unexpected this morning has been."

She grinned. "You could say that again. I was just trying to go ice skating."

"Oh yeah? How'd that work out for you?"

She leaned in, dropping her voice so only he could hear, a playful spark in her gaze. "Best morning ever."

Liam's smile lingered, but inside, he was watching her closely, looking for any flicker of doubt in her eyes. Making sure she didn't regret what they'd shared. Making sure he hadn't pushed her into something she wasn't ready for just because the pull between them was too strong to ignore.

He knew about her vow, and he understood why she'd made it. From everything she'd hinted about her ex, the guy sounded like a real piece of work. Liam could understand needing space, needing to find your own footing before letting someone else in.

He didn't want to be another guy who took more than he gave.

Liam pulled into his driveway. He lived in a small, two-bedroom house on the outskirts of town, not far from his family's farm. The house had had solid bones when he'd bought it three years ago. "Charming, cozy bungalow" had been the real estate description. It had conveniently left out the popcorn ceilings and a family of raccoons living in the attic.

Zoe had helped rehome the raccoons, and Zach had helped with renovating the rest.

Liam tried not to watch Cassidy too closely as she took in the space—worn leather furniture, a woven rug he'd picked up at a market last fall, the empty dog bed still sitting in the corner like it was waiting for Chance to come back.

She didn't say anything about the lack of Christmas decorations.

But he could feel her noticing.

Her gaze lingered just a moment too long on the bare mantel. The undecorated windows. The stretch of wall where a tree might go, if he'd put one up.

He waited for the question. For her to ask why his house looked like December hadn't even arrived.

But she just smiled a little, soft and understanding, and carried the bags into the kitchen like she hadn't seen a thing.

He was sure then that she knew about Avery. Or, at least, she suspected. And she gave him the space anyway, to tell her in his own time. No pressure. No digging.

Liam swallowed hard and busied himself with unpacking the eggs.

"You want me to do pancakes or bacon?" she asked, pulling her hair into a loose bun.

"You do pancakes. I'll tackle the bacon."

She got to work with the confidence of someone who knew her way around a stove, humming quietly as she whisked. He brewed coffee and set the bacon sizzling. It was warm in the kitchen, the windows fogging slightly from the steam, the smell of maple and sugar filling the air.

After the pancakes were done and the bacon perfectly crisp, they sat at his tiny kitchen table, knees brushing, sharing bites and pouring too much syrup.

Midway through breakfast, the conversation shifted.

"So… tell me more about Paris. Do you miss it? Your friends?"

She paused like she'd hit an unexpected wall inside herself.

He poured her a glass of orange juice and handed it over gently. "What's wrong?"

Cassidy took a sip before answering. "It sounds awful, but I don't miss them. Any of them."

She looked up at him, eyes wide like she was only just realizing it.

"All my friends were Jean-Paul's. Before that I had a few close friends—Claudia, Noah—we met in culinary school. But once I started dating Jean-Paul, I kind of drifted away from them. They didn't like him. Said he was controlling. And I just stopped hanging out with them."

Liam's grip tightened on the table.

Her voice cracked, and she looked away. "I didn't even question it. I thought he knew better. That I was the problem."

A slow burn started in his chest.

"I didn't see it then, but now..." She exhaled shakily. "He pulled me away from everything that made me feel like me. He constantly cut me down. Never made me feel seen. Not in bed, not in life."

He clenched his jaw.

"Sounds like a real narcissistic asshole," he said.

What he didn't say was that he wanted to punch Jean-Paul in the face. That he wanted to find him and make him pay for what he'd done. For the pain he'd caused Cassidy. Thank God she'd found her joy back. He couldn't imagine her not being the bright, beautiful Cassidy he knew.

Cassidy gave a sad laugh. "I was with him for three years. Three years of thinking I wasn't enough. That I needed to be smaller. Quieter. Easier to love."

She looked up at him then, vulnerable and brave all at once.

"But I'm starting to remember who I was before him. And I like her."

Liam reached across the table, tucking a strand of hair behind her ear. "I like her too."

She held his gaze for a moment, then smiled.

They didn't say anything else. Not right then.

It was quiet. Warm. The kind of morning he hadn't known he was missing until it was here.

He wanted to slow it down, for her sake. He didn't want to push her. He wondered if she'd realized she'd been in an abusive relationship. He didn't need to know any more than she'd already said to call it like it was.

Part of him didn't want to know more, afraid of what he might want to do to the man.

But he would still listen, if that's what Cassidy needed.

TWENTY-SEVEN

CASSIDY

Wednesday, December 10th

Cassidy was doing everything in her power to focus on her holiday display and not relive every moment with Liam earlier that morning. Her cheeks flushed at the memory. Dear God, she didn't know pine trees could be so erotic. And then afterwards? He'd offered breakfast, coffee, and a chance to really talk. It had all been perfect. No wonder she'd said to hell with her vow.

She wiped her hands on her holiday apron, the one with dancing reindeer, before refilling the toppings station—marshmallows dusted with powdered sugar, chocolate curls, peppermint sticks, and spiced candied orange peel that glistened in the warm light. She glanced around to make sure the café tables in the window nook, with their tiny vases of holly and pine, were wiped down.

Customers came and went, some stopping to sip cocoa while chatting, others picking up boxes of chocolates wrapped in festive ribbon. She moved through it all, greeting regulars with a warm smile, recommending her grand-maman's Parisian spiced cocoa to newcomers, taking payments, and dashing back to the kitchen to check on another batch of chocolate-dipped candied oranges cooling on parchment.

It was busy. *She* was busy. And that was exactly how it needed to be.

And yet, despite the flurry of spiced cocoa orders, chocolate buying for Christmas gifts, and light-up display prep, she still caught sight of Liam outside his shop across the street, hauling crates or fixing a wreath, or pausing to wave through her window with a crooked smile that made her heart flutter.

She rolled her eyes, suddenly annoyed with herself. She wasn't some easily distracted woman who fell in love with the first man that made love to her in a forest.

No, she had a competition to focus on.

Cassidy looked down at her cocoa tags and Advent reveal boxes. They just weren't going to be enough.

She racked her brain, trying to come up with something else, something that screamed Christmas but was still unique.

Outside, she heard the whistle of the holiday train, and an idea struck her. What if she had a hot cocoa train? Not a full-size one like the train outside, but a model train. She could picture it now: little cars carrying hot cocoa toppings like choco-late chips, crushed peppermint, cinnamon sticks, flavored marshmallows, and meringues. She'd pour the cocoa, and customers could top it with whatever their hearts desired. She could build an elevated village out of marshmallows and gumdrops, a pine forest, too.

She felt herself blush. She would never look at white pines the same way again.

"No more fantasizing," she told herself. She didn't want to end up on Santa's naughty list. Liam's, maybe…

Cassidy was just about to grab her phone to see how quickly she could get a model train delivered when the shop door chimed.

Mrs. Bishop and Mrs. C. stepped inside, and Cassidy did a

double-take when she saw what they were wearing—bright red sweaters embroidered with the words "Team Cassidy" across the front.

"What is this?" she asked, motioning to their sweaters.

"This?" Mrs. C. did a proud spin in the middle of the shop. "Just a little something us crafting club ladies cooked up. Competition sweaters! What do you think?"

Cassidy came around the counter. "You made these for all the businesses?"

Mrs. Bishop hesitated. "Not exactly all the businesses..."

"Just you and Liam," Mrs. C. chimed in matter-of-factly. "Because let's be honest, the competition's really between the two of you. Everybody loves a romance story."

"What?" Cassidy's eyes went wide.

"Come now, we all know you two have a thing for each other," Mrs. C. added breezily.

"We saw you skating on the lake this morning," Mrs. Bishop said with a knowing smile.

Cassidy cleared her throat and silently prayed that was all they had seen.

"Oh, don't be too flustered, dear," Mrs. Bishop said, patting her arm with a wink. "It's all in good fun. We haven't seen this town so excited about the competition in years."

"Honestly, people are placing bets on who's going to win," Mrs. C. said, chuckling. "Gary over at the hardware store's running a bracket, and Kit tells me the Maple Leaf Café has a Team Liam and Team Cassidy tip jar situation going on."

Cassidy covered her face with her hands. "Oh my gosh."

Mrs. Bishop laughed. "It's all in the spirit of Christmas. And all the proceeds from the sweater sales will go to the winning charity," she added more gently. "Just a nice way to add a little more excitement to the competition."

"That's actually a great idea," Cassidy said, her tone softening. "My charity means a lot to me. It's the children's hospital in

Mount Holly. When I was little, I spent a Christmas there, and some kind stranger donated a bunch of toys to all of us kids. I've never forgotten it. I always thought it would be amazing to return the favor—to spread some holiday joy to kids who are having a really hard Christmas."

"And that's exactly why we're wearing Team Cassidy sweaters," Mrs. C. said with a smile.

"Now, about that spiced cocoa," Mrs. Bishop said, leaning on the counter. "Think we could get a cup?"

"How about it's on the house if you tell me where I can get one of those sweaters," Cassidy replied.

"The crafting club's set up a stand right in front of the town Christmas tree," Mrs. Bishop replied. "You can't miss it. There's already a line."

"Perfect," Cassidy said, her grin growing as her competitive spirit kicked into gear. "What do you think about me adding a hot cocoa train to my window display?" Cassidy asked, valuing the women's advice.

"Well, that would be different," Mrs. C. said thoughtfully.

"Different good or different bad?" Cassidy asked for clari-fication.

"Different good. Most definitely," Mrs. Bishop answered for the both of them.

Cassidy handed over their spiced cocoa, watching as Mrs. C. took a sip and smiled in approval. They weren't just customers. They were part of something bigger now, a web of people who looked out for one another. And she was one of them.

Cassidy paused, her hand resting on the warm wood counter, the scent of vanilla bean and toasted hazelnut wrap-ping around her as laughter drifted in from the sidewalk outside. She didn't know when it had happened, but for the first time in a long time, she felt steady. Like she could finally exhale.

TWENTY-EIGHT
LIAM

Liam was sorting through a bin of oversized white bulbs, prepping for his Christmas light-up display. He was thinking of all the ways he could take the farm shop's holiday setup out front to the next level. He'd already set aside a handful of six-foot blue spruces from the farm. He'd haul them in at the weekend, decorate each one top to bottom in a rustic theme. No plastic. No cheap imports. Just wood, cotton, soft flannels, and handmade ornaments from local artisans. His light-up might not be for two weeks, but he'd need all the extra time to pull out all the stops.

He wanted to make the shop feel like home, like his family's farm. Like a place built on heart and hard work.

The air inside already smelled like an evergreen forest, thanks to the candle burning behind the counter with notes of pine, peppermint, and vanilla curling through the room.

It reminded him of Cassidy.

Of the woods.

Of that morning, spent tucked away beneath the snow-dusted pines.

So much for taking it slow, he thought, raking a hand through his hair.

He hadn't taken things all the way. Not the way his body had wanted to.

But he'd made it good for her. That's what mattered.

Through the front window, he could see his reflection—flannel sleeves rolled to his elbows, hair mussed from hauling crates, a smudge of sap on his wrist as he adjusted the wire display stand for the ornaments. Beyond that reflection, across the street, he could see the Cocoa Corner, its windows glowing softly with twinkle lights and frosted garlands, the chalkboard sign for the pop-up advertising "The Spiced Cocoa Café."

His eyes kept drifting there, catching glimpses of Cassidy moving behind the counter, her wavy blonde hair falling forward as she took a tray of steaming cocoa to a young couple. She laughed at something they said, head tipping back, eyes bright.

"Knock, knock." Zach's voice cut through the soft hum of the farm shop's old heater, the bell above the door jingling.

Liam cleared his throat, hoping it would take his thoughts of Cassidy with it.

"Do you think two thousand bulbs are enough?" Liam asked, but he stopped short when he looked up and saw Zach wearing an emerald-green sweater with the words "Team Liam" knit across the front.

"Don't worry, buddy—I got you one too." Zach tossed a sweater at him. Liam caught it with one hand and dropped it into the box with the rest of the bulbs.

"Man, what in the world? Please tell me there aren't more of these."

"More? There's a whole line of people in front of the town Christmas tree, lined up to buy theirs."

"You've gotta be kidding me."

"Don't worry. There are Team Cassidy ones too. It's a limited-edition collectible. Future generations will talk about the time Liam Hawthorne wore a sparkly sweater and smiled in public at Christmas."

"Keep talking and I'll make you climb the ladder and hang all two thousand bulbs by yourself."

Liam was about to say it was completely over the top and that there was no way in holly-jolly heck he was wearing one of those sweaters...

Then he glanced out the window and spotted her strutting back to her shop in her bright red Team Cassidy sweater, like she'd already won the whole competition. Her face was glowing, her smile smug and sparkling.

She looked entirely too pleased with herself.

And yeah, she looked gorgeous too, but Liam mostly saw a challenge.

Game on, Sugarplum.

He tugged the sweater on over his head.

The sweater was soft, absurdly festive, and smelled faintly of Mrs. Bishop's lilac perfume. He looked ridiculous—and, surprisingly, didn't mind.

"Alright," he said. "Now, where were we?"

"You were asking me about some bulbs," Zach reminded him.

"Right. You're right. Two thousand isn't enough. Better make it five thousand."

"I don't know... are you sure you don't wanna make it ten thousand?" Zach motioned across the street. "Do you see how much work your girl over there is putting in?"

Liam was about to object and say that Cassidy wasn't his girl—until he realized Zach had said it more as a friendly term than a relationship status update.

Zach was still looking outside. Liam followed his gaze. Across the street, Cassidy stood in front of her shop with a measuring tape. She dragged one of the chairs over to the window and stood on it so she could reach the top of the window. They watched her measure the window vertically, then horizontally, then diagonally.

"What do you suppose she's doing?" Zach asked, arms folded as he leaned against the front counter.

Liam mirrored him on the opposite side. "No idea. But she's got to be freezing. She's been in and out of there all morning."

"Maybe she's working on reinforcements."

"Reinforcements? That seems a bit dramatic, don't you think?"

"Not if you don't want your decorations destroyed or stolen. That Gingerbread Jerk still hasn't been caught. Didn't you see what happened to the nutcrackers at the Kettle?"

"No. What happened?"

"They cracked more than nuts," Zach said. "Both of them toppled. Busted right up. And you know those suckers weighed a ton. I think they ended up tossing them."

"Are you kidding me?" Liam asked, standing straighter. He'd been hoping the Gingerbread Jerk wasn't here to stay. Things like that didn't happen in Maple Falls no matter how intense the holiday competition got.

Maybe Cassidy was trying to make her light-up plans thief-proof.

He was just relieved she hadn't marched down to the hardware store to interrogate poor Mr. Alders. He could picture it now, Cassidy, all fired up, pointing a finger in Mr. Alders' face with one hand and holding a candy cane in the other. It definitely wouldn't end well, and it wouldn't help her new business either. If Liam knew one thing about living in Maple Falls, it was that you wanted the older folk on your side.

Liam continued to watch her. She measured once more, putting notes in her phone.

She's going to burn herself out at this rate, he thought. More concerned for her than anything. *Or maybe she'll win—and leave you wondering how you ever thought you stood a chance.*

TWENTY-NINE

CASSIDY

Wednesday, December 10th

Cassidy was feeling pretty accomplished. She'd managed to overnight a holiday train set—complete with a train table—that was scheduled to arrive tomorrow. She planned to spend the evening working on a tiny marshmallow village to accompany it.

She'd also decided to paint the front shop window with snowflakes and rolling hills. Everything would be done in white, with touches of glitter to catch the light. It was going to be beautiful. Liam's rustic charm and farm-boy swagger didn't stand a chance.

She was outside in between waiting on customers, measuring the length of the front window for the third time to make sure she had enough paint, when Liam strolled up.

"Oh, it's getting serious if you've got the measuring tape out," he teased.

Cassidy looked up and smiled, her eyes immediately landing on the bright green sweater stretched across his chest.

"I wasn't sure if you were going to wear it."

"What, this old thing?" he asked, mock-casual, tugging at the hem. "Figured I should rep the winning team."

Cassidy raised a brow, one hand still on the measuring tape. "That's funny. I thought Team Cassidy sold out twice as fast."

"Nah, that's just what they want you to think. You wait and see, come tomorrow, there will be a sea of green for as far as the eye can see."

Cassidy laughed.

"What are you up to?" Liam motioned to the window. "Zach thought you might be adding reinforcements."

"Reinforcements? What would I need those for?"

Liam rocked back on his heels. "Ah, so you don't know. I figured..."

"Wait, what? What's going on?"

"Apparently, someone knocked over the nutcrackers in front of the Kettle."

"I wondered what happened to those. It was the Gingerbread Jerk, wasn't it? Wait, when did this happen? And does Mr. Alders have an alibi?"

He grinned. "I knew you'd jump right to him. First of all, Mr. Alders has a bad hip and scoliosis. I doubt he's going to tip over hundred-pound nutcrackers and risk throwing his back out."

"He could've paid some high schoolers to do it!" she suggested.

"Doubtful. He's really a nice guy. I think you just caught him on a bad day."

"I still think somebody should interview him—"

Before she could insist any further, a familiar voice interrupted.

"Oh, there they are—our favorite hometown rivals!" Mayor Bloomfield said, approaching them with his assistant in tow. Today, he looked rather reserved in black slacks and a sport coat

—until he slid his hands into his pockets, revealing a silver-blue satin vest embroidered with snowflakes.

"What can we do for you, Mayor?" Liam asked.

"Just wondering if we could borrow the two of you for a moment," Mayor Bloomfield said. "Elsie can tell you more about it." He motioned to her standing beside him with a smartphone in one hand and a clipboard in the other. "She wants to put something on Instant-something, or... what was that again? Tickity Tockity? I don't know. Social media, she tells me. I wouldn't even bother with it if Elsie didn't insist on how important it was."

Elsie stepped forward, clearly exasperated with the mayor but trying to hide it. "It's for the town's holiday social media post. We're calling it 'The Great Maple Falls Holiday Rivalry.' Thought we'd capture a little photo-op magic."

"Oooh, I like it." Cassidy smiled.

"We thought it would be great to help boost holiday tourism, showcase a bit of everything—the competition, the tree lighting, the lantern garden walks, the Midnight Silent Night coming up. And when I saw the Team Cassidy versus Team Liam sweaters, it was too good to pass up. Do you guys mind doing a quick photo?"

She hesitated a beat, then added lightly, "It's not how I'd do things, but if this is how Maple Falls really wants to celebrate the holiday, I'd like to give it at least a decent press kit."

Cassidy exchanged a curious glance with Liam, but before either could ask, Elsie was already lifting her phone and shifting them into position.

"I think it's a great idea," Cassidy replied honestly.

Liam shrugged, his gaze steady. "What do you need us to do?"

Elsie had them stand back to back, arms folded, facing the camera, their Team Cassidy and Team Liam sweaters bright under the shop lights. They tried to mean-mug for the camera, but Cassidy kept cracking up, especially when Liam's arm brushed against hers, or when she caught his reflection in the window, winking at her.

But this wasn't just for show. Cassidy *wanted* to beat him. She needed to. She was fighting to prove herself, to build something lasting, to show she could do this on her own.

And Liam? She knew he wasn't backing down, either. She could practically feel the energy radiating off him, that quiet determination that made him so annoyingly attractive.

"Come on, Cass," he murmured out of the side of his mouth. "Don't tell me this is too much for you."

She narrowed her eyes, leaning back against him, refusing to give an inch. "You wish, Hawthorne."

Cassidy dug deep and put on the most determined look she could muster. Or that any woman could muster with felt reindeer antlers on and temporary glitter star tattoos.

"Perfect. That's the one." Elsie beamed. "I'll make sure to tag both of your shops when I post it."

"Thank you—that's perfect," Cassidy said, clapping her hands. This was exactly the kind of publicity she needed.

She turned and stuck out her hand, her grip firm. "May the best business win, Grinch," she said with a confident smile.

"Don't worry, Sugarplum," Liam replied, his thumb brushing over her wrist before he let go, a playful smirk curving his lips. "It will."

The touch lingered like a spark. Cassidy's pulse skipped, her breath catching slightly as heat curled low in her belly.

She straightened her antlers, doing her best to look composed.

But deep down, she wished they were alone, with nothing but the sweet heat of their bodies between them.

THIRTY

LIAM

On Thursday night, Liam met Zach and Tyler at the Kettle for a round of darts and a couple of beers. Jackson didn't want to come of course. He thought about inviting Cassidy, but Tyler was single and Zach hadn't said anything about bringing Madison. It felt like a guys-only night.

That might be the case now, but earlier, his phone was blowing up with the group chat.

Madison: Okay, okay I need to know... how did I miss the Team Cassidy vs. Team Liam sweaters? 😅

Kit: You were literally in the room when the crafting club talked about it!

Madison: Yeah but I thought they were joking?? Now they've already been made somehow and it's all over Elsie's social feed!! I just saw two middle schoolers arguing over which team to join. 😂

Cassidy: It's so cute, OMG.

Emily: I give up! Anyway, I won last year. 😂

Zach: I'm Team Whoever Brings Me Food. I can be bought.

Zoe: All jokes aside, I don't care if I win. I've got a whole fundraiser planned for my eco project with the greenhouse kids and Mrs. C.'s Sunday Club. We're good. 🩶

Emily: Same. Honestly, the more the town hypes this rivalry, the more people turn out. That means more sales for everyone. Win-win.

Madison: I love this town so much. Also I want both sweaters.

Liam hearted the last message and shoved his phone back into his pocket. The Kettle was packed, as usual. The tavern had gone all-in for Christmas. Silver tinsel was draped along the walls and around every beam, catching the glow of red and green twinkle lights strung from the ceiling. The mirror-backed bar reflected the lights, making the uneven cobblestone floor seem brighter than usual. Framed pictures on the walls—snapshots of locals, vintage beer ads, and old concert posters—had been wrapped in festive holiday paper and rehung like presents on the walls.

The scent of wood-fired pizza and fried everything filled the air. They'd demolished a plate of chicken wings, devoured a deep-dish pizza, and played more than a few rounds of darts. Thankfully, Cassidy's name hadn't come up once yet. If Liam glanced at the door more than once or twice, hoping she might walk in, Zach didn't say anything. Liam remembered a time not long ago when Zach had done the same thing. Liam had left his friend alone then—and Zach was returning the favor.

. . .

It wasn't until an hour or so later, on his way home, down the streetlight-lit street with the snow crunching under his boots, that he spotted her.

She was still outside, working on the Cocoa Corner's window display. From a block away, he could see her shivering despite her red puffer coat and a white beanie hat dusted in glitter.

Liam picked up his pace.

"Not again," she muttered to herself.

"You're not locked out again, are you?" Liam tried to joke.

Cassidy startled, jerking at the sound of his voice. The cup in her hand flung upward, splattering him right in the face. A white, chalky substance splashed into his beard and dripped down his coat.

"Oh my God, you scared me!" Cassidy cried, reaching out with the end of her scarf to dab at his face.

Liam cautiously tasted the corner of his lip. "That's not chocolate."

"No, it's paint. I was trying to touch up the window, but everything keeps freezing." She sneezed and sniffled again.

That's when he really looked at her. She had dark circles under her eyes, her hands were red from the cold, and she couldn't stop coughing. She was clearly getting sick.

He caught her hands gently, stopping her attempts to clean him up. "Have you been out here all day?"

"Pretty much, whenever I had a customer break," she admitted. "There's just so much work left and not enough time. I don't know how you're managing it all."

"Leave the window. Come inside," he said firmly.

"But if I don't finish—"

"You'll finish it tomorrow," Liam cut in.

There was no room for argument.

"You're doing too much," he said. It wasn't a question.

Cassidy gave a weak smile.

He guided her firmly through her shop, toward the back, and up the staircase.

Muff greeted them with a bark and a tail wag when she opened the door.

"Hey, girl, you need to go out?" he asked the pup.

"You don't have to. I can go back down—" Cassidy started to say.

"It's alright. Just let me wash this paint off my face, and I'll take care of her," he insisted.

"The bathroom is the first door on your right," she said, clearly not having the energy to argue, for once.

Cassidy's apartment was a small, one-bedroom, one-bath flat. A galley kitchen and living room took up the main living space, with a bathroom and bedroom down a short hall.

Liam made quick work of washing up. Cassidy's bathroom was like the rest of her apartment. It wasn't designer chic; it was more homestead Christmas.

Her bathroom had little green Christmas tree soaps in a white porcelain soap dish, hand-painted with festive green holly. He didn't want to use her good soap or dry his face on her good holiday towels, but that was all she had.

Out in the living room, she had a four-foot pink tinsel tree in the corner. Liam knew that if she'd had the room, the tree would have been ten feet tall. As it was, the tree was filled with mismatched, homemade ornaments. He didn't linger; he only had a moment while Cassidy fetched Muff's leash, but in that brief minute, he saw crocheted cocoa mugs, a painted gingerbread man, and cinnamon dough stars.

The couch was draped in a bright blue knit blanket with palm-sized white snowflakes added to the squares and white faux fur throw pillows. A felt Advent calendar hung on the wall. It was the kind with a wooden Christmas tree that you moved daily from pocket to pocket.

Cassidy's voice croaked as she reappeared, leash in hand, a box of tissues tucked under her arm. "I might've gone a little overboard with the decorations this year. It was the first time I'd been able to unbox them for a few years," she apologized before punctuating the sentence with a sneeze so sharp it startled Muff, who gave a tiny bark in response.

He wanted to say something about how unfair that was, how she should've been able to decorate her Parisian apartment however she wanted, but he didn't because Muff was jumping up and down, prancing around the living room like she needed to go out, *now*!

So, he clipped on the pup's leash and promised Cassidy they'd be back in a few minutes.

Liam dialed Zach's mom, Anita, who lived nearby, on his way down the stairs.

"Liam, what's up?" she asked when their lines connected.

"Cassidy's sick. I was hoping you still had some of that chicken noodle soup of yours?"

"I have plenty. Some fresh bread too. I'll meet you at the front door in fifteen minutes."

Oak Way was quiet, the kind of quiet that only came after closing time, when the shops had gone still but their windows still glowed with twinkle lights set to timers. Even from down the road, Liam could see the Cinnamon Spice Inn. The lights must've been set to stay on until at least midnight. Madison had strung lights on every tree and bush, and along the roofline, making the inn appear warm and inviting even in the freezing cold.

Liam hadn't noticed that before. But he noticed it now.

Just like how he noticed the fresh snow that covered the sidewalk, clean except for a trail of Muff's pawprints as she walked around, nose to the ground, taking her time.

He gave Muff a few minutes, watching tiny flecks of snow drift through the air, catching in the light like silver glitter. The gaslit fireplace on the street corner was still going, firelight flickering behind the screen, even if no one sat in the Adirondack chairs tonight. The street was silent. Not another soul in sight. It was peaceful in a way that only Maple Falls could be. Liam thought Cassidy would've called the moment magical. He didn't disagree.

Anita opened the café door right on time and handed over a brown paper bag. "There's enough for two," she said, her eyes meeting his. "Take care of her."

He nodded. "Don't worry. I will."

Anita didn't let go of the bag right away. Her hand lingered for a second, her gaze soft but steady. "You're a good boy."

Liam grinned, not allowing the moment to get too heavy. "Keep it down, will you? I don't want my reputation ruined." He thought for a beat before adding, "And don't tell my mother."

Anita smiled, letting go of the bag. "Your secret's safe with me."

He knew that to be true. Zach's mom heard plenty of small-town gossip at her café, but she tended to listen to it rather than spread it. He appreciated that about her.

"Thanks, you're the best." Liam gave a tip of his imaginary hat and headed back down Oak Way, making one more quick stop along the way.

Back at Cassidy's, he knocked and opened the door, announcing himself as he did. "It's just us," he said, unclipping Muff and following her through the kitchen into the living room. Muff wasted no time climbing up on the couch and tucking in next to Cassidy, who was curled up in the corner, shivering under the knit snowflake blanket.

"I got you some soup," Liam added, taking the bag to the

kitchen and getting down a bowl. He'd save the rest for her for later.

"You didn't have to do that," she said. "I could've made some ramen or something."

"I doubt you want to do much of anything," Liam replied. She was looking worse by the minute.

"I think I'm getting a fever," she admitted.

"I picked up some cold medicine too—pick your poison," he said, taking out some nighttime cold medicine along with Tylenol and some flu and cold capsules. "Wasn't sure what your go-to was, but I generally like to knock myself out when I'm dealing with the crud."

"You didn't have to do all this," Cassidy said softly when he returned with the warmed-up soup, and set up cold medicine, a fresh bottle of water, and a mug of tea beside her.

"I know. I wanted to," he said.

Cassidy shivered.

"You need a pillow. Do you mind?" He motioned back down the hall to her bedroom.

"No, a pillow would be great," she replied, eyes closed.

He moved quietly down the hall, his boots softened by the rug. Her bedroom door was slightly ajar.

This was the first time he'd let himself step inside. Before, the idea of being alone in her space, the place where she slept, dreamed, and rested, had felt too intimate. Too tempting. But she needed him. He was here for her, not himself, and somehow knowing that made it even harder to breathe.

The room was small but warm, with a red-and-white holiday quilt tucked over the bed. A few Christmas throw pillows were arranged neatly, and soft white twinkle lights were draped around the window frame. It smelled of vanilla and peppermint.

Liam stopped when he spotted the full-length mirror in the

corner. He couldn't stop the flash of images, of the things he wanted to do with Cassidy in front of that mirror.

Swallowing his desire down, he grabbed the pillow from the bed and turned to go, but not before letting himself glance around once more.

Someday soon...

THIRTY-ONE

CASSIDY

Friday, December 12th

The next morning, Cassidy still felt like trash.

She'd slept on the couch all night, only getting up once to take Muff out. Her poor pup must've sensed she wasn't feeling well; she hadn't left her side once.

She hated how awful she felt. Tonight was Zoe's light-up night, and Cassidy was most likely going to miss it.

She knew Zoe had special-ordered dozens of roses, deep-red carnations, frosted white mums, and all kinds of winter greenery. Whatever Zoe had planned for the Cherry Crush, she'd kept it tightly under wraps, but it was going to be stunning. Zoe had a gift for turning flowers into magic. And even though they were competitors, she wanted nothing more than to be out there supporting her friend with the rest of the town.

But instead, she was stuck here.

She glanced down at the thermometer in her hand: 103.2.

Yep. Still a walking furnace.

Even if she could summon enough energy to bundle up and

shuffle down the street, she'd just end up coughing on everyone. And no one wanted a mystery virus for Christmas.

The best thing she could do, the only responsible thing, was stay home, drink lemon and ginger tea, and keep her germs to herself.

Still, her heart ached knowing she wouldn't be there for her friend.

She was feeling pretty low, thinking about how much she wanted to see Zoe's display, when her phone chimed from the end table.

It was a text from Liam:

Hey, Sugarplum. How you feeling?

She shook her head at the nickname. She knew he'd started using it to tease her, but somehow it had become... endearing.

Cassidy stared at the screen. She didn't want to lie and say she was fine, but she also didn't want him to think he had to rush over and take care of her again. He had his own shop to run, his own Christmas display to finish. Still, she knew he'd want to know the truth.

Still a bit rough, Grinch, but your soup and company worked wonders. I owe you one.

She read it over twice, making sure it was honest but warm, letting him know how much she appreciated *him*, not just the soup.

A few moments later, Liam replied:

You don't owe me a thing. Just get better. And if you need anything just say the word.

She smiled at the message, then curled back up on the couch. Her favorite holiday rom-com was on, the one she'd seen a thousand times. The soft music and familiar dialogue lulled her back to sleep in no time.

By the time she woke up, the sun had shifted. It was well into the afternoon, and Muff was pawing gently at her leg.

"Alright, girl, I hear you," Cassidy murmured.

Still in her pajamas, she threw on her heavy-duty puffer coat, slipped on some boots, and grabbed Muff's leash. She'd planned on using the back exit, but as she passed the front window, she paused.

Liam was out there with a drill in one hand and a couple of two-by-fours in the other.

"What in the world...?" she muttered.

Muff barked softly and wagged her tail, already heading for the door. Cassidy followed, stepping outside into the crisp air.

"Liam?" she called, her voice hoarse. "What are you doing? Everything okay?"

He looked up, startled to see her. "Hey. Yeah. I'm just finishing something."

She stepped closer and realized what he was working on: her display backdrop. The one she'd been too tired to finish last night. He'd added brackets to reinforce the base and threaded a length of chain through a cinder block to weigh it down.

"I didn't want all your hard work to go to waste," he said, tightening a bolt.

"You did all this... for me?"

"And for poor Mr. Alders. Hate to see what you'd do to the man if your display toppled over."

She let out a weak laugh. "Ha, ha. Very funny."

But the chuckle turned into a coughing fit that left her

doubled over and wheezing. Her chest ached, and even just standing upright made her feel like she'd run a marathon.

"Thanks again," she managed between breaths. "I think I'd better head back in and lie down."

He straightened and gave her a once-over, eyes full of concern. "Call me if you need anything. Seriously."

"I will," she promised. "Oh, and can you tell your mom I won't be able to make the cookie decorating?" She doubted she'd feel better in the next day.

"Don't worry, I'll let her know."

"Thanks." She gave him a small, grateful smile before heading back inside with Muff at her heels.

She downed some cough medicine and crawled onto the couch, where she promptly fell asleep.

When she woke, night had already fallen. The living room was dim, the TV screen frozen on a Netflix prompt asking if she was still watching.

Muff lifted her head hopefully from the end of the couch, tail thumping once.

Cassidy sat up and leaned forward to scratch behind her pup's ears. "You're a very good nurse," she said with a tired smile.

But the truth was, she still felt awful. Her head throbbed, her body ached, and her fever hadn't budged. This was clearly one of those colds that needed time to run its course.

She checked her phone and saw that her brother had called her as well as Mrs. Bishop. She didn't even know how the older woman had her number. She played the voicemail and listened to Mrs. Bishop promise to drop off her homemade cold remedy.

Cassidy decided to call back her brother later. No sense in getting Julian and Miles worried about her once they heard how sick she was, and if she texted them, it would only lead to questions.

She texted Zoe instead, wishing her good luck for the night.

Sorry I'm sick. I'm sure it'll be beautiful. Good luck!

Zoe replied almost instantly with a heart emoji and a *Feel better soon.*

Cassidy wrapped herself in a blanket and shuffled toward the front window. The Cherry Crush flower shop was just down the block, and a small crowd had already started to gather out front. She pressed her forehead gently to the cold glass, trying to see, but the angle wasn't great. And the condensation on the windowpane blurred everything.

Still, it was something. At least she could support her friend in spirit.

Her phone buzzed in her hand again.

Liam.

She answered, her voice rasping. "Hello?" She hadn't realized how scratchy and rough her throat was until she went to talk.

"I see you're feeling better," he replied sarcastically.

"I feel like I've been run over by Santa's sleigh."

"I bet. I'm sorry. Zoe's light-up is about to start. Want me to FaceTime you from the street so you don't miss it?"

She fumbled for her words. He knew her so well. "Would you? Really?"

"Already walking down there. Hold tight."

Her FaceTime notification began to ring a few moments later.

Cassidy walked back to the couch and propped the phone up against a nearby mug.

And there he was. Liam's face filled the screen, his breath clouding the camera in puffs as he turned it toward the crowd.

"Evening," he said with a wink. "Reporting live from the second official Maple Falls light-up extravaganza."

She chuckled, coughing slightly. "You're ridiculous."

"And yet you're smiling," he said. "And I like those glasses."

Cassidy had forgotten she was wearing her red frames. She'd been too sick to bother with her usual contacts.

"They look great on you." He'd dropped the comment nonchalantly, but it meant everything to her. Jean-Paul's disparaging remarks floated in her head, but she quickly shut them down.

"Okay, hang on. I'll flip the camera so you can see the magic," Liam said, getting right to it.

The view shifted, showing Zoe's shop, where her display had just been revealed.

"Merry Christmas" was spelled out in giant block letters— each one overflowing with blooms. Red roses, white carnations, green mums, and sprigs of holly packed every letter, the colors rich and festive, like something out of a holiday card. Twinkling lights outlined each letter, making the flowers glow against the snowy backdrop.

Cassidy leaned closer to the screen, smiling despite the ache in her head. "She filled the letters with actual flowers?" She gasped. "Zoe outdid herself."

"It's pretty awesome," Liam agreed, angling the camera so she could see the crowd clapping and cheering. "Everyone's loving it."

She leaned her head against the cushion, a smile tugging at her lips despite the fever. "Thank you for this. I didn't realize how much I needed to feel part of it."

"You are part of it," he said quietly. "Even if you're watching from the couch wrapped in a blanket burrito."

Her eyes filled with sudden tears. "I really like you, Liam."

"I know," he said, grinning. "I like you too. Now rest. I'll call you in the morning, yeah?"

She nodded. "Yeah."

He gave the screen a little salute. "Goodnight, Cassidy."

The call ended, but she didn't move. She sat there watching the last flickers of Zoe's lights from her window, Muff's warm body curled against her side, her heart full despite everything.

She may have missed the crowd, but she hadn't missed the moment.

And the truth was, Liam had been her favorite part of it all.

THIRTY-TWO

LIAM

Liam hadn't been sure if he should call Cassidy or not. It was hard not to worry, hard not to imagine her curled up on the couch, pale and sniffling, trying to wave him off with that stubborn little smile of hers. He hadn't wanted to wake her if she was finally getting some rest, but he knew how badly she'd hate to miss Zoe's light-up night.

Even after he hung up the phone, he stayed out front, leaning against the lamppost across from Zoe's flower shop. Kids were running around, laughing and throwing snowballs at each other. Zoe beamed, her cheeks flushed with pride. She was taking photos with the mayor and a couple of excited tourists, clearly in her element.

Jackson stood off to the side, helping Zoe adjust a strand of twinkle lights that had slipped, his hands steady as he looped it back around the post. Liam was surprised to see his brother there, but then again, Jackson and Zoe had always been close.

Liam wasn't sure if it was Zoe's grounded, down-to-earth personality or the way she somehow made every space feel calmer, but Zoe was good for Jackson. She always had been. Even as kids, she was the one who coaxed Jackson out of his shell, convinced him to play pretend kitchen and decorate mud pies with "sprinkles" (which were actually pine needles). Seeing them together now—Zoe laughing at something Jackson murmured as they worked side by side—gave Liam a rare sense of relief. It was like watching his brother come back to life, piece by piece.

Watching them made Liam realize how much he missed not having Cassidy there with him. It hit him harder than he expected. He crossed his arms, more to keep his feelings in than for warmth. He liked having her beside him. She made things brighter. Warmer. He wanted her there, not just tonight, but always.

As the crowd shifted, Liam moved down the street. He waved at Mr. Alders, then Edith, Madison, and a dozen other familiar faces. Everyone seemed to be in good spirits, chatting over cider and stopping to admire the flower display.

Near the town's Christmas tree, a group of elementary schoolers, Emma included, were lining up, all wearing lopsided Santa hats. Liam stopped to watch. Their teacher clapped her hands and called out a quick countdown. On three, the kids launched into a loud, slightly off-key but completely joyful version of "Deck the Halls."

He really needed to head back to the shop. There were orders to pack, displays to straighten, and inventory to go through. But something rooted him here.

He listened to the kids sing, and somewhere in the crowd, Mrs. C. waved him over.

"You look like a man with something on his mind," she said, handing him a warm cup. "Mulled wine. Helps with heartbreak."

"Thanks, Mrs. C. But I'm not heartbroken." He paused, then added, "At least not yet."

The older woman peered up at him knowingly. "You mean Cassidy?"

"Is there anyone else?" Liam took a sip of the mulled wine. It was the first time he'd drunk it in years. It tasted like Christmas in a glass. It was warm, fruity, and just a little bit boozy. Liam had a feeling Mrs. C. had added even more brandy than the recipe called for.

Mrs. C. patted his arm. "She's special, that one," she said. "And I've lived long enough to know that special doesn't come around often. Not for everyone."

Liam stared off, eye catching the icicles that hung on the bookstore across the street, the glow from the holiday lights making them sparkle.

"I'm scared I'm not good enough for her," he admitted. "She deserves everything, and I... I don't know if I know how to give it."

Mrs. C. gave him a sharp look. "You fixed her broken display when she was too sick to stand. You called just to show her the flowers. You show up, Liam. That's how you give it."

He didn't respond right away. The words sat heavy in his chest, like something he needed to absorb one beat at a time.

The crowd applauded as the kids finished their song, their teacher looking relieved no one had fallen off the stage. Zoe was passing out red carnations to each student. They beamed, accepting her gift.

"Thanks, Mrs. C. You have a good night."

"You too, dear."

Liam took one last look and then slowly turned back toward the Cocoa Corner.

He walked in silence, hands in his pockets, boots crunching softly against the salted sidewalk. When he reached his shop, he looked across the street at Cassidy's. The curtain in her window had shifted, and for a second, he imagined her silhouette standing there.

Maybe she really was watching.

He paused, letting himself feel it. That connection that tugged at him even from a distance.

He wanted to be the one to make her laugh when she felt like crying. To bring her soup every time she was sick. To see her eyes light up on Christmas morning. He wanted to be the one she trusted enough to let go with.

The fact that she hadn't yet didn't make him feel like a failure. It made him feel protective. Not of her body, but of her heart.

Jean-Paul had failed her in every single way. Liam wasn't going to be that man. He would wait. Learn her rhythms. Earn her trust. And when the moment came, and it would come, he'd make damn sure she felt seen.

THIRTY-THREE

CASSIDY

Two days later, Cassidy was feeling like herself again. She was only bummed that she'd missed so much—baking cookies with Liam's family and the Jingle Bell 5k. Not that she had planned to run, but she'd wanted to cheer on Madison, who had come away with gold.

But now, there'd be no more missed festivities.

Whatever had been in Mrs. Bishop's cold concoction had worked. It tasted like something between spicy ginger beer and Christmas potpourri, with an afterburn that could probably clear sinuses for a mile. She'd barely managed to get the stuff down, but she had to admit it had done the trick. Her fever had broken that night, and by morning, she'd felt human.

She was still in her flannel pajama bottoms and Christmas tree socks when Zoe stopped by.

"Florals for the flu," Zoe said cheerfully, stepping inside and holding a bouquet of deep-red roses and snow-dusted eucalyptus wrapped in brown paper. "I brought you something to make you feel festive and not dead."

"Oh... that's so sweet. You can put them next to Liam's."

Zoe stopped mid-step. "Wait. What?"

"Yesterday afternoon," Cassidy said, glancing sheepishly toward the other bouquet on the kitchen counter. "He stopped by with soup *and* flowers."

Zoe narrowed her eyes and crossed the room to examine the blooms. "Are you serious right now?" She plucked out one of the signature twine-tied name cards from the stems. "These are from my shop. How did I not know about this?"

Cassidy laughed. "I guess he's sneaky."

Zoe turned around slowly. "Cassidy. I own the shop. I made these."

Cassidy winced. "Well, they're beautiful. So technically, you still helped."

Zoe let out a dramatic sigh and tossed her own bouquet onto the counter. "Figures. I try to be a good friend, and your lumberjack boyfriend ruins my grand gesture."

"He's not my boyfriend," Cassidy said, blushing.

Zoe raised an eyebrow. "You sure about that?"

Cassidy sat down on the couch and pulled a blanket over her lap. "Honestly? I don't know. But I'm definitely falling... Like, really falling. And it's not just about sex, although I'm not going to lie, he's very, very good."

Zoe covered her ears dramatically. "Nope. Stop. Do not talk about Liam and sex in the same sentence. He's basically my brother; we went to preschool together!"

"I don't know if I'd call it sex... well, maybe..." Cassidy admitted, her cheeks flushing. "We did this thing in the pine tree forest where I—"

"NOPE!" Zoe shouted. "If the next word is 'ride,' I'm leaving. Doesn't matter what you were riding. My brain is already scarred."

Cassidy snorted. "Okay, okay. But I'm just saying, I've never done anything like that in my life. And it's not just that. It's how he shows up. Like, without asking. Without expecting anything. He secured my display for me. Didn't even tell me, just did it because it needed to be done. No angle. No 'oh, now I'll win since she's sick.' Just... helped. I'm not used to that."

Zoe shook her head with a smile. "That's because your last boyfriend was trash."

"Liam is nothing like him." Cassidy sighed. "I made this vow, you know? Not to be with a guy for a whole year. I wanted to work on myself, so I wouldn't ever lose myself in a relationship again. I needed to take time for me. And I've done that. But Liam has never once made me feel weird about the stuff I love. He hates Christmas, but he's still shown up to stuff. When I don't wear a festive sweater, he thinks something's wrong."

Zoe smiled. "If you're trying to convince me Liam's great, don't bother. I've known that for twenty-five years."

Cassidy tilted her head. "You think he's definitely a good guy?"

"Did you even listen to yourself? You know he's a good guy. And if you're wondering if you can trust him with your heart, I'd say yeah. You can."

Cassidy exhaled, the weight of it all sinking in. "Thank you. I needed to hear that."

"But for the love of all things holy, do not share any sexy details with me. Please, I'm begging you."

"He can do this thing with his tongue—"

"STOP!" Zoe threw one of the fuzzy throw pillows at Cassidy.

She caught it. "Okay, noted. No sexy details."

"Thank you," Zoe said, settling into the couch.

Cassidy drummed her fingers on her leg, thinking. "The only thing is... I can't figure out what chocolate suits him. I've tried. Twice. Nothing's landed."

Zoe laughed. "What are you saying, he's your chocolate mystery man?"

"I'm really good at this," Cassidy said. "I know what flavors fit people. But Liam? He's... complicated. Sweet, salty, deep. I think I need to make one from scratch."

She clicked her tongue thoughtfully. Flavors danced through her mind—orange and caramel, coffee and cherry—but none of them felt quite right.

"I need to get back in the kitchen before I open," she said, eyes lighting up. "Start experimenting."

"While you do that, I'm going back to the flower shop," Zoe said, gathering her things. "Good luck with the chocolate. And the man."

"Thanks, girl. And thanks for the flowers."

That afternoon, Cassidy pulled out her phone and opened a new text.

Hey, want to come over for dinner tonight?

She hit send before she could overthink it.

No, she wasn't going to confess her love. Not yet.

But the vow? It was officially off the table.

She was done hiding from her feelings. Done forcing herself to slow down. Done being afraid.

She was ready to fall. Fast and free. For real this time.

And if Liam was the one catching her... well, maybe she'd finally landed in the right place.

THIRTY-FOUR

LIAM

Liam hadn't expected to hear from Cassidy that day—honestly, he hadn't thought he'd hear from her much at all that week. She would be deep in prep for her Christmas light-up event on Friday.

So when her name lit up his phone with a new message as he was walking back inside his house from Sunday lunch with his family, he stopped mid-step. Shifting to balance his mom's leftovers against his hip, he freed his thumb to read it.

Hey, want to come over for dinner tonight?

She didn't say what she was making, but he figured she had it covered. Still, he wasn't going to show up empty-handed.

He texted back:

Just tell me when. Want me to bring anything?

She replied:

Don't worry about it. I've got everything taken care of. 😉

That winking emoji should not have made his stomach do what it did. Liam gave himself a stern talking-to, reminding himself that tonight wasn't about crossing any lines. He wasn't going to tempt her with anything more than good conversation —maybe a goodnight kiss if the mood was right. He respected her vow, even if it was getting harder and harder to ignore the way she looked at him sometimes.

He still couldn't believe she'd stayed with Jean-Paul as long as she had... and yet, in a way, he could. That's how people ended up in toxic relationships, wasn't it? They didn't realize how far they'd drifted until they could no longer see the shoreline.

Guys like Jean-Paul were master gaslighters. They made you second-guess everything—what you heard, what you felt— until you were the one apologizing for their behavior. Liam had never even met the man, but he could see it in Cassidy. In the way she apologized for being "too much," as if her brightness was something to tone down. But she wasn't too much. She was perfect.

He decided to bring a bottle of wine—maybe a little cliché, but Cassidy would appreciate it.

The sun set early in December in Maple Falls. It wasn't even six o'clock, and stores had already switched on their Christmas lights. Families were arriving, bundled in scarves and hats, heading toward the Santa House or snapping photos in front of the town's giant Christmas tree.

Liam imagined standing there with Cassidy, his arms wrapped around her waist as someone took their picture—not for social media, not for the town's Christmas Countdown page

—just for them. She wasn't ready for that, but maybe next year. Yeah, next year Liam could see that.

Maybe they'd even send out holiday cards.

He chuckled to himself. Holiday cards? Christmas trees?

Who in the hell was he?

He was about to step into the general store for that bottle of wine when he spotted her.

She wore her red wool coat, the one with the oversized buttons and faux fur trim. Her black stocking cap was slightly crooked, the way it always slid when she rushed somewhere. She was gorgeous. And he smiled, knowing he was having dinner that night with the most beautiful woman in Maple Falls.

He lifted a hand, ready to call out to her, to cross the street and surprise her.

But then she stopped.

She hadn't seen him. She was standing near the town's Christmas tree, where the warm white lights glowed against the softening blue of early evening. Snow fell in gentle flurries, catching in the streetlights, turning the square into something out of a snow globe.

That's when Liam saw him.

A man stood in front of her. He had a thick mess of dark hair, tousled in that effortless way Liam had always found infuriating. The kind of guy who looked like he walked out of a magazine shoot without even trying.

The man turned his collar up against the cold, and he was smiling at her. Smiling like he knew her. Like he had a right to stand that close.

Liam's smile slipped, confusion tightening into something heavier in his gut.

They were talking, and even from across the street, Liam could see Cassidy's face shift—her eyes wide, mouth parting, her breath visible in small white clouds. Her hands came out of her pockets, fluttering like she didn't know what to do with them.

And then, without warning, the man dropped to one knee.

The world around them slowed. People in the square paused, their conversations cutting off mid-sentence, cider cups frozen halfway to lips, eyes widening as they turned to watch. The lights from the tree twinkled above them, the snow falling thicker now, a perfect, cinematic backdrop for what was happening.

Cassidy's hands flew to her mouth, her eyes glistening in the glow of the Christmas lights.

Liam took a single step forward, heart hammering, a dull roar in his ears. He couldn't hear what the man was saying, but he didn't need to. The look on Cassidy's face—shock, confusion, something like disbelief—told him enough.

The man rose, slow, confident, and then he pulled Cassidy into his arms, pressing his mouth to hers in a passionate kiss.

Liam felt the ground tilt.

His chest felt tight, the cold air suddenly sharp in his lungs, burning with every breath.

He didn't need to get closer. He didn't need to see any more.

Because there was only one man who would show up out of nowhere, who would kiss her like he owned her, who would look at Cassidy like she was a prize he was claiming.

Jean-Paul. Who else could it be?

All this time, Liam had assumed Cassidy's vow was about healing. About reclaiming her independence. About moving forward. That's what she'd said, wasn't it?

And he'd believed her.

But maybe... maybe it was about waiting.

Waiting for him.

For the man she'd never gotten over.

Liam had seen it with Zach and Madison—the way feelings, when buried, never really went away. Deep down, Madison had always wanted Zach to fight for her. To chase after her.

Maybe Cassidy wasn't so different.

Maybe she'd been holding out hope all along.

He couldn't breathe. The woman he was falling for—who he was imagining a future with—had never really been his.

And Jean-Paul? God, everything Cassidy had told him about that guy screamed red flags—narcissistic, controlling, manipulative. The kind of man who could shatter a woman's confidence, piece by piece, until she didn't even realize it was happening. The kind of man who would show up like this, in the middle of town, making a spectacle, pulling her back into his orbit like she owed him something.

What was he supposed to do? Run across the street and drag her away?

If this was her choice... he would just never be able to understand it.

A familiar tightness pressed against his ribs, creeping up his throat. He hadn't had a panic attack in over a year, but he felt one coming on now. It suddenly felt like this time of year was cursed for him. He'd just started to let go of the past, and to fall in love again. He should have known better than to tempt fate by allowing happiness to get a foothold at Christmastime. Now he was going to have a panic attack here, in front of everyone, in front of her. No. He needed out. Out of town, out of the crowd, away from the lights and the cheer and the image of Cassidy being kissed by someone else.

He turned to walk away and found himself running.

He had to escape Maple Falls.

THIRTY-FIVE
CASSIDY

"What? No. I won't marry you!" Cassidy exclaimed in French as she pushed off Jean-Paul's chest, her voice sharp and echoing across the town square. She couldn't believe he'd just shown up like this—out of nowhere—and dropped to one knee as if the last year hadn't happened. "In what world does that make sense?"

But it was too late.

The whole town was staring. Looking at her like she was some wicked Christmas Jezebel who'd just stomped on their hometown hero's heart. Mr. Alders glared from his bench. Mrs. C. was tugging off her Team Cassidy sweater.

"Stop, I'm not marrying him!" she shouted in English now, looking around, trying to get everyone to believe her. "I don't even like him!" she added, hoping that would help.

Jean-Paul looked incredulous, as though he genuinely couldn't believe she was rejecting him.

"What is the matter with you?" He gripped her by the arm, reverting back to French. "You didn't even look at the ring." He held open the box, hoping to charm her by the massive diamond twinkling up at her.

She hated it at first sight.

"I don't care about the ring! God, what is the matter with you?"

Jean-Paul dropped his voice. "You are making a scene. Let's get out of here. I booked us a room. We can talk this through."

"You booked a room at the Cinnamon Spice Inn?" she asked, baffled.

"What? God, no. I booked a five-star hotel about fifty miles from here. That's how far I had to go to find a decent hotel, if you can believe it. And what's with the sweater? Were you forced to wear that as part of your uniform?"

"Uniform?" she repeated, stunned. "No. I happen to love this sweater. And for the record, no one tells me what to do. I own my own chocolate shop."

Jean-Paul laughed. A hollow, condescending sound.

"That isn't a chocolate shop. That is selling basic sweets to a bunch of unsophisticated Americans. What we have together in Paris—that's a chocolate shop."

His French was rapid now, sharp, cutting insults that the crowd couldn't follow—but Cassidy could. And even if they couldn't understand the words, the tone was unmistakable. The anger in his voice made people shift uncomfortably, even without knowing the language.

"I'm not going anywhere with you," Cassidy said firmly back in French, her voice clear and rising above the noise. "In fact, I never want to see you again. You won't believe it, but I'm happy—really, truly happy. I love my life. And it doesn't have you in it. I never want it to again."

Before Jean-Paul could respond, Zach stepped in, coming up beside her like a silent shield.

"I'm pretty sure the woman just told you to leave," he said flatly.

Cassidy glanced at Zach, grateful. The translation wasn't exact, but it was close enough.

Jean-Paul narrowed his eyes and took a step back, sizing Zach up.

They stared each other down.

Cassidy held her breath, watching. Jean-Paul had always preyed on anyone he could control—people who felt small, uncertain, unsure. But he knew he couldn't control Zach, and he couldn't control her anymore. She saw it in his eyes. He knew it.

But she also knew what he was capable of. He fought dirty, always had. She'd seen him coax others into throwing the first punch so that he could cry victim and press charges. He was smarter than he looked—and slippery. But here, in this town, it was clear to everyone: He didn't belong. And no one was buying his act.

"You're going to regret this, you stupid bitch," Jean-Paul spat out in French, and by the gasps, she could tell enough people had heard and understood.

Before Zach could even move, Madison appeared—her fist flying.

She punched Jean-Paul square in the jaw. He dropped like a wet towel. A wet towel in an expensive suit.

"That's for insulting my friend," Madison said coldly. "And for disrespecting our town."

She turned to Cassidy. "I took French in high school. The swears are about all I remember." She cracked her knuckles. "You alright?"

Cassidy nodded, still trying to process everything. "Yeah. I'm fine."

"Good," Zach said. "But Liam's not. He saw the whole thing."

"Well... not the whole thing," Madison corrected, glancing

at Zach. "He saw the part where Jean-Paul got down on one knee, everyone clapped and cheered... and then he bolted."

Cassidy swore under her breath. She fumbled for her phone, her fingers flying across the screen, dialing Liam's number. She pressed the phone to her ear as the ringtone droned on, over and over again.

No answer.

She pulled the phone away, her fingers trembling as she typed:

Liam, I can explain. It's not what you think. Please call me.

She hit send, staring at the screen, willing the three dots of a reply to appear. Nothing. No text. No call.

Nothing.

She looked up, her reflection in the café window catching her off guard—flushed cheeks, wide eyes, panic etched across her features beneath the twinkle of holiday lights.

"I have to find him," she said, almost apologetic, to Madison and Zach.

She didn't wait for them to reply as she half walked, half jogged down Oak Way, scanning for his truck.

She reached his shop, breathless, heart hammering, and tried the door.

Locked.

She cupped her hands around her face, peering into the darkened interior, hoping—praying—to see him moving inside.

Nothing. No lights, no movement. Just her reflection, pale and frantic, staring back.

Cassidy's breath fogged the glass as she leaned her forehead against the door, her eyes closing.

She had no idea where he was.

THIRTY-SIX

LIAM

Sunday, December 14th

Liam didn't tell anyone where he was going—except Jackson. And even then, it was more of a text than a conversation.

Liam: Going off grid for a couple days. I'll be back soon—just need some time.

Jackson: Got it.

That was the thing about his brother. He didn't ask questions. Didn't press for details. He just gave Liam space. Even better, Jackson would tell their parents, and their mom would take care of the farm shop while Liam was away.

Liam packed a small bag, grabbed his sketchbook and pencils, a thermos of black coffee that would go cold before he drank it, and drove north, away from Maple Falls. Away from the festive lights, cheerful music, and the image of Cassidy— wrapped in someone else's arms. The image twisted in his gut and he wished he could burn the memory away.

His truck wound up the mountain roads, tires occasionally slipping on the icy concrete. He didn't care. He just kept on driving in silence, not even bothering to turn on the radio. Liam didn't want the noise. Just the engine, the wind, and the steady drumbeat of *you should've known* pounding in his head.

Two hours later he turned off the main road onto a two-track trail. This was the part of the trip where four-wheel drive was a must. The log cabin had been in his family for four generations. A place for hunting trips, weekend escapes, and summer nights with bonfires that lasted until the early-morning hours. Liam had tagged his first buck in those woods. Had his first sip of whiskey afterwards around the fire with his granddad.

Now it stood quiet, tucked between tall pines and heavy snow, far from cell towers and town gossip. A place that didn't ask anything of him. It was all he could ask for.

He stepped inside the two-bedroom space and didn't bother turning on the lights. He dropped his bag, let the door swing shut behind him, and stood in the center of the empty room. The air smelled of old cedar and cold ash from the last fire, layered with the faint scent of pine that seeped through the drafty windows.

He braced his hands on the worn kitchen counter, staring at the frost etching along the windowpane, breath clouding the glass.

What had he expected? That a woman like Cassidy—with her spark and softness and light—would really want someone like him?

His breath hitched.

God, he was such an idiot.

He ran a hand through his hair and paced the length of the cabin, jaw tight, heart thudding while he tried to get a fire started. He needed to keep his hands busy.

He gathered the dried wood from the side grate, twisted old newspaper, wedging it between the logs, before finding the jar of wooden matches on the mantel.

He hadn't been here since the year before Avery died. They'd talked about coming up after Christmas that winter, just the two of them. No pressure, no expectations—just snow, quiet, and each other. She'd wanted to skate on the lake, bake something from scratch, sketch beside him in the mornings with too much coffee and not enough sleep. He remembered how her eyes had lit up when he'd told her about the cabin. "I want to see it in the snow," she'd said. "I want to see *you* in the snow."

After lighting the fire, the flames licking up the newspaper, he sank onto the edge of the old couch and dropped his head into his hands, cataloging every error he'd made with Cassidy. He'd thought he'd protected himself. Thought the walls he'd built were strong enough. But she had slipped past them without even trying. She'd made him hope again. And that was the real betrayal—he'd let her.

"Maybe I deserve this," he muttered to the empty room.

He pulled his sketchbook out of his bag, but his fingers trembled. He tried to draw. Anything. The slope of a mountain. The edge of a tree branch. But it all blurred.

The page stayed empty.

Just like his chest.

Just like the damn holiday.

Christmas. What a joke.

It used to mean something. With Jackson and Lily, sneaking downstairs to see what Santa had brought them. With his mom, who sang along to the old Bing Crosby records while she baked cinnamon rolls. With Avery, who insisted on making her own wrapping paper out of decorated craft paper.

She'd loved Christmas, too.

Sometimes he still heard her laugh in the cold. Saw her in

his dreams. He wondered what she'd say now—what she'd think of Cassidy.

Would she tell him to stop pushing people away?

Would she tell him it was okay to try again?

In some ways, Cassidy reminded him of Avery. They were very different people, but at their core they had the same warmth. The same love of life and fierce determination.

He let out a rough breath and dropped the pencil. Leaned back against the wall and stared up at the wooden beams of the ceiling.

This was what he got. For letting his guard down. For falling for someone who was still waiting around for someone else. For thinking, for one stupid second, that maybe he could have more.

Outside, snow fell steadily, softening the world into silence.

Inside, he closed his eyes.

And let the darkness settle in.

THIRTY-SEVEN

CASSIDY

Cassidy felt sick to her stomach. She couldn't believe Liam would just disappear like this.

"Does he do this often?" she had asked Madison.

"No, not often. But he's not himself this time of year, and when he needs a moment, it's best to give him one."

She was wiping down the cocoa bar for the third time that morning, glancing out the window at his darkened shop across the street, when the bell over her door jingled.

Beth Hawthorne stepped inside, bringing a swirl of cold air with her, followed closely by Mrs. Bishop and Mrs. C., who was already unwrapping a butterscotch candy.

"There she is," Beth said warmly, pulling off her gloves and walking straight over to give Cassidy a hug. "Honey, don't you worry about a thing."

"Beth, I—"

"We all saw what happened," Mrs. Bishop cut in, her cheeks flushed from the cold. "That slimy ex of yours dropping to one knee like he was in some cheap holiday movie."

Mrs. C. sniffed. "If I'd been closer, I would have whacked him with my purse. Hard."

Cassidy let out a strangled laugh, tears pricking her eyes.

Beth squeezed her shoulder. "Liam just needs a little time, honey. He'll come around. He always does."

Mrs. C. nodded, rummaging in her purse. "And when he does, you tell him we said he better not let a two-bit French soap opera villain ruin what you two have."

Mrs. Bishop was peering around the shop, taking in the scent of warm cocoa and the soft glow of the twinkle lights. "You keeping up okay here, dear? Need us to run deliveries? I've got nothing but time now that my knitting club is off for the holidays."

"I-I'm okay," Cassidy stammered, overwhelmed by the kindness. "I'm thinking about pulling out of the competition though. After everything, I'm just not sure—"

"What!" Mrs. Bishop shouted. "You can't do that!"

"Nonsense. Do you know how many Team Cassidy sweaters we've sold? This town loves you!" Mrs. C. added.

Beth smiled. "It's true, and the competition has been so good for the town. Don't you worry about Liam, and don't you dare worry about what anyone else thinks."

"Are you sure?" Cassidy knew winning was a long shot, but after the drama she'd caused, she wasn't sure if she even had a chance. Not that she wanted to quit...

"Quit talking like that. You're going to win. You just wait and see!" Mrs. Bishop said, putting an end to the conversation.

Mrs. C. clapped her hands. "Now, who wants spiced cocoa? Because I, for one, think this situation calls for extra whipped cream."

Cassidy let out a watery laugh, the tension easing from her shoulders for the first time all day. She glanced outside at the falling snow, then back at the women crowding around her cocoa bar, fussing over marshmallows and stirring sticks.

She still didn't know when Liam would come back.

But at least, in that moment, she knew she wasn't alone.

It was that evening when she noticed something very wrong. She was outside, getting ready to step out for a walk with Muff, when she looked over and saw Liam's shop.

"What in the world?" Cassidy murmured as she saw the trees Liam had set up in front of his shop knocked over. Ornaments were shattered across the sidewalk from the force of the fall. Liam had spent so much time making sure her storefront was secure that he hadn't protected his own.

She looked up and down the street. It wasn't windy. Not in the least bit. Snow was falling, sure, but it wasn't a blizzard out. This was more of a lazy snow shower, just passing through.

Liam had been creating an enchanted forest in the green space beside his shop, using real trees potted in rustic wooden containers. Each tree had a small "For Sale" sign. Some were live potted evergreens, ready to be replanted after the holidays, while others the town would donate to be repurposed as mulch for the community gardens come spring.

It was Zoe's idea—she'd rallied the crafting club and the local schools, encouraging families to give their Christmas trees a second life instead of tossing them to the curb. Cassidy loved it. She'd never liked the idea of cutting down trees just to throw them away after a couple of weeks, even if it was for Christmas. This way was better. It felt hopeful, like a promise of new roots and second chances—something she found herself craving more and more lately.

As Cassidy approached, she realized it was worse than she'd thought. Not only had the Christmas trees been knocked over, but someone had cut the lights. The wires were mangled and torn—not just snipped, but unraveled, as if whoever had done it wanted to make repairs impossible. The lights had been disconnected in several places. It would be easier to toss the whole thing than to try and fix it.

She felt as guilty as she was appalled. Would this have happened if Liam had been around? She knew it wasn't her fault Jean-Paul had shown up and proposed, but she shouldn't have let him kiss her. She should've pushed him away sooner. But the truth was, she'd been too stunned to react. One minute she was on her way to pick up a bottle of wine from Gourmet Goodies, and the next, Jean-Paul was in front of her, down on one knee. It had been like a nightmare, and in that split second of silence, he'd taken her hesitation as agreement.

If that hadn't happened, maybe it would've been Liam punching Jean-Paul in the face, not Madison. Although Cassidy had to admit, Madison had done a hell of a job.

Cassidy created a new group chat so Liam wouldn't see it.

Cassidy: Anyone free to help? Looks like the Gingerbread Jerk targeted Liam's shop. Front display ruined. I'm going to try and fix it.

Within seconds, the chat lit up:

Madison: What time do you need us there?

Kit: What the hell??

Emily: Not his shop too!

Zach: I'll swing by the farm and grab new trees.

Soon, they had a plan. Everyone would meet at Liam's shop in thirty minutes.

While she waited for her friends to arrive, Cassidy quickly pulled out her phone and searched for farm-inspired holiday décor. One of the first ideas that popped up was a set of reindeer made from birch logs.

"Perfect," she murmured, taking a screenshot of the directions and calling Zach. "Any chance you know where we can get some birch logs?"

"Probably at the farm. I'll see what I can do."

"Thanks." She clicked off with Zach and figured she could grab the rest of the supplies at the hardware store.

Without a moment to lose, she beelined for the shop and almost walked straight into Mr. Alders.

"Well, if it isn't the girl who scared off poor Liam," the gruff older man muttered.

Cassidy tensed. "It was just a misunderstanding. Jean-Paul is an ex who had a hard time accepting no. Nothing else." She glanced across the street. "You didn't happen to see what happened to Liam's display, did you?"

Mr. Alders looked away. "Might've seen something."

She tried to bite her tongue and failed. "What do you mean by that?"

"All I'm saying is I saw it was tipped over. Looks like it was wrecked. Like young Emily's. Ha." He gave a smug little snort, as if he might've added a bow to the wreckage himself. It was a shame she didn't have any evidence. She couldn't go around accusing people based on a hunch.

One thing was for sure: Mr. Alders didn't exactly radiate Christmas cheer. She brushed past him and entered the hardware store, quickly collecting what she needed.

On her way out, she bumped into Mayor Bloomfield. He was just the man she was looking for.

"Oh! Hello there, Cassidy," he said, adjusting his green sport coat. His red tie and white shirt gave him a festive, holly-jolly look, like a Christmas elf in retirement.

"Hi, Mayor. Did you see what happened to Liam's display?"

His smile faded. "No. Don't tell me—it's been messed with?"

Cassidy nodded. "Just like Emily's. Just like the bookstore. I know Maple Falls isn't exactly a big fan of surveillance cameras, but something needs to be done." She shifted the shopping bag to her other arm. "Have we at least brought it to the sheriff's attention?"

Mayor Bloomfield chuckled. "Oh, Cassidy. I know people have been worried about the so-called Gingerbread Jerk, but the more I've thought about it, the more I think we're just seeing a string of odd coincidences. Something more innocent is going on. Nothing to get worked up over. Maple Falls is still a safe place."

Her eyes drifted toward Mr. Alders again.

The mayor followed her gaze. "You know, big-city living can make the imagination run a little wild. Maybe you're still adjusting."

Cassidy liked Mayor Bloomfield, truly. And she loved the way he dressed, but right now, she did not like the way he was dismissing her. She realized she wasn't going to get any further with him.

"Thanks, Mayor. Have a good night."

He tipped his head. "You too, Cassidy."

Outside Liam's shop, Zach, Madison, Emily, and Kit were already waiting. Zach made quick work of tossing broken ornaments and snapped lights into a trash bag while Madison swept up the scattered debris. Cassidy and Kit worked together to assemble the reindeer from the saved directions.

They worked in silence, trying to recreate the magic Liam had so carefully crafted.

Zach had only been able to bring a couple of trees from the farm. The potted ones sold out fastest. Thankfully, not all had been destroyed. A few were just damaged. Cassidy, wearing thick gloves, carefully snipped broken branches and helped string the new lights. The side of the building, thankfully, was untouched. A big wreath still hung in the front window, centered with a bright red bow courtesy of Liam's mom. Zach had picked it up when he'd gone to get the trees—turns out, she'd been working on it all along.

"I don't know," Madison said, stepping back, hands on her hips. "I think it looks even better than before."

"High-five to the best Christmas decorators in town," Kit agreed, going up high.

Cassidy had to agree.

There was something simple and beautiful about it. The farm-style reindeer, the warm lights, the hometown charm... It reminded her of his family farm. Comforting. Real.

A place where she could see herself belonging.

And now he was gone and she flat-out missed him. It was crazy how used she'd gotten to seeing him, spending time with him. And now it was just silence.

She knew he had to be hurting, and even though part of her was furious for jumping to conclusions, she hated that for him.

Cassidy looked at the storefront one more time and silently wished he could see it.

Maybe then he'd know how much he meant to her.

THIRTY-EIGHT

CASSIDY

Tuesday, December 16th

Cassidy flipped the "Open" sign to "Closed" at the Cocoa Corner, pressing a hand to the glass for a moment as she looked out at the softly falling snow. The glow from the twinkle lights around her window reflected back, dancing over the trays of truffles and the cocoa mugs she'd just hung up to dry.

It was crafting night at the Cinnamon Spice Inn. Cassidy thought she might have to miss it with all the chocolate orders coming in and last-minute Christmas prep, but tonight she promised herself she would go, even if just for an hour. She needed it, needed the connection, the laughter, the warmth.

She tugged on her red wool coat and black stocking cap, locking the shop behind her before stepping into the winter night. Snow crunched under her boots as she made her way down Oak Way, passing the twinkling lampposts wrapped in garlands, the darkened windows of Liam's farm shop, and the warm glow spilling from the bakery next door.

The Cinnamon Spice Inn stood at the end of the street like something out of a storybook. Its white clapboard exterior was strung with warm white lights, and evergreen swags draped the porch railing, tied with crimson bows that fluttered in the cold breeze. A wreath of pinecones and dried oranges hung on the door, the scent of cinnamon and clove already reaching Cassidy before she even stepped inside.

Cassidy had loved the Cinnamon Spice Inn from the moment she'd laid eyes on it. She hadn't seen it before Madison and Zach renovated it in the fall, but they'd done a beautiful job.

Inside, a deep green rug with gold swirls greeted guests at the door. Off to the side, a charming Christmas village had been set up, complete with fake snow and miniature houses that lit up. There was even a tiny ice rink with animatronic skaters. She couldn't help but think of the time she and Liam had gone skating together, and everything that had followed afterward.

She shook the thought away, allowing her senses to ground in the present. The inn always smelled like the cinnamon rolls it was famous for. Cassidy didn't know if it was from Kit's baking or if they had fresheners plugged into every outlet.

With snow falling outside and a roaring fire in the hearth, she could see why everyone in the town loved the inn so much. And that wasn't even counting the twelve-foot spruce in the great dining room, wrapped with thousands of white lights and blown glass ornaments.

"Careful," Madison said, pulling Cassidy back. "I'm pretty sure it's a Norway spruce."

"Don't have to tell me twice." She took a step back, allowing Madison to lead her upstairs and down the hall to Edith's private apartment.

The door looked like the rest of the guest rooms on the floor, plain white with a numbered plaque on the front, but when Madison opened it, it revealed the combined living and dining space of a quaint little apartment.

The living room was cozy and inviting, centered around a

small fireplace. A plush wingback chair sat angled beside it, with a floral footstool tucked neatly underneath. A soft, white quilted throw was draped over the back of the couch, which faced the hearth. To the left, an oak dining table dominated the remaining space. She could tell the table wasn't usually that long. Edith had added the leaves to expand it for company. It made the whole apartment feel like the kind of place where stories were swapped over games of cards and second helpings were expected.

Off to the right was the kitchen, partially closed off by a set of upper cabinets and a central island that created a small sense of separation without feeling cut off from the rest of the apartment.

Edith had gone all out for tonight's crafting club gathering. She had trays set out with bite-sized ham and Swiss pinwheels, bacon-wrapped dates, miniature quiches, and a bowl of rosemary-spiced nuts. A wooden board held an assortment of cheeses, crackers, and red grapes, while a tiered stand was stacked with gingerbread men and snowflake-shaped sugar cookies.

"I have mulled wine!" Edith said by way of greeting once Madison and Cassidy reached her.

The scent of warm red wine, cinnamon, orange, and clove filled the room.

"I'd love a cup," Madison said, joining Edith in the kitchen.

"Make that two," Cassidy said, still taking in all the food before her eyes wandered to the supplies for tonight's craft.

The dining room table was a crafter's paradise. There were white socks, baskets of buttons, felt hats, glittery sequins, hot glue guns, fabric scraps, and even a few crochet hooks with yarn if anyone wanted to really go all out.

The rest of the women arrived right on time.

Kit had baked cinnamon rolls, of course, and paired them with Zach's homemade apple butter.

"I'm sorry," Cassidy said, seeing everyone walk in with something. "I should've brought chocolates. My head's just not where it needs to be."

Mrs. C. waved Cassidy's concern away. "It's probably a good thing you didn't. We have enough food to feed an army."

"And then some," Mrs. Bishop said, adding a cream cheese veggie pizza to the table.

Cassidy took a sip of the mulled wine, letting its warmth seep through her chest. The room buzzed with chatter and laughter as the women gathered around the table, pulling supplies closer with their plates of goodies. For a moment, she let herself soak it in, the easy conversation, the delicious food, the smell of the glue guns heating up.

She needed this.

That was, until Mrs. Bishop gave her a pointed look over the rim of her wine glass. "So," she said casually, "any updates on the Liam front?"

The room went quiet, too quiet. Even the snowman heads seemed to lean in.

Cassidy shook her head. "Wow, okay. We're just diving right in, huh?"

Mrs. C. waved a dismissive hand. "No sense in pretending otherwise."

Cassidy let out a sigh and reached for a glittery top hat, as if gluing tiny felt accessories might shield her from the truth. "No, I haven't heard a peep." It had been two days without a sound from Liam.

Kit pointed her glue gun like a weapon. "If you ask me, he should've talked to you before running off like that."

"I know. I agree. I get it that he was hurt. I just really want to talk to him and straighten things out."

"And tell him about his shop," Madison added.

"What happened to the Hot Honey Farm Shop?" Edith asked, brows lifting as she paused mid-sip of her wine.

"The Gingerbread Jerk struck again," Kit said, gluing on her snowman's head.

"No!" Mrs. C. said at the same time Mrs. Bishop asked, "When?"

"Yesterday sometime. And Liam's switch-on is next week," Cassidy said.

"I'd be more worried about yours in three days. Don't want something happening to your display now," Kit added.

"No, I know. Trust me, I've tried to figure out who's behind it. I still think it's someone local. Someone who knows these displays mean something, how important they are," Cassidy said.

"You know what I think?" Mrs. Bishop said, leaning back in her chair and adjusting her holiday brooch with purpose. "I think it's up to us to solve the case!"

"What? Now why would you say that?" Edith asked.

"Well, if the mayor's too busy to figure out who's behind all the vandalism," Mrs. C. said, "then we're going to do it. What do you ladies say?"

"I say I want to build a snowman," Edith replied, carefully dabbing glue on a tiny pom-pom hat. Then she added with a sly grin, "But I'd like to solve this mystery too."

"How about we do both?" Madison suggested.

The women got to work decorating their snowmen while tossing out ideas and theories.

"I've said from the beginning that something with Mr. Alders felt off," Cassidy offered. "He came into my shop on the first day I opened, complaining that Maple Falls was too over-the-top about Christmas and that things were changing. He didn't sound happy."

Mrs. C. snorted. "Sounds like Gary. The man can't handle change."

"I'll second that," Mrs. Bishop said. "He's retired, and yet he still shows up at the hardware store every day. Maybe he's finally lost his marbles."

"Alright, I'll add him to the suspect list," Edith said, taking a pen and piece of paper out of her kitchen drawer. "But have you all seen Hank's niece lately?"

Mrs. Bishop turned to Edith. "Now *that* I didn't think of, but you might be onto something..."

"Elsie?" Kit asked. "Why Elsie?"

"She and Hank have been fighting nonstop. She's mad he won't adopt her ideas to modernize Christmas in Maple Falls. She wants everything livestreamed and 'on-brand' for Instagram," Edith explained. "Thinks our traditions are outdated. She's even trying to convince him this should be the last year for the festive light-ups. She wanted a drone parade and less emphasis on Christmas or something equally awful."

"That would be horrible," Mrs. C. said, scandalized.

"She does seem stressed out lately," Madison added. "She came into the inn last week looking like she hadn't slept in days. Muttered something about branding synergy and walked into a door."

"If that's true," Cassidy said slowly, "I could actually see her sabotaging things to get her own way. She's so driven. Maybe hoping we'll give up and just go with her plan."

The group of ladies nodded.

"Okay, so we've got two suspects. Anyone else?" Edith asked, clicking the end of her pen and looking around the table.

Everyone paused, frowning thoughtfully over their glitter-strewn snowmen.

Then Edith straightened. "I think it's time we do a stakeout."

Cassidy raised both brows. "A stakeout?"

"Of course," Mrs. Bishop said brightly, as if it were the most obvious next step in a crafting night. "We've got the mulled wine, lawn chairs. All we need is a thermos and a set of binoculars."

Mrs. C. leaned back and patted her knee. "I've got a heated blanket and a husband who snores. Count me in."

Kit grinned. "Do we get walkie-talkies?"

Mrs. C. tapped her pen to her chin. "We should. I'll check the garage. George used to have some for hunting."

Cassidy cracked a smile for the first time all day. "Let's do it tonight."

THIRTY-NINE

LIAM

The drive back to town was icy and dark, the kind of darkness that swallowed everything beyond the thin glow of his headlights. Snow swirled across the two-lane road, drifting in from the fields on either side. There weren't streetlights out here, not like in town, just the silhouettes of bare-limbed trees lining the ditches.

Liam's truck's headlights cut through the darkness on the road, but not inside his mind.

His hands tightened on the steering wheel, thumbs drumming absently. The rhythmic swish of the wipers against the windshield was the only other sound, cutting a path through the snow and sleet that clung to the glass.

He knew he couldn't stay away from his shop forever; he just really needed some time to gather his thoughts. He had a sneaking suspicion that when he got back to Maple Falls, he'd find one of two things: Either Jean-Paul had moved in with Cassidy, or there'd be a "For Sale" sign in the window of the

Cocoa Corner, replacing the sign advertising her Spiced Cocoa Café pop-up.

Probably the "For Sale" sign.

There was no way a man like Jean-Paul would call Maple Falls home.

Liam was wondering how long he could hide from Cassidy if she was staying. Maybe he'd never have to see her again.

Ha. That was wishful thinking. She literally lived across the street from his shop.

He hated confrontation. Hated talking about his feelings. But she had to know, didn't she? She had to know she'd broken his heart, that he'd been falling for her. Hadn't he made it clear how much he cared?

He hadn't been looking for anything serious for years. Hadn't wanted to fall in love again. Then as soon as he met her, he started falling faster than ever before.

But how well did he really know her?

Maybe he'd gotten ahead of himself. They'd only met at the beginning of the month. Liam shook his head. It was just like him to fall head over heels after avoiding an emotional connection with any woman for the last four years.

Now, here he was. Exhausted. He hadn't slept in two nights. And all he'd done was stare at a blank sketch pad.

No inspiration. No creativity. No spark.

As he pulled into town, he wondered, not for the first time, how long this heaviness would last. How long before the sadness let go of him. Before he felt like himself again.

He found himself, once again, praying for the holiday season to end. If he could just get through the next week, through his shop's light-up night, he could disappear again. Go off the grid until New Year's. That was when things started to feel normal again. When the lights came down and people stopped pretending everything was merry and bright.

Maybe he'd feel normal then, too, after some time away from Cassidy.

But first, he needed to stop by the farm shop, check on things and locate some details about orders and deliveries for his mom, who'd been covering the shop for him. He'd buy her an extra present for all the work his absence must have caused her—not that she'd ever complain.

He had a black hoodie pulled tight over his head and just wanted to jog in and out, unnoticed before he lost his nerve. He didn't even register the new decorations until he almost walked into a Christmas tree that shouldn't have been there.

He took a step back, eyeing the rest of his shop, when—

"Ah-ha! Gotcha!" A fishing net came down over his shoulder.

"What in the world?" Liam tried to lift the net over his head, but the woman wasn't letting go.

"I got him! I got him!" Mrs. C. hollered. "Somebody call the sheriff!"

"You haven't caught anything. Mrs. C., it's me."

"Liam?" Mrs. C. looked at Liam and raised the net.

Cassidy ran up, the beam of her phone flashlight catching him in the eyes. He winced at the sudden brightness—and at the expression on her face. Not apologetic. Not embarrassed.

Angry.

Furious, even.

He didn't think he'd ever seen a woman look that angry. And he'd known Madison since first grade.

"Cassidy?" he asked, glancing around the shadowed street. "Can someone tell me what's going on?"

"What's going on is that we're in the middle of a Gingerbread Jerk stakeout," Cassidy snapped. "And you walked right into it."

"Stakeout?" It was then that Liam took in the women

standing around him. Cassidy, Mrs. Bishop, Mrs. C., and Edith were all standing around him, dressed head to toe in black. Even their stocking caps were black. Mrs. Bishop had gone so far as to bring a ski mask. He would've laughed if he wasn't still trying to make sense of it all.

Liam looked up and down the street. It was quiet. He'd even say peaceful if Cassidy wasn't looking at him with daggers in her eyes.

He looked back at his shop, seeing the new decorations, the trees, the birch log reindeer. "The Gingerbread Jerk targeted my shop."

"Yeah, but don't worry, I fixed it up real nice," she added, hands on her hips, voice sharp. "Although I don't know why I bothered."

His jaw tensed. "I don't know—maybe you felt guilty because you strung me along for weeks only to get back together with Jean-Paul the Douchebag?"

"Strung you along?!?" Her voice rose up an octave.

"I say we back up and give the two of them a moment," Edith suggested, gently tugging Mrs. C. and Mrs. Bishop back by their coats.

"What else would you call it?" Liam crossed his arms over his chest, stance wide.

Cassidy's chest heaved, cheeks flushed with cold and fury. She stepped closer, jabbing a finger at his chest.

"Are you kidding me?" Her voice cracked, high with anger. "You disappeared, Liam! Since Sunday! Do you know what that was like? I was worried sick, pacing my tiny apartment, checking my phone every five minutes, praying you were okay. Then you show up here like this? What were you going to do, sneak in and back out? Hope I didn't see you?"

He opened his mouth, but nothing came out.

She shook her head, her breath coming out in harsh white

clouds. "Don't you dare stand there and accuse me of leading you on when you're the one who ran away."

"The man kissed you, Cassidy. What was I supposed to do?"

"I don't know, talk to me?"

Liam suddenly realized why she had looked at him like he was the bad guy. Because maybe... maybe he had been.

"You're not engaged?"

"No, I'm not engaged. Why would I get back together with someone like that?"

He dropped his face into his hand, rubbing his temples with his finger and thumb.

"I was worried about you," she continued, more quietly now. "I didn't know where you'd gone. And I hated that you thought I'd betrayed you."

"I told Jackson where I went," he said, but even to his own ears the excuse sounded weak.

"Jackson? The man who's never said two words to me?"

"My family knew I was safe," he mumbled. His excuses weren't doing him any favors.

Liam sighed and closed his eyes for a beat, trying to get his thoughts straight.

He opened his eyes and looked into Cassidy's. The anger was still there, but he hoped there was room for something more.

"Look, this is all coming out wrong. I freaked out. I took off. I'm sorry. I just..." He exhaled sharply. "It scared me. How much I care about you. And I clearly made all the wrong moves."

She crossed her arms, still guarded. The street was quiet around them; the only sound was that of Mrs. Bishop unwrapping a peppermint from her pocket.

"It's freezing out here," Liam added, rubbing his hands together. "Could we maybe take this inside?"

He was well aware that the entire crafting club was currently getting a play-by-play of one of the most vulnerable moments of his life.

Cassidy's glare finally softened. Just a little.

"Sure," she said. "Come on. I'll put the cocoa on."

FORTY

CASSIDY

Cassidy was both relieved and furious at the same time. But the longer Liam stood in front of her, the relief began to win out. When she looked at him, really looked, she saw how tired he was. Dark circles clung beneath his eyes, and his beard had grown a little longer.

"Are you hungry?" she asked gently.

"Not really," he replied, pulling one of the black café chairs back. The sound scraped across the hardwood floor. "Just cocoa would be great."

Cassidy turned back to the stove. She stirred the cocoa, watching the swirl of cream disappear into the dark chocolate. Her fingers clenched the whisk a little too tightly as she added a splash of whiskey to the batch. The scent of melting cocoa, ground cloves, and whiskey filled the air. It was warm, familiar, grounding.

The space was dim, with the only soft light coming from the twinkle lights twinkling overhead. She allowed the silence to stretch between them, giving them both space to think. Her shoulders rose and fell with a breath she didn't even know she'd been holding.

She knew Liam felt awful, gutted really, for how wrong he'd gotten everything. She'd been so angry at him, not because she didn't care... but because she did.

It had been a misunderstanding. And if they didn't have real feelings for each other, it wouldn't have mattered so much.

You didn't get this angry if you didn't care.

You didn't hurt this much, either.

Cassidy wondered how she would've reacted if the roles were reversed. If she somehow thought Liam had gotten back together with an ex. She would've been devastated. And yeah, she'd probably want to leave town for a few days too.

He sighed behind her. It wasn't loud, but she felt it.

She didn't turn. Not yet. Her hand slowed on the whisk, and she added another splash of cream. She needed the buffer, to drag out the moment. She needed the chance to calm her racing thoughts.

She heard the scrape of the chair, the hollow knock of his boot against the leg of the table.

"I really messed things up," he said quietly, voice rough with fatigue. "I'm sorry. I don't know how to make it up to you. I shouldn't have overreacted. I hope you know that I care about you so much." His voice cracked slightly. "Hell... I've only known you for a few weeks. But I've fallen in love with you."

That made her freeze.

Slowly, she set the whisk down on the spoon rest and turned to face him.

Liam sat hunched at the café table, elbows on his knees, head bowed like he didn't expect her to believe him. But when he lifted his eyes to hers, her heart stopped. His expression was wary, searching. Cassidy saw everything. The vulnerability. The fear. The truth of what he'd just said.

The words hung in the air like ornaments on a Christmas tree until Cassidy said, "I've fallen for you, too."

His face lit up. It was the first time she'd seen him truly smile.

Tears welled before she could stop them. Not the same tears she'd cried when he'd left. These were different because the man she was falling in love with was here, finally letting her see a side of him that she knew was hard for him to share.

"How about this?" he said, his voice steadier now. "I make a promise to you, right here, right now. If something's on my mind, bothering me, weighing me down, if I'm ever worried about us, I'll talk to you before I react. Deal?"

Cassidy nodded, her voice catching. "I think that's a pretty good deal."

It was a good thing she'd already turned off the cocoa burner, because the next second, Liam was standing and closing the space between them.

For a moment, they just stood there, inches apart, the scent of cocoa and peppermint between them, the tension of everything unspoken pressing close.

His thumb skimmed her cheekbone. His touch was featherlight and made her breath catch. When his lips met hers, they didn't rush. They lingered. Like he was memorizing the shape of her mouth, the sound of her soft sigh, the way she leaned into him without hesitation. And when she kissed him back? It felt like the world narrowed to just the two of them.

"I missed you," he murmured. "I thought... I thought I'd never get to kiss you again."

Cassidy said nothing, just wound her arms around his neck and pulled him back in.

Where he was hesitant, she leaned in, deepening the kiss. When she sucked his tongue, he groaned into her mouth. The sound sent a ripple through her, right to her toes.

He broke away a breath later, forehead pressed to hers, eyes closed. "Alright," he said roughly, "that's not fair. I'm trying to be respectful here, take things slow like you said, and you're driving me absolutely wild."

Cassidy smiled, her hands still looped around his neck. "I don't want to take things slow anymore," she said, letting the words linger as she gathered her thoughts.

She took a breath, her voice steady. "I want you, Liam. Emotionally. Physically. All of it. I don't want anything else in the way."

"Are you sure?"

"I've never been more sure about anything in my life, except... maybe my undying, slightly OTT love for Christmas," she teased.

Liam didn't hesitate. He lifted her up. Cassidy wrapped her legs around his waist as he kissed her, deep and slow.

She didn't know exactly what she'd expected—maybe for him to lose control and take her right there on the chocolate shop's counter. Honestly, the image of him lifting her onto the marble surface in her kitchen with melted chocolate nearby was more than a little tempting.

But Liam surprised her.

He took his time.

"Does this mean... you'd be okay if we went upstairs?" he asked, voice low and rough.

"Is that where you'd like to go?"

"Truthfully? I've been fantasizing about you in your bedroom since the tree lighting ceremony."

Cassidy's smile was slow and sure. "Then let's go upstairs."

FORTY-ONE

CASSIDY

Cassidy had never wanted anyone the way she wanted Liam.

She loved the way he looked at her, like she was a gift to be slowly unwrapped. The way he never rushed her or made her feel like she had to be anyone but herself.

She was still learning how to let go. That had always been the hard part.

But she had a feeling Liam wouldn't mind the work.

She could feel his patience in every glance, every touch, like he already knew that her body needed more, that her mind had to be coaxed. Her senses lit up one by one. He didn't ask her to switch off the world. He helped her sink into it.

The bedroom was warm and still, faintly scented with cinnamon and chocolate from downstairs. It felt like stepping into a dream she hadn't let herself hope for.

Liam kissed her again. It was slow and unhurried. Her hands slid beneath his hoodie, beneath his shirt, seeking skin. Heat. The thud of his heart beneath her palms.

More. She wanted more.

She lifted the hoodie over his head, then lifted his shirt, needing him closer. He let her undress him piece by piece, her breath catching as more of him was revealed.

When she reached for the button of his jeans, he stilled.

"Are you sure?" he asked, voice low and steady.

She nodded, her pulse thudding in her ears. "Trust me. I've thought about this... a lot."

Liam stepped out of his jeans. She shivered. Liam was simply a gorgeous man. Broad shoulders, flat abs, and the outline of his boxer briefs left nothing to the imagination. He looked sinfully delicious, and he was all hers.

He moved through this like he already knew the map of her body. Like he'd memorized every slow turn and detour.

Like he understood she wasn't going to fall apart easily. That she needed time. Sensation. Safety.

His knees sank into the bed, and she fell back into the pillows.

She loved the feeling of his weight above her. Her back pressed into the pillows, her body on the soft quilt. Outside the window, snowflakes drifted past the twinkle lights still framing the glass. Inside, her bedroom was quiet. The only sound was that of their breathing and the faint creak of the bed beneath them.

She reached up and traced the muscles on his stomach. He kissed her, slow and deep, his hand cupping the side of her face as he braced himself above her. His touch was sure but unhurried, like he had all the time in the world.

And maybe he did. They'd already said the hard things. And now, there was only this. Only them.

He kissed lower, down the column of her throat, then across her collarbone, making her squirm beneath him. His hand roamed under her oversized Christmas sweater. It was bright pink with Rudolph and a jingle bell nose, and she absolutely loved it. He found the hem of her camisole beneath. He pushed it up slowly, dragging it over her ribs, exposing inches of skin and kissing every one of them.

She tried to sit up, to help undress herself faster, but Liam gently guided her back down.

"Patience," he said. The word alone made her shiver.

He peeled her sweater off carefully, followed by her camisole. Her skin was flushed, her breath uneven, and still he moved with infuriating control. Liam pressed kisses along the curve of her breast, his hand brushing lightly down her side, fingers pausing at the waistband of her candy-cane underwear.

"Still sure?" he asked, voice low and serious.

"If you stop now, I'll kill you."

Liam chuckled against her skin.

He tugged her panties down, over her hips, down her legs, slipping her free until she was bare. Then he looked at her, studied her, like he was trying to memorize every inch of her.

"You're beautiful," he murmured, his voice rough.

Then Liam kissed his way down her body, slowly, until his mouth found the heat between her thighs. She cried out softly, her hands tangling in the quilt, her back arching as his tongue circled her clit, teasing and relentless. When his fingers joined in, she thought she might come apart completely.

But every time she got close, every time she thought that this time would be the first time she'd orgasm with a partner, he pulled back, just enough to keep her right on the edge.

"You're evil," she whispered, breathless.

"That's one word for it," he said, his voice thick with desire.

Cassidy wasn't sure what Liam was doing.

One minute he was devouring her, and the next he was standing, offering her his hand.

"Come here," he whispered, helping her up, guiding her around so she was standing in front of the mirror.

Her heart fluttered as she joined him. She could see herself, fully exposed, Liam close behind her, his gaze locked on her through the mirror.

"I want you to see what I see," he murmured, his breath hot against her damp skin.

He kissed the back of her neck, slow and purposeful, letting his mouth linger at her pulse. She shivered as his hands slid around her torso, rough palms against soft skin, thumbs grazing the underside of her breasts.

Then he touched her properly, cupping her, kneading gently before rolling her nipples between his fingers. She'd never been touched this way. Never stood still and watched herself be wanted.

Her body arched instinctively into his hands. Liam didn't rush. He tugged, circled, pinched just enough to send heat zipping straight to her core. His mouth never left her neck, dragging open-mouthed kisses across it.

She moaned softly, her eyes locked on their reflection. She barely recognized the woman looking back at her. She was flushed, hungry, wild with want. But she loved the way Liam's hands moved over her, demanding, controlling.

She loved being at his mercy. Being the object of his desire.

When he was done with her breasts, his hands drifted lower, skimming her belly, then trailing down to the place she needed him most.

In the mirror, she watched as he parted her with achingly slow precision.

One finger slipped inside, followed by the gentle press of his palm against her clit.

Liam's voice was warm against her ear. "Good girl."

Nerves shot through her body.

She whimpered, her hips rocking forward without conscious thought.

"You like watching what I'm doing to you?"

Her lips parted, but she couldn't speak. The only sound was her breath. It was ragged, unsteady, alive.

He added the slightest pressure with his thumb, and her knees nearly gave out.

"Do you like the way it feels?" he asked, fingers curling just right.

She nodded, barely able to whisper. "Yes... God, yes."

Her knees buckled slightly, and he steadied her with one arm around her waist, never letting her fall. His other hand continued its gentle torment, filling her, circling her, coaxing her body into a rhythm that was uniquely theirs.

She couldn't look away.

In the mirror, she saw her skin flushed, her mouth parted, her nipples peaked from his earlier attention. And behind her, she saw him. His jaw was tight with restraint, eyes burning into hers.

He was watching her watch herself.

The vulnerability of it sent a shiver down her spine... but also something else. Power. She wasn't just reacting; she was part of this. He wasn't performing on her. He was with her, meeting her in this moment.

He kissed the curve of her shoulder, his beard grazing her skin. "You're breathtaking," he murmured. "Every sound you make. Every time your body moves against mine. You have no idea what it does to me."

Her breath hitched as his fingers slid out slowly and then back in, pressing deeper this time, curling just enough to make her legs tremble again.

"Liam..." she whispered, her voice full of need.

He drew her even closer, pressing his hips gently into her from behind, letting her feel his arousal, thick and ready, pressed to the curve of her backside. The heat of him, the weight of him... it made her pulse thrum.

"You're so responsive," he whispered. "So sensitive. And I

want to give you everything. But I need you to stay right here for me... just like this."

His hand moved faster now, not rushed but with intent. She moaned again, louder this time, as pressure built inside her. Her body chased something just out of reach. Her hands found the edge of the dresser for balance, her palms pressing into the cool wood as her thighs began to shake.

"I've got you," he said softly, kissing the back of her neck. "Don't hold back. I want you to fall apart in my hands first."

She whimpered, thighs trembling.

"I don't know how," she choked out. "It never—"

"Don't think," Liam cut in gently, his fingers moving in slow, sure circles. "Just feel."

His lips brushed her ear. "You're safe with me. No one's judging. There's only this..."

He kissed her shoulder.

"Only me..."

Another kiss.

"... and you..."

He curled his fingers just right, and she gasped.

"... and the way you fall apart when I touch you like this."

She let her head fall back onto his shoulder, her hips pushing into his hand, eyes fluttering shut, and then forcing herself to open them again.

Because he'd told her to see what he saw.

And what she saw was a woman on the edge of unraveling, adored by the man behind her.

With every stroke of his fingers, every whispered word, he took her higher until she finally came completely undone.

The orgasm ripped through her like a crashing wave, powerful and raw. She cried out, her fingers digging into the wood, her body jerking, breath catching. Every part of her pulsing, shaking, and she wanted to ride that wave as long as possible.

And through it all, he held her steady.

"That's it," he whispered. "That's my girl."

Her legs nearly gave out again, but he caught her, lifting her carefully into his arms. She buried her face in his neck, still trembling, tears stinging her lashes—not from sadness but from something else. Release. Relief. The overwhelming feeling of being known and wanted, exactly as she was.

He carried her back to the bed, laying her down on the soft quilt. Then, he climbed in beside her, brushing damp hair away from her forehead and kissing her softly.

"How are you feeling?" he asked, voice warm.

She opened her eyes, breathless and still floating. "Like you just rewired my entire nervous system."

He laughed gently, stroking her cheek. "Good."

He then added quietly, "You're everything, Cassidy. Everything."

She reached for him, heart full and body still humming. "Then come here."

FORTY-TWO

LIAM

Wednesday, December 17th

Liam woke the next morning to find Cassidy's side of the bed empty, but he still had a smile on his face.

If anything could make him believe in the magic of Christmas again, it was the look on her face when she'd finally come undone. The memory twitched through his body, heat rising as the images replayed in minute, vivid detail.

He found her downstairs, the radio on, soft Christmas music filling the space. Liam paused at the entrance to the kitchen, leaning against the doorframe, arms crossed, just watching her as she sang about it being cold outside and how she really can't stay.

Cassidy sang, unaware she had an audience, while Liam continued to hum under his breath and watch.

Cassidy wore an apron patterned with little Christmas trees, tied snugly at her waist, her hair twisted into a messy knot. She swayed her hips while whisking chocolate in a large metal bowl tucked beneath one arm. The picture of holiday domestic bliss, and yet he found it completely erotic.

He leaned against the doorway and took a second to memorize the scene. Because all he wanted was to come up behind her, slide his hands around her waist, and whisper everything he planned to do to her if they didn't have a day full of responsibilities waiting.

He cleared his throat and walked forward. "If you keep swaying your hips like that, Sugarplum, I'm going to forget all about work."

She smiled over her shoulder. "You think you can distract me that easily?"

Liam stepped closer, lowering his voice. "I know I can."

She arched a brow. "You clearly underestimate how seriously I take today. There are display lights to test, chocolates to prep, and exactly zero time for your very distracting mouth," she teased, handing him a mug. "Now sit, drink your coffee, and no distractions. I have cocoa to mix up."

"Is that so?" he asked, watching her work.

"It is. I'm testing out flavors for my cocoa Advent calendar," she said, pulling out a Mason jar labeled "Cinnamon Swirl" and setting it next to "Peppermint Bark" and "French Lavender."

He raised an eyebrow. "You made all of those?"

She nodded, a little proudly. "From scratch."

He leaned on the counter, sipping slowly. "What else you got?"

She pointed to the jars as she lined them up. "White Chocolate Snowfall, Gingerbread Spice, and Black Forest Gateau. Kit swears it tastes like chocolate-covered cherries."

Liam took another sip of his coffee, eyes still on her. "You know, most people would've just stuck with regular cocoa."

"Most people don't care as much as I do," she said lightly, but there was something deeper in her voice. She opened the lid of the Gingerbread Spice and inhaled deeply before spooning a bit into a mug.

"You trying to win over the competition or the entire town?"

She shrugged, pouring milk into a saucepan. "Both. Is that so wrong?"

"Not at all." He stepped behind her and kissed her cheek. "Just don't forget to save some of that care for yourself."

She glanced at him over her shoulder. "What do you mean?"

"You're putting all this magic into other people's cups," he said. "Make sure there's still some left for you."

"Maybe I'll make my own, call it Cassidy's Secret Blend."

"Sounds delicious."

She smirked. "Oh, it will be. If you're lucky, I'll let you try it on my light-up night."

He leaned back and grinned. "I'll bring the whipped cream."

FORTY-THREE

CASSIDY

Late afternoon the next day, Cassidy and Liam were trying to decide what they wanted to do after closing up their shops. They had spent plenty of time alone together last night, and the only way she could describe it was as a sexual awakening. She felt herself blooming. The way he coaxed her with those wicked words of his undid something in her. She had never felt more beautiful or desired in her entire life. She wanted to explore that side of herself more. She trusted him. Maybe it was because she knew he was just as vulnerable as she was.

But there were only so many orgasms a woman could have in twenty-four hours. And with her light-up tomorrow night, and everything ready after a lot of hard work, Cassidy wanted to go out first.

"We could go Christmas shopping?" she offered.

Liam closed his eyes. "Not my favorite thing. I know I need to get started with it—"

"Get started? You haven't even started?" She was incredulous.

"Hey, I still have a bit of time. I'm one of those last-minute shoppers. Nothing like a deadline to help me feel inspired."

"So no shopping?"

"Is that alright with you?"

She loved that he was looking to her for her opinion. She knew that if she said she really wanted to go, he'd agree if only to make her happy. Which was exactly why she didn't push it.

"No, you're right. What would you like to do?"

He got a wicked grin and a glint in his eye.

"Other than that," she said with a laugh. She knew better than to playfully push his shoulder because then he'd pull her close and tumble her onto the couch, and then they wouldn't be leaving to go anywhere.

Poor Muff must have been quite shocked by the sounds coming from her bedroom. Cassidy would've felt embarrassed if it had been with anyone else. But no, not with Liam.

The way he talked, the way he worshiped her. The props he used, because really, what else was she supposed to call them? They weren't sex toys, but she blushed thinking about it. Maybe they'd try those too. And a blindfold. She had always wanted to try a blindfold... and obviously something with chocolate...

"I know you're thinking about it," he said.

"Of course I am, but a girl needs air too. Which is why we gotta go—now."

She grabbed her phone and pulled up the town's social media page to find out what else was happening for the Christmas Countdown that night. "What's the Festival of Trees?" she asked.

Liam, who had been scratching Muff behind the ears, stopped. "It's actually not a bad event," he admitted.

"A Christmas event you don't hate? Tell me more."

"The high school on the other side of the lake does a fundraiser where students and community groups can buy a tree spot. They decorate it however they want, then people bid on them. Most of the money goes back to the school, minus the cost of the trees."

"Oh, I like that, but wait..." Cassidy did not need to walk into an allergy nightmare.

"All the trees are artificial," Liam added.

She relaxed. "I say it sounds perfect then."

They decided to take Muff with them. Her pup loved getting out and about in the community, and she and Liam had spent a lot of time indoors. They took Liam's truck, Muff hopping up on the bench seat to sit between them. She wagged her tail and stared out the windshield, her little pink tongue panting and fogging up the glass.

Liam wrapped his arm around the dog, keeping her close. Seeing how affectionate he was with her pup made Cassidy fall in love with him a little more.

The high school parking lot was packed, headlights gleaming off patches of icy snow. Cassidy tugged her coat tighter as she stepped out of the truck, Muff hopping down beside her. Warm light spilled from the gymnasium doors.

"Wow, this is quite the event."

"Wait until you see the trees." Liam guided her forward with a hand on her back. "Some of our locals are really crafty."

"I'm a member of the crafting club, remember?"

"Oh, I remember alright."

Inside, the gym had been transformed into a winter wonderland. The gym perimeter was set up to look like a Christmas tree stand, with black poles and white lights strung across them, crisscrossing the gym. The student orchestra played renditions of Christmas classics from the stage, and the scent of fudge and cookies drifted from the bake sale table near the entrance.

Cassidy's eyes widened. "Oh my gosh... this is amazing."

She couldn't decide where to start as she stared at row after row of artificial Christmas trees, each one decorated to reflect the personality of its sponsor. Some were traditional, decked in red and gold ornaments with shining angels on top. Others went bold. One was covered in neon lights and rubber ducks; another was themed after a retro diner, complete with tinsel milkshakes and vinyl records as ornaments.

"Oh no," Cassidy said dramatically, eyes sweeping the room. "I want them all."

"Why do I feel like you're not joking?"

"Because I'm not," she said, nudging him with her shoulder. "You should be thankful I only have room for three trees."

She wasn't lying. She had the pink one in her living room, a four-foot green one in her bedroom, and a little glass porcelain tree on her kitchen counter.

They wandered through the rows, occasionally pausing to admire clever themes. One tree shimmered in lace and pearls; another featured coastal vibes, with starfish, shells, and sea-glass ornaments.

"If only..." Cassidy said dreamily, taking in the trees.

"Bid on one."

"What?"

"Bid on one."

"Why? I don't have any more room. I suppose I could fit one downstairs in the shop, but I already have the photo backdrop, the train table, and my cocoa stand. I'm not sure where I'd put it."

"Not for you. For me. I don't have a tree."

Her heart melted. "You want a tree? And I get to pick it? You're seriously going to put up a Christmas tree in your house?"

He shrugged. "I've been meaning to get one anyway."

Cassidy wasn't sure if she believed him or not, but she wasn't about to talk him out of a tree.

"Alright then..." She was on a mission now. They walked hand in hand, analyzing each one. Some were too glittery, others too whimsical, and some were downright gaudy. Cassidy couldn't believe she was even thinking that.

But then she found it—a tree that screamed Liam.

It had burlap ribbon, wooden ornaments tied with red ribbon, and pinecones dipped in white. No glitter, nothing flashing, just a simply beautiful tree.

"This one," she whispered.

He tilted his head. "Really?"

"It's all woody and wild, like you." She went up on her tiptoes and kissed his cheek.

Then, before he could beat her to it, she scribbled down a bid and folded the slip before he could peek.

"How much?"

"You'll see."

"That's not how this works."

"It's your Christmas present," she said, slipping the paper into the ballot box.

He tugged on her hand, pulling her forward. "You don't have to do that."

"I don't know, you've been pretty good to me this season," she said, bumping his shoulder as they walked.

They made their way slowly toward the exit, Muff trotting beside them. Outside, snow had begun to fall again in big, fat flakes. She could see them clearly in the fluorescent glow of the parking lot's lights.

There was something about being surrounded by families, laughter, and beautiful trees that made her want to open up to Liam. She wanted him to realize how much he meant to her this year—how special Christmas had been. Her first Christmas in Maple Falls.

They climbed into the truck, Muff settling between them.

"The last two nights? They were everything. I didn't know it could be like that," she said. "You're the only one I've ever been with who's made me, you know..."

"You know I love hearing you say that," he said, voice low and rough as he started the truck.

"Actually, it's all been new."

Liam was about to put the car into drive but stopped. "What do you mean?"

Cassidy promised herself she wouldn't blush. There was nothing to be embarrassed about. "I mean, I've had sex before, but like regular sex. Vanilla sex. Nothing like oral sex or dirty talk... Jean-Paul is the only other guy I've ever been with."

"The only other guy?"

"Why, is that not okay?"

"It's just... Christ."

She felt a chill crawl across her skin.

"Liam?"

He shook his head, as if trying to clear it. "Cass, I didn't know... I shouldn't have assumed you were comfortable with everything."

"What?"

"All of it," he said quietly. "The stuff in the kitchen. Upstairs. The mirror. The way I talked to you. I thought... I guess I just figured you'd tell me if I was going too far."

"I would've," she said quickly. "Liam, I wanted all of that."

"Did you, though?" he asked, finally looking at her. "Or did you just not know how to say no?"

Her stomach twisted. "That's not fair."

"I'm not trying to accuse you," he said, voice tight. "I just... You're still figuring out who you are, Cassidy. What you like. What you want. And I've been treating you like you already know. Like you've done this before. And maybe that wasn't fair of me."

"I do know what I want," she said, her voice shaking now. "I want you."

He looked at her like he didn't believe her.

"You're not a mistake," she whispered.

"But what if I become one?" he asked. "What if I'm rushing you into something you'll regret?"

She shook her head, tears burning now. "I haven't regretted a single second."

But it didn't matter. She could see it in his face—he wasn't hearing her. He was stuck in his own head, tangled up in guilt and doubt.

And just like that, the warmth between them turned brittle.

"Let's go," he said after a beat. "I'll drive you home."

Cassidy nodded, but her heart ached.

FORTY-FOUR

LIAM

Liam knew Cassidy was looking for some kind of reassurance on the drive home, but he couldn't give it to her.

Instead, he gripped the steering wheel like it was the only thing keeping him grounded and kept his eyes fixed on the road, pretending the patches of ice demanded his full attention. The truck's heater hummed low, fighting against the cold that had settled in their clothes from the walk across the snow-dusted parking lot. He turned the radio on, hoping it would fill the silence between them.

The same holiday station that had played on the way to the Festival of Trees was still on, only now it was Bing Crosby crooning "Have Yourself a Merry Little Christmas." The irony wasn't lost on him.

Outside, Maple Falls was washed in the soft glow of Christmas lights strung across porches and storefronts, twinkling like tiny stars against the snowy streets, already dark in the early evening. Neighborhood houses were decked in long strands of colored bulbs, some blinking in cheerful patterns, others glowing steadily in warm golds and soft whites. Icicle lights dripped from eaves, looking fragile and delicate dangling above the snowbanks below, while inflatable snowmen and Santa Clauses swayed gently with each gust of wind.

None of it helped ease Liam's mind.

He couldn't help it. His mind was replaying the last twenty-four hours—not a highlight reel of passion, but a slow, creeping worry that he'd pushed her too far. The way she had trembled and moaned, how she'd come undone for him again and again. It had felt like shared desire in the moment. But now? Now he couldn't stop wondering:

What if it was too much, too fast?

What if she didn't know how to say stop?

He thought about what she'd told him—how she had frozen when Jean-Paul kissed her. How she'd stayed with a narcissist for three years. Liam refused to ever put her in a position like that again.

He prided himself on being someone people could trust, especially her. Especially the woman he was starting to imagine a future with. But now, the idea that he might have unintentionally pressured her? It wrecked him.

Yes, she'd said she wanted it. Every time. But maybe she'd just been trying to keep up. Maybe he hadn't listened hard enough. He'd been focused on her pleasure, but he couldn't deny that his ego had loved it too. That it had done something to him, knowing he could unravel her like that.

But Cassidy... she wasn't just anyone.

How could a woman so beautiful, so smart, so full of life and light, have only ever been with someone like Jean-Paul?

Liam had fallen for her fast. He could admit that now. He wanted her, in every way, but she didn't need someone like him rushing in, piling intensity on top of intimacy before she'd even figured out what she wanted.

That was why she'd made the vow.

It wasn't just about saying no to men; it was about finding herself again. And she'd been smart to make that vow. She needed space to learn what she liked, what she craved, what felt good on her own terms.

Not what he gave her.

Not what he thrust onto her.

His jaw clenched. His desire for her ran deep—too deep. And it terrified him.

She wasn't a prize to be won.

She was a woman who deserved more.

And yet again, he wasn't sure he was what she needed.

Even Muff seemed to pick up on the tension in the truck, glancing between Liam and Cassidy like she was trying to make sense of what was happening.

"Come here, girl," Cassidy said, patting her lap. The pup scooted closer with a soft whine, resting her head on her thigh.

Thankfully, the drive from the high school back to downtown was short. Liam pulled into a parallel spot right in front of the shop and shifted the truck into park.

Cassidy hesitated. "Do you want to come in?" she asked softly.

He let out a slow breath, still looking at the windshield. "Sorry, but not tonight."

She didn't budge. "I'm not just going to get out of the truck and pretend like everything's fine. Didn't you just say you were going to stop keeping things to yourself? That you'd tell me what you're feeling instead of shutting down?"

He was caught off guard by her calling him out—but she wasn't wrong. He turned to face her, jaw tense.

"I'm uncomfortable."

Her eyes widened. She clearly hadn't expected that.

"Things have happened... fast. Intense. And I think we need to slow down."

"Slow down?" Cassidy repeated, her voice sharp.

He could already feel the heat rising between them. He didn't want to make things worse.

"You asked me to be honest, and I am. I'm not saying this to hurt you, Cassidy. I'm saying it because I care. But if you're going to twist it into something else—if we're about to fight about this—I can't. Not right now. Can we just... talk later?"

Cassidy shook her head, stunned. "Yeah. Sure. Whatever."

She opened the door and climbed out, Muff hopping down behind her. The only thing colder than the air was her voice.

Liam didn't blame her. But he had to believe he was protecting her—protecting them both.

He didn't flinch when she slammed the truck door.

But he did wait.

He sat in silence, watching until she and Muff were safely inside the shop, the front door clicking shut behind them, before easing off the brake and pulling slowly away from the curb.

FORTY-FIVE

CASSIDY

Cassidy was too restless to just sit in her apartment. She could use a drink, but there was no way she was going to the Kettle. Knowing her luck, that's exactly where Liam would go, and she couldn't guarantee she wouldn't cause a scene.

She still couldn't figure out how everything had gone so sideways so fast. One minute she was trying to tell him how happy she was, how seen and alive she felt, and the next, he was telling her they needed to slow down. Their communication was so off-track it was laughable.

Cassidy started to think that things would never work between the two of them. They were just too different. They couldn't seem to stay on the same page for more than a few days.

She pulled out her phone and called Zoe. It was either that or make a vat of hot cocoa and binge Christmas movies, but she was too keyed up for that.

"Are you free?" Cassidy asked without preamble.

"If by free do you mean am I making thirty centerpieces for the Clawson wedding this weekend? Then yeah, I'm free."

Cassidy groaned. "Never mind."

"No, I'm kidding. I mean, I do have the centerpieces to finish, but what's going on?" Cassidy could hear the snip of Zoe's floral scissors in the background.

"I do not understand men," Cassidy said, flopping onto her couch.

"Uh-oh. This is about Liam, isn't it?"

Cassidy sat up. "Is there any other man in this town that drives me crazy?"

"No?" Zoe guessed with a laugh. "What did he do?"

"He put the brakes on, that's what he did. And now I'm too restless to sit still. I was hoping you wanted to hang out."

"Want to walk down to the shop and help me with these? I have all this red ribbon and holly..."

"It's a Christmas-themed wedding? You're killing me." Cassidy sighed dramatically.

She'd always dreamed of a Christmas wedding with a strapless white satin dress, beaded bodice, maybe even a velvet inlay. She still had a page ripped from a bridal magazine tucked somewhere in an old journal. She used to dream about that day.

But then she thought about Liam and how much he hated Christmas. It would almost be comical if it wasn't so depressing.

"Please?" Zoe begged as if she'd been the one to call. "I could really use some extra hands..."

"Alright, alright. I'm coming down," Cassidy said, grabbing her coat before she could change her mind. "Care if I bring Muff?"

"No, of course not. Whiskers is upstairs," she said, referencing her gray Maine Coon kitty. "I'll prep the front window seat for her."

"Okay, we're on our way."

The outside of Zoe's flower shop had a large bay window. The corners were frosted by nature, framing a gorgeous seasonal display of white and red poinsettias tucked into birch bark vases, twinkling twinkle lights woven through fresh evergreen garlands, and a hand-painted sign that read, "Let Love Bloom—Even in Winter."

Cassidy dropped Muff's leash after stepping inside.

"Come over here, girl," Zoe said, luring Muff to her window seat with a dog biscuit.

"You thinking of getting a dog?" Cassidy asked, eyeing the treats.

"What? No, Whiskers would kill me." She shook her head. "I was helping Kallie at the pet shop. She wants to make homemade dog treats and sell them. They're loads better than the commercial ones, and you know me, the more natural the better."

The pup sniffed around for a minute before taking up residence in Zoe's window seat as promised.

Cassidy inhaled deeply, letting the scent of pine and eucalyptus calm her. A rustic wooden counter ran along the back third of the shop, covered with ribbons, shears, spools of floral wire, and mugs of tea in varying degrees of fullness. Chalkboard signs labeled galvanized buckets brimming with winter blooms such as white amaryllis, snowy roses, deep-red ranunculus, blue thistle, and soft-green eucalyptus.

The shop had a small corner devoted to custom bouquet wrapping, with kraft paper, silk ribbons, and gift tags that read "For You," "Winter Wishes," and "Just Because."

Zoe was adding a sprig of holly and sugared berries each to an array of vases.

"These are gorgeous," said Cassidy. The centerpieces had red roses in the center, with evergreen, holly, and sugared berries tucked around them. The round glass vases were tied with red satin ribbon.

"Thanks. Five done, only twenty-five more to go." Zoe beamed.

Cassidy rolled up her sleeves. "Just tell me what you need me to do."

A little while later, after Cassidy had tied all the ribbons, she sat on a barstool in Zoe's flower shop, pizza in one hand, a glass of red wine in the other, watching her friend fuss over a bouquet of red roses.

"Alright, enough with work. Now, do you want to tell me what's going on with you and Liam?"

Cassidy finished chewing the bite. "I'd love to, but you don't want to hear about his ding-dong, so..."

"Don't suppose you could skip over his ding-dong?" Zoe asked hopefully.

"'Fraid not. It's literally the crux of the problem."

"Fine, fine," Zoe said, waving a pair of scissors in her direction. "What's so important about Liam's ding-dong that's got your whole relationship messed up?"

Cassidy wiped her hands with a napkin. "All I was trying to do was tell him how good things have been between us. How he's opened my eyes, if you know what I'm saying."

Zoe tilted her head. "Not really."

"I told Liam I've only ever been with Jean-Paul, and Jean-Paul never did anything like what Liam does." Cassidy's cheeks flushed. "Zoe... he's like a sex god. He's wicked with his mouth, his fingers, those dirty words of his. Plus, I'll never be able to look at a scarf the same way again."

Cassidy clenched her fist, trying to suppress the heat rushing to her face.

Zoe held up a hand. "Okay, okay! I get it. He's good."

Cassidy let out a dreamy sigh. "Like really good. I feel like a completely different woman with him. There's this whole other side of me I didn't even know existed. And when I started to tell him that, he shut down. He thinks he's pushing me too fast or that I'm just going along with things I wouldn't normally want."

"Are you?" Zoe asked carefully. "Doing things you didn't want to do?"

"No!" Cassidy said, a little too loudly. She lowered her voice. "I loved all of it. I don't even care how that makes me sound. I tried to tell him that, but he didn't believe me. Or maybe he didn't want to believe me. I honestly think *he's* scared. So now he says we should slow down."

Cassidy reached for another slice of pizza.

"Don't throw your pizza at me," Zoe said, "but if you do think Liam is scared, and he's asking you to slow down, what's so wrong with that?"

Cassidy opened her mouth, ready to fire back, but shut it. That wasn't the question she'd expected.

"He's not saying it's too much for him; he's putting it on me," Cassidy said after a moment. "He's making me the one who isn't ready. Like I can't know what I want. And I just don't think that's fair. If he's the one freaking out, then he should say that. Own that. Don't try to spin it like he's doing me a favor."

Zoe leaned back, considering. "Okay, I'll give you that."

"Thank you! And no, I'm not throwing pizza at you. This stuff's too good." Cassidy took a big bite of her veggie lover's slice—black and green olives, peppers, mushrooms, onions, and bubbling cheese. It was her favorite combo, comfort food at its finest.

"You know this time of year is hard for him," Zoe said gently. "Maybe you guys should just pick things up again in the new year. Give it a little breathing room."

Cassidy sighed, leaning back against the counter. "Yeah. Maybe we should. I just... I don't know."

Cassidy stared at the ceiling, her heart caught somewhere between disappointment and longing. Part of her wanted to scream, *Why does it always have to be this hard?* But another part—quieter, more vulnerable—still clung to the way Liam looked at her when he thought she wasn't watching. The way he touched her like she mattered. The way, just days ago, he made her feel more seen than she'd ever felt in her life.

But now? He was backing off. Calling things "too fast." As if she didn't know her own mind. As if her desire, her joy, and her very self were something to second-guess.

Maybe Zoe was right. Maybe a break would give them both space. But Cassidy didn't want space. She wanted him. And worse, she'd started to believe she could have him. That this town, this business, this weird, wonderful, cozy life she was building could include Liam.

Now, she wasn't so sure.

The warmth of the room, the soft instrumental carols playing in the background, the scent of the flower shop, none of it soothed the ache in her chest.

Zoe opened her mouth to speak again, but before she could, Muff started barking and jumping around the room.

"Muff, knock that off!" Cassidy stood, not wanting Muff to knock over something of Zoe's. Her pup rarely went nuts when people walked by, which was one of her most endearing traits. It would be hard to own a business if your dog went crazy every time she heard a noise or a strange voice.

But Muff was not listening, paws up on the window, barking like crazy at whatever was outside.

Muff's barks were followed by a loud *CRASH*.

Both women were now on their feet.

They rushed to the window. Outside, one of the large planters had been knocked over, its ceramic base shattered across the icy sidewalk. Winter greenery spilled out across the snow.

Cassidy yanked the door open, but the street was empty. The only noise was the sound of a dog barking in the distance.

"How is that possible?" Zoe asked, looking up and down the street.

Cassidy folded her arms tightly against her chest. "I have no idea, but this has to stop. Now."

Zoe looked at the determined glint in her eye. "What are you going to do?"

"I'm setting up security cameras. And we're going to catch this Gingerbread Jerk once and for all."

FORTY-SIX

LIAM

Thursday, December 18th

Liam had opened up the farm shop for any evening gift shoppers and was keeping busy at his counter, doing a poor job of pretending he wasn't watching Cassidy across the street. She had come back to the Cocoa Corner and was stringing the last row of lights along the edge of her shop awning, or maybe she was moving the lights out of the way? He wasn't sure exactly what she was doing, but she had moved the ladder under the awning at least five times. Tomorrow was her big light-up event, and she was clearly determined to make it perfect.

Snowflakes clung to her red beret, but she didn't seem to care. Just like she didn't seem to care if Liam was watching her.

Liam shook his head, wondering if he had made a mistake earlier that evening. He missed her already, and it had nothing to do with the sex. Although, that had been mind-blowing. It was everything else. The way she hummed when she stirred her cocoa, the way she smiled so warmly at everyone who came into her shop. The way she looked at him, like he was someone worth loving.

He'd had that, had her, and then he'd pulled away.

Mrs. Bishop was browsing the shelves, holding up a scarf in one hand and a bundle of evergreen-scented candles in the other. She'd been in the store for a bit. Liam had done his part, asking if she needed any help. When she'd insisted she didn't, he'd gone back to his sketch pad that he kept under the desk.

He didn't need to think. Didn't even need to see a picture. He just drew. His pencil traced the curve of her cheek. Shaded in the knots on her braid. He gave her a peppermint-striped scarf that she hadn't worn since last week, and he smiled without realizing, adding the faintest smudge of chocolate to her cheek. Because, of course, she had chocolate on her cheek.

Mrs. Bishop approached the counter, and he quickly flipped the sketch pad closed.

"Find everything you need?"

"Oh yes, you have some lovely gifts."

Liam had made sure to go all out, offering a little bit of everything. His favorites were the Rustic Winter Jam Trio with mini jars of cranberry pear, spiced apple butter, and bourbon cherry jam packaged in a wooden crate. And the Hot Honey & Cheese Pairing Set. It included a jar of his family's signature hot honey, a wedge of aged local Cheddar, and rosemary crackers, all tied with twine and a sprig of pine.

His personal life might be a mess, but when it came to this shop, he knew exactly what he was doing—simmer pot kits, DIY wax ornaments, a reusable winter market tote featuring a hand-drawn sketch of Maple Falls; Liam wanted his shop to represent the heart of the town.

He went to tell Mrs. Bishop thank you when he spotted the Team Cassidy sweater peeking out from under her unzipped coat.

He replied with a small, involuntary grunt instead.

"Nothing personal," she said brightly, catching the look on

his face. "I just think the children's hospital is a really good cause. I've already donated to your family's llama sanctuary. And Cassidy really is the sweetest thing."

He nodded without meeting her eye, wrapping her purchases and sliding the items into a brown paper gift bag.

"You're right, she is."

After Mrs. Bishop left, Liam slipped his sketch pad out and got back to work, adding wisps of hair framing her face, an extra sparkle to her eye.

The bell jingled overhead, and Liam cursed softly, closing the pad a beat too late. Zach stepped inside, stomping snow off his boots, and gave him a look. "Drawing her now, huh?" he said, arching a brow.

He scowled. "Don't start."

It was too late. That was the only reason Zach had stopped over in the first place.

"I haven't seen you around much the last couple of days," Zach said, glancing at the empty shop. "What've you been up to?"

"Work," Liam replied, opening the inventory software on the computer. He might as well check and see how many jams he needed to order.

"Ah, of course. Work," Zach replied sarcastically. "Takes a lot out of you, doesn't it?"

"Sure does." Liam kept his eyes trained on the computer screen. "Do you need something?"

"Just wondering how long you plan on acting like an ass."

That got Liam's attention. "Who said I was acting like an ass?" He expected Zach to say Zoe. Or Madison. Maybe even Kit.

"Cassidy. She told me I should come over and smack some sense into you."

"She did not."

"No," Zach admitted, "but she did ask my advice. She was wondering how much space to give you. That part required a little explaining... You want some advice?" Zach asked.

"No," Liam replied flatly.

"Excellent, 'cause I never wanted your advice either, but here you have it—talk to her."

Liam sighed and rubbed the back of his neck. "I don't know what to say. I'm not even sure that I'm wrong."

"What do you mean?"

"She's been through a lot. I'm not sure if you knew about it, but after that French asshole, she made this vow: no dating, no men, just time to figure herself out. I respected it, or tried to." His jaw tightened. "She came to me, Zach. She told me she was tired of letting Jean-Paul's shadow control her. She wanted to take her life back. She wanted to break her 'no men for the year' vow—on her terms. All in. Physically, emotionally, everything."

Zach studied him. "And what did you do?"

Liam let out a breath, shaking his head. "I let her. I went there with her." His voice dropped, rough with feeling. "Wouldn't you?"

He paused, staring past Zach toward the snow-covered sidewalks outside.

"I thought everything was good. Better than good. There's something about her that just snaps something loose in me. Makes me want to give her everything. But I didn't realize how new all of it was to her. How little experience she really had."

Zach folded his arms. "So now you think Cassidy doesn't know herself? Doesn't know what she wants?"

Liam hesitated. "I just... I don't want to be another guy she goes along with. She's got a history of choosing people who don't treat her right. I didn't want her to feel like she had to say yes to something just because I wanted it."

Zach raised a brow. "I'll give you that, but maybe that's how she used to be. But the Cassidy I know? She knows you hate

Christmas and still parades around here full of jolly and holly like an elf at the North Pole. She knows you despise Christmas music, and she still sings carols whether you're in the room or not."

He leaned in slightly. "She's not changing who she is to make you happy. She's being herself. All she's asking is that you accept her as is. And from the looks of things, you already have. If anyone's not being fully honest in this equation, it might be you."

Liam let the words settle. Zach wasn't wrong.

Cassidy hadn't changed, not once. Sure, there'd been that one time she'd worn a boring beige sweater, but that was it. She still showed up with tinsel tangled in her hair and glittery snowflake tattoos on her cheeks. Her Christmas sweater collection was enough to give Santa secondhand embarrassment. And despite her tiny apartment, she had three Christmas trees.

She sang "Baby It's Cold Outside" while she stirred chocolate. She wore candy-cane-striped pajamas and, God help him, coordinating panties.

"Something tells me," Zach said, standing up straight again, "you owe someone an apology."

Liam exhaled, long and low, but he didn't say a word.

Zach grinned. "Good talk, man. I'll catch up with you later."

Liam didn't answer.

The bell over the door jingled behind him, but Liam stayed still, surrounded by the scent of cedar and beeswax and regret.

Outside, Cassidy had taken a step back. She was admiring her handiwork, and knowing her, she still wouldn't think it was enough.

He opened his sketch pad. The drawing was rough but unmistakably her with eyes bright, striped scarf, and the cocoa on her cheek. He traced the corner of the page with his thumb.

It had only been a few hours, and he still missed her so much.

He kept turning things over in his head, second-guessing everything he'd said, wondering if there was any way to make things right.

FORTY-SEVEN

LIAM

Late that night, with the stars crowding the sky and a thin crescent moon hanging low, Liam went for a walk down Oak Way. The street, usually buzzing with chatter and foot traffic, had gone quiet. Not silent exactly. He could still hear the scrape of a snow shovel in the distance, a car engine starting, muffled laughter as a couple hurried down the sidewalk, but there was a hush settling in. It was the kind of hurried silence that came before a snowstorm hit. People wanted to run their errands and get home before the roads became too bad.

Liam didn't mind. He liked having the street to himself. He'd spent the whole evening thinking about what Zach had said, and the worst part was, he knew his friend was right.

But that didn't mean he could just walk over to Cassidy's and blurt out an apology. He didn't want to tell her how sorry he was. He wanted to show her. To find a way that would mean something.

But still, doubt crept in. *Maybe she's already asleep. Maybe she doesn't want to see me. Maybe I should give her more time.*

He walked on, looking at the icicles glittering under the streetlights, listening to the snow crunching underfoot and hearing nothing but silence.

At the end of the street, the town Christmas tree shimmered. Somehow, Liam found himself standing in front of it, looking up at the star on top, quietly asking for guidance.

Or maybe, just maybe, for a little of that Christmas magic to rub off on him.

Liam chuckled softly, scratching the back of his neck the way he always did when he felt unsure. Before Cassidy had come into his life, you would've never caught him talking to a Christmas tree star, but here he was.

"There's this girl," he said aloud, voice low and a little hoarse. "I care about her. A lot. More than I think I've let myself admit. And I keep screwing it up."

He sighed before he went on. "She's got this way about her. Lights up a room without even trying."

He paused, eyes still fixed on the star.

"And now I've gone and hurt her. Again. Backed off when I should've leaned in. Said the wrong thing. Hell, maybe I'm the wrong guy. But she makes me feel like maybe I could be something better. Someone better."

The wind picked back up, blowing down the street, carrying the scent of freshly fallen snow and something that felt a little like hope.

"I don't know if you grant wishes or give second chances," Liam said quietly. "But I could use both."

Taking a deep breath, he let the icy air fill his lungs. It was sharp and clean, a brisk kind of cold that made him feel awake, maybe even a little brave.

Then he turned and walked toward the Cocoa Corner.

Her Cocoa & Kisses-themed photo booth was cloaked in heavy black fabric, as were her front windows. She clearly wasn't taking any chances with last-minute sabotage.

Liam respected that. But... could it really hurt to take a peek?

He crouched down and gently lifted the corner of the cloth, curious. He was proud of her, of everything she'd created. He couldn't wait to see the final display in all its glowing glory.

That's when his foot hit a slick patch of ice.

His boot skidded and his arms flailed. He grabbed the first thing his fingers landed on, which was the display.

The brace he'd built cracked, and he went down hard, the heavy fabric going with him. He landed flat on his back with the display on top of him.

Liam groaned, trying to take a breath. The wind had been knocked out of him and his hamstring screamed in protest. His pride didn't fare much better.

He sat up slowly, wincing, lifting the display off him, thinking maybe Cassidy wasn't the only one around here prone to clumsy missteps.

Thankfully, the main backdrop wasn't broken, just the supporting brace. He could fix that.

He was still untangling himself from the fabric when Cassidy ran through the door, fire extinguisher in hand, pointed at his face like she was ready to do some damage.

Liam went to put his hands up in surrender, but doing so meant letting go of the display. It pitched forward. He dropped his hands to keep it from falling.

"Liam? No! It can't be. You're the Gingerbread Jerk?"

"What? No, of course not," he said quickly. "That doesn't even make any sense. Do you think I'd trash my own display? And I wasn't even here when that happened." He tried to keep her backdrop from falling over, but it definitely needed a new bracket. "I was just trying to see how it all turned out. I slipped on some ice."

"You set off my cameras..."

"Cameras?"

"You didn't know I had them, did you?" Cassidy's eyes narrowed, and she leveled the hose of the canister at his face.

He stepped back. "Are you crazy?" That probably wasn't the smartest thing to say, but he couldn't believe the way she was looking at him. "I wasn't trying to destroy anything. I just wanted to look at it. I know how hard you've worked."

"I'm not so sure I believe you," she said coldly.

That stung. "Seriously? Just because I said I wanted to slow things down doesn't mean I'm out here sabotaging your shop. You know I'm not like that."

"Do I?" Her voice cracked slightly. "Do I even know you at all?"

The words hit him like a punch to the chest.

"Never mind," she said, shaking her head and stepping back. "I'm not having this conversation right now. My brother's coming into town tomorrow, and I've got a hundred things to do. I'm exhausted. I need sleep. So, if you don't mind, cover it back up and go home. I'll fix it in the morning."

She turned without waiting for a response.

Liam stood there a moment longer, the cold sinking through his jeans, the sharp ache of regret crawling deeper. So much for apologizing. So much for making things right.

Things weren't just bad; they were worse than ever.

FORTY-EIGHT
CASSIDY

"Wait, you caught him red-handed?" Madison looked unconvinced, eyebrows raised as she curled her hands around her travel mug of coffee. She'd brought it with her on the walk down from the inn, steam still rising from the lid.

Even though it was late, Cassidy had invited Madison, Zoe, and Kit over for emergency hot chocolate and a Christmas movie. After what had happened with Liam, she needed something, anything, to pull her back into a festive headspace.

The snow had started to fall down in thick, puffy flakes. It wasn't just flurrying anymore. These flakes were thick and heavy, the kind that stuck to everything they touched. Cassidy watched as they piled on the rooftops and drifted into soft mounds along the sidewalk. It was beautiful, sure, but also the kind of snow that could either turn the town into a winter wonderland or keep people curled up inside. She just hoped it added a little magic to her display—and didn't scare folks off before tomorrow's big light-up event.

Madison was wearing soft black leggings, an oversized cable-knit sweater in deep forest green, and cozy wool socks. Kit had shown up in holiday pajama shorts with gingerbread men on them, even though it was freezing out, and her Team Cassidy sweater. Zoe had brought her peppermint tea with her, along with her fuzzy slippers in the shape of foxes. But Cassidy was probably the coziest of all. She wore her vintage candy-cane-striped pajama pants, a graphic sweatshirt with a reindeer sipping cocoa on the front, and red fuzzy socks. Muff was curled up beside her like a warm blanket.

"I mean, what else was he doing?" Cassidy asked, still stewing.

"Maybe he was telling the truth," Zoe offered gently. "Maybe he really was just curious," she said while casually eating popcorn.

"Or sabotaging it," Cassidy grumbled.

"Do you think he'd do that?" Zoe's question was directed at Madison.

"No, and Cassidy doesn't either." Madison put her mug on the coffee table and gave Cassidy a level stare. "You know he'd never do something like that. You're just mad about him running away."

Cassidy didn't respond. Madison always had a way of cutting to the truth, and Cassidy hated how much it stung. Yes, she was mad. Mad that Liam had pulled away. Mad that he blamed it on her.

She'd been waiting for him to make the first move. And apparently, that first move had been sneaking around her display at night. It rattled her. She was already on edge with all the vandalism. She couldn't afford to have her hard work ruined before the light-up.

The movie played on in the background, some cutesy couple decorating a tree with matching flannel pajamas and suspiciously perfect hair. Cassidy stared at the screen but wasn't really watching.

Alright, so it had been her turn to overreact. She could admit that, if only to herself. And she got that Madison was annoyed with her. She probably should've thought it through a bit more before she'd invited Liam's childhood friends over to complain about him.

Cassidy was about to ask the group what she should do next when an alarm cut through the air.

BEEP. BEEP. BEEP.

The security alert on Cassidy's phone made all four women jump.

Kit spilled her cocoa. Zoe dropped the popcorn bowl. Madison grabbed the remote, fumbling to pause the movie as Cassidy lunged for her phone.

"It's the camera," Cassidy said, heart in her throat.

They all rushed to the screen as she pulled up the app.

It felt like forever for the screen to load. For a second, the feed was all shadows and snowfall.

Until...

"Oh, come on," Kit said, peering over Cassidy's shoulder. "Is that...?"

"A raccoon," Madison confirmed.

"Not just one," Zoe added, counting the number of critters on her screen. "It's a whole crazy trash panda family."

On screen, the fuzzy bandits scampered across Cassidy's front display. Two of them climbed over the edge of her Cocoa & Kisses photo booth, treating it like a jungle gym. Another pawed its way up the side of the window, using the eavestrough like monkey bars.

Muff must have sensed the commotion because a moment later, she started barking like crazy. She ran over and put her paws on the window ledge, barking, pawing at the glass, desperate to chase the intruders away.

Cassidy stared in disbelief as the raccoons tackled her display again. One launched itself from the wooden backdrop to the window ledge and then scurried up onto the roof. Another followed close behind, their tiny claws scrabbling as they disappeared out of sight. In a matter of seconds, they'd unstrung half her lights and almost broken her backdrop.

She shuddered to think what might have happened if Muff hadn't gone berserk.

"Well," Madison said, folding her arms tightly across her chest. Her gaze didn't soften as it landed on Cassidy. "Looks like Liam was telling the truth."

Cassidy winced. "I know. I-I need to apologize."

"You think?" Madison's voice sharpened.

Kit sucked in her breath.

Cassidy knew Madison loved Liam like a brother, and she was not happy with Cassidy for hurting her friend. She got that.

Cassidy's stomach twisted. She didn't have a defense. Not one that would make sense. Not when Madison was right. She'd let her hurt speak louder than her trust.

"I didn't mean to," she said quietly. "I was just... upset."

Madison's arms stayed crossed, her voice sharp. "Being upset doesn't give you the right to hurt people. Especially not someone like Liam."

"He hurt me too, you know. He pushed me away first. I just reacted."

That gave Madison pause.

Cassidy's voice dropped to a whisper. "I'll make it right. I love him."

Madison's expression faltered, softening at the edges. "You love him?" she asked, voice lower now.

Cassidy nodded. "More than I've ever loved anyone. That's why it hurts so much."

Madison sighed, arms slowly uncrossing. "Liam's not

perfect. He's stubborn, and when he gets scared, he shuts down. But you're right. He pushed you away." She looked Cassidy in the eye. "So go tell him that. Tell him you love him. Tell him you're not scared. And this time, don't let him run."

She would.

But not tonight.

Tonight, Cassidy needed a moment to collect herself, to let her thoughts settle. Her emotions had been a mess lately. That was nothing new when it came to Liam. They'd always had this strange mix of tension and chemistry, equal parts competition and connection.

And now, with part of her display needing to be rebuilt, she just wanted to focus. She needed quiet. Some clarity. Then she'd find Liam and make things right.

Because deep down, she'd never truly believed he was the one behind the sabotage. Madison had seen it too and called her out on it. Cassidy had let her frustration speak louder than her heart. She'd been hurt when he had pulled back from her, confused by his sudden shift.

But she wasn't scared of what they were becoming. Not anymore.

She needed him to know that.

She liked what they were doing together. She liked how it felt to be with him, how safe he made her feel when things got messy. No one had ever taken the time to learn her the way Liam had. No one had ever made her feel so comfortable in her own skin.

So she hated that Liam had said he was uncomfortable. But deep down she knew it was because he cared about her and he didn't understand that she was ready for this. That he was the right man for her.

Being with him had felt more natural than anything else in her life.

She didn't want to hold back. Not now. Not with him.

Liam helped her feel things she'd spent years pushing down. He made her want more, not just passion, but presence. A real connection.

And she needed him to know that she was finally ready for it.

FORTY-NINE

CASSIDY

Cassidy was lucky. The raccoons hadn't caused any permanent damage, and it only took her about thirty minutes to fix everything. Thankfully, she'd had the foresight to cover her front window with a heavy drape, saving her hand-painted mural. And she had plenty of extra light clips on hand to replace the ones those little bandits had broken. Even the weather seemed to be on her side—the snowstorm had passed by morning, and Julian and Miles arrived right on time.

"Cass, this is amazing," her brother-in-law said, pulling her into a tight hug the moment she opened the door to the Cocoa Corner. He was dressed in a bright red sports jacket that matched the frames of his glasses and a pair of slim-fit jeans. Julian followed close behind in black dress pants and matching wool coat. He didn't say anything at first. He just looked around the shop in quiet awe, his eyes wide.

She hadn't realized how much his opinion mattered to her until that very moment. She wanted him to see the dream she'd been chasing, to understand why she'd taken such a leap to do this on her own.

"This is amazing, Cass. You're incredible," Julian finally said, grinning at her. And just like that, the knot in her stomach loosened.

Julian and Miles took a delighted Muff for a walk through the snow-dusted streets of downtown while Cassidy worked on her display. The pup absolutely loved it of course, and when they got back, the little fluffball curled up on a cushion behind the counter, paws twitching in a dream.

She was adjusting the lights on her window when the bell over the door jingled and Julian stepped back inside after another wander round town. He shivered, his nose red from the cold.

"We went to the most amazing farm shop," he said, taking his stocking cap off. "It's right across the street. Have you been in there?"

Before she could answer, Miles barreled in behind him, holding a brown paper bag like it was a precious artifact. "Cass, that place is incredible. It's got everything. And it's all local. I mean, look at this!"

He started pulling out goodies like he was doing a show-and-tell.

"Hot honey infused with chili flakes. It smells insane," he said, holding up a small glass jar with a rustic black-and-gold label. "And look, cranberry orange jam. He makes it in-house. The hot guy behind the counter said it sells out every weekend."

He reached in again. "Oh! And these. Peppermint-dusted chocolate bark? Handmade. I already had a piece."

Julian shot him a mock glare. "You opened it without me?"

"I was hungry," Miles said, unapologetic. "Also? I got this balsam fir soy candle that smells like an actual Christmas tree, and one of those beeswax lip balms with the cinnamon oil. My lips have never felt this hydrated."

Cassidy wanted to say that she knew all about Liam's shop. That she'd been in there dozens of times, but that wasn't true. She'd only stepped foot in there—once. And she hadn't stayed more than five minutes.

How was that possible?

Her own shop was such a big part of her; surely his was the same. And she still hadn't apologized to him. But she would. Tonight. She promised herself that no matter what happened, she'd make things right. Maybe he wouldn't forgive her, but at least everything would be out in the open.

Two hours later, it was showtime.

Outside, Mayor Bloomfield was setting up with his microphone, and Elsie was livestreaming the event.

"Have you seen how many likes and followers we've picked up?" Elsie asked Cassidy excitedly.

"No..." Cassidy looked over at the screen. A hundred people were watching, with the number steadily climbing by the second.

She turned the camera onto Cassidy.

Cassidy played along and waved. Miles joined her.

"What page is this?" he asked Elsie once the camera was off of him.

"I'm TheMidwesternGirl—but I'm streaming this one from the Maple Falls town page."

Miles smiled. "I think I've seen some of your content. Pretty sure I've commented on a few."

Elsie tilted her head. "Yeah? What's your handle?"

"NYCChocolate," Miles said casually.

Elsie's jaw dropped. "Wait—you're *the* NYCChocolate?"

Miles looked pleased. "You've heard of me?"

"You're like... famous!" she said, wide-eyed. "I love your behind-the-scenes chocolate videos. Everything you post looks amazing."

Cassidy stared at her brother-in-law, stunned. She'd had no idea he had an Instagram page. But then again, she never spent much time on social media. She knew she had to step up her social posting for the Cocoa Corner, but her focus had been on laying down the roots of her business in the real world, here in Maple Falls.

"I started it after you left," Miles explained. "No face shots —just my hands and the chocolate. It's done amazing things for our business."

"It sounds like it," Cassidy said. If Elsie knew about it in Maple Falls, Miles had done an amazing job of promoting their shop. "You'll have to show me," she added.

Miles was already taking out his phone and bringing his profile up.

"I think you might need to do a social media workshop while you're here," Elsie urged him. "And maybe talk to my uncle a bit? I'm still fighting to get him on board."

Mayor Bloomfield, dressed in a baby-blue suit embroidered with silver snowflakes and a matching satin cummerbund, turned to the crowd.

"I do like his style," Miles murmured, and he wasn't joking. He and Cassidy shared a flair for dramatic fashion, and he was now proudly sporting his Team Cassidy sweater.

He wasn't the only one. As Cassidy scanned the crowd, she couldn't count how many locals were sporting the bright red sweaters. She beamed looking at them all.

"Okay, ladies and gentlemen, gather round! It's time for our third Christmas light-up event!" the mayor called, and the crowd cheered. "Cassidy, would you like to say a few words about your display?"

Cassidy froze. The other shop owners had only shared their chosen charities. She hadn't expected to speak.

The crowd quieted as Mayor Bloomfield passed Cassidy the microphone.

She could paint a mural across a storefront window, decorate an entire chocolate shop and charm customers one-on-one all day long. But this? Standing in front of a whole crowd with every eye on her?

Nope. No thank you.

She swallowed hard. Her mind, which had been buzzing with ideas just minutes ago, suddenly emptied. Like someone had hit a mute button in her brain.

Elsie stood in front of her, just off to the side, still livestreaming the whole event.

Her heart pounded in her chest.

Say something. Anything.

She opened her mouth, but no words came. The silence stretched a second too long.

Then her eyes caught on something. Someone.

Liam.

He was standing near the back, arms crossed over his chest. He wasn't smiling, not exactly, but his gaze was steady. Sure. Safe.

Like he saw her. Not just the woman fumbling with a microphone, but her.

He gave a small nod, almost imperceptible. Encouraging.

She smiled.

Cassidy lifted the mic, her voice still wobbly but finding its footing.

"Oh-kay," she said with a soft laugh. "I wasn't expecting to give a speech tonight. I'm way better with cocoa than crowds."

The crowd laughed.

"But... when I started planning this display, I kept thinking about old-fashioned chocolate shops. The kind where you'd step inside, and everything just... slowed down. Where you weren't in a rush, and you could savor each flavor like a memory. That's what I wanted to bring to Maple Falls. A little bit of sweetness. A little bit of nostalgia."

She glanced at Liam again. Relaxed.

"And hopefully, a reminder that Christmas isn't about how fast we move, but about how deeply we feel. I hope this display gives you a moment to pause and just enjoy."

She exhaled, her shoulders finally lowering from her ears as she handed the mic back to the mayor.

"Oh, before I forget," Mayor Bloomfield said. "What is your charity of choice?"

Cassidy cleared her throat. "For my charity, I chose the children's hospital in Mount Holly. I spent a Christmas there as a kid after my parents died, and I've always wanted to pay the kindness I felt there forward."

A soft murmur passed through the crowd. Some seemed surprised, others, touched.

Cassidy wasn't sure how many people knew that she had lost her parents at Christmastime. She had told Liam and a few people around town, but she didn't think it was public knowledge. Then again, news traveled fast in a small town.

Mayor Bloomfield stepped up. "A beautiful sentiment. Without further ado, Cassidy, please reveal your lovely chocolatey Christmas display."

She took a steadying breath and nodded to Julian and Miles.

The crowd hushed.

A moment later, the curtain began to lower—and just as it fell away, the display behind the window lit up in an instant.

Gasps rippled through the crowd.

Behind her painted front glass window was a miniature chocolate wonderland framed in warm white twinkle lights. The window display looked like something out of a storybook with handmade buildings, marshmallow trees, and gumdrop forests. It was Maple Falls come to life in cocoa and sugar.

A hand-painted village scene stretched across the back wall, snowy rooftops glittering with sugar-dusted shimmer. The shops of Oak Way were there, hand-sculpted out of chocolate. There was the Cinnamon Spice Inn, the Pumpkin Pie Bakery, the Hot Honey Farm Shop, the Little Lantern Bookshop, the Cherry Crush Flower Shop. Soft warm lights glowed from within each shop, casting flickering shadows that made the whole village feel alive. Each one was decorated for Christmas with miniature decorations—three-inch Christmas trees with real working lights, tiny, multicolored bulbs along the roof line. Even the chocolate streetlamps glowed onto the sugary snow.

But at the center stood Cassidy's crown jewel, the idea she'd finally settled on after wavering over the train set idea for a while. It was a charming, old-world chocolate shop, complete with a golden sign that read "The Cocoa Corner." She had a tealight inside of it, so it glowed from within. Icicles strung from above sparkled in the light, catching the movement of the softly falling snowflakes drifting down from the hidden blower above. The smell of chocolate wafted through the air from the hidden scent diffuser Cassidy had hidden nearby. It worked like a charm.

On the outside of the window stood a photo station. She had found an antique wooden sleigh and draped it in cozy tartan blankets. Nestled beside it was a sign that read "Cocoa & Kisses." A bucket of candy canes sat to the side, and another sign encouraged visitors to snap a photo and donate to the Mount Holly Children's Hospital.

For a long moment, no one said a word.

Cassidy couldn't move, couldn't breathe.

Then Tyler's daughter, Emma, whispered, "It's magic."

Julian let out a low whistle. "Cass... this is insane. Like, next-level chocolate shop fantasy."

Miles stepped forward, crouching to get a better look at the tiny truffles in the window. "Are these handmade?"

She nodded, wordlessly.

"I can't believe it. Even the brushstrokes... Wow, Cass, this is art," Miles continued.

Someone behind them clapped. Then another. And suddenly the street was filled with warm applause, as if the whole town had just exhaled all at once.

This. This was what made it all worth it. The stress. The hours spent pouring chocolate into molds. The late nights.

The townspeople were smiling. People were pointing, whispering to one another, taking photos in front of her display. Children tugged at their parents' sleeves, asking for cocoa, for a picture, for just one more look.

And Liam was there too. He was standing a few feet back, smiling, really smiling. Hands tucked in his coat pockets, like he didn't have anywhere else he'd rather be.

He held her gaze for a moment. Nodded, once.

Then he turned to walk away.

Cassidy didn't even hesitate in following him. Her heart was already moving before her feet.

FIFTY

LIAM

He heard Cassidy's footsteps, quick and steady, as she jogged to catch up with him. He glanced over his shoulder right as he reached the front door of his shop.

"You came," she said a bit breathlessly.

"I wasn't sure if I should," he said, not meeting her eyes.

"No, you should've," she said quickly.

Liam glanced up and congratulated her before he could stop himself. "I'm glad I did. It looked great. Congratulations."

He turned back around to unlock his shop's door.

"I was wrong last night. Even before I found out the Gingerbread Jerk was raccoons," Cassidy blurted out.

He blinked. "Raccoons?"

She nodded, cheeks flushed from embarrassment. "That's who's behind all the damage. I caught them on camera. Zoe's trying to figure out how to trap them, but... I owe you an apology. It wasn't fair of me to accuse you. I know you'd never sabotage my shop."

She paused. Her voice softened. "I said those things because I was hurt."

Liam looked down the street. There were too many people milling about. Lights glowing in windows, tourists passing by, chatting. People admiring Cassidy's display.

He wasn't about to pour his heart out on the sidewalk.

"You want to come inside?" he asked, keeping his voice low.

She glanced through the window, then nodded. "I'd love to."

He unlocked the door and held it open for her.

Inside, the shop was quiet, the air warm and filled with the soft, spiced scent of the simmering pot sachets stacked by the register. Wax candle kits lined the far shelves. Honey gift sets shimmered in their jars, arranged with care beside rows of seasonal jam. The lights were soft and low. Comforting.

He watched her as she took it all in. She paused by a display of hand-poured candles and glass-blown ornaments, fingers tracing the outline of one.

This was his place. A reflection of everything he loved. His family. His roots. His work. He wanted her to see it all. To feel it.

"I owe you an apology too," he said, leaning against the counter. He crossed his arms over his chest and let his eyes settle on her.

She turned to face him, still holding the ornament, her expression wary.

"You were right," he said. "I got scared. I thought I was pushing you too fast. That I was asking for too much. I told myself I was giving you space, but really, I was running."

She stayed quiet, eyes locked on his.

"You're not the same woman who dated Jean-Paul. You've never once backed down from who you are. Not even when I rolled my eyes or refused to go caroling or acted like a grinch about your sweaters. And for the record, I still won't go caroling."

A hint of a smile tugged at her lips.

"But decorating cookies with you? Watching those cheesy movies while drinking cocoa in your Christmas pajamas? Cuddling up under way too many blankets? I actually want all of that. I can't promise I won't be scared again and I can't promise I'll ever be as into Christmas as you are. But I swear to you, I won't run. I will listen to you."

He uncrossed his arms and reached out his hand.

"I want that too," she said quietly, stepping closer. "I know how hard this time of year is for you..."

He let out a breath. "I figured you did. I wanted to tell you about Avery myself. Not because I'm still stuck in the past but because I needed you to understand the fear that comes with trying again."

She opened her mouth, but he held up a hand.

"You don't have to fix it. Just... let me say this. Avery died on her way to Maple Falls. We were going to spend the holidays together anyway, but I told her I missed her, and she left early, driving through a snowstorm to be with me. And she never made it. That's a fact I have to live with."

The silence stretched. The weight of it was still sharp.

"I didn't think I'd ever feel anything close to joy at Christmas again. But that night you asked me over, the night Jean-Paul proposed? All I could picture was decorating a tree with you. Hanging stockings. Sending out the cheesiest Christmas cards."

His voice dipped. "You made me want those things again. And sometimes I want them so badly it terrifies me. I start thinking I'll lose it all again, that I don't deserve it. I know that's not how life works, but it's hard to shake."

Her voice was soft when she finally spoke. "I know you're scared. So am I. I've made plenty of mistakes. But you're not one of them. You undo me, Liam. You see me. There's no one else like you. And I don't want to lose what's just starting between us."

Liam stepped forward. Slowly. Carefully.

And when she didn't pull away, he leaned in and kissed her.

It wasn't urgent. It wasn't rushed.

Just the soft press of his mouth against hers, warm and steady and sure. It was the kind of kiss that said, *I'm still here.*

She swayed toward him, her hand brushing his chest. Her fingers curled into the soft flannel on his shirt.

That was all the permission he needed.

Without breaking the kiss, he walked her to the door, pulled down the shade, and felt along the wall for the latch. A soft click echoed as he turned the lock on the front door. The sound felt final, like shutting the world out.

Cassidy was breathless, her cheeks flushed pink. "What are you doing?"

He cupped her jaw, his thumb tracing just beneath her bottom lip. "Making sure I don't lose you again."

"Here?" She looked around, realizing that the front windows were covered, and no one could see in. She relaxed.

"Is that okay?" He backed up, giving her space to decide.

"It's more than okay." She smiled seductively.

His hands slid to her hips as he guided her backward, her body bumping gently into the wooden counter. The scent of beeswax and cinnamon hung in the air, wrapping around them.

He kissed her again. It was slower this time, with a hint of reverence, like he was tasting something he thought he might never have again.

"I missed you," she said. Her voice was steady, but her hands trembled slightly where they rested on his chest. He covered them with his own, pressing them flat over his heart.

"Feel that?" he said quietly. "That's what you do to me."

Liam leaned in and kissed her again, her mouth, her cheek, the soft skin of her neck. "Let me help you feel."

Cassidy nodded breathlessly.

He took his time undressing her. Not rushed. Not greedy. Just gentle, deliberate movements—the brush of his knuckles against her side as he slid the zipper down, the soft rustle of fabric pooling at her feet.

His own clothes came next, piece by piece. He wanted her to see him, to know there was no part of himself he was holding back from her now. When they were bare, skin to skin, he cupped her face again and kissed her like he'd been waiting years for this moment.

Her breath came faster, her skin heating under his touch. "Liam..."

He trailed one hand down her spine, slow and sure, anchoring her with every inch. "You feel incredible," he whispered. "All soft and warm and mine."

He helped her up onto the counter, kissing her thighs, her stomach, her collarbone, all the places that had gone unnoticed for too long. When he finally reached between her legs and touched her, it made her gasp with desire.

"You've been wanting this, haven't you?" he murmured against her skin.

She nodded, eyes fluttering shut. "So much..."

"Tell me how you want it, sweetheart." His fingers slid against her, slow, coaxing. "Soft and slow? Or hard and fast?"

Cassidy whimpered, her back arching. "I just want you. All of you."

Liam's control nearly cracked, but he held on because this was Cassidy. And she deserved more than just release. She deserved to be seen.

He reached into the drawer beneath the counter where he kept emergency first-aid and seasonal extras, finding the small foil square he had stashed months ago.

Cassidy watched as he rolled the condom on, her pupils dilated with desire.

And when he stepped between her legs, hands firm on her thighs, Liam looked into her eyes. "Are you ready?"

She wrapped her arms around his neck. "Yes. Liam, please."

He entered her slowly, shuddering as she took him in. Every inch felt like a promise—one he wasn't afraid to accept anymore.

Liam held still once he was fully inside her, his forehead pressed to hers. "You feel like home," he whispered.

She kissed him, sweet and deep.

He started to move: long, slow strokes that dragged soft sounds from her lips. The counter beneath her creaked faintly with each thrust, but neither of them noticed. It was just the sound of connection, of something real being built between them.

Her legs wrapped around him tighter, pulling him closer.

Liam could feel her getting closer. The way her breaths came faster. The way her body clenched around him, already fluttering with anticipation.

"You're doing so good," he whispered, his voice thick. He slid one hand between her legs, his thumb circling gently. "Let go for me. Let me feel you fall apart."

Her hands gripped his shoulders, nails biting into his skin as the pressure inside her coiled tighter and tighter.

Liam held her through it, slowing only slightly as he watched her come undone in his arms. "That's it," he murmured. "You're so beautiful like this."

He didn't last much longer. The feel of her still pulsing around him, the sound of her voice, the way she held him so tight—he couldn't hold back.

"Cassidy," he groaned, burying himself deep one last time as he came, his whole body tensing as pleasure surged through him. His forehead dropped to her shoulder, his arms wrapping around her like he never wanted to let go.

For a long moment, they just breathed.

She ran her fingers gently through his hair, still catching her breath. Liam kissed her collarbone, then her neck, then finally her lips.

He was quiet for a beat, then smiled and brushed her damp hair from her face. "You know, the first day I met you, I pictured this."

"This?" she asked, motioning to the counter.

He nodded, still a little breathless. "Yeah. Right here."

"Oh really. What about now?"

"Now?" He grinned. "Now I want every surface. Every damn one."

She laughed. "That sounds like a challenge."

FIFTY-ONE

CASSIDY

The next morning, Cassidy found herself replaying the night before. She would have loved nothing more than to explore all the different surfaces Liam had hinted at, but she hadn't been able to ignore Julian and Miles, especially with them only in town for one night. She'd even tried to convince them to stay longer, though she understood why they couldn't. Owning a business meant every day off was a sacrifice.

She'd found them back at her chocolate shop, waiting and wondering where she'd snuck off to. Miles had lifted his brows when she told them. *So that's who you're dating? The farm shop hottie?* Julian had crossed his arms in mock offense, but Miles's easy grin and teasing shoulder squeeze had smoothed it over. Even Julian's attempt to hold onto his scowl hadn't lasted long before it gave way to a grin. Cassidy could still hear the warmth in Miles's voice when he turned back to her and said, *We're happy for you.*

Letting them go that morning hadn't been easy, but she hadn't fought too hard. Now that her light-up night was behind her and Christmas was less than a week away, Cassidy finally felt like she could exhale. The worst of the pressure had passed. Liam was still working on the final touches for his display, hammering and fussing over details. She'd offered to help, but he'd waved her off, reminding her she'd already done plenty when she'd stepped in after the raccoons had wrecked everything. She was still reeling to think that after all the gossip and rumors, after all her suspicions and anger about the Gingerbread Jerk, the answer to the Maple Falls Christmas mystery had turned out to be so innocent.

Later that afternoon, a message buzzed on her phone.

How do you feel about lasagna?

She replied right away.

Lasagna sounds perfect. I'll bring the wine.

She packed an overnight bag and tucked it into the backseat of her car. She didn't want to assume anything, but she also didn't want to be caught unprepared.

When she stepped inside his house later that evening, the first thing she noticed was the Christmas tree standing in the corner of his living room. Her heart jumped.

It was the tree. The one she'd bid on at the Festival of Trees.

Her face lit up. "You got it," she said, walking toward it slowly, taking in the warm lights and mix of ornaments. "Although... it looks a little different."

"I added a few things of my own," he said from the kitchen,

glancing over as he used a corkscrew to open the bottle of wine she'd brought.

She moved closer, brushing her fingers along one of the new ornaments. A small wooden honeybee nestled near the top. A carved ornament shaped like a tiny saw. She smiled. They were so... him.

For the next hour, they cooked together in the glow of the tree lights and the hum of soft holiday music playing in the background. Liam browned the meat, a dishtowel slung over his shoulder, while Cassidy stirred the simmering sauce. A pot of noodles bubbled gently on the stove.

They worked in tandem, layering the noodles, sauce, and cheeses—ricotta, mozzarella, and a sprinkle of parmesan. She laid down the noodles, he followed with a generous spoonful of sauce, and together, they scattered handfuls of shredded cheese.

It wasn't fancy, and it wasn't fast. But it was warm and unhurried and full of shared glances and soft laughter.

Once the lasagna was safely tucked into the oven, he rinsed his hands and reached for the wine glasses. Her fingers brushed his as he handed her the glass.

"To finally being able to slow down," he said, raising his glass.

"I'll drink to that." She clinked her glass gently against his.

Cassidy hadn't realized how much she'd craved this kind of quiet. There were no expectations. No pressure. A feeling of contentment bloomed in her chest.

This man had been worth breaking her vow for. This man was the kind of man who would love her forever.

FIFTY-TWO

LIAM

Tuesday, December 23rd

Liam thought that if every night with Cassidy could be like the days and nights they'd shared together in the last few days, then he would be the happiest man for the rest of his life. She gave her whole heart; she was selfless and giving in ways he still had to get used to, ways he didn't always feel like he deserved. But he'd promised himself he would show up for her, love her, and support her.

Tonight was his light-up night. They stood outside, bundled together. Cassidy in the red wool coat that he loved, hair in two braids, green tinsel woven through. Him in his black puffer coat, no tinsel, but a bright red scarf. It was a gift from her and he loved wearing it.

"You know what today is?" She grinned. "It's Christmas Eve Eve! And it's going to be the *best* day of the year."

"Because I'm going to win?" he asked playfully.

She leaned and whispered in his ear. "You'll win something, for sure. I'll show you later."

Liam laughed. The look in her eye wasn't just teasing—it was a promise. And suddenly, he couldn't wait until later that night when it would be just the two of them.

But right now, they were surrounded by a packed crowd. His parents were there, too, and his mom was smiling ear to ear. They were set to go over to his parents' house for Christmas dinner. When he'd asked his mom if he could bring Cassidy, she'd squealed into the phone. He'd considered that a yes.

Liam didn't know if his rustic "Down on the Farm" holiday theme could compete with Cassidy's whimsical chocolate display, Zoe's floral magic, or Emily's heavenly dessert extravaganza. But it didn't matter. What mattered was that it was him. It was real. It was his story woven in lights and handmade ornaments and a little surprise he hoped would charm the crowd.

"Welcome to the final switch-on," Mayor Bloomfield boomed. "Our last contestant needs no introduction, but I'll give you one anyway. Let's hear it for Liam Hawthorne and his Hot Honey Farm Shop."

Liam walked to the front and waved, taking the mic from the mayor. "I just want to thank you for coming out tonight. For all the support you've shown me and the new shop. And I hope you like what I've created for you." He nodded his head and then disappeared around the side of the shop.

The shop slowly came to life. First with the pine tree forest Liam had staged near the front, each wrapped in warm white twinkle lights.

Then the rustic garland that framed the doors. It was made of fresh pine, dried oranges, and cranberries, tied with burlap bows. A wooden sleigh leaned against the front wall, stacked with wrapped boxes in brown paper and twine.

A spotlight shone on his interactive touches. The hot cider station he'd created in a hollowed-out barrel, self-serve with a ladle, cinnamon sticks, and branded Hot Honey Farm Shop mugs. A mailbox labeled "Letters to Santa" for the kids, with stamped kraft-paper envelopes and pencils tied with twine. His donation box, a handmade beehive box with a sign that read "Sweeten Someone's Season" beside it.

And if that wasn't enough, when he reappeared, he had Jackson with him, and two llamas.

Cassidy burst out laughing. "You brought llamas? Oh, come on."

"I brought llamas," Liam said with a proud grin. "You didn't think I'd forget about Daisy and Tinsel, did you?"

"I haven't seen them since that day in the barn," she said, her voice softening.

"That was a very good day," Liam said, voice low.

"It was the best," she agreed.

"It was the beginning," he added.

Beside him, Jackson adjusted Daisy's lead rope, scratching the llama's neck with an absentminded tenderness that softened the usual guarded lines of his face. His dark hair was ruffled by the wind, and he wore a Hot Honey Farm Shop beanie pulled low over his ears.

Zoe stepped forward with a handful of cut apple pieces, her eyes bright. "Mind if I...?"

Jackson's lips quirked. "Go for it. Daisy loves attention."

Zoe giggled as Daisy nuzzled her palm, careful and gentle, her long lashes blinking slowly. "You're gorgeous, aren't you?"

Daisy loved the attention, leaning into Zoe so she could scratch under her harness.

Jackson watched, something vulnerable flickering in his eyes, before clearing his throat. "She's not usually that affection-ate. Takes a bit to warm up."

Zoe glanced up, cheeks pink from the cold and maybe something else. "That's alright, I can be patient."

Jackson's mouth twitched. "I've noticed."

Cassidy's eyes darted between them, a slow smile spreading across her face. She looked like she wanted to say something to Liam, but the crowd surged closer, drawn in by the glowing lights, the smell of warm cider, and the llamas. Daisy shook her head, the bell on her halter jingling. Tinsel sniffed a toddler's mitten and looked like she wanted a little taste before the tyke offered her some hay.

"That's a crowd-pleaser if I've ever seen one," Kit said, appearing at Cassidy's side with a cider mug in each hand. She passed one to her.

Zoe followed, eyes wide as she took in the display. "Liam, this is beautiful. It feels like Maple Falls. Like home."

Madison nodded. "It's exactly what Christmas should be."

Liam was overwhelmed by the attention. He rubbed the back of his neck, muttering a quiet thanks as more neighbors approached to shake his hand or clap him on the shoulder.

That's when he noticed Mr. Alders—pushing his way through the crowd in a bulky green coat and... *Is that...?*

"Is he wearing...?"

"A Team Liam sweater," Madison confirmed, eyes twinkling.

Sure enough, the old man had purchased a Team Liam sweater. He walked straight up to Liam and gave a stiff nod.

"This is the best damn display I've seen since oh-four," he said, voice gravelly with emotion. "Don't tell anyone I said that."

"Thanks, Mr. Alders. Glad you like it."

"You used dried oranges. My mama used to do that." He looked up at the garlands, eyes misting for just a second before he cleared his throat and turned away.

"Merry Christmas," Liam said to the older man's back.

He replied with a wave above his head without turning around.

Liam nudged Cassidy. "And you thought he was the Gingerbread Jerk," he teased.

"He sure was doing a fine job of acting like it," she replied in her defense, but smiled when she said it.

A flash of light caught his eye. He and Cassidy turned and spotted Elsie, standing off to the side, phone in hand. Her livestream was still running, but the look on her face had shifted. It was less smug, more thoughtful. Like she couldn't believe how many people had turned out for Liam's display, and how many people were watching her livestream.

Cassidy followed her gaze.

Families were gathered around the cider barrel, children slipping paper letters into Liam's handmade Santa mailbox. A group of teens took selfies with Daisy the llama. Mr. Alders stood chatting with Liam's parents with a smile on his face. Every inch of the storefront felt like a scene from a storybook.

Cassidy brought up her phone, joined the livestream, and showed Liam, who couldn't help the feeling of pride that bloomed in his chest. The comments were flooding in faster than Elsie could keep up.

I wish my town did stuff like this.

The real Christmas spirit!

Where is this?! I want to move there!

Following just for this vibe 🤍

Elsie looked down at her screen, then back at Liam's display —at the wooden ornaments, the handmade sleigh, the burlap and dried oranges. Her mouth parted slightly, like she was realizing this was what people actually wanted.

"She sees it now," Zoe murmured beside Cassidy. "It's not about flashy or new. People love things that feel traditional at this time of year. It's about feeling connected."

Cassidy nodded. "She thought she needed to reinvent Christmas to make it special."

Zoe tilted her head. "Turns out it was already special. She just hadn't seen it yet."

Now the only thing that was left to do was wait until tomorrow night to see who the winner was.

FIFTY-THREE

CASSIDY

It was the annual Christmas Eve walk, and Cassidy was nervous. She was trying not to be. It didn't matter who won, she told herself. Yes, she wanted to give to the hospital. And yes, of course she wanted to win Business of the Year and host the New Year's Eve party. But she also knew how important the llama sanctuary and the farm shop were to Liam.

She couldn't very well root against the man she loved. That wouldn't be very in the Christmas spirit, now would it?

She knew all of this. But still... she wanted to win.

She tugged her scarf higher around her neck and exhaled, her breath puffing in the cold air. It was frigid tonight, barely above twenty degrees, yet Cassidy had never felt warmer. She was wrapped in layers with her red wool coat and green stocking cap with a pom-pom on top, and walking hand in hand with Liam while he walked Muff. Her pup was in doggy heaven, getting pets from all the kids and plenty of ear scratches.

Just like Muff, there was nowhere else Cassidy would rather be.

Lanterns flickered all around them, carried by children in puffy coats and mittened hands. At the front and back of the procession, volunteers held old-fashioned torches, their flames flickering against the still night air. Further ahead, a brass band played "O Come All Ye Faithful."

The whole town had turned out for the walk. It was a Maple Falls tradition—part light-up tour, part caroling, part party. And to her, it felt like something magical.

She grinned when they walked past the bakery, and she saw Emily had managed to rebuild her famous pie tin tree. It looked bigger and shinier than ever, stacked high in glinting, silvery layers.

The café had a cute window scene, too. Anita had run a snowflake coloring competition. Dozens of snowflakes were colored with markers, paint, crayons, and glitter. They dangled inside her front window by invisible string, fluttering in the café's circulating air. Cassidy smiled, watching the children point out the ones they'd made.

By the time they reached the town square, the sky had deepened into inky blue and stars had begun to appear. The town's Christmas tree lit up the square. As did all the surrounding holiday lights.

Clusters of townspeople gathered around in thick coats and colorful scarves, but what stood out most was that everywhere she looked, people sported their Team Cassidy and Team Liam sweaters. Cassidy couldn't help but smile. It looked pretty evenly split.

The Boy Scout troop had set up a hot cocoa pop-up that was nothing like Cassidy's. It was only powdered cocoa mix with hot water, but she couldn't resist. She loved supporting the local kids. She and Liam both got a cup.

People milled around, greeting neighbors, waving to friends, humming along with the brass band as it assembled for one final round of carols, leading off with "Jingle Bells." She found herself singing along, letting the warmth of the moment wrap around her like a fresh blanket out of the dryer.

Liam leaned in close, just enough for her to hear, and deliberately sang the alternate words to the chorus. She elbowed him, laughing at his Batman rendition as he grinned down at her, unapologetic.

"What? They're the only words I know," he said, and she was sure he was lying.

"You're incorrigible." Cassidy grinned.

They found their friends hanging out on the sidewalk near the café. Zoe had just finished stringing up a cluster of mistletoe on the streetlight, hoping to inspire some holiday romance. Kit stood nearby, spiked cider in one hand, the other waving animatedly as she told a story to Rachel, the girl she was now lowkey seeing. Madison and Zach were tucked in close, stealing a kiss in the shadowed doorway of the Kettle. Cassidy slid in beside Kit, Liam at her side, the gentle brush of his arm against hers grounding her like always.

Then the microphone screeched softly, and the crowd hushed.

Mayor Bloomfield stepped up onto the platform, cheeks pink from the cold, his long wool coat buttoned to the neck. He adjusted his Santa hat and tapped the mic again.

Cassidy's stomach fluttered.

"Ladies and gentlemen," he said, "I have to say, this has been the most spirited Maple Falls Christmas Light-Up Display Competition in recent memory. And it was close. Real close."

Someone in the crowd started chanting, "Llamas! Llamas!" while others shouted, "Cocoa Corner!"

Cassidy felt Liam's hand slide into hers. He laced their fingers together and held tight.

"But the winner of this year's light-up, by just one vote," the mayor added with a dramatic pause, "is Liam Hawthorne and the Hot Honey Farm Shop!"

The crowd erupted into cheers and applause. Cassidy clapped, then stepped back to let him have his moment.

But he turned and tugged her forward.

"What? No," she said, surprised. "You won."

"And I want you up there with me."

He didn't let go of her hand as he climbed the wooden steps to the small platform stage. She followed, cheeks flushed, eyes wide. He stood before the town, not nervous at all, just certain.

"Thank you, Mayor. And thank you to everyone who came out and voted," Liam said, his voice steady. "I'm proud of what we built here, and I mean that. Not just the display. But the community. The heart behind it."

He glanced at Cassidy, giving her hand a gentle squeeze.

"I know many of you know about the children's hospital fundraiser Cassidy was running," he continued, turning back to the crowd. "And I also know how much you've supported the expansion plans for the llama sanctuary. I'm grateful for that. Truly."

He took a breath. "So, I wanted to say the prize money is going to the children's hospital. Because that's what matters most of all. Our kids."

A quiet hush swept the crowd before it broke into another round of applause, louder than before.

"And thanks to the support you've all shown my shop this season, my family can still move forward with the sanctuary expansion. So, in a way... we both won."

Cassidy felt her throat tighten, tears burning at the corners of her eyes as she looked at Liam.

Then he looked down at her, and everything else faded.

"None of it would've happened without this beautiful, magical woman," he said.

A soft "aww" rolled through the crowd, but she hardly noticed.

"You made me believe in Christmas again, Cassidy," Liam continued. "And not just with your spiced cocoa and whatever magic potion I'm convinced you add to it. With the way you give. With how you show up, not just for me, but for this whole town. You reminded me that it's okay to want more. To want love. To want you."

A tear slid down her cheek. Liam brushed it away with his thumb.

"I know I'm not perfect. And I know I've been scared," he said. "I worried I wasn't enough for someone like you. And I wasn't ready to open up my heart again. But you've made me feel more me than I ever have before."

She wanted to say something, but her heart was too full.

He smiled softly. "Remember that first day I walked into your shop?"

"Yes?" Cassidy said hesitantly, not sure where Liam was going with this.

"She gave me a chocolate," he said to the crowd, then turned fully to face her. "Told me she could guess anyone's favorite."

"No..." she said softly.

"Yes." His smile deepened. "That chocolate you handed me that very first day? It was absolutely my favorite. It was perfect. You got it right."

"Are you kidding me!" She laughed and playfully pushed his shoulder. "I thought I'd lost my touch."

"Not even close. You've been right since day one. About the chocolate. About everything."

He took both of her hands in his. "I want you to know that I love you, Cassidy. And I'll keep showing up, every day, in every way I can. If you'll let me."

Cassidy stepped into him. "I love you too, but..."

"But?" He cocked an eyebrow.

"But *Die Hard* will never be a Christmas movie."

And right there, in front of the glittering Christmas tree and the entire town, Liam kissed her.

The town cheered as snowflakes began to fall.

And in that perfect, glittering moment, it felt like the whole world had shown up just for their love.

EPILOGUE

Christmas Day

Liam stood near the fireplace and scanned his parents' living room. His mom had stacked an impressive number of presents underneath the Christmas tree. The gifts were wrapped in mismatched paper, topped with shiny bows and tags written in varying levels of legibility, thanks to his dad's help. The stockings were so stuffed, they couldn't even hang on the mantel. They were propped under the tree as well.

Even Muff had a stocking. Hers overflowed with treats, a new sweater, and a chew toy. He'd helped Cassidy wrap everything last night. The pup didn't seem to notice the stocking as she was too busy sitting like a good girl next to the kitchen table, watching Beth finish prepping the holiday meal and taste-testing whatever scraps Liam's mom slipped her from time to time.

Everyone was home for the first time in six years. Lily had surprised them all, flying in last night from Honduras. And Jackson was spending his first Christmas home since returning from Syria.

Cassidy stood beside Lily, both of them bent over a tray of iced sugar cookies they were decorating like it was a serious art form. Cassidy wore a vintage green sweater dress with red buttons shaped like holly berries, and red tights with tiny gingerbread men on them. She'd opted for a side braid and pinned her bangs in place with a glittering snowflake barrette. It was a look that only Cassidy could pull off.

She glanced over at Liam just then, caught him staring, and gave him a wink before turning back to her conversation with Lily. They were already thick as thieves.

Liam smiled, letting the warmth spread in his chest. His parents' house had never felt this full. This alive. And that was before Jackson had announced that Zoe would be stopping by later to hang out. They were first going to head out in a little bit to release the raccoon family she'd managed to catch. Then they'd spend some time at the farmhouse with the rest of the family. *There's something there*, he thought, remembering seeing Jackson and Zoe two nights ago. He'd have to talk to Cassidy and see what she thought.

The dining table in the next room was laid out with all the traditional Christmas Day staples: a perfectly browned turkey at the center, buttery mashed potatoes, stuffing with herbs and sausage, green bean casserole with crispy onion topping, roasted carrots glazed with maple syrup, and two types of pie, pumpkin and pecan. His mom had made the cranberry sauce from scratch, and the bread rolls were still warm. It smelled like home. Like childhood. Like the kind of future he hadn't dared to hope for until recently.

He'd done it. When December 1st had rolled around, he had only been trying to survive. But he'd done a lot more than that this year. His business had done a lot more, too.

The season had been more profitable than he could've hoped, and even after donating all the prize money to the children's hospital, he had enough to start the llama sanctuary expansion. It felt like a miracle. And for the first time in a long time, Liam believed in those again.

He looked down at his red socks. They were bright with reindeer and candy canes. Cassidy had bought them for him, more as a joke, said he didn't have to wear them, but Liam had wanted to. The smile on her face when he took off his shoes was worth it.

After dinner, Liam's mom called them all into the living room. "Present time!" she shouted, clapping her hands like a preschool teacher as everyone piled into the living room, plates of pie in hand.

He settled beside Cassidy on the floor, his shoulder brushing hers, and passed her a slice of pecan pie. "Just how you like it, with extra whipped cream," he murmured.

Her eyes sparkled as she took the plate, leaning in so only he could hear. "Careful, or I'll start thinking of other uses for that whipped cream."

Liam choked on a laugh, his ears going pink, but the smirk he shot her was pure trouble. "Don't start something you can't finish, Sugarplum."

Then his mom clapped her hands, commanding their attention, and the moment slipped into something softer, sweeter.

He watched Cassidy open her gifts: the handmade apron from his mom embroidered with "Cocoa Queen," a set of vintage chocolate molds that Liam had found on eBay, a book of Christmas cookie recipes from Jackson, who never bought gifts for people.

Cassidy laughed through her tears, touched by every gesture. She slipped the apron on right then and there, tied it around her waist, then headed over and gave Beth a hug, both of their eyes shining.

The gift-giving continued until there was only one more.

"Hey," Liam said, pulling the box out from behind the tree. "I have one more."

She looked up.

His whole family seemed to stop what they were doing to watch her open the gift.

Cassidy carefully tore back the paper and opened the small box. Inside lay a hand-painted silver bulb with her name in white script.

She looked up at him. "It's the same as the rest of yours."

"You're part of us now."

Her laugh broke through a teary breath. "You're going to make me cry in front of your whole family."

She slipped the ornament out of the box and stood. "Will you hang it with me?"

Liam rose, taking her hand as she led him to the tree. He gently helped her loop the red ribbon over a waiting branch near his own bulb.

There it was.

Proof she was his.

Proof of his love.

Proof that this cozy, love-wrapped moment next to the Christmas tree was only the beginning of their story in Maple Falls.

A LETTER FROM HARPER

Thank you so much for visiting Maple Falls and reading *The Spiced Cocoa Café*. Cassidy and Liam's story was such a blast to write. Their voices were so strong in my head that it made telling their story effortless—or as effortless as writing a novel can be!

If you enjoyed the book and want to stay up to date with my latest releases, you can sign up for my newsletter at the following link:

www.bookouture.com/harper-graham

Your email address will never be shared, and you can unsubscribe at any time.

If you could also leave a review, I would greatly appreciate it! Reviews help new readers discover my books and take a chance on Maple Falls. Plus, I love hearing your favorite part of the story. Did I make you laugh? Cry? Chuck the book across the room? Let me know!

Want to connect? Feel free to reach out through Facebook, X, Instagram, or TikTok.

Until next time, and happy holidays,

Harper

ACKNOWLEDGMENTS

Once again, the entire team at Bookouture has been brilliant! A special shoutout to my editor, Rhianna Louise, for pushing me in my craft and polishing the story until it shined; my publicist, Jess Readett, for her behind-the-scenes work and social media magic; and the rest of the team—including rights, marketing, production, copy editing, and proofreading—bravo, guys!

To my agent, Cindy Bullard, for continuing to work her business magic so I can focus on the creative side. Let's be honest, contracts and negotiations aren't my strong suit. Thank you, Cindy, for overseeing all of that and more!

To my husband, for giving me plenty of Liam inspiration. I'm one lucky girl.

And to the reader—whether this is your first time visiting Maple Falls or you're a repeat guest—thank you for stopping by our charming Midwestern town, where cozy vibes, plenty of spice, and happily ever afters are only the next book away.

PUBLISHING TEAM

Turning a manuscript into a book requires the efforts of many people. The publishing team at Bookouture would like to acknowledge everyone who contributed to this publication.

Audio
Alba Proko
Sinead O'Connor
Melissa Tran

Commercial
Lauren Morrissette
Hannah Richmond
Imogen Allport

Cover design
Alexandra Allden

Data and analysis
Mark Alder
Mohamed Bussuri

Editorial
Rhianna Louise
Ria Clare

Copyeditor
DeAndra Lupu

Proofreader
Becca Allen

Marketing
Alex Crow
Melanie Price
Occy Carr
Cíara Rosney
Martyna Młynarska

Operations and distribution
Marina Valles
Stephanie Straub
Joe Morris

Production
Hannah Snetsinger
Mandy Kullar
Nadia Michael
Charlotte Hegley

Publicity
Kim Nash
Noelle Holten
Jess Readett
Sarah Hardy

Rights and contracts
Peta Nightingale
Richard King
Saidah Graham

Dear Reader,

We'd love your attention for one more page to tell you about the crisis in children's reading, and what we can all do.

Studies have shown that reading for fun is the **single biggest predictor of a child's future life chances** – more than family circumstance, parents' educational background or income. It improves academic results, mental health, wealth, communication skills, ambition and happiness.

The number of children reading for fun is in rapid decline. Young people have a lot of competition for their time, and a worryingly high number do not have a single book at home.

Hachette works extensively with schools, libraries and literacy charities, but here are some ways we can all raise more readers:

- Reading to children for just 10 minutes a day makes a difference
- Don't give up if children aren't regular readers – there will be books for them!

- Visit bookshops and libraries to get recommendations
- Encourage them to listen to audiobooks
- Support school libraries
- Give books as gifts

There's a lot more information about how to encourage children to read on our websites: **www.RaisingReaders.co.uk** and **www.JoinRaisingReaders.com**.

Thank you for reading.